FALCON HEART

CHRONICLE I

Azalea Dabill

Dynamos Press
Chiloquin Oregon

Dynamos Press
www.azaleadabill.com
Publisher's Note: This is a work of fiction. Names, characters, places, and incidents are a product of the author's imagination. Locales and public names are sometimes used for atmospheric purposes. Any resemblance to actual people, living or dead, or to businesses, companies, events, institutions, or locales is completely coincidental.

All Scripture quotes from NASB except for a few words substituted for meaning. "Scripture quotations taken from the New American Standard Bible®, Copyright © 1960, 1962, 1963, 1968, 1971, 1972, 1973,1975, 1977, 1995 by The Lockman Foundation Used by permission." (www.Lockman.org)

Book Layout ©2015 BookDesignTemplates.com

Cover Designer: Derek Murphy

Keywords: Crossover: Find the Eternal the Adventure, Teen and young adult fantasy books, Young adult fantasy series, Christian adventure books for teens, Epic fantasy romance, Coming of age fantasy, Fantasy literature for children and young adults.

Falcon Heart Chronicle I/ Azalea Dabill. -- 1st ed.
ISBN 978-1-943034-00-0

Contents

Falcon Heart

To all my readers and my loving family, who gave me a place to grow and still encourage my adventures.

And to the Creator of adventure and joy, Who made me all I am and will be. Without Him Falcon Heart would not be written.

The Falcon Chronicles

Falcon Heart Chronicle I

Falcon Flight Chronicle II

Falcon Dagger Chronicle III *

Lance and Qull - A Novella

Falcon's Ode - Poetry Companion

Suggested Reading Order

Two prequels in *Falcon Dagger* *Coming 2024

Falcon Heart a novel

Falcon Flight a novel

Lance and Quill a novella

Falcon Dagger three novellas.

PROLOGUE

Seeker

This child . . . ~Exodus 2:9

Wind gusted around Kyrin. Heavy with the smell of rain, it flattened the dry grass under her horse's hooves in the evening light, whispered and rustled across the cart track leading to the guarded gate. Wide as a man lying down and thrice as high, her godfather's out-wall circled his stronghold with dark stone.

Between the stronghold wall and the sea, mist rose from grassy hollows to meet the clouds looming behind Kyrin in the lowering sun. She straightened her back.

The armsmen guarding the north gate knew who they were. Their choices were made, their position and allegiance accepted. If she could but choose her own . . .

The grizzled, older armsman bowed as her mother's mount passed him. "Lady of Cieri." With a grin and a touch of his spear to his helm, he motioned Kyrin through the heavy portal after her mother. The younger guard raised his arm toward Lord Fenwer's stronghold.

The hood of his cloak tossed in the wind, tangling with his black hair. There were thoughts of her lands in his eyes, and that her form did not displease him. He dropped his arm and turned back to his post, a silent witness to choice.

My fight does not touch him. Kyrin rubbed her sleeve across her eyes and tightened her hood. The wall at her back was mossy and solid, murmuring of a shield and of time. Here there would be quiet from the voices that clamored, incessant—if she did not let them follow her inside her godfather's walls. Such as Aunt Medaen's strident advice, "Act your age and position, child!"

As if position gave one everything. But Father said Aunt Medaen had naught else. Kyrin lifted Aart's rein and nudged him up beside her mother's dark bay.

"Mother, why did you send back Father's armsmen?" Not that she agreed with old Medaen, that it was not fit for a lady to ride without escort.

Lady Willa Cieri tilted up her chin, guiding her horse with a firmer rein, her face shadowed within her hood. "Medaen is *not* mistress of Cierheld, and we are *not* at war. Lord Fenwer patrols his lands with every sunrise. And your Father and our armsmen were with us until York!"

Kyrin bit her lip. Mother felt old Medaen's discontent, yet for Father's sake she did not toss Aunt Medaen out on her ear. Surely Lord Fenwer would not seek to weave his will around them as Aunt Medaen did, though he had been present at Kyrin's birth. "Did Lord Fenwer truly hold me when I was born?"

Her mother's grey gaze sharpened. "It is a godfather's duty. Why are you wary of him? He is a good man."

Yes, but it had been thirteen summers since he heard her first cry, and to be first-daughter of Cierheld and of age was to be caged. She did not need another cage and keeper.

She had no sisters—and no brothers. No brothers was worse. A brother would take the mantle of inheritance and release her to the woods and the wild wings of the falcons. It was not likely she would hunt again after she had hand-fasted. Truly hunt, that is—astride Aart—unless she found a lord she could meld to her will.

But she did not want a lord like Myrna's father who turned tail for his solar, his books, and his parchments to escape his wife's scythe-sharp tongue. Nor would she take a lord who left bruises to prove his strength, or treated her as his prize mare. If Father had not needed Roman stone for Cierheld's wall, and a solid line to inherit . . . But the wall was being built, and Lord Fenwer quarried the stone, a friend. Kyrin sighed.

"No, mother, I'm not afraid of him. He is kind, as you say." Was he interested in her coming lord, the lord who would some-day hold the key of Cierheld? Kyrin wound a strand of hair about her finger.

If she must hand-fast she would ride beside a true lord, nei-ther a tyrannous master nor a besotted slave. But it was better to hold her own honor. Safe from blows and shame—and bars hemming her in—bars that seemed grey as death the longer she looked at them.

Her mother sighed and patted Kyrin's knee. Kyrin steadied her cold hands against Aart's soft neck, warmth blooming inside her. Mother seemed to sense when words would give no help and gave her the quiet gift of nearness.

From the gate to the small entry in the yard wall ahead stretched more than a bowshot of grass. Cold bare emptiness for defense against fire and enemies.

Catching her mother's weary smile, Kyrin nudged Aart forward. There was nothing to gain, dawdling on the killing-ground. Aart's thudding hooves quickened. He stretched out his neck with a snort, eager for meadow hay and a stall out of the wind.

Kyrin slowed him at the yard wall. The high walkway was deserted, and no guard or armsman called within the yard. Lord Fenwer did not have the armsmen Cierheld boasted, and he had his great out-wall. But should not his inner walls be watched?

Twisted iron bound the young oak trunks of the gate. Kyrin stretched out her hand. Old and loyal, the rough oak held; the iron was cold, under cloud-shadow. Pulled from within, the gate creaked open.

Kyrin yanked her hand back and Aart shied. Her mother moved up beside her as Aart trotted forward. Kyrin shifted on his back with a frown.

A few servants lingered about the yard. No one waited to greet them on the wide stone steps that rose to the threshold of Lord Fenwer's hall, or stood in the double-leaved open door between the high towers. Had her father's messenger not come?

A hale old man before the gaping arches of the stable on Kyrin's right watched them. A bit of hay winked in the twisting fingers of a retainer leaning against an arch behind him. On his right was a man stolid as a tree: a farmer, most like. A fourth man clad in dark wool rocked on his heels, armed with sword and dagger, assessing Kyrin for threat and dismissing her.

The old man's blue gaze caught her, level and sharp. He did not offend. His white hair was thick, his coarse knee-length tunic brown wool. She lifted her chin. Perhaps he was the steward? Cross garters wound about his calves saved his wrinkled hose from puddling around his shoes. Gold gilding glinted on the worn leather ties.

Kyrin tensed. *Gilding—Lord Fenwer. It must be, and I thought him a servant.* Her ears heated and she bowed her head.

"You are well come to my hall and my hearth." Her godfather's voice was quiet, as if he noticed nothing.

Kyrin raised her gaze. The quirk of his mouth was quick.

She could not help her grin. *He* did not seek a lady for his hall. *He* did not see Lord Dain Cieri's first-daughter, to weigh for her worth of blood and land, and her ties to power, such as they were.

Lord Fenwer smoothed his white mustache with weathered fingers, his craggy face solemn as a moor-rock. "Tomorrow you can fly any of my hawks and falcons you wish, goddaughter, and I will show you my walls. I think you will agree with your lord father—the Roman Eagles' stone wards my stronghold well."

She somehow did not think he would name her goose for concerning herself with neighbor stronghold's foolish sons and their allegiances, or worse, call her hill-sprite because she loved the woods of Cierheld. He also held the falcon's soul-piercing call to freedom close to his heart.

"Yes, my lord," she said to Aart's mane. His coarse hair flicked her wind-chilled fingers. But she did not wish her godfather to escort her around his stronghold walls, under the eyes of servants and others who might laugh behind their hands. She wanted to be alone, with wings beating high above her, and not think. At the silence, she looked up.

Laughter lines gathered around Lord Fenwer's mouth. Kyrin shivered in sudden doubt. Did he smile because Father told him she could ride and shoot a bow as well as his armsmen in training, or because she, the heir who bore the key and the future of Cierheld, was so awkward?

Lord Fenwer gestured. His dark-garbed armsman closed the gate, the oak bar thunked home, and her godfather strode to her mother's mount. "Well come, I say again!"

He led the bay toward the hall steps, and Kyrin followed on Aart. He did not laugh at her.

Lady Willa said softly, "It is good to see you, old friend, in this time of trouble." Her bay stretched its neck and whuffled in Lord Fenwer's chest.

"Your Lord Dain has an eye for a beast." Lord Fenwer stroked the bay.

"My lord is akin to you, milord! His loyalty cannot be bought, and the beasts know it."

Kyrin worked her cold fingers in Aart's mane. A chicken cackled contentment, scratching at the dust below her stirrup. A boy with a pup at his heels made his way toward the hall door, but stopped on the bottom hall step to stare.

Kyrin smiled at him. Though not a lord's son, she could respect him. Respect.

She frowned. Men gave respect and allegiance to her father, a just lord who paid his men with trust, besides their due coin. He kept his blade clean between himself and his armsmen.

Her father would see that she was well-kept by the lord who claimed her. Kyrin's smile slipped and she ducked her head. Mother said she need not answer any lord's son until she reached fifteen summers. She hugged herself.

Uncle Ulf would tell her to pray. And she had, but—Kyrin sniffed. The scent of hot bread and roasting meat with sage pulled at her.

In the hall the last red-gold light glowed on Fenwer's great chair at the end of a long table. Benches lined the sides. Servants crossed to the board, balancing enormous stacks of trenchers and cups.

The boy on the steps wiped his dirty hands on his trousers, his barley-straw hair bristling.

Kyrin grinned. He looked as hungry as she. Then he sneezed.

The chicken cackled in alarm and burst from under Kyrin's stirrup on pounding wings. Kyrin wrapped her legs around Aart's stiff sides and whispered to his cocked ears. Now would not be a good time for him to leap away from a chicken-wolf and dump her in the dust. Not in front of her godfather and his men and women, who would not laugh at her if she did not give them cause.

"Darin!" cried a sharp voice. The boy jumped, and Aart threw back his head with a snort. Aart danced. Kyrin held with her legs and argued for the rein.

In the hall doorway a girl with a yellow braid wiped her hands on her apron. She frowned. "The wood, remember loose-wit, for the oven?" She turned away, her voice drifting back. "I even have to tell you to tie up your trews—!"

Darin's thin shoulders sagged.

Kyrin scowled at the girl's back. *As horrible as old Medaen and Esther.*

The boy glanced at the thin column of smoke rising above the low thatch roof of the servants' long quarters that adjoined the hall. The kitchen must lie behind, built apart from the main hall, with a hungry oven Darin had forgotten. Kyrin urged stillness into Aart and abruptly held out the reins.

"Darin, hold him for me?" First cool drops of rain pattered down, dampening her outstretched arm, flecking the dust.

Darin wiped his nose on his sleeve, struggling to keep back his grin. He took his charge in a hand that trembled—only a little. Kyrin twisted in her saddle to loosen her haversack.

There. She dared honor a serving boy. Let Esther make of it what she would.

"Come, come inside from the wet!" Lord Fenwer reached up, his hands on Kyrin's waist warding her like iron. He set her on the ground beside her mother, sack in hand, while Darin led Aart away. Darin's head was up, and his eyes shone.

On Lord Fenwer's threshold warmth met Kyrin like a wall, and she leaned into its comfort. At the head of her godfather's table she steadied weary legs and gulped steaming sweet cider from Lord Fenwer's silver guest-cup. The heavy oak board was smooth and shiny from use.

Kyrin wished it was laden with the thick gravy, roast meat, and golden bread of supper. There might even be honey-oat cakes. She swallowed.

Her godfather winked, and Kyrin blushed. She set the still warm guest-cup in his hand, began to bow but remembered he was not her father, and ducked into a hasty curtsey. Lord Fenwer inclined his head gravely, the lines about his eyes crinkling.

He turned. "My Lady Willa, we will see if the room in the north tower is to your taste."

"My lord, I know it is your best. There is no need. We will do excellently. You should hear at what length my lord speaks of your hospitality." Willa smiled.

Flame-light played on her mother's fair skin and black hair, tousled by her cloak. It was good to hear her low, pleasant laugh. The servants paused in their tasks about the table to listen. The cook's grin was wide. Kyrin lowered her gaze.

Lady Willa of Cierheld fit her name despite her left hand. Once broken, it had healed awry and now curled in a fur glove at her side. She could not use a quill and ink but could grasp a wooden spoon to stir the batter-cakes as her other hand busily shook in salt. She was as graceful as Kyrin was ill-favored, as Esther so often reminded her. Kyrin scowled.

"Even so." Lord Fenwer beckoned to one of his people. "Calee!"

With a curtsey—proper and swift—and a merry greeting that revealed crooked teeth, Calee led them to an open stair on the far side of the hall from the table. Two flights of steps, a short landing, and then Kyrin hung her cloak beside her mother's inside a small room.

There were enough pegs for her haversack of hawks' jesses and hoods. She had brought Samson's spare jesses and the hood with the blue feathers for feast days. Father said Lord Fenwer raised the finest line of falcons among the northern strongholds.

She withdrew the jesses and touched the worn leather. She missed Samson's bright eyes and glorious feathers. Still, it would be good to fly a falcon, a queen of the air, far over the trees, the cliffs, and the endless ocean. Far from suspicion and laughter and choice.

Calee lit the fire in the hearth and left them.

Kyrin moved past the bed with its smell of autumn-grass mattress and opened the wide shutter. Misting rain sprinkled the sill. How did one ride the wind and conquer anything from a cage? A hundred lengths across the roof of the hall, the south tower rose opposite hers.

She wanted to sleep here, as Father said he had. To watch the sea as an Eagle sentry in her father's tales of long ago—to catch the forest appearing beyond the wall, mysterious in the dawn.

But grey hid Lord Fenwer's out-wall. Beyond the approaching storm-veil, the cold waves of the North Sea thundered against the cliffs. The raging echoes shivered in her ears. Storm-wind scented with smoke, damp leaves, and the grass of the hills swept the grey mist away from yard, tower, and wall. The sudden cold vastness of grass and stone called to her. To see the Eagles who had passed so many seasons agone.

She could almost catch a bit of red cloak—hear the shish-ing of swords from sheaths—see the eagle they carried as their standard. Lords of decision and battle, prey of their choices. The wind taunted her, a falcon imprisoned in her eyrie.

Pursued

The snares of death. ~Psalm 18:5

With a deep breath, Kyrin shook back her long hair. She had not thought to watch the sea from her god-father's tower without Celine this leaf-fall. Falcons were true—but friends cut sharp as a treacherous blade. Lord Fenwer's tower gave her a high eyrie from storm for the second time in two years.

Another gust of wind batted shorter locks about her face. A chair creaked. Her mother padded across the stone behind her. Kyrin heard the sigh of a tunic dropped to the floor, the rustling of a dinner tunic donned. Rain spattered the window sill and misted on the floor, a breath of coolness wafting against her ankles.

Father was not here to tickle her mother's ear with a kiss and a low laugh on the morrow—to seal her freedom for a day in the woods, thick now with yellow-clad willow and birch and green pines. He could not tell Mother she would be safe outside Lord Fenwer's stronghold despite the sea-mist and the cliffs, flying her hunters of the air. The sea-thunder boded ill. The moaning wind around the tower would batter any hawk or falcon to a bolt of wet feathers hurtling to ruin under the trees.

"What do you think, Kyrin?"

Kyrin started and turned, with a swift smile.

Her mother's tunic, the rich ochre of autumn, flowed to the tips of her doeskin shoes. The saffron sleeves of her over-tunic brushed her girdle, and from the braided linen swung the key of Cierheld. A beautiful, handspan-long, angular piece of iron.

Kyrin stared at it grimly. Before many more sunrises she would hand her own key to a lord. And she had not yet found him.

"Are you well?" Lady Willa sat, her crippled fingers gripping the arm of her chair, living wood curling about a tree-knot. *She can be hard as a knot too, when she settles her mind on a thing.* Her concern enfolded Kyrin with the warmth of fur in winter. *She said I had until fifteen summers to choose.* Kyrin shivered. Her mother's grey gaze sharpened. "What is it?"

"Nothing, Mother. You will bring honor to Father this night, and Calee's tongue will wag in the kitchen—the sleeves are most becoming." Kyrin moved to the bed and dropped her tunic, which smelled of Aart, around her feet. She dug for a clean one in her mother's saddlebag. "Do not think of me, I'm well, truly. It was a long ride. But Lord Fenwer is as kind as ever."

She tugged at a strand of hair that had escaped the bonds of her leather circlet. Mother said her hair shone with glints of honey in the sun. It was not "drab as a draggled wren just in out of the rain"—as Myrna of Jornhold declared once, with a disdainful sniff.

Kyrin's fingers tightened. Wren or not, she had time to show Esther and Myrna that hunting a falcon was about swift beauty, about something of use in her hand, and something she could not name that rose inside her on their wings. Esther, the nearest stronghold first-daughter, would not laugh at her again.

And Mother must never know what Esther whispered of her hill-blood.

Everyone in the three strongholds knew Esther was the beauty among their first-daughters, with hair of gold and straw-flower eyes. Round faced Myrna was winsome in her ways, and cried over the rabbits that Kyrin's hawk, Samson, hunted for the stew.

But Kyrin of Cierheld was too small, with all the sharp angles of her blood, as apt to stumble into one with a scowl as to curtsey and smile.

An orphan and the stronghold daughters' companion, colt-ish, red-haired Celine was a born mimic—sure to find her place despite a rough beginning—if she stayed close to the others. So Aunt Medaen said. "High blood will call to blood."

As if old Medaen knows anything about high blood, or those of the blood of the hills—she followed Father from peasant to mercenary, and despised Lord Edsel until he repaid Father's protection with Cierheld. Now the other lords look at Father and Edsel's wall with suspicion. And Medaen can't see past her long nose. She insists I ready myself for Lord Bergrin Jorn. That I guard his suit as I can against Lord Edsel.

But Edsel makes me laugh. And he is as old as Father—and Lord Fenwer. With Edsel I am safe.

Kyrin smothered a grin. *Fenwer's stone* did *ward me well. Old Medaen need not fear. I will not hand-fast any but a true lord. Though I have not found one.*

But Esther—she could not wait for the lords or their sons to seek her out when she came of age. She sought them with wile and wit, and always Kyrin was the one caught stumbling over her feet, or missing the proper greeting and conversation. Kyrin clenched her hands.

Along with the usual bards' songs and tales, the scops brought to Cierheld the rumor of short, slant-eyed master horsemen from the Steppes—archers without compare—who drove all before them on the far side of the world.

Father would give a field for one of their bows. He said in battle their arrows fell like rain. Their horse-archers could strike a man's spine at two hundred paces as his mount galloped, and topple him from the saddle.

Capture by the Steppe barbarians *might* cure Esther. Hauling endless loads of dried horse dung to barbarian fires would bend her mind from the men's glances she drew behind her at every feast. After she escaped, with due trouble, (for not knowing how to ride astride or anything useful) she would gather with Celine and Myrna in Kyrin's room, and humbly ask Kyrin how she came to be so sensible. Kyrin smiled.

Myrna would wring her hands and cry over Esther's ordeal and take a cake from the platter on Kyrin's table for comfort. Celine would listen wide-eyed, but soon beg Kyrin to show her how to fly Samson as she had promised.

The tower shutter rattled. Esther was not here. Kyrin grimaced and fished her wrinkled tunic from the saddlebag. She would be a lady for her godfather tonight, though at her first guest-cup two seasons agone he'd caught her between a man's bow and a curtsey. Following guest-cups and another leaf-fall had taught her better. She was no longer so awkward in manners, though Esther seemed able to make her stumble with one cool lift of an eyebrow.

The pine-green tunic Kyrin held slid soft over her shoulders. Cut high above her breast, the soft wool fell to her ankles, secured by the girdle that held her pouch and Cierheld key, twin to her mother's. She could shoot and ride better than many of the lords' sons. She shook out her wide sleeves, edged with blue thread.

No matter what Myrna said of her fitted sleeves, they made shooting a bow possible. No wind could swell them like blown glass, to startle her hawk or her falcon. She never told Myrna of her riding trews and running through the grass below her hunters of the air. She donned her trews alone, when she reached the friendly trees. She flopped back on the bed and twisted the beads of her necklace.

The delicate carved fish of green-and-rose seashell leaped amid oak beads that she liked to think were peat-dark river bubbles. Her father's gift for her fifteenth name-day went well with her green tunic. Kyrin sat up to slip off her shoes. Rain drummed on the slate roof and in the window.

Mother would have something to say if the wet dampened her tunic—though she wanted the shutter open for the fresh air. She said storms made her feel alive.

In the morning the sun might be shining. Who can tell? I will fly with Lord Fenwer's falcons, high and far. Wind ripped the shutter around and slammed it against the outside wall.

A winged shape hurtled past the sill with a shrill cry. Was it one of Lord Fenwer's birds? Kyrin leaned out and twisted to stare up, blinking against the almost dark and the rain.

"Kyrin, your tunic—"

Again the call came—the harsh echo of a lone gull. Kyrin saw nothing but wind-blown rain.

"Yes, mother." She wiped her face and reached for the shutter. The wind pulled at it, and she struggled.

Along the east side of the out-wall a small door opened onto the cliffs. It flapped in the wind, a crow's wing. A torch bobbed through it. All else along the wall was dark.

A shout came, far and distant. Flames licked up the side of the stables and grew swiftly, as if fed with invisible fuel more potent than wood. Pale-robed figures crossed the yard below in a rough line. The spikes on their pale mushroom-like helms glowed silver and red in the firelight. Kyrin caught her breath.

None of Lord Fenwer's men had spiked helms. Raiders from the far Steppes? Had her wicked wish for Esther called them? No, no bows shone among the silent rushing shapes, flickering in and out of shadow. They streamed toward the servants who carried splashing buckets and pans from the hall door.

Kyrin gripped the sill, her breath frozen. Were they passing traders who had seen the fire? They would help, take the buckets in ready hands . . . The men drew a flickering line of swords, and the servants scattered—quail fleeing a falcon's shadow.

Lord Fenwer's shouting armsmen poured down the steps, their ranks met and swelled by guards running from the wall. The gleaming line of swordsmen broke and surged to surround sudden knots of struggling, screaming men and women. The chair squawked behind Kyrin. Her mother's grip hurt her shoulder.

Lady Willa stared down a moment, her breath harsh. She spun toward the door. "Kyrin—we must get to Lord Fenwer!"

She snatched Kyrin's wool cloak from the pegs, tossed it to her, and slung her own about her shoulders.

From another peg Kyrin grabbed a belt with the plain arm-length sword her mother wore. Father had stood at the edge of York on the tree-shadowed road, looking up at her mother on her horse. He held the sheathed sword in his outstretched hand. "At least take a blade. When one is needed, it is better you wield one."

Her mother wrapped her crippled hand around the leather-wrapped hilt with a blush and a smile, and Father released her bay's bridle and waved as he turned to the bustling meet. York did not wait for sun or storm, and Lord Dain Cieri must need bargain for steel for weapons.

Now a sword was needed, and Kyrin did not know how to swing it. She wordlessly held the blade out to her mother, who took it and jerked the belt tight under her cloak.

The top of the stair was dark. Kyrin looked back at the tower door, streaming warm firelight. She should have grabbed the leather falcon leashes and hoods from their hook: they would make a stone-sling. But the roar of conflict grew, and she turned after her mother.

They slipped past a guttering torch, staying close to the wall, away from the open side of the stair and the long drop. Lord Fenwer's rooms lay at the far end of the hall below. A yell of triumph rang out. Kyrin faltered.

Men at the foot of the stair held raised swords. One had a spear. They sprang up the steps, their mud-stained robes slapping their legs. Spikes gleamed above cloth-wrapped helms.

Her mother dragged her to the side of the steps. "Jump!"

They leaped, and the raiders gave a wordless shout. Feet stinging from impact, Kyrin scrambled up and plunged after her mother, who spun under the stairwell and through a small, lightless door. Kyrin ran blind, cold air wafting against her face. Behind her, curses echoed over the sound of slapping feet.

Her mother pulled her on, her hand hot and damp. Kyrin reached out and brushed chill stone. The air was dusty and stale. She strained to hear over her thudding heart—were the men following unseen and unheard, like rats?

Sometime later her mother thumped into something with a grunt. Kyrin groped around a bend after her. A red spark shone ahead, a baleful eye. Dim and jumbled, stones had collapsed on the floor below the red glow near the roof. Kyrin stopped. A torch; and men gathered behind the corner.

The pool of light widened. Liquid voices echoed down the passage. Her mother clutched at her. Kyrin put her sleeve to her mouth to muffle the sudden rasping of her breath in her ears.

The "shush" of her feet as they ran back sounded loud as Aart's hooves. *Caught between a burrowing badger and a hound. If only I had my bow.* The pursuing light outlined a black, broken doorway ahead. If only it led far away . . . Kyrin peered in.

Rough-hewn stone, the alcove was ten strides deep and fifteen long, an abandoned room. Her mother slipped in and ran her hands over the shadowed floor and up the walls. Kyrin did not see a crack in it big enough for a rabbit.

Her mother yanked her inside and slid Kyrin's hood around her face, her fingers chill. Kyrin put her arms around her, breathing in the familiar smell of wool cloak and chives and sweet herbs. "Mother, I can . . ."

"Shhh, my little one. Quiet." Lady Willa hugged her with fierce strength, touched her cheek with a feather-light finger, and pushed her back against the wall. Kyrin leaned down and fumbled at chunks of a broken wall-stone that nudged her heels. One piece scraped the other, sharp in her hands.

Her mother drew her eating dagger from her girdle with her twisted hand and slid her sword free with the other. She swung it. The blade whispered, severing the gloom. She lifted her hood and shrugged her cloak around her, blotting out the faint shine of her weapons. She stepped to the shadowed side of the door. A foot scuffed without.

Kyrin's mouth dried. *Be still, keep still. Father!*

Two men walked lightly past, glancing in. They passed from sight beyond the edge of the broken doorway. Six raiders shuffled by after the front guard, several with torches. Light fingered Kyrin. She glimpsed dark hands and eyes and sweating faces.

Some of them wore helmets and some not. Their straight swords were as tall as her mother's waist. Wide daggers with hooked blades were thrust through lengths of bright cloth they wore for belts. Leather and chain mail whispered. Their robes swirled about their feet, wafting sickly sweet perfume, mud, and sea-smell. Then they were past.

She started forward but shrank back at a solitary footfall and the whisper of a dragging limb. In the dimness of the retreating torchlight a raider stumbled into the doorway with a grunt and braced himself, gripping his bloody ankle.

Squinting in pain, he turned his head. Kyrin gripped her stones and pressed back as if she could sink into the wall. His eyes widened. He lurched up, pulling his blade from his sash.

Kyrin's mother slid her arms from under her cloak. The raider raised his sword. Kyrin drew back her rock, but her mother slid between, her blade up to block his, thrusting with her dagger.

2

Taken

Let the sighing of the prisoner come before Thee. ~Psalm 79:11

Kyrin's mother straightened explosively from her crouch, and the raider fell before her slash-and-thrust with a yell. There were answering yells and thudding feet. Another raider sprang into the doorway. He crumpled with a cough, and her mother slid her sword loose from his belly. The wide doorway was empty. Voices cried out in rage. The torchlight bathed Kyrin in red-orange.

"Back!" Fear hollowed her mother's face—then it strengthened into stone. She nodded, acknowledging a command from someone who stood at her shoulder—in the sword-brother place that was empty. Then she glanced back at Kyrin and her stubborn mouth quirked. As when she had all to gain, stealing out of Cierheld with her under old Medaen's nose—both of them after woodland flowers with the dew on them.

The raiders rushed. Her mother whipped about with a ringing yell, facing a storm of weapons. Kyrin twitched against the wall, driven by the skirling scream of metal on metal as blades met and parted. Smoke gathered, shadowing stark grimaces and the tangled dart of blades.

Her mother spun, thrust to deflect an overhead blow, and countered, her blade darting in to strike a raider's thigh. She never stopped moving. Kyrin dared not throw at the men struggling to flank her.

Two of them squeezed around their fallen in the doorway. Her mother stabbed the first and slid around him, pulling her dagger across his stomach as she brought her sword up into the belly of a bull-like man behind him. A thin raider pushed through, jumping at her angled back. Kyrin threw a rock with all her might and hit his elbow. His weapon dropped from his slack fingers.

Kyrin's mother lost her dagger in his chest, then her sword was up, guarding. She moved back, reaching under her cloak. Her leg slid, buckled, and her sword arm swung wide. She thudded back into the wall beside Kyrin.

Kyrin raised her last stone, shivering. With a harsh noise in the back of his throat, another raider swung his sword up two-handed. With a hoarse cry, Kyrin threw. Her rock took him in the neck and he staggered. His blade fell, but numbness held her, and his sword struck her mother. The blade grated free, across the wall, and tangled in Kyrin's cloak at her throat. Her neck burned.

The raider gurgled, dropped his sword, and grabbed his throat. Kyrin could not move. Her mother sucked in a choked breath and her sword clattered on the floor. She slid toward Kyrin, her hand twisted in her cloak at her breast. She wrapped her arm around her, pushing her down. Kyrin's head knocked against the stone floor. Sweet-metal blood smell filled her nose.

She must grab the sword—the sharp edge resting a hand-width from her eyes. Her mother's hair fell across her in a smothering curtain. She groped for her shoulder; she could not breathe.

"Jesu. Jesu . . . Kyrin." Her mother's breath warmed her cheek like soft summer. Then she sighed and her head dropped against her. There was pain, and nothing.

§

Kyrin opened her eyes on light shining through strands of darkness that trapped the warmth of her breath. She tried to lift her head and whimpered. Her neck was afire; her head pounded. Something heavy lay across her. She wriggled away, pushing back handfuls of hair.

Her fingers brushed cool skin. She struggled free to crouch on the floor. Flames licked a dropped torch near her mother's feet. She lay on her side near the wall, her cloak tangled about her.

Kyrin's hand brushed the front of her tunic, stuck to her in a wide wet patch. Her fingers came away dark. Her stomach surged. Her mother was not sleeping.

A low cry tore her. If she had fought for her as a falcon defends its nest, her mother would not lie so pale and still. She dropped to her knees and clutched her mother's crooked hand. She should have thrown her rock sooner; she should have leaped at the man. Her mother fought for her, then, when the sword fell . . . she did not. Kyrin lifted her mother's head onto her knees, smoothing her hair with shaking hands, her heart twisting on itself. The torch flickered, beating at the dark.

A fallen raider's callused feet extended through the doorway. Dust caked the cracks in his heels. Kyrin swallowed, her dry eyes aching. The raiders would come back for the last of their dead. They must not find her.

She laid her mother on the floor and stood. Her legs were full of needles. So Esther and Myrna despised her for hunting in her high valley. It did not matter.

Mother said her bow was useful. And she would be useful—against any man with a weapon. She gritted her teeth on a shudder—part tearless sob, part anger beyond heat or cold. She would shoot until she could hit an ash leaf at a hundred and fifty paces instead of forty. No matter. She would bring down any man who raised a blade to harm. She would get the strength to swing her mother's sword . . . But the floor was empty—the sword was gone.

She lifted the edge of her mother's cloak to make sure the blade did not hide beneath. The cloak tightened, pulling at a long, slender shape near the bronze cloak clasp. She unfastened the red oak leaf and laid back her mother's cloak.

A sheathed dagger lay on her breast, tangled in her hair. *She reached for this when she fell.* Kyrin freed the weapon and slid the blade from the leather. She opened her hand, and blinked. The brazed dagger was a cunningly shaped falcon.

Torchlight played over the bronze feathers. Beak open in a defiant scream, the falcon's eyes penetrated hers, amber lurking in the ebony depths. The falcon's body and shoulders formed the haft, etched wing-tips brushing the reddish blade. The reaching talons and fanned tail formed a down-swept hand guard on either side. The blade was straight, sharp and clean. Kyrin shivered, drawn again to the falcon's far-seeing eyes.

It saw her ugly shrinking, her fear. Where was the hunter of the woods? But unfaltering warmth enfolded her: the falcon gently called her to fly higher. Kyrin's tears came in a rush.

Sometime later, she wiped her face and slid the falcon dagger through her girdle. Faint hope made a nest in a corner of her mind. Maybe Lord Fenwer was beating off the raiders—but he did not know where she was. She had to get away, to get to him, and then to her father. But she could not leave her mother so, twisted on the floor like a downed deer.

She pulled her straight, coiled her hair into her hood as best she could, and tucked her cloak about her softly. She could not cover her face: somewhere else her mother lived. The torch flickered and went out.

Kyrin sneezed at the bitter smoke. She leaned against the wall, biting her lip against a sudden bloom of pain. "Jesu, help me."

Clutching the falcon dagger, she staggered toward the door, feeling her way over the dead man. The dark felt full of hands, ready seize her. Her feet on the stone were loud as Aart's. If he was free outside . . . But raiders prized horses. She must find her godfather, anyone.

She stumbled along the silent passage, feeling her way. Mustiness pressed in on her, tainted with blood; everywhere she smelled it. The floor slanted down. At the end, a wood door was rough under her fingers. The line of light under it shone steady. All seemed still beyond.

She pushed through slowly. The door scraped. Her arms prickled.

She pulled back inside the passage and listened so hard to the emptiness that her ears rang. Torches guttered in crude iron brackets on the opposite wall.

If there was a draft, there was another door. Perhaps a well-used servants' passage? She left the door as it was, stepped around tunics strewn on the passage floor, and peeped inside a plundered room. She saw no bodies. She looked in seven more rooms, all empty. A sudden scuttling was a raider's rush at her back.

She whirled, slamming her elbow into the wall. Her numb fingers almost lost the falcon. A rat scurried away between the angle of wall and floor, ears pinned and tail whisking behind. Kyrin gasped in a breath and rubbed her tingling arm.

A whisper of damp air blew from a doorway at the bottom of a stair. Long and windowless, the chamber smelled of grain, candles, and wood. Light from the passage did not reach far within.

Clutching the falcon, Kyrin crawled past jars large enough to hold her. Jars of wine and pickled meat, and smaller jars of spices. She skirted stacks of dry hides looming above bundled arrow-shafts, and ventured into the shadows. Her fingers found a heap of empty sacks, the rough kind her mother used for grain. Kyrin rubbed her throat and jerked back at the sting. Her head hurt so. She climbed up the mound and curled under the cloak.. She would rest a moment, then she would find her godfather.

§

Light spread like moonrise over the chamber ceiling. Kyrin stared past the top edge of the sack pile, pain pounding through her. Someone spoke in a quick rill of words. Kyrin rolled over— and stifled her cry of pain. She must get away without the voice's notice. *Crawl.* She eased around a jar.

Near the first bundle of arrow-shafts a stray bit of wood cracked loudly under her knee. She flattened like a rabbit gone to earth. Feet rushed across the stone behind her, and many voices murmured. Silence.

She peered between the hides and bristling shafts. Across a stretch of floor, before barrels and a blacksmith's pile of raw-cast pigs of lead, two hands of raiders stood in a circle, their swords drawn, facing outward. They guarded a man behind them. Kyrin glimpsed a turban above a fish-belly pale face.

Three raiders left the wary circle and spread out across the chamber, stepping through the goods, their heads turning, eyes quick, faces fierce as eagles'. The sword of the man in the center chinked against a stone jar; then his blade tugged at the sacks she had left.

A jet-skinned man with a wide, heavy sword went to bar the door. His nose was strong above a generous mouth, and his slightly bared teeth gleamed like his robe, white and startling. His eyes narrowed, and he thrust his head forward with a deep sniff, as if he would smell her out. His head near touched the door lintel; his tree-trunk body filled it. Kyrin swallowed. No escape that way. She tucked the falcon inside her tunic.

The nearest searcher cursed under his breath and stabbed at a hide. Trapped midway between her hunters and the door, Kyrin looked down. Father said light-gleam in the eyes gave rabbits away.

Pain spiked, battering her; for a moment she could not move. Five paces away, the nearest raider grunted. Kyrin's huffing breath stirred the dust; it tickled her nose. She pinched hard. The man turned away. She sighed.

Someone landed on her back, pinning her to the floor, smashing her cheek into the stone.

Fool! She strained to reach the falcon dagger but could not move for the weight crushing her. Her girdle pouch was jerked away. Iron hands dragged her wrists behind her and bound them. Her neck protested when she turned her head.

A man with tawny skin, dark eyes, and a wide mouth grabbed her cloak, snagging her hair. He dragged her up. Her cloak choked her; her fish necklace broke, and fell.

With a chuckle, the raider scooped it up before it reached the floor and tucked it into his sash with her girdle pouch. He pulled her, struggling, toward the waiting raiders. The circle parted.

Kyrin fell where her captor dropped her, hitting her chin on the floor hard enough to lose sight a moment. The falcon bit into her chest. She blinked back tears, gulping for air.

In front of her nose, the edge of a white robe swayed above crimson shoes. The pointed toes were embroidered with stylized vines of gold. Thread so costly she had seen it once: among a trader's stolen goods. Goods stolen from a Saracen. *The mushroom helms.*

Her Arab captor kicked her in the side. "Look up!"

Kyrin obeyed. The owner of the shoes had snapping black eyes. The white-soft skin of his cheeks was high but well-fleshed, and his brown hair curled loosely to his neck. He was not ill-looking. His dark eyes sifted her, chill with disdain. She swallowed back a sob. His thin lips smiled.

Her captor nudged her with a hard toe. His pale robes on his tanned body could belong to any of her mother's murderers, but she did not recognize the tight-pressed generous mouth below his flowing head-cloth, a cloth like to her mother's hair-wrap but bound about his brow with a black cord.

He watched her with an enmity she did not understand, with the intentness of a cat eyeing a fly buzzing about a closed window. He the cat, about to swat her down. "The last of the whelps. One of the unbelievers." He stepped on the hem of her cloak as she tried to roll away, and she struggled against his scornful hand, which shoved her flat again.

"She had this."

Kyrin raised her head. Her oak necklace lay over his palm; he closed his fingers and shook his fist.

Father bored those beads with a burning rod, and with love.

"Peace, peace, Umar. By Allah, this one is older, but she is young enough. I will take one for my service from this house." The black-eyed man turned to run his hand over the pile of rect-angular lead pigs, then said over his shoulder, "Have the healer see to her."

Umar let her go. His hand dropped to his sword hilt. She gathered herself, whimpers in her throat. He cocked his head, his mouth eager. Waiting for her, the fly, to flee and draw his wrath.

Kyrin did not move. Umar growled and yanked her to her feet. Encouraged by his cuffs, she stumbled across the room and past the black giant, who moved aside impassively, and up the stairs. In Lord Fenwer's kitchen she passed bunches of herbs, crushed fragrant on the flagged floor among scattered bronze cauldrons. She pattered across the bit of yard behind the servants' wing and into the great hall. Lord Fenwer had kissed her and her mother in greeting, and lifted the wide-bowled guest-cup in salute, grinning at her, glad to see her again.

His carved seat lay broken on its side, the long benches overturned. Bodies were piled upon the oak board, tumbled over scattered eating knives. She did not see her godfather's white hair in the grisly heap. Shivers shook her. The tower stair lay across the hall.

Her knees wavered. A wind roared in her ears.

Umar struck her hard. "Stand!"

She was first-daughter of Cierheld, Lord Dain's daughter, she was of Cierheld. A falcon, and she must fly. . . . Kyrin fell, gasping. *Mother stood against them.*

Umar dragged her over the great hall doors of nailed oak, splintered on the steps. The tree that had rammed them lay to the side, deserted.

Umar yanked, and Kyrin stumbled to her feet again. She felt her tower rising behind, empty. The yard, hours ago holding children, servants, and contented hounds, was wind-swept, dark and slick with puddles. Umar forced her through the yard gate, the oak bars yet whole, and over the endless killing ground to the forlorn, flapping side gate. Without the great out-wall, the sea growled. Kyrin looked back, wind thrumming in her ears.

Against the grey clouds tipped with dawn her godfather's stronghold crouched like a powerful beast, fallen, its heart ripped from it. Umar cuffed her again; her head rang. At the cliffs' edge she faltered.

Pink from the east blanketed the fog spreading away at her feet. A thin path went down into the mist, toward the thundering ocean. Muddy and scratched from falls, she at last reached the bottom. She scrambled down to gravel and the sea that swirled inside a protecting curve of rock. A gaggle of boats rocked and spun on the foam-flecked swells. Round marsh-boats.

Umar tossed her inside the nearest and stepped over her to the woven withe bench. Seawater slapped over the side and soaked Kyrin, cold and bitter on her lips. There was nowhere to run—water left no tracks for Father.

She levered herself up on her bound hands, panting. She could not swim. Her wool cloak pulled on her aching throat, and she wriggled her shoulders until it eased.

Mist fenced her in on a spinning island of skin and wood. It beaded on Umar's black hair. She stared at his back while he paddled. By his breadth of shoulder and cast of face he had at least twice her summers.

A wave welled toward them, and the skin boat rushed up it and fell, to swoop up another mountain and smack down at the bottom with a jolt. Kyrin rolled, and shoved her feet wide, wedging her toes against the boat's curving sides. Thin hide rippled under her shoulders, the cold water outside squeezing her against Umar's bench. She gulped.

Umar paddled harder. The boat spun, and her stomach with it. Kyrin closed her eyes, swallowing. A solid thump against the boat and raucous hails roused her from stupor.

She squinted through gouts of spray at the wall of a ship, and up, and up. Grinning brown-skinned men, many beardless, peered down at her through patches of mist from a deck above. A fat man with a silver hoop dragging at his ear bawled an order. Men tossed ropes to Umar.

He knotted a thick rope around her middle, and his gesture sent her sliding up the slimy side of the ship. Batted by the waves, she swung and bumped to the top, her middle sawn near in two by the prickly rope. They dumped her on the deck.

Kyrin lifted her head. The last breaths of the storm chilled her. Her bound hands were stiff, her skinned elbows and stomach burned. She rolled over and laid her cheek on the wet wood. The mist wisped away. Dawn spangled the deck with red and silver drops, as with blood and water.

3

Slaves

They ... bow down ... are gone into captivity. ~Isaiah 46:2

A sail rippled with a loud pop above Kyrin. It could wrap the ship around with canvas to spare. Near the far end of the deck squatted a small structure, so rough-hewn the cracks showed. She turned her throbbing head. Behind her rose another shelter of weathered, tight-joined planks with a low door.

Boisterous men called excited questions down to Umar. With his feet braced against the hull, he climbed the side of the ship and stepped over the rail to the deck. Shouts of triumph rose.

Kyrin shrank back from the edge, straining at her bonds. Any moment Umar did not see her was a good moment. The rest of the raiders arrived with more noise, fending their boats from the heaving swell that sought to drive them against the ship's side. They passed sacks of dry goods, furs, weapons, and small handbags of gold and silver jewelry up to their companions who pulled the goods over the rail, across the deck, and through a dark hole into the ship's belly. The pigs of cast lead swung in their coarse sacks, giving the men trouble. Their curses made Kyrin's mouth curve. Her mother's blade was solid and warm against her under her tunic, and she drew a breath. The falcon had stayed with her.

Umar slapped the back of the man with the silver hoop earring and walked toward Kyrin, smiling. She gripped her cold fingers together. *Please, not the dark hole.* Father would never find her there. Umar slung her over his shoulder as if she were a sack of barley. Her head pounded. Kyrin clamped her lips shut. She must not be sick or he would kill her.

Gripping her ankles in a large hand, he bore her through the cargo hole, stepping down a ladder, his lamp shining on a wood wall. It fled past her face as he moved down the passage. The ship squeaked around her with the high pitched voice of a sea creature. Blackness and pain crowded out her vision.

Umar stopped, and a stench of old sweat and pain coiled around Kyrin. Hoarse breathing echoed around them, impossible to tell where it came from. Umar shrugged his shoulder from under her and dropped her.

Kyrin landed on a body that twitched with a hissing grunt. She bit her tongue on her own cry, twisted about—and jerked back from a man's face a hand-span from her nose. Pain dizzied her. When she could see again, he grimaced, but made no further move, staring at her.

His rye-dark, round face was stark measured against Umar's paler length. His short hair of straight black bore the first frost of years.Sweat-beaded skin crinkled around his almond shaped brown eyes. He gasped a gentle word she did not understand, and his full mouth tilted at the corners.

Thin ropes tied to posts stretched him an armspan above the floor, racking his wrists and ankles with his weight and hers. Blood wove down his arms from his purple hands.

Choking, suddenly aware of her weight against his wrists, Kyrin twisted to roll off him, but he pulled up on one side and heaved his shoulder in the way. She slumped back, without strength, and the man clenched his jaw, slowly letting himself pull equally on all four limbs again, breathing hard, his eyes briefly closing. Slanted eyes—a nomad Steppes' archer—and their bows. If they did this to one of them, what of her?

Through a terrible ringing in her ears, Umar laughed. "She is yours to keep alive, one of the people of the Book, an unbelieving Nasrany. Filthy *hwarang*—fighter for flowers and undying spirits! See if you can obey our master in *this*. Keep her life."

A knife rasped on rope. The man's feet thudded to the floor beneath Kyrin. She slid and opened her eyes, grasping with her bound hands at the man's tunic. The cloth pulled through her weak fingers. He raised his knees with a grunt, halting her fall.

Umar cut the man's hands free, his laugh biting as vinegar. The man worked his arms under Kyrin without using his hands and pushed himself to his feet, panting. When he swayed, the floor dipped under Kyrin with a sickening lurch. He turned from Umar's satisfied smile, and a door gaped before them.

Their tormentor's steps retreated, then Kyrin was inside a stinking black place. The man let her down. And the dark took her away.

§

She woke on her face on a mat that smelled like it had not seen water since its woven birth. Grey light came from somewhere above. Cold water dribbled over her neck, tickling.

Someone hummed, deep and soft. Hands gripped her shoulders and turned her over. Kyrin stiffened and scrambled away from the man with the almond eyes. The dawn-cold wall nudged her back.

A slant eyed Steppes' horse-lord, here? They did unspeakable things to their enemies: skinned them alive, drank their blood . . . yet they kept falcons.

He had kept her from the hard floor, but for Umar, for Umar's snapping-eyed lord, or for himself? He might be a hand or two of years older than she. His legs were not bowed from riding from birth, as the horse-lords' were said to be. He had no bow in this room, only a leather bag behind him on his pallet.

The room smelled of sharp herbs, old sweat, blood, and the faintest scent of sickness. The man's eyes were intent despite their half-lidded appearance, in a face as smooth as her father's. Yet he looked weathered. Maybe it was the finest of wrinkles about the corners of his eyes, or his mouth that smiled even in pain. The white in his hair above one ear did not match the strength in him. Mother said white hair sometimes came early, but men did not lose their desire—Kyrin's throat tightened. If she were a falcon she could fly—out—far over the ocean.

He was staring, then looked away, and his sigh did not comfort her. At last he cupped her cold hands in his, leaving her room to escape. His grasp was warm. He had washed away the blood from the biting ropes, and one of his wrists was thick as both of hers. She might die in those hands, or find room for her wings. Kyrin bit her lip till the blood came. *Jesu!*

§

Pity shook Tae. He reached for her and she cringed. "I will not hurt you." His Master above had sent this one. Not quite a child nor yet a woman. A bruise marred her forehead above amber eyes wide and dark with desolation. Thick, honey-dark hair frustrated its woven band, cupping her pale cheeks and sharp chin. By her wool cloak of heavy green cloth she was well-born.

He leaned forward, keeping his hands down, and kissed her forehead, hoping her father did so. Her face crumpled, and she leaned forward and wrapped her arms around his neck hard enough to strangle.

He had been right, then. He rocked her, his hand on her back, cradling her head on his shoulder. "Shh, shhh." After a while she hiccuped between softer sobs and pulled free. He let her go.

"This—must come off." He prayed his pain-roughened voice was kind, as his commanding fingers tugged at her soaking cloak. He had feared earlier, by Umar's word and the blood smell about her in the dark, that she was mortally hurt. But her skin had been unbroken under the wide red stain on her tunic. He was glad she had been asleep for that, or she might fear him yet more. He pulled the filthy cloak away.

She rubbed her nose with a sniff, and her fingers wandered down to a thin red wound gaping across her neck. He reached out instinctively, and she flinched. Her cloak had hidden that cut—made by a blade. He rummaged for his jar of salve in his herb bag and opened it, dabbed some on her fingers and motioned to her neck. "Put it on."

She spread the thick salve to his satisfaction, biting her lip white, and then let him wind a loose bandage around her neck without protest. No more tears.

He eyed her. One of the people of the Book, Umar said. It might mean much, or nothing. He thought it meant much, but she did not need his questions after Umar's heavy hands.

Weary in every bone, Tae dragged a wooden bucket close and lifted out a dripping rag. His hands were swollen, and it dropped back with a splash into the seawater, so he fished again.

The girl sat with her arms around her legs. He hoped no ill humors of water swelled her head as often happened after a severe blow. Under the early light from the crack of the open hatch, her gaze followed his hands while he bound his ankles and wrists, and hissed between his teeth from the seawater sting. He should be used to stares, but he wished she would turn away. As if she heard his thought, the others, visible in the growing dawn, pulled her attention from him.

His seven companions occupied the other rush mats. Two of them were from the girl's land, and five had been Moor pirates who attacked off the coast of Andulus. Tae shook his head. His master was foolish. Pirates did not make good slaves, and soon they would recover.

Two of the men watched Tae, always. The woman from the village some way up the coast that Ali had raided muttered in her corner. Listening to Winfrey's labored breath, Tae squeezed his rag hard. The other girl taken with her had been unmarked. Alaina would stay whole, at least while he lived.

He sighed. Sick or whole, all were in his charge. Unfit slaves were thrown into the sea. He had not seen any thrown yet, and the Master of the stars willing, he never would.

Ali might order him to make the youngest Moor a eunuch. He hoped not, for the operation often killed. And Abul's arm was healing fast.

And this little one. She shivered, fingering her throat. Tae set a dry bandage around his ankle. "That strike was a near kill. It is a bad place for a scar, for you."

She swallowed when she caught his eyes. From his herb bag he offered her part of his barley bread and a salted fish.

"I thank you." Her voice was raw and soft.

What would she sound like when she healed? Would she train for a singer? But that blade wound—he shook his head. The other one, Alaina, had red-gold hair and eyes not often seen: hazel-green, full of mischief. This one's eyes were amber in the light. They darkened to jet when she looked past him into shadow, at Winfrey. He peered closer. It must be the head blow. She shifted uneasily and turned her head.

Tae tied up the rest of his food; he would wait till his stomach quieted. The girl needed good voices now. Huen would do better, but she was not here.

"You are well come." His voice sounded loud even to him. She started then put a hand to the side of her head, and Tae winced.

It was harder for him to speak without command than it was to understand her tongue.

"I am Kyrin Cieri," she whispered. "Who are you?" She stared at the food in her hands, and gnawed at the fish, watching him.

"I am Tae Chisun." She stopped chewing. Did she catch his formal tone? He must not forget himself again. He bowed his head. "I am a healer—a slave." He leaned forward. She no longer had a child's soul, and he would speak to her so. "How did you come here, daughter of Cieri?"

She told him of the raiders in the storm and her mother. "I should have hit his arm—then she would have her sword, and we—we would be riding home." Her whisper trailed away.

"You have no training in the sword."

"I should have tried . . ."

"You would have fallen. Let your heart rest. There were too many." He stared at his hands. Ali Ben Aidon, master and man stealer: let him die with no one to give him honor. Tae rubbed his chin. That was not a forgiving thought. *Creator of all, cover me.* Kyrin's father was a lord and a warrior by her word, but with no knowledge of the sea. He would not come in time.

Ali raided Kyrin's shores to make up his loss of food and furs that the first storm had taken. He would burn her stronghold, it was his way. Tae snorted.

His master went nowhere without his *hakeem*, his esteemed healer, and then there were the pirates. And now three women.

To his master's eyes, Winfrey was spoiled goods, with nothing but the strength of her arms to bring him gold at her sale, but the other two were virgin. It did not mean a peaceful voyage. Ali would be almost pleased to find them spoiled, to bring him pain, to throw his lack of honor and the weakness of the Master of the stars in his face.

"Why do they hurt you?" Kyrin pointed at one of the posts visible outside the door.

Tae's smile felt crooked. But he need tell only enough for her need, and the tale might comfort her.

"I am a hwarang of the Silla Kingdom in the East, far beyond the seas. I left my land, for I offended my Huen's father, my *kuksun,* my general." Her way of tilting her head like a listening bird was very like Huen. What he would trade to touch Huen's loving face. He cleared his throat. "I journeyed to the Holy City seeking Hebrew poetry, herb culture, and a higher knowledge of medicine, for I am a healer, a hakeem. I stayed with a merchant and his family for the summer, winter, and spring until a trader, jealous of the gold I brought my friend, seized him. He dragged him before the court on false charges. The Master of the stars decided; the judge listened, and my friend and his family were spared. I went with the desert caravans to Baghdad to draw my enemy's jealousy away."

There was pain in her intent eyes, in her finger that scratched agitatedly at her bandage; pain for him. Tae said in a lighter voice, "You may see the round city, when our master Ali Ben Aidon trades there. The *caliph's* city is rich with merchants and goods and learning—and poetry.

"In the caravanserai outside Baghdad, I guested with a merchant who wanted a draught for his wife. After a cup of farewell tea, I woke on Ali's ship, far from the round city; I still do not know the drug the merchant used. Ali traded so far north as the North-men, then we turned back. A storm seven sunrises ago swept everything on deck into the sea. We were hungry. Ali found a village on your shore, and his men killed—many.

Two boys ran by me. I hid them under a slaughtered cow left to bleed out in a cart of straw. Some of Ali's men saw them climbing out. Eager for sport, they were too quick for the boys.

In the dusk the men did not see me. Not quickly enough for two of them. I had a sword, but still there were too many."

Kyrin eyed him up and down. Tae held his quirking mouth still with effort. At most, he guessed the top of his head might reach her warrior father's shoulder.

"On his last raid, Ali ordered Umar to use the ropes. I make a good warning before the door." He made himself smile. It hurt less than hitting the floor with his fist. The boys had been—barely—men. "I am a healer who can also scribe, and Ali tells me his wife needs my herbs. So I live, Ali Ben Aidon's hakeem."

Her eyes slid to his bandages.

"I will heal. It is my skill. You sleep here." He patted her mat. "The others are not safe."

She nodded, her eyes dark again.

Turning on her side, she put her rolled cloak under her head, drawing up her feet in their small skin shoes. Tae laid another mat over her and settled, easing himself down cross-legged. He would do what he could about her fear. This was the last raid, if Ali listened to the shipmaster about the damage to his vessel and the coming storms.

Tae stared out the door, humming a martial tune Huen composed and played for him the night they bound themselves to each other. How her small hands had danced over the strings! Her voice, soft as a dove, lilting as a lark's, held poetry of rhythm to the full.

4

Falcon

The Lord is near to the brokenhearted . . . ~Psalms 34:18

Mist surrounded Kyrin in an abandoned room. Cold stone gritted in her hands. The raider lifted his sword—she threw. The blade fell—she ran and gained no ground—and her mother tumbled.

Light bloomed red in the mist around Kyrin. She was alone. The light grew into a blaze of cliffs under the sun, swallowing her sight. She covered her face, stumbled, and steadied herself against a mossy tree trunk.

She stood in a spread of alders and young oaks bordering a sunny glade. In the grass under the king oak her mother leaned down, picking wild flowers. She cradled bluebells and delicate stars of white and pink in a living heap in her left arm. Her crooked hand was straight and whole. She raised her head with a laugh, her smile glad.

Kyrin's heart leaped—she opened her mouth.

Under a clump of sapling oaks behind her mother, tall ferns stirred in the shade. Green-gold eyes stared from the fronds. The tiger crept forward, his viper head low, black and orange striped body tight to the earth, tail flicking, flicking. His eyes locked on Kyrin with desire for more than her flesh. In him was an endless hunger: to bring her nightmares and swallow her dreams.

Kyrin's mother straightened. With a buzzing snarl, the tiger whipped by her. She smiled at his back and sat in the bluebells under the oak. She laid her flowers in her lap, her fingers stained with green. "The Master of all stands with you, Kyrin!"

Ears flat, the tiger reared, his massive forepaws flashing fingerbreadths from Kyrin's face. He roared, "Coward!"

The stench of the meat-eater made her sick. She could not move; she was made of ice. Kyrin screamed against the numbness holding her. In the king oak a falcon lifted her wings. She dove toward Kyrin with a shriek.

Leaning back, Kyrin raised her arm in helpless defense. The falcon screamed again, brushing the tiger's ears with her passage; then her wingbeats whipped Kyrin's hair, and her fierce talons gripped her arm to alight.

With a spitting yowl, the tiger turned from Kyrin and sprang toward her mother, his snarling mouth wide. She laughed in his teeth, a joyous strong peal.

Kyrin reached out. "Mother!"

Fog twisted her mother, the tiger, and the falcon in dark wool, pulling them into nothingness. She was falling.

She opened her eyes, her heart thumping. A shaft of sun heated her cheek. The mats across from her were deserted. The wood floor dipped, loosing her stomach. The ship.

Her head pounded with an echo of "coward, coward, coward." Her eyes pricked with grit and thorns. Her mother was gone, like the dream. But oh! She had been so full of joy and not afraid of the tiger. She had laughed—laughed in the face of death.

Kyrin sat up, and froze.

On her other side a girl studied her, her hazel eyes deep as a summer river. Studying her as if she were a dog making out whether Kyrin was a friend or an enemy. Kyrin smoothed her tunic over her knees.

Gold curls blew above the girl's freckled nose, tumbled around her heart-shaped face by a breeze wandering from the hatch. Her slim legs peeped from a too-short linen tunic. Impossible to tell what color it had faded from, if it had ever been dyed. Gooseflesh bumped her brown calves, scarred with harvest and berrying scratches. Kyrin's clean cloak lay folded in her lap.

"You are awake. I'm glad. It has been . . ." Her eager voice fell on Kyrin's raw heart with the cleansing sting of honey, until she stopped short and peered at her.

Kyrin dropped her gaze, sitting again in her mother's airy chamber beside Celine, each bent over a yard-wide embroidery hoop. Rain pounded outside. Esther and Myrna sat with Lady Willa under the light of the thin window.

"Kyrin, let me see your work." Her mother smiled, and Kyrin hesitated then held up her robin's-egg-blue pillow cover, destined for her dower chest. Her mother pushed a dark strand of hair out of her face. "Good. Your stitches are smaller than your wont. Aunt Medaen will be pleased."

Esther's absent nod of approval was sweet as mead to Kyrin until she bent her head to Myrna's loud whisper, "Falcons, again? Does she want to be one?" And Esther smiled with a corner of her mouth, stifling her laugh without disturbing her summer-straw rope of thick hair. Celine giggled.

Kyrin pressed her lips together and laid her embroidery in her lap as if it were a robin's egg in truth, staring at her birds.

Why was it so horrible to love falcons? They were beautiful and strong and true. True to themselves and the one who created them. She raised her hoop between her and the others and turned her head; she would not get wet spots on her birds. With hot, sticky fingers she tied off her black thread and knotted it.

One clumsily stitched talon, done. She rethreaded with silver, and slid her needle among steely feathers.

Parchment rustled. Esther, unrolling her precious list of lords, most of them beardless, who *might* allow Kyrin to brush the dust from their boots, since Cierheld lay in the power of her hand in the shape of her stronghold key. But Mother insisted she did not have to look at those names. Kyrin glared, wishing the parchment would go up in flame.

Her bow and the fields and forests of Cierheld meant more to her than any alliance. And much more than proud lords who did not wish to hear her speak, but for her to admire their breadth of shoulder or their lands or their taste in cloaks. And beneath their wishes lay darker things: the desire of the hunt, and of power. Kyrin fingered the key on her girdle.

Celine left her and rose on her toes to peer over Myrna's shoulder. Kyrin blinked, staring fiercely at her hoop. Riding among the trees she might find deer or hares, or spot a boar for her father's men. At least the leaves rustled with peace or out-right danger of storm, not with honeyed words she must search for snares.

Esther pounced on her whenever she caught Kyrin staring with amber-black eyes when she was angry or sad or thinking. Esther said her blood was tainted. And Myrna looked aside, wondering softly if Kyrin was "sprite-get." Blood, blood, blood! Kyrin almost wished she had none. But it was her mother's blood too, the blood of the denizens of the hills and the old forests.

Celine once asked her if she spoke to Samson in the bird-speech of the old ones, if that was why he followed Kyrin with-out her having to call him. Kyrin's eyes burned. She would give much to speak with a falcon or dance like the thistledown sprites in the wood in the tapestry in Myrna's room. But she was not like them: the girls or the sprites. It did not matter. *Falcons fly*

alone, not in a flock like crows. If only they did not laugh. A blade would hurt
less. If Esther would bear one against me . . . but she would never dare.

But the strange girl who stared rudely as the ship rocked beneath them was not a first-daughter. Kyrin balled her hands in
her cloak and looked aside, waiting for the girl's halting laugh,
or the mat to rustle as she shrank away. A rough palm lighted
on her arm, a butterfly. Kyrin lifted her head. The girl meant to
speak her scorn.

"Your eyes are fair as a red deer's. I'm Alaina." Her smile
crinkled at the edges. "How is your head?" She scooted closer,
reaching a hand to gently brush Kyrin's hair from her forehead.

Kyrin swallowed past her dry throat. "I—it is well."

Later, Tae interrupted their whispering with fish and bread
he brought, and sat down to eat with them. The bread disappeared quickly, though its hardness made Kyrin's teeth ache,
and the ache spread to her head.

"How long has it been . . . Tae?" She was not sure from the
sun slant.

"It is midday, a day and a night after you fell asleep." He
mopped fish bits from his fingers with the last of his bread. "I
am glad to see you are over your fever." He grinned at her and
ate his last bite without losing a crumb.

Fever. The dream of the tiger. "My thanks. Where are we?"

"Sailing the great sea to Ali Ben Aidon's home in Araby."

"Ali Ben—Ben . . ." She frowned.

"Ben Aidon," said Alaina. "Our master. A Saracen of Persian
blood, not of Araby. He pays Allah with his tongue and his taxes,
but not much else. And nothing pleases him."

"Yes," Tae said. "Umar, who brought you, hates us for Allah's
sake, and because—I am who I am. And Ali—I took his men."

So Ali Ben Aidon was lord to the raiders. Umar, who sought
her as a fly, was one of his. And Araby—she had heard of the hot

land of hellish warriors. How she wanted the sturdy wood walls of Cierheld instead of the ship's wall at her back. If, *when* she got back, she would not complain of cleaning the pig's pen. Father would look for her, but so far, over so much water . . . Did he know she lived? If her godfather's stronghold burned, he might mourn her bones. Kyrin wiped her eyes hard.

Her father had stood in a circle of his armsmen in Cierheld's woods. "Think," he said. His cinnamon eyes stared past his attentive men at her. "Be ready to give your life; know He holds the battle." He spread his hands. "I named our stronghold Cierheld because we of Cieri are held by Him." He nodded, grave at Kyrin's frown. "It is easier to reach forward to attack, and attacking is its own form of warding. Think, and use every strength you have." His armsmen nodded quietly, and Kyrin smiled.

Father defended Cierheld's walls once in his youth, and several times after he had led his men to help neighbor strongholds. He was always interested in new weapons and tactics. He grinned then, at her. "Someday you will ward Cierheld, my daughter, and our people."

Attacking worked for father. Now she must deal with Ali, an enemy it was not safe to beard. She needed a weapon, and she did not feel the falcon dagger in her tunic.

Tae caught her anxious hand, his own a blur. "Don't touch your throat! It must heal." Startled, Kyrin didn't move. His fingers were steel; she could not have moved if she wanted to. In the doorway, Umar eyed them. After a moment his lip curled, and he turned away.

Tae slid his bag from the head of his mat. Among the dry herb bunches nestled a hare's pelt. He held the brown bundle between his knees and untied the furry legs. One had been sewn into a sheath. The head of the falcon dagger peeped from it. It looked ruffled, its eyes wary in the streaming sun. Kyrin swallowed a laugh.

"Hide it well." Tae set the blade in her hand. Its balanced haft fit her grip. The handspan bronze blade fell to a double-edged point.

"No one down here will harm you or Alaina, for I mend their hurts. But they might take this." Tae touched the falcon's head with one finger. "The haft is crafted with skill. Up there"—he nodded toward the sound of pattering feet over their heads— "they take what they want. Carry it after we get to Araby, then they will have other things on their minds. Did you see the great man with the night-black skin?"

Kyrin nodded.

"Good. The Nubian will not hurt you. He will give you food and water and let you keep your robes. But stay out of Umar's sight and keep busy with our master's tasks. Wash yourself every sunrise with seawater; Ali cannot abide slave-stink. The Master of the stars protect you up there. I cannot."

Alaina blurted, "You protected me!" She turned to Kyrin, her words flowing fast, eyes shining. "He is a warrior, and with his hands and feet he is terrible. He and my brother, Owin . . . Well, when Owin and the baker's son fell, it took more than three of Ali's men to hold him. He killed one of them after they knocked his sword away."

Kyrin flinched. *Oh, Alaina.* Tae could not save her brother. But killing without a weapon? That was curious. She had grown up with warriors and their tales, and she had never heard of anyone but wrestlers or tumblers fighting without a blade, be it but a spear or a two-handed sword.

"Feet and hands do not have all power," Tae said. "A sword gives much advantage, and a spear or a bow, more. The mind gives most."

That was something Father might have said. Kyrin stared at Tae. He was shorter and slighter than any warrior she knew, muscled as a hart. He had walked up with their bread and fish quiet as a fox; she had looked around when she smelled the fish. His brown feet were short and broad, callused, and not unmarked. The white scars on his hands said they knew many things. She shivered at his slow, sure smile, but not for herself.

Any who opposed him would not find what they wished. There was more to him than a simple warrior—and he knew the sword. Would he teach her? But she could not ask yet. Kyrin held out the falcon for him to put in his sack. Who did he speak of, this "Master of the stars"?

Tae sheathed the dagger and slid it inside the bag. His herbs were different than her mother's, both sharp and heavy, wormwood and something sweet she did not know.

"Ali summons you to get your earring, his mark." Tae pulled her cloak around her, careful of her throat. "Come, this way."

"Do what Ali says, and you will be well." Alaina tilted her head, showing Kyrin a bronze ring the size of a penny in her left ear, and scrambled to her feet. "I'm coming too!"

"Come, then. Patience is not one of our master's virtues."

Tae led them out of the hold, up to the deck. Kyrin thought the passage shorter than when Umar carried her down. Ali's low weathered hall loomed against the silver face of the rippling sea. The air was salt and fresh. Kyrin stepped after Tae through the low doorway, down below the level of the deck.

The door closed with a creak. Three Arab raiders lounged about a low table on a rug, their swords lying against the wall. Each man wore a headcloth, bound about his brows by a twisted dark cord. Frankincense rose through the dim closeness of the room in curls of sweet smoke from an iron brazier. Silk hangings gleamed on the walls.

At the end of the room, beyond the brazier, Ali sat between Umar and the Nubian. The black giant reminded Kyrin of a lion, light on his feet with the grace of power, his head covered with minute curls. His dark eyes saw all, considered all. His sword reached his hip, wide as his leg. Kyrin swallowed. One of his hands would cover her face. On Ali's other side, Umar watched her with a slight smile. All eyes were on her.

Ali leaned forward on his throne of bronze and red cushions. Tae nudged Kyrin. She stepped toward Ali against the will of her legs. His long pale fingers tapped his blue-robed knee. He had the wanting in his face that she saw in the storage room; she did not know the name of his yearning, but feared the hunter, the gloating coldness. *Mother would stare him down.*

In a tapestry behind her master a great tiger paced in a small room with carved white arches and rich hangings. The tiger's green and bronze-flecked eyes followed Kyrin. Black and orange striped his sides; fangs glistened in his quivering mouth.

On his heavy shoulders sat a hooded falcon, her wing feathers steel grey-and-blue against a creamy breast speckled with black. A gold chain linked her saffron-hued foot to a silver torque about the tiger's neck. A wide torque, etched with wings and set with round amber stones, in places dark as jet.

"Hmmm. You admire my tiger?" Ali said in a smooth, accented polyglot of her tongue.

Kyrin blinked, breathing fast. It was a likeness, a good one, but only a likeness. She tore her gaze from it.

Ali beckoned. "Come, slave, my belly does not seek meat."

He *was* hungry, but for something she could not name. She obeyed, and his eyes wandered over her, noting every smudge, wrinkle, and lacking curve. Kyrin flushed. Myrna giggled often enough at her boy-like straightness.

Ali frowned. "Why the cloth on her neck, my hakeem?"

Kyrin forced herself not to touch her bandage. She licked her lips and glanced over her shoulder. Tae knelt, his forehead on the floor, his voice muffled. "One of your men's blades, my master."

"Will the scar fade, O my Hakeem?" Ali stood.

Kyrin stayed very still. Ali loosed the cloth bandage, dropped it, and touched the hollow of her throat. It hurt. A shiver tore through her, and her blood beat against the light pressure of his fingers. She had to move away; she must not.

"No, my master. The mark is small and can be hidden—"

Ali seemed not to hear. "My buyers come for perfect slaves. They choose the sign to be branded in their flesh and worn for the glory of Allah. This one is . . . worthless."

Kyrin stiffened. If only she had not left the falcon behind.

"Worthless, but for one thing."

Hope beat at the coiled iciness in her stomach.

Ali dropped his hand and walked to the brazier, his blue robe rippling. He lifted a pair of tongs. Thin white ash fell to the glowing coals.

"Stand there, worthless one." He pointed at a red circle on the floor near the brazier. Kyrin stepped into it. Ali brought the tongs to her ear, and she bit her tongue against the cold then searing heat. *I am not thrown over the side, I am not thrown over the side.*

The pain eased, and Ali tugged at her earlobe—the earring. Kyrin opened her eyes.

Ali raised his hand, his pursed lips thin, his face flushed. "Will this cover my warriors lost to the Nasrany dog who whelped you?" Across his fingers dangled the fish carved in nacre, its sea-green, wild rose, and pearl swirling between beads of dark river bubbles.

He shoved the necklace at Kyrin. "Its worth is but shell and wood, worthless one."

She made her uncertain fingers grasp it. *Mother—he has no right to take my key, touch my necklace, to speak of you.* Something of her thoughts must have showed in her face.

Ali snorted. Umar swept a thong whip from behind his back and handed it to Ali.

5

Defiance

He knoweth what is in the darkness,

and the light dwelleth with him. ~Daniel 2:22

"My master, please, I will teach her," Tae said low. "Dancing, singing, scribing, or—"

Iron bits were embedded in the leather strips of the whip. Clutching her necklace, Kyrin backed away. She tripped over Tae, the whip swept forward, and Alaina cried out.

Kyrin curled on the floor, in darkness, bound in ropes of fire. Then hands were on her, Tae's hands, rolling and spinning her, his knees digging into her side. Kyrin took a shuddering breath, tears hot on her cheeks. *Mother laughed at the tiger.*

"Master, her voice is like a bird's. She will silence the lark." Tae's voice rumbled in his chest above her ear.

"You were master to hundreds, fighting those from the North who overran your land, and you deem your hand worthy to teach this scarred one? Was it not to be thousands to command, O warrior of flowers, fighter for spirits, except for your treachery?" Ali's voice was full of honey and spit.

"She will learn martial skill and weapons. Wonders of my land that your guests and brother merchants will whisper of in the caliph's ears. You have seen a hundredth of my skills, O my master."

"Why pity, for a whelp not your own?" Beyond the curve of Tae's stomach, Ali's slippered foot tapped the floor.

"She will be a treasure." Tae's middle was armor against Kyrin's side. He drew his knees closer and hooked her legs beneath him with a shift of one arm.

"Ahhh. The Light of your Eyes that you left behind; maybe this scarred one is the dark pearl to her moon, eh, O my hakeem?" He laughed, and Kyrin's skin prickled. Tae tensed.

There was a hissing swish and a *"swap,"* and Tae jerked, a catch in his breath. Kyrin flinched and squeezed her eyes shut. Five blows, Tae huddling closer over her after each. Would Ali kill him?

No, no. Nothing but a whimper came from her. The tiger in her mind lifted his head, his ears twitching forward, lips pulled swiftly back from his teeth. The falcon's feathers were in disarray, her eyes dull, head sunk to her shoulders.

Ali snapped an order. The Nubian pried Tae from Kyrin and he slumped at the Nubian's feet near the brazier, then struggled to his knees. Alaina darted to Tae's side. The black giant wedged Tae's arms behind him.

Kyrin wiped tears from her chin. She would go into the cold sea and follow her mother. But the tongs in the brazier would take Ali's eyes, before his guards' swords reached her.

Ali stalked around her, thoughtful. He stopped beside Tae and nudged him with his toe. "You are foolish, but useful, Hakeem. And you, Nasrany whelp—are fit to teach him his place, and his unbelieving manhood." He grinned, his mouth wide as an eel's with prey in sight. "My hakeem will yield to a tender blossom. You would not refuse your protector, scarred one? No, you would not deny him when he comes for his nectar."

Umar stood beside the hot coals, his mouth a stiff line, arms crossed. Kyrin sniffed and wiped her nose. Good, he could not reach his blade so easy.

Ali's whip hand trembled.

One leap to the tongs in the brazier beside Tae. Two more to reach her master.

Ali raised his arm.

Kyrin gathered her legs. The whip swung back. *Help me!* She leaped.

Tae cried, "No, my master! I will—"

Umar stepped clear of the swinging thongs, and his foot caught a leg of the brazier. He reached for the tottering burner and snatched his hand back with an oath. The brazier slid down his thigh. Coals rolled bright and whispering.

The Nubian yanked Tae out of reach of the bright cascade. Ali held his whip wide, wordless, his mouth sagging open. Kyrin scuttled over the wood floor on her hands and knees—she must find the tongs. They were nowhere.

The coals spat and popped at Ali's feet. He yelled for water, and the whip thongs whistled. Kyrin flung up her arm.

Flames crackled and roared hungrily.

Ali yelled louder than Umar and beat at whirling sparks, glowing and black on his blue robe. The door slammed open.

Slaves and warriors rushed inside in a thunder of feet and excited voices. Buckets of thrown seawater crashed on the floor and splashed around Kyrin, hissing over the flames.

She blinked. Her eyes stung, and the blackened floor ran with water and charcoal. Smoke choked the incense.

Tae drew his hand across his forehead, staring at Kyrin. Alaina crouched beside him, her hands on his shoulder, hazel eyes round.

Ali made a harsh sound in his throat, his eyes black as a winter bog. He picked the tongs from the floor. *"You* will show my Shema her worth. But I must bind your eye of evil . . ." His voice was soft.

He kicked Kyrin down. She glimpsed another ring in his hand, a shining black oval, and ground her teeth, closing her eyes. The biting tongs yanked at her other ear, the right.

Falcon ... she was ... a falcon. She must climb this wind to get ready for her stoop. Someday her master would be alone, a rabbit.

"Not fit to serve any but my Shema, with those marks." Ali moved back, pursing his mouth, and gave the tongs to the Nubian to put in the empty brazier. He chuckled without mirth. "Yes, yes, such a scarred one will gladden my Shema's heart. She pines as a gazelle, but claims a night with me lasts a moon. You, worthless one, will show her the counter-balance of the scales she has chosen."

Kyrin's heart pounded. Arms rigid, thrusting his scrawny neck forward, Ali grated softly, "Hakeem, see you teach the whelp to follow her dying god. If she curses me with the eye of evil again—you will beg. The jet will swallow and bind dark power. Do not remove it."

Kyrin's mouth dried. What dying god—oh, the leaping fish meant Jesu. But what "curse"? She could not use such power, even if Esther thought different. The eye of evil? Did her gaze frighten him as it did Esther?

"She is yours, Hakeem, and the other dog's daughter." Ali's voice rose. "We will see how long you follow your weak god with two virgins beside you. Wife, concubine, I care not. The evil that might dry your seed is bound. Your sons are mine. When these two come into the way of women—but that small thing will not hold you back, O flower of all warriors." He snorted. "You know the signs that call the bee. Now see to your wounds."

"I am a hakeem, my master, as you say." Tae dropped his eyes, stifling a groan.

Kyrin wanted to hide, but was trapped by a thicket of legs. Not drowning in the sea, but married, given, to Tae. Three together—it could not be—it was abomination. She swallowed hard, but the sourness came up anyway, and spattered the floor and her hands.

Ali turned his back and motioned to a red-haired slave with a bowl of rosewater. He raised his arms, his blue sleeves slid back, and he dipped his hands. He shook away the drops.

"Go," The Nubian ordered Kyrin, his nostrils flaring, his eyes on Ali. The Nubian raised Tae to his feet and shoved him toward the door. A gentle shove.

Beside the brazier Umar held his sword in his unburned hand, his strong face pinched. He met Kyrin's eyes and his mouth flattened, his knuckles white on his sword hilt.

§

Alaina tended Tae in the slaves' quarters, salving his back and laying a bandage on it at his direction. His clammy skin twitched under her hands. The other slaves trailed in, glancing at him and skirting Kyrin, who sat hunched on her mat. Alaina wished they would speak, say something. If she opened her mouth, she'd scream at them—the dogs, afraid of their shadows.

Red-haired Winfrey settled on her mat and whispered to the young Moor, Abul. "I know her kind, from the wild places, the heath and the forest. They say such as she can lay words on us— burn us to black husks, floating to our graves, the ship never to reach shore. Even the master sees it." She lowered her voice.

Alaina pounded her knee with her hand and turned her back on Winfrey. Kyrin was no threat, but Winfrey saw only her heritage, the dark hair and penetrating eyes of those of the blood of the hills, the mystery and the magic woven by loose tongues. Alaina snorted.

Ali feared his new slave: he marked Kyrin with black jet, an earring of the eye, sigil of evil. And he shamed her, setting her to serve his wife at home, his unworthy wife. Alaina wiped her face. Her throat felt thick.

What would happen to her and Kyrin and Tae, three threads woven on a loom of loss? Her master had destroyed Owin. Was any of her family left? She did not think so. She was alone. But she did not have the strength to hate Ali, and Kyrin . . . she huddled on her mat, clutching a cloth spread with salve to her ears, shivering. Alaina almost touched her shoulder but pulled back. The necklace Ali had taunted her with graced her neck, shimmering. Beautiful. She had never touched such a thing.

Alaina reached out again, and drew back reluctantly. Kyrin was high-born, not used to a rough peasant's hand. And Kyrin obeyed Ali because a peasant advised her so—and came near to death. Alaina looked at the floor; Owin had called her simple, once. She must be wiser. Such a necklace belonged with such a one.

How small Kyrin had looked when the Nubian pulled Tae away, her brown hair tossed around her pale face. Her unearthly eyes seemed to pierce body and spirit. A wild, untamed creature of twilight and the airy heights. Alaina wanted to stay close, to shield that wild spark. Somehow, Kyrin warmed her against Ali's coldness. She scrubbed at her drying tears. It was like her master to bind her and Kyrin to Tae with an awful oath. And Ali would keep his promise to make Tae beg.

But Tae in his turn would keep her and Kyrin, bound to protect his—his own. Alaina bowed her head. Ali bound them, but she had not heard Tae agree to his bed-right. Tae first belonged to his Master of the stars. But was he strong enough to keep his oath?

"Water. Please, water." Tae's voice was stronger. Alaina padded out to the barrel next to the ladder and returned with the dipper. She paused, water dripping on her toes.

Lying on his mat, Tae's wide, muscled back was striped with her neat bandaging, spotted with blood. A pale scar stretched from his shoulder blade to his hip, running in and out under the bandages, disappearing at his trouser line. A sword scar from his fighting days in the lower *rangdo* ranks of hwarang, before Huen? Flecks of white swirled in his dark hair about Ali's ring of ownership, snow at night about bronze flame. He was not so old.

Alaina closed her eyes. *Lord of all, help us.* Tae tried to help her brother, Owin: he did not break oaths, even those unspoken. Tae licked his lips, and Alaina lowered the dipper.

§

Kyrin turned her throbbing head to ease her cramped neck. *Lord, not the wife-right.* When the ship made land she would run. Would Alaina come?

Alaina sat with her back against the wall at the head of Tae's mat. In the hatch's last light, her breath ruffled her hair that hung in her face, sticking to smudged tears.

The red-haired slave muttered of Kyrin's shame in the growing dark. Kyrin tried to think of nothing. At last Winfrey fell mercifully silent. The sun was going.

Kyrin's eyes opened on a dream of darkness and shadows. Across the room a vague swordsman swung at her mother, who cowered against the wall. Kyrin screamed. The raider's eyes snapped open. Ali's dark eyes in his pale face were pitiless.

Kyrin swung the stones in her hands. They smacked against warmth and wet, smashing those dead orbs of vision. He fell.

Mist rose thick around him then wisped away in a breeze she did not feel. The tiger stood where Ali had lain, one paw lifted, his huge eyes green-gold. The falcon clung to his fur, a loop of her chain tinking, her wings spreading in alarm.

Kyrin sprang to her feet. The tiger took a stalking step, tail lashing, and crouched. The falcon flapped and shrieked, bobbing her head. The tiger opened his cavernous mouth. "Coward!" He roared.

Kyrin ran. She did not feel the ankle chain shackling her foot until it snapped taught, slamming her to her knees and elbows on unforgiving wood outside the door of the slaves' quarters. She rolled to her back, facing the door, her arms and free leg drawn up to shield her.

A wind rushed through her, stirring every fiber, blood-beat, and bone. Then it was gone, and she was lighter, her heart and breath faster. Something bound her face; she smelled leather. She thought of a falcon's hood and struggled to lift her arms. Air resisted her, pushing, pulling—at feathers. Her feathers. But she dared not fly. His claws would find her.

She unfurled her wings and crouched, hoping her talons did not prick him to madness. No, there was a silk pad on his shoulders: the threads caught at her talons. His chest vibrated with a rumbling cough. He stretched out his neck, sniffed, and snorted. Her ankle chain she had left behind clinked on the deck under his shifting body; he pawed at it, a claw scritching against metal. He would smell her, chained again, this time on his back, and . . .

With a stretching of unfamiliar muscles, she raised an unwieldy sharp-tipped foot to the hood that barred her sight.

Kyrin blinked muzzily. She lay on her mat, Alaina at her feet. No feathers, no hood.

Alaina nudged her ankle and tipped her head toward the door. Tae's breathing was quiet where he slept on his mat. Umar, a tall, black shape, waited in the doorway.

At his gesture, Kyrin got up, stiff and slow. So this was how a slave's sunrise began. The scabbed lash marks pulled at her back, stinging. She was glad Umar let Tae be, though she wished for his warmth at her back. Alaina did not seem alarmed. Kyrin followed her. The other slaves' feet pattered behind them.

The deck was cold under Kyrin's toes. Umar barked an order. The men and Winfrey scattered to buckets and bundles of rags beside the rail. Rags plunged into icy water and plopped wetly onto the deck. Kyrin helped them wash the endless wood planks, hauling fresh buckets of saltwater from the sea, dumping the dirty back.

Gauzy bands of red and purple lightened the sky. The sea slapped the hull. Kyrin wiped her warm face on her arm and rubbed the bronze ring in her itching ear. The jet earring dragged painfully heavy on the other side, and she touched it with one finger. When the others' eyes fell on it they looked away, like Esther. She was a changeling this morn.

Umar cleared his throat and gave her a lizard grin, slapping the whip in his hand gently against his thigh. Kyrin scrambled back to Alaina and rubbed her rag hard over the planks. The pitch between them stuck to her fingers and did not keep out splinters. She flinched. It was worse than trying to reap grain with a straight-sword.

The wood deck gleamed before the sun grew hot, and Ali's warriors brought spoil to be counted while Umar valued the heaps and tallied them. Aching from so long in one position sorting and piling, Kyrin watched for the warrior she had struck in the throat with her rock. She did not see him. So, one of her godfather's men must have killed him. *Good.*

When the sun dipped below the horizon she rose from before the heap of brooches, rings, and arm rings ripped from Lord Fenwer and his men. Umar released her after the others with a cuff. "Nasrany dog!" She went to her mat, her hand over her stinging ear with the black ring, imagining the falcon dagger warm in her fingers. She went to sleep touching Tae's herb bag.

§

Alaina woke. A muffled sob broke the blackness. "Kyrin, what is it?" She reached, found Kyrin's shoulder, and slid an awkward arm around her.

Kyrin sniffed. "Alaina, are you—hand-fasted—at home?"

"No." She sucked her lip. She had been friends with Aldhelm, though he felt more for her. His bread was good and light, as wholesome as his kindness, for all he was an apprentice baker. Had been, before he fell with Owin. Her breath quickened. "Ali is a pig!" she blurted

"Yes. He will fall to a hunter someday." Kyrin's voice cracked.

Alaina held her tight. "Do *you* have someone?"

"No. But better Tae than the others."

"Yes, burn it." Her voice wavered, with a sorrowful, bitter sound. They could jump from the ship, never mind if they drowned. But she did not truly wish death.

Oh, Owin, I am glad you are not here, but I wish you were. You would cut down Ali like the pig he is. And I—I would finish learning to read with Sister Ethelbert, and not have to marry both—no, don't think of that. Tae may keep his oath. My sister—she would be free.

Kyrin whispered, "I will ask Tae not to touch us. He knows we are pure."

Alaina pulled back. "Do not say so. Tae has not spoken. Do not ask him!" If they never spoke of it, it never happened. If they never spoke of it, they could not betray each other if Ali found out.

"I must, Alaina. I must find my father. But—don't hate me."

Alaina squeezed her shoulder. "I won't. Sister," she added under her breath.

A voice came out of the dark. "It seems we agree before the Master of the stars."

Alaina jumped, and Kyrin stifled a cry.

Tae's mat rustled, and his voice held solemn promise. "Huen waits for me. I think of her at sunset and sunrise. To me, you are the daughters she longs for."

He was not taking the wife-right. He was keeping his higher oath. Alaina gripped Kyrin's arm hard in hope. But what would Ali do? Drowning would be gentler.

"Do not fear. Ali knows you are too young. I will make you herb draughts to strengthen you for sons. You will drink them; they will improve your digestion. Then, when you become women, we will find another reason, another way."

"But how can you keep—what you say?" Kyrin's voice wobbled.

"By this, for you. I will think of something for me, for the nights."

The herb bag crackled. Tae's warm fingers holding a sharp, cool edge skimmed Alaina's arm. Kyrin's falcon blade: beautiful, farseeing, deadly. Alaina drew away with a shudder. It spoke to her of death, maybe because Kyrin was so full of anger when she looked at it.

"It is well," Kyrin said, a lord's daughter again. "I did think you might know him who gave us the sign of the fish. Is he the Master of Heaven you speak of?"

"Yes. Sleep now."

"Yes, Tae."

"My thanks." Alaina smiled in the dark, her voice faint, but her heart leapt. She pressed Kyrin's hand and whispered, "Whatever happens, I am of your hearth and salt."

Kyrin pulled her hand away. "You are not my servant."

"I did not seek to be." Alaina's heart thudded. She dared much, but to not be alone . . .

"What *do* you mean?"

"We mean to rise together, to stand, bound to each other's good," Tae broke in.

"He has said it—sister." Alaina dared to loose the word to the waiting air.

"But you know what I did. My mother fell because I feared—I'm not . . . worthy." Desolation choked Kyrin's voice.

"Oh *that,"* Alaina said airily, and held her close. Kyrin cried, drawing a shivering breath in her arms. Had Kyrin never had a sister? Alaina hugged her hard.

Sniffing, Kyrin raised her head from Alaina's shoulder. "Tae, what did Ali mean, calling you 'flower warrior, fighter for spirits'?"

Tae was silent then he sighed. "You know I am hwarang. It means one of the flowering youth of my land, flowering warrior, though my years pass. I fight for him whose sign you carry at your neck, since my people deem me unfit to raise my hand beside them against the riders of the North."

Alaina touched her throat. The iridescent necklace she had envied Kyrin. She smiled slightly. She had known such a graceful thing signified something beautiful. "Jesu," she said softly.

"And our Father and his Spirit."

"It is good," Kyrin whispered.

"Yes." Their voices mingled.

Alaina lay down and wriggled joyously closer to Kyrin's warm back. "Well then, good night to you, sister. Good night, Tae."

"Good night, daughters."

It was good. Alaina sighed. Kyrin had huddled amid the streaming ash and dead coals, defiant, sure of her death at Ali's hands. Now she was her sister. Alive.

Alaina shivered. Ali would have to go through her to get to Kyrin again. And if the last scop she had heard gossiping in the village before the raiders came was to be believed, though the horse lords trampled the land of silk and dragons in the East, Tae's hwarang, even if they were ten to their enemies' fifty, would defend their country and triumph. Never give up. Tae said it, and he was hwarang.

$\underline{6}$

$\mathcal{O}aths$

O mine enemy. ~Micah 7:8

Ali leaned on his elbow beside the table, a half-eaten date on his plate. His new slave watched him and the ship's master at their gambling, her face pale, her eyes the color of the jet eye of evil in her ear. He beckoned, and his worthless one stood beside him, her bare feet noiseless enough, holding out a silver serving platter.

Ali grunted. She was too quiet. A slave should go unnoticed by all but her master, who must know where every slave stood around him. The angry, finger-long cut at the base of her throat glistened with the hakeem's salve, and her fingers that clutched his platter were torn. They had bled. She was learning, and she gave him a way to instruct another. Kef had questioned him about his sailing course.

Ali raised his eyes to his opponent. Sweat rolled down the shipmaster's nut-brown cheeks where he bent a shrewd gaze on the ivory markers on their polished board on the table. He moved his marker, pulled it back, and studied the board again. He cursed, fingering his lip.

Below the table, Ali switched a loaded mark with one from his sleeve. He cast, and won three marks. Kef would not rebuke

69

him again for the brazier being lit while *his* ship was under sail. Umar could frown until his forehead stiffened. Allah knew such a game was to him the wager of his horse against another's, a lawful bet. His worthless one sniffled, and Ali gave her a chill glare.

She ducked her head and muffled her sneeze in her arm, lowering her watering, dark, unsettling eyes to the floor. A strange curse caster: incense and rose water tormented her.

He shook his head. A foolish thought that the heat in her hungry spirit called to the fire and it answered. Where had he heard the whisper that such evil dried up the seed of men for children? The eye of evil would not work now through one so marred as she. The beauty of the moon on a silken black night or the light grace of a gazelle: those drew the regard of the eye. But if the source of darkness sought to hide its intentions for his house?

Ali shook his head. His house was known as the merciful. Yet—the ring in the slave's ear shivered, glistening. Blessed be Allah, his robe had been blue, and deflected her intent from the seat of the continuation of his house to the brazier. Dry spoke to dry. He would get a worthy heir, and no power would stop him.

He cuffed the slave and grabbed her neck, pulled to her knees. She was so slender, a twig under his hand. She steadied and submitted, quivering. Her fingers whitened on her wide dish, her arms sagging under the burden of dried fruit and almonds, and the milk in her bowl rippled. She refused to look at him. Ali sighed his regret, cradling his markers in one hand. Umar had instructed her. She did not allow a date to fall or a drop of milk to spill.

"You see, Kef, this"—Ali flicked the jet ring in her ear—"is her glorious binding. It marks her among those who serve me.

The cautious eyes of many make the most careful master. Until such a time as she comes under the mark of her future lord."

Kef glanced at the slave, grunted, and shrugged.

Ali scowled and shoved her away. His worthless one stood without meeting his gaze. The evil was quelled. He grinned and cast his markers, slanting a look at her. She bent her head, rubbing her black earring viciously against her shoulder. An intuitive one, who divined his words without needing his hakeem to interpret.

Ali grinned. His new slave's eyes were almost black, her hatred for him a river. The roiling flood quite overcame the dying god's forgiveness. Ali flicked a crumb from his sleeve and smoothed away the resulting wrinkle. That god did not compare to the evil eye, and the eye was a mote to Allah, who favored the righteous.

Ali glared at Kef. There had been fear in Shema, and anger, when he inquired why she desired the desert of his absence instead of their son. He had thought a son might comfort her, one who carried their blood, his rich heritage. But this worthless one was a flawed jewel, to be set in Shema's lap both as gift and warning. Ahh, yes, a warning. One was due.

Ali lifted his hand, palm down, and spread his fingers. His guards flanked the worthless one in an instant, their hands on their blades. She shrank, wilting before Umar's smile. His bandaged hand quivered on his sword.

"Ahh, such eagerness, Umar." Umar was his blood, indeed, though of low stock. Ali smiled, then nodded, and Umar dropped his hand, reluctant. The Nubian had not touched his hilt. Ali frowned. Did he think to read his master's mind so easily? It was a danger if he thought so—

"Aha!" Kef crowed.

Ali jerked back to the markers. Kef was grinning, taking a marker in triumph. He burped, his stomach straining over his red sash, and drained his tea-cup to the dregs. An older, red-haired slave leaned over to pour for him. The steaming brown drink hit the table and splattered.

Ali drew, reversed the dagger in his hand, and struck. The slave cried out and retreated, rubbing her thigh. She should be grateful—it was but the haft. Instruction remained in a slave's soul if given while the gold was hot, malleable. Ali chuckled, stabbed a date off his worthless one's dish, and dipped it in the milk. It was sweet. He mouthed it in delight.

The red-haired slave licked her lips, crouching against the wall, tears on her face. A small seed of wisdom was hers. Ali's lips quirked. She might be of use in his house, or if the price was right, he might regain some of his loss from the worthless one. He laid his dagger beside his bowl and reached for the apricots.

The worthless one's mouth quivered, her eyes on the red-haired slave. She seemed a reed that would break at a tap, but grasped at the wrong angle, she would cut the hand that wielded her. Ali frowned.

If he heeded the North-men's tales, they coveted the gold and silver that flowed through the veins of his worthless one's barbarous frozen land. The Britons' silver was bright as the moon, their furs thick as choking summer, but nowhere had he caught a whisper of a wise one who might change silver to gold. Even among the North-men, who gathered so much of both.

Sirius Abdasir desired information. Did he send him after a moonbeam that vanished under the sun? Why had the caliph's guardsman sent him to the North Sea, discontented with the gold of Africa? At all times the guardsman's designs held more than one strand of a desert spider's sand-web. News, he said.

News was power. He wished to know if any man of the caliph's traveled this part of the world.

Ali snorted. Proud servant of the most blessed caliph, Sirius Abdasir had the caliph's ear. He sought more. With a twist of his mouth, Ali waved the red-haired slave out.

Gold shone the brighter, the fewer the touching hands. The older slave would not make up this wasted voyage, to him or to the caliph's guardsman. He sighed. He could not afford buyers who frowned in displeasure. Umar needed the rod of patience to cool his blood.

None of these slaves was fit to present when Sirius guested at his table. There were edges to cut and polish if these barbarians were to be jewels with ears, set in high places at court. At court, on the board of power, where pieces moved under the caliph's watchful gaze.

Ali turned his smile on Kef until Kef shifted on his heels, then to Shema's worthless slave. She twitched her face straight, empty and dark.

Hah! Ali spat a date pit. He would cow his worthless one before his hakeem could.

§

Kyrin found Tae on deck. He stared over the rippling water at the last edge of the sun. Some of the crew crouched on their heels in the prow around marked sticks that one or another of them cast to the wood. Their murmurs were indistinguishable. Markers and coins changed hands. A game similar to the one their masters played below.

Kyrin hesitated and touched her neck. It was a small pain. The sword cut was healing.

What had her mother felt when the sword struck her? For her mother, Ali would meet the falcon dagger and feel its edge. On Tae's back the lash marks were already ropey looking scabs.

"What is it?" He did not turn.

She laced her fingers tightly together. In a short, hard rush she said, "Ali murdered my mother and everyone in my godfather's stronghold. I will kill him—but I do not know how to find my way home—after."

Tae turned then, a dark shape against the last of the sun. After a long moment his voice came low. "God avenges. He tells me to defend the helpless. When I would take Ali down for the kidnapper and murderer he is"—his smile slid to one side—"I do not have the seal to do so. You do not. We can defend our lives, but Ali has said he will keep you for Shema. Though he breaks the royal law of God, that does not give us warrant to do so."

Kyrin ached to hit Tae. If Father were here, he would fight Ali, execute him, and take her away. It would be just. But she could not touch Ali with a blade in the dark? And Tae would not, unless it was kill or be killed?

A wind whispered through the rigging, rustled over the tight sail. Her mother's warm hands, her kiss, were gone, never to come again. And Ali was well and fat, sailing home.

She wiped her eyes. *Mother, oh Mother.* Her mother's throaty voice came again as clear as the night she bent over the Vulgate in her lap, the tome golden under candlelight. "He that hates is in darkness. . . ."

Tae's hand was warm and heavy on Kyrin's shoulder. "Do what he commands, daughter. Then you will understand. Some obediences come to us so. Each time Ali closes his heart to the one who fashioned him, to the Master of the star's law, he bargains more of himself to darkness."

Kyrin stifled her snort. *I hope the tiger finds him quickly.*

"Hate seeks you. Do not let it eat you."

The sea heaved under the clouds, as swift as Kyrin's eyes rose to his. He could not see her thoughts. He could not see the tiger.

She lifted her chin. "You killed to save Owin, and the other boy you hid—and Ali hung you in the ropes. You are afraid, afraid!"

"Yes. I am." It was calm, dangerous.

She swallowed.

"I am afraid for me and for Alaina and for you. Ali's country will not judge him for killing what is his, for *instructing* a slave." In the prow the crew's laughter erupted.

Tae regarded them, and then her. "I serve Ali in my body, but I serve first the Master of the stars." The planes of his face were sharp against the orange and black sky, cut by a pale blue horizon.

"Yes, I was angry at Ali's men. I did not know I could not save Owin—until I tried. You never know, before." His hands closed on the rail convulsively. "Wanting to defend them, to stop the raiders' evil, stormed in me. As it should. Now—they are gone, and a blade in Ali's back will not return Owin. The Master of the stars works here. I must love my earthly master as he says. I choose it. I will not murder Ali." His mouth twisted against the black shapes of rope and rail.

Kyrin wrapped her arms around her sore ribs. Cooling deck pitch sucked at her toes. Tae could not save Owin, but he took her whipping.

Father would weigh Tae's words and think on them, and he might agree with him. Uncle Ulf would throw out his arms, his voice strident, "You commit sacrilege!" A warrior who refused in God's name to fight for her. A warrior who was not a monk, but spoke of the Master of the stars most familiar, as if God were a sword-brother.

Kyrin sighed. The Master of all would not forgive her if she did not forgive. Besides, his vengeance would be better; his bill of debt was longer. And her mother had said not to stare behind at past evil, for it would taint the path ahead. Kyrin bit back a sob.

She would watch her path and grow strong, strong enough not to fear Ali. "I will try—to serve him." Her voice broke. He had better never threaten Tae or Alaina; she would kill him then.

Tae pulled her into his arms. "You will do well, daughter. You serve the Master of the stars—who waits to help you."

She clung to him. Tears slipped down her face.

He wiped one away with his thumb. "I know, little one. Do not fear your fear. Do the right you know to do."

She pulled back. The strength in him was honest, and comforting, and grasshoppers scuttled up her back. "I—please Tae."

"What, daughter?" His arms tightened.

Lead weighed her bones. "Mother said touching—any man— is not safe. I know what you said, but—" He would hate her. And there was no one else to be strong for her and Alaina. Kyrin held her breath against more tears.

Tae was still. "You do have troubles tonight. But be easy." He lowered his arms. She shivered and stepped away.

"You are tired. Come, I want to show you something." Ali's men wandered toward their sleeping places. The slaves' hatch thundered shut.

With a hiccup, Kyrin rubbed her face on her arm. Tae wanted her to go with him. He did not hate her. She pattered after him, feeling strangely light.

After a few scrapes and sparks, a flame grew in the lamp Tae lit in the slaves' quarters. The slaves crowded close, shielding its light from the door. Alaina sat up, rubbing her eyes.

Tae rummaged in his herb bag and drew out his hand. On his palm rested a slender woman as tall as his forearm, with coiffed, thick black hair. She smiled if she looked on joyful things. Her lips curved with a hint of mischief. She extended one foot in a swan's delicate step, toes touching first. A pale dove rested on her fingers, in its beak a scarlet-dipped thorn. Her wrap-around brown robes were sticky with glue when Kyrin reached out a cautious hand.

Tae caressed the figurine's face with a gentle finger. "This is my Huen. My wife will stand between our mats every night until I see her again." He stared from Kyrin to Alaina, and around the watching circle of slaves, and every man straightened.

Kyrin let out her breath. Someday she hoped to find a man such as Tae. The lords on Esther's list did not reach his mark by a bowshot. She rubbed her tear-damp face. The doll was so real. She wanted to meet her. Huen. She sounded gentle and kind.

Tae set Huen near the head of his mat and turned. "Ali has decreed that I teach you my way of the warrior. I will teach you more than he knows. You will never be without a weapon again, even if you have no blade in your hand."

Outside in the hold, Umar shouted, "Quiet!"

In the slaves' sudden silence, Tae snapped straight and clapped his fist to his breast. His eyes were wide in mock fear. Then he slumped against the wall and nodded to his brethren in feigned relief. His smile was fleeting. "Knowledge is your greatest weapon."

Alaina's shoulders shook. Kyrin smiled. Tae did not fear Umar, despite the pain he could inflict. The others muffled their glee.

She looped a bit of hair around her finger and tugged, her heart rising. Tae would teach her. She would not fear a sword. She would use it—and she would destroy those of Ali's ilk.

$\mathcal{L}earning$

Like wolves tearing the prey. ~Ezekiel 22:27

Two seven-days later water was rationed, salt encrusted every surface, and the clouds hung over an ocean of iron plate. The westering sun poured through the lowering clouds. Kyrin sat in the ship's prow. A breath of air teased her hair around to tickle her sore cheek. Ali had cuffed her for his meat, over-salted by Winfrey. Sometimes the air alone seemed kind.

If only the wind did not bear her further from Cierheld with every puff. Point her home and she would be a white dandelion, ready to part her seed cradle at the least pull. If only what Esther said about her power to change shape and fly with the birds was true. Under each new sun, the water in her deck-washing bucket made a wavering cameo of her pointed chin, elfin face, and the slave rings in her ears—bronze and jet. Kyrin sighed. So she was Ali's slave. At least she lived.

Tae called his fighting art Subak, the warrior's way of hand and foot fighting. He said it took years to ingrain the killing art to instinct. She would learn weapons after the unarmed skills. No one would die by her side again, and a man who touched her would rue it.

Above her the sail snapped, the deck rolled under her feet, and the prow dug into the grey waves. The calm was breaking. *Father would set his own sword in my hand, if he could. He would hire Tae in the blink of an eye.*

Frowning, Kyrin traced the grain of the shivering wood with her toe, lifted her chin, and walked down the deck against the roll. Her father's light voice was strong in her inner ear, his deep brown eyes as clear in her mind as when he had smiled down at her, his great yew bow slack in his hand. "Kyrin, take aim."

She raised her bow and held and shot.

"Good!" His arm had warmed her shoulders. He pulled her close, and she had laid her cheek against him. The side of her face that hurt now. If only he could be here, with her. Her memory of his warm cinnamon smell dissolved in her tears.

Kyrin rubbed her cheek gingerly. Tae had the salve for it, and her new trousers and tunic for Subak practice, which began with the next sun.

Next morning, she ran across the deck, dodging sail ropes, out of breath and sore from stretching near in half. A crowd of Ali's men and the crew gathered to watch.

"Move!" Tae yelled, and Kyrin sprinted after Alaina, her legs cramping. Alaina seemed to flit from one side of the ship to the other, glancing over her shoulder at Kyrin with a teasing smile.

"Peasant," Kyrin muttered, tripped, and almost sprawled over a coiled rope.

About to duck through Ali's door, Umar glanced at her and paused.

Tae called something, and Umar frowned, jerking his head as at a pesky fly. He crossed his arms, and his hand dropped to play with his sword hilt.

The bandage was gone, but a wide red scab peeped between his thumb and forefinger. His hand tightened convulsively. He stared past Kyrin as if she were invisible, his mouth thin.

Tae went down the ladder into the hold, and one of the crew helped him lift up a bale of wool. Kyrin wrinkled her nose. The washed wool smelled of lanolin. What did Tae want it for?

They settled the dense bale on the hatch, grunting. Tae asked the man to brace it. Then he spun.

His foot flashed out behind him, faster than a horse's kick, driving deep. The bale skidded, shoving the man back while he scrambled to keep his feet. Tae bowed his thanks, ignoring the man's wide-eyed startlement and the other men's laughter. Umar looked away across the deck, unsmiling.

Kyrin closed her open mouth.

Tae waved Alaina over. She eyed the bale, spun and kicked, and her foot sank inches into the "enemy." Tae showed her how to snap her knee up to paradoxically thrust her foot higher behind her. The bale shuddered under Alaina's ruthless attack. Her back kick would take a man in the face.

When Alaina tired and her heel struck wide, Tae turned to Kyrin. Kef and the others turned with him.

Kyrin's blood pounded in her head. Did they wonder what the slave with the eye of evil would do? She lifted her chin.

Raising her hands, she took her place before the bale, turned slowly, pulled her knee up, leaned forward, and kicked back. She hit low, where the wool was packed hard. Pain exploded through her foot, and she almost fell. With a small gasp, she hopped about, teeth gritted.

Umar's lips pulled back from his teeth. Beside him, Kef's belly shook with his chuckle.

Kyrin rubbed her foot hard. How dare they? Murderers. She turned to the sea to hide her face.

"Hit with your heel, not your toes," Alaina offered.

Tae nodded. "A back kick is your strongest kick. You will learn."

Five kicks later Kyrin's foot struck the depression Alaina's heel had left. The bale caved slightly around her blow. Panting, wet with sweat, she smiled. When she could kick like Tae—what would that much force do to a man's knee? That man might never walk again. And if he could not walk, he could not swing a sword. He could not kill. She smiled.

§

That night in the slaves' quarters, Tae bristled with badger intensity under the closed hatch. "Here in this place you are rangdo, students. Watch, and listen." He pointed at the deck above. "Show what you learn to no one. Winfrey, keep the door." His tone was forceful, yet courteous.

Winfrey walked to her post with a smile. Her red hair was bound back with a thong. One of the older men shifted against the wall, among the others.

Tae's gaze moved from face to face and rested at last on Kyrin. "You will never be stronger than the enemy attacking you. You must strike fast. Abul!"

Dark and lithe, Abul moved forward. His left arm bore a scabbed-over wound. It stretched from his elbow, down, and across the back of his hand. Kyrin hated to think of the blow that gave that weal. It was a wonder he could use his arm. Tae had healed him well.

"Victory can spring from as small a thing as redirecting your enemy's strike." Tae drew a wooden dagger from his tunic and handed it to Abul with a bow.

Abul studied the blade. Kyrin bit her lip. Was it safe to teach a pirate the way of the warrior?

As if he heard, Abul lunged for Tae's stomach without warning.

In one smooth, flowing movement Tae struck Abul's throat with his hand, took the blade and was behind him, the wood point nudging the soft spot behind his ear.

Kyrin forgot to breathe. Dark and smoke. Blood in a small room, her mother heavy across her chest, torches and fear.

Alaina elbowed her. "Look, Kyrin, the dagger is blunt. Abul won't hurt Tae."

Kyrin shoved back the dark tide. *Don't look at the blade. Watch Tae—he moves, he breathes, he is not hurt.*

Tae inclined his head. "Again, slow." Abul extended his arm in a slow lunge. "If you want the blade—do so." In slow motion Tae deflected Abul's hand, trapping his wrist in a steel grip. He tugged the dagger sharply toward himself. Abul instinctively resisted, pulling back to keep his weapon, and Tae reversed with Abul's motion, twisting in toward his shoulder. The dagger levered free in Tae's hand.

"If you want to knock him out"—Tae pretended to hit Abul behind the ear with the haft—"or kill"—he drew the spine of the blade across Abul's throat—"all are easier if you are behind your enemy."

Kyrin swallowed hard. The raider's blade fell, and the burn of it bloomed at her throat again.

Tae twisted Abul's wrist and he fell, pulling Tae down after him. "If you are driven down or lose your blade"—Tae dropped the dagger and slithered over Abul's chest like a crab, bringing all his weight to bear—arms, head, and legs locking down—controlling Abul's wild blows. Shifting, he slid astride Abul's stomach, staying on despite his desperate bucking. Abul subsided, panting, then struck at Tae's arms and face with his fists.

Tae drove his elbows down at Abul, striking at the bones above his eyes. "You can blind your attacker with blood, if you hit him, so."

Abul grunted acknowledgement and smiled crookedly from the floor, his wooly hair darker than ever. Tae helped him up, wiped his sweating face on his arm and glanced around the circle of rangdo. Kyrin let out her breath in a long sigh and heard the echoes of others.

Tae bent in a courteous bow and held out the wooden dagger. "Abul, yours is the blunt blade." Abul returned the bow and took it. "Kyrin, you work with Abul. Winfrey, you and Alaina drill beside them."

Kyrin moved to her place. *The blade is wood, only wood. Abul is not an Arab—though a pirate, he speaks from his heart.* She clenched and unclenched her hands.

He was about her size, but far faster and stronger. She could see a sword in his hand, the bright blade slashing down . . . and red blood spilling from its bite. She would not be sick—

"Are you well?" Tae touched her shoulder. Kyrin shrank away, then straightened with an effort and turned to Abul, rubbing her damp hands down her trousers. He grinned and handed her the polished wood blade.

Tae's voice rose to include every rangdo in the room. "You must see your attacker as a whole. Let the power of your blow snap into your enemy, into the point you attack. You are a whip, loose until impact. But slow now, slow. Speed comes after you set the pattern in your limbs."

Kyrin gripped the dagger's wood haft, knuckles white. She remembered Samson's warm, soft feathers, his daring dives. A falcon was swifter yet.

She set her jaw. *Don't see the sharp edge—watch Abul lick his lips, shift back. Someday an Arab will stand where he does.* She struck, the blade sliding before her.

Abul stepped back, trapped the dagger in a sure grip and slid forward in the correct maneuver. He did not twist her arm past the point of submission, but released her. She almost smiled. He had played this game many times with Tae.

Abul nodded gravely. She cocked her head. He did not fear her. They were rangdo, together, learning the way of the warrior.

Every sunrise and sunset, sore and sweating, falling on unforgiving planks and kicking till her legs were like lead, Kyrin learned to strike when her muscles burned, to defend against an enemy when her breath came short—or not at all. A hard palm strike to an attacker's arm was both a defense and an attack. Sharp blows to the nose, brow, temple, or neck with open hands in the right number and sequence could drop a man senseless. Mock-kicking Abul's knee with the blade edge of her foot at the precise angle to break it was harder yet.

In their practice bouts, Abul beat her most of the time. He grinned when he dumped her on the wood. She rubbed her sore behind, scowled, set her jaw and tried again. No one but the night saw her tears.

She bested Alaina at hand to hand a few times, though Alaina drubbed her and Abul with the staff. Alaina had practiced with Owin since she was five summers, at first copying his quarterstaff drills in the field, then practicing with him before his competitions at local fairs.

Kyrin thirsted to try the falcon dagger with Abul. "I know I can, Tae. I'll take the blade and 'kill' him without pricking his skin." Then it would be time to wield a true sword; she would never be sick at thought of an Arab's blood.

Tae regarded her, his dark face still. "You must have the right motion, without thinking, without stopping. My rangdo learn unarmed fighting, then weapons." He paused, looking far beyond her in thought, and nodded. "But Ali is not patient, so now you learn stick and staff, and how to defend against a dagger. The sword must come after." He smiled, the skin crinkling about his eyes. "Dream of your falcon, for you have only begun. It is too soon for a bare blade. In the end you will know both dagger and sword."

He motioned at the wool bale. "Watch, daughter. A stick alone can kill." He seized a spear waiting for repair against the men's hut, twitched the point from the broken shaft and dropped it to the deck, then whirled the shaft in and out around the bale, punctuating the humming of its passage with sharp 'thwacks' into the wool. Dust rose from the rocking target.

The wood haft swept through the air in a blur, struck the knees, poked out the eyes, and came whistling down atop the bale's head with a splitting thump. Tae lowered his arm. "That is the first stick drill."

Kyrin's heart sank. He wasn't even breathing hard. He wrapped the end of the stick in a strip of linen and set it in her hand.

She repeated his twelve-stroke drill awkwardly, whispering, "Temple, temple, collarbone, collarbone . . ." She hit with a tenth of Tae's power. She stopped, for she could not recall the next target. Tae showed her again, swifter than before. Soon the stick was a bronze bar in her trembling, hot hand.

Tae stood back, his arms crossed. Weary moments passed. He rapped, "Keep your elbows in. Wrist loose, loose! Don't hold your breath! Guard your face with your other arm!"

Kyrin gulped, ignoring her dry throat, her burning arm and wrist. *Just get it up to his ear, hit the temple, sweep up—and down to the collarbone. Then the eye—*

"No, no, not the eye, the stomach!"

Her stick dropped too far for the following blow to the knees, and caught her own shin. It stung but carried no weight. She bit her lip. *I'm so tired I can't break a twig.*

"Enough now." Tae held out his hand for the stick. "Go on, Ali is calling. You have done well."

Kyrin went. Done well? She was weak and slow, her thoughts thick as a snail's. Learning the sword would take a lifetime.

Next day Tae set a different stick in her hand. It was silk-soft, black as swamp mud, and thick as three fingers. The heavy weapon would make a dent in anyone's head. Kyrin grinned, swung it back and forth, her wrist loose, and went at the bale with a will.

Tae watched a while and then stopped her, the corner of his mouth twitching. "You hit hard, yes. But your wrist is stiff again. Let it whip, loose the power through your hand, through the wood—to snap into your enemy."

Kyrin tried. And the stick rebounded the smallest bit against her palm with each strike. She had gained force.

In a few moments it was Alaina's turn. The stick hummed for her, and sheep smell rose thick from the bale with the dust. Kyrin flexed her aching hand.

She *had* done better. Someday Tae's stick would sing for her. It would.

But Subak was not all about fighting with a stick or her hands and feet.

One evening Kyrin knelt beside Ali's table, a bit of broken bowl in her hand. She scooped up spilled rice with another shard of the bowl she had dropped. The ship rolled, breasting the cold ocean where it wrestled with the warm Mediterranean. Kyrin swayed and braced herself.

She would not touch the bowl again to the wood or to her master's carpet. What had Tae said about balance? Grow roots. Be a tree. Give way and return, don't fall.

"You don't have the sense Allah gave a camel!" Ali snorted.

Kyrin wiped a drop of his spittle from her cheek, locking her giggle behind tight lips. Tae said camels did spit.

"Watching the sea and dreaming, or dropping dishes!" Where he sat on his cushions, Ali thumped his knee with a fist. "Not that I could get gold for you. Do you hear, worthless one?"

"Yes, my master." She lowered her forehead to the rug. It prickled. *Let him think me a reed. Wield misdirection.*

His voice thickened. "Serve well, and reward will find you. Serve ill, and you become a flawed jewel. If your flaw has not already marked you beyond healing," he muttered. "But we will see. A flawed jewel will be ground to gem dust, not wasted, be it diamond or jet. . . ." His voice trailed away.

She dared lift her eyes. He gazed over her head, his lips curved, almost in happiness.

There was something of the tiger about the confidence of his thin mouth—the pleasure that his thoughts of destroying brought him, and the power of using others.

The tiger stared past Ali's shoulder. She looked into those bottomless gold-green eyes, then down. *When the time is right I will run. Tae and Alaina will come with me. Home—to the beech leaves rustling under the trees. Cierheld will be warm with fires to ward off the rain. There will be hot food and enough furs. Father will wait for me.*

Ali frowned and hitched himself up with a sigh. He nudged her forehead with his foot. "Go, Nasrany—and take the rice with you. Do not let me see your foul gaze till light."

Kyrin crawled backward, rose, and chased the last sticky grains from her hands, struggling to keep her thoughts from her face. Thoughts of the falcon blade pricking Ali's skin, of his bobbing throat, his clenched hands, the pleading in his eyes. Above Ali's red cushions the tiger kept his captive, the falcon's chain sliding across his shoulder. His panting mouth gloated. He hunted the falcon, and her.

Kyrin turned her head. Safer not to see the monster. If only she dared stick out her tongue at his ugly fangs. When she broke the chain, how the falcon would surge up on beating wings and its cry ring across the sky.

Araby

Discretion will guard you,

Understanding will watch over you.... ~Proverbs 2:11

On deck, eager for a first glimpse of land, Kef's men sang about their work and Ali's warriors joked, their robes fresh washed and white. Their swords gleamed in their sashes.

The slaves crowded against the rail. Misted by distance, an uneven line rose against the blue-white horizon. The hills grew.

Kyrin could not decide if they were green or grey. The ship moved around an arm of land and into a large bay. A stone quay glided over the water toward them, a mossy sea serpent. Two ships moved with it.

Kyrin felt a slight shock as rolling waves slapped the quay and her vessel, the stone itself forever still. She was the one moving, speeding towards them. Docked on the far side of the grey stones, a slender Greek vessel with a triangular lateen sail sprouted oars, an ocean creature of many legs. Ali's vessel gained like a gull on the closer ship.

Tae eyed it. "Egyptian."

Everything interested Tae. Kyrin sighed. It would not carry her home.

91

Wide, with a shallow draw made for peaceful waters, it had a square sail, at present furled and lashed. A man with square-cut midnight hair and a short white cloth wrapping his waist, stared at Kyrin with haughty, kohl-lined eyes. His generous nostrils flared.

Kyrin caught a strong whiff of fish and looked down.

A boat bobbed between the ships' hulls. A blue-eyed, dark-skinned figure in a grimy turban held a limp fish in one hand and an eel in the other, his gap-toothed smile flashing, his pale eyes sharp and darting. "Sale, sale!"

A heap of strange, round orange fruits in his boat shone bravely in the midday heat, mingling tangy sweetness with the smell of fish. Kyrin's stomach did a slow flop and gurgle with the gentle sway of the heavy eel that strained the man's skinny, high-held arm.

She touched Alaina's hand where she leaned over the rail, met her grin, and pointed down. Alaina glanced at the fish-seller, shrugged, and turned back to the approaching white shore.

"Alaina!" Kyrin huffed out her breath. Of course Alaina did not mind the fish; she was drinking in their new world of pale sand. Kyrin's mouth twisted, and Ali's vessel bumped the heat-blurred stones.

"What is it?"

"Nothing."

The Egyptian on the deck across from Kyrin snorted, his dark lip curling. She glared at him. The fish seller hastily poled his vessel out of the narrowing crack of water to slip under the Egyptian's prow and around the far side of the quay, out of sight. A few people walked to and from the docked ships, their steps slow and languid under the sun. The heat was a lion, and the sea breeze was dead.

Kef yelled and one of the crew jumped to the quay. Swaying a moment to get his land-legs, he tied a thick rope to a stone, mortared upright among the others. It was worn about the middle with use, like an open clamshell or a woman's shapely waist.

Dry earth. Kyrin's breath came faster. For the first time in moons the ship was still. Like Alaina, she longed for grit under her toes. *It is not my land. No. But I must know my enemy and his land.*

Her chance might come in those lumpy, drab hills—before Ali began his long journey to his home in southern Araby. In summer, Tae said most of Araby was skin-blistered rock and sand and spiny plants. To journey then meant death. In winter there was cutting wind, ice, and even snow.

Kyrin's tight jaw hurt. Araby was more forbidding than Tae's tales, and she was already thirsty. She licked her lips. The autumn here was hotter than she had ever felt, even in wheat harvest. Her mouth was dry as chaff.

Parched, sparse trees hugged the brown hills beyond the sandy crests around the bay, shrubby looking beside her majestic forests of Britannia. There were no stately oaks or laughing brooks. Rowans did not chuckle here. Some places in the Oman mountains were green and pleasant in spring, so Tae said.

Marching over the closest hill of sand, a grove of tall trees with tufts of huge, fan-like leaves clustered above sword-bare trunks extended a finger of green down the hill. It almost touched the quay.

Ah. Tae called them palms.

Two figures struggled upward under the trees. Kyrin squinted. The boys' ragged robes flapped about their limbs. Likely they carried news of Ali's arrival. They topped the rise then their close-cropped heads disappeared below the crest.

Above the edge, the tops of square buildings wavered in the heat. Southward, brown, desolate mountains cut the sky, their spear tips thrusting above the round shields of hills.

Kef's men furled the sail and stowed ropes. With a bang, they lowered a plank to the quay. Ali strode forward, slow and stately. He hummed.

Umar stalked a little ahead of him, his hand on his sword. Ali stepped onto the stone quay, the Nubian at his heels, his Arabs behind. The heavy-laden fish seller waddled away from the Greek ship, followed by the sound of curses. His voice high and beseeching, he held out his arms to Ali, knelt, and bowed his forehead to the stone.

Ali walked by so close that his hem brushed the man's arm. The man tried to kiss Ali's sandals. Umar turned on his heel, circled back, and kicked the fish seller off the quay into the water. The old man's yowl choked silent.

Kyrin flinched, glad she was not the fish seller. It was not right. The crew around her laughed. He must know how to swim, he had not seemed that simple.

The Nubian moved forward to prowl before Ali, guarding his way. Tae was silent, and Winfrey muttered.

"Move! Back, sons of infidels!" Umar raised his arms. His men on the deck herded the slaves away from the quay to the opposite side and against the rail. "Make your way to shore in the water. Your stink rises to heaven!"

Abul yanked Kyrin to his side. The rail dug into her ribs.

White light blazed off the water and blinded her. Far under the dancing surface lay a blue-crystal sea bottom. She gripped the smooth wood and pulled herself up.

"I will sink." Winfrey whispered, her knuckles white beside Kyrin's brown ones.

"Yes, but you will come up, and we will help." Kyrin tilted her head at Alaina and Tae on her other side. Tae nodded and climbed up on the rail, riding the swelling breath of the ocean, legs flexing. A warrior indeed.

Winfrey eyed the water. "My thanks." Her fingernails dug into the wood. One of the older pirates behind her was also tight-lipped.

Umar snorted. "Go, daughters of dung beetles!" He drew his sword and swatted about with the flat. He laughed when Abul sprang away from the sting and half fell over the side. A splash came from below.

Tae dived. Umar drew back his blade, turning it slightly, his eyes on Kyrin, half-lidded.

Kyrin let her legs fold and plunged after Abul and Tae.

Hot air beat at her through her tunic, then water thundered around her. She came up spluttering and treading hard, her nose stinging. The water was warm. It felt silky and fresh. She hoped the fishy orange seller enjoyed it as much. Where were Abul and Alaina?

A shadow slid near under the sparking surface. A sea-grey beast burst into the air before Kyrin in a shower of spray. Gracefully standing on its tail, it squeaked in a creaky-sweet voice.

"Tae!" Kyrin yelled, spluttering when water poured into her mouth. Alaina popped up in reach of her arm. Where was Abul?

The sea beast arced over them in a leap, its body glistening. It had fins like a fish's, except solid and thick, and its body resembled a small, skinny whale. Alaina treaded water, head tipped back as she watched, open mouthed. The creature slid into the water again, blue beak first, sending a wave over Kyrin's head.

"It is a dolphin. It will not hurt you!" Abul swam beside them, his dark arms graceful in the sea foam.

"You can swim, you eel!" Kyrin yelped, and shoved Abul. He pushed down on her shoulders and dunked her. The sea beast slid by under the water; sunlight played over its back. Abruptly it turned to a speeding shadow, disappearing toward the depths. Kyrin pulled herself to Abul's ankles and clung, dragging him under. She ran out of air, and came up. Alaina and the ships wheeled by. Abul grabbed her from behind, and they went under again, spinning.

Would the dolphin come back? Kyrin broke the surface, and pulled her clinging hair from her face, laughing. She stopped short. Dolphins ringed them in a great circle, splashing in and out of the water.

Leaping and crying in their creaky voices, they parted the waves around the scrambling clot of swimming slaves in a great, flashing wheel. For a moment one sea beast stood on its tail five yards from Tae, who towed Winfrey toward shore with an arm about her. Winfrey's eyes shone.

One blink and another—and the dolphins dived and were gone. Alaina looked after them with longing. Kyrin ducked her head under the heaving swell.

Retreating clicks, wails, and squeaks came to her over the sea-sound. She held her breath as long as she could and came up with a great gasp. Panting beside her, Abul leaned back with a sudden whoop, water dripping from his chin. With a mock scowl she chucked a handful of seawater at him to cover the warm wet welling in her eyes.

The dolphins were free and beautiful. While they wove through the water the slaves were taken out of themselves, caught up by that power, that beauty. Winfrey smiled, floating on her back, and Tae nodded at something she whispered.

Did they feel the surge of sweetness, the almost-sorrow of longing, as if something here would dance in them forever? It stirred in the depths of her, surged into her throat.

The flip of a grey-blue fin, water running from its edge, drops sparkling in a joyful swathe under the beast's leap—somehow it all mingled with the softness in Tae toward every person in pain, with Alaina's mischievous grin that lit her face, with the falcon blade, the edge sharp against evil, in the fight for goodness and courage.... Everything all suddenly mattered intensely, though Kyrin could not shape it in words. Purpose was all around her; every moment a part of eternity.

"Go on, dogs!"

Kyrin kicked at the water and turned. Scowling, Umar pointed a long arm toward shore, the tail of his white kaffiyeh dangling undone from his turban. Kyrin smiled.

He could not take this moment. It lay in her mind, a jewel of green and blue, of sea salt. She would remember.

Reaching shore was a rushing, breathless tumble of sand and wave that whirled her over and over, scraping her knees, leaving the sting of salt. In high spirits for the good omen of the dolphins, Ali's men roared with amusement as Kyrin and the rest staggered out of the waves, leaving footprints in ragged curves that the water wiped out behind them.

Kyrin walked up the hill after Tae to set up camp under the palms. By the time she made the rise, she needed another bathe. She grimaced. It was probably too much to hope Umar would stay with the ship.

When Ali called Tae inside their master's tent, Umar followed. No one else was watching, busy with their tasks. Kyrin crept close to the undulating black felt and laid her ear against it. The stiff wall radiated scalding heat. She pulled back a little.

Within, Ali said, "Do my budding flowers begin to give their perfume?"

"Soon, my master. One cannot force a flower to unfold." Tae said nothing more. There was a long pause. Kyrin held her breath.

"The bee is shy to sample his flowers under the sun," Ali said with a longsuffering sigh. "And there is no nectar yet."

Kyrin stifled her snort. Tae was no oath-breaker, whether she became a woman soon or late. The Nubian's impassive voice came clear. "It is so, my master. Their bloom is not something they could hide."

"Ahh." Ali was satisfied. "It is time for my meat. Go, hakeem, I tire of your inauspicious news."

Kyrin slipped away. Beside the slaves' tent she stamped her heel into the sand. That-that eel, who never let go after he got his teeth into his prey. Most of the slaves slept under the grove of palms, only Winfrey taking to the patched tent. She joined them. The leaves above fringed the starry sky, rustling in the moonlight, blending with the lonely, whispering surf.

She woke with the sun and pushed her hair, damp with dew, behind her ears. Ali's tent rose black behind her at the palm grove's edge. The sea below framed the felt walls, the blue rollers crowned in white, the sound of their crashing drowned by a ceaseless babble of nearby humanity. Kyrin rolled over on her mat.

Three arrow flights down the inland slope, people ate, bartered, and squabbled around booths of palm fronds. A bustling market had sprung up before the walls of the town like mushrooms in a night. She leaned over and shook Alaina. Alaina rose on her arms with a groan, then paused, riveted. Kyrin held her knees and rested her chin on her hands.

Gaily robed sellers chanted their wares and sold to buyers, both sides arguing, hands flitting, fingers stabbing the air. The smell of roasted meat, fermented drinks, sweet fruit, and warm bodies drifted to her. Sword-bearing Arabs strolled from booth to booth, their sashes bright against pale robes. Light-skinned Persians stalked to and fro in trousers and turbans, attended by watchful guards.

Most of the women wore dark veils and bore baskets of vegetables or fruit on their heads. Some carried fat clay jars, balanced with a graceful hand, or cradled delicate vessels in their arms, or tended booths beside their husbands. A few bare-headed tribeswomen wore red and green, their faces and hands twined with painted flowers and designs of vivid henna. Bangles tinkled as they led goats and sheep to the market or toward the hills.

A few Egyptians roamed in white cotton shentis, coarse or gauze-thin according to rank. An arrow-straight Moor in a crown of parrot feathers and a long-bearded Hebrew in a striped robe bartered, protesting a date seller's price. Kyrin's mouth watered.

She could almost taste the short, sticky brown fruits. She had smelled them, serving Ali. They were sweet like honey, but not, Tae said.

Slaves were everywhere, bearing goods or watching riding beasts for their masters or mistresses. Some were ill kept, others Kyrin knew apart from their masters only by the way they obeyed. It tired her, seeing their quiet watchfulness for another man or woman's word to go, to fetch, to carry.

The palms stretched northeast from Ali's tent in a thin line, across the market to the town wall. Near the top on both sides of the thick, double-leaved gate, the high mud defense was pierced by rectangular holes for bowmen or spearmen. The finer mud brick houses within the wall each had a square wind tower, airy as lattice—riddled with fanciful windows to catch the idlest breeze and funnel it within. The airy wind towers, crafted in intricate geometric designs, as if a djinn had been let loose with cerulean blue and green, watched over courts filled with leafy trees. Apricots scented the air, and the tang of the orange fruits the fish seller had carried.

Before the town sprawled a group of black tents around the south and east side. Tall-legged beasts with wedge-shaped heads on snake-necks grunted near the tents, kneeling in their places on the sand. Camels could be disdainful animals, but Abul had warned her never to strike one in anger. They were part of the Arabs, bone and blood and breath.

Kyrin rubbed her chin across her knuckles until it hurt. Past the black tents, down the stony road through the blue-brown mountains, the caravan would travel two-and-a-half thousand Eagle miles around a great desert to Ali's home near the Oman mountains.

Thorny growth crawled around the beginning of the path to the plains, the wadis and rocky mountains where bears and lions prowled. Kyrin licked her lips. She had never seen a lion.

At least in caravan she would be protected. Ali did not tolerate threats to his goods. Last night Tae had said that no ship sailed near her land in winter. She could not ask for passage even if she did find a vessel willing to risk the sea.

She had no gold or silver. And if she ran, with her light skin she would stand out like a pomegranate in a bag of dates. So she would ride a camel. But spring came after winter, and there were ports on the Oman coast.

Our flesh had no rest....

without were fightings,

within were fears. ~2 Corinthians 7:5

Alaina stared at a line of patterned rugs of blue, purple, and white hung on a tent rope fifty lengths off. "Those women know how to weave."

"They're beautiful, but we better move before Umar catches us."

Alaina frowned. "A good thought."

At the head of Ali's camel line near the bottom of the hill, hands on his hips, Umar bellowed, "Abul!"

A few heads turned in the market. Abul came out of Ali's tent with a bulging linen sack over his shoulder and waved to Umar. He struggled down through the sand toward the line of pack camels, the heavy sack sliding back and forth across his back. Two ragged Arab youths ran up from the market and swarmed around him, throwing taunts.

Alaina nibbled a fingernail. Umar was in a foul humor, cursing at Abul. Poor Abul, he worked hard.

She bent beside Kyrin and snatched up her palm mat, her hair flying thin and pale beside Kyrin's rich darkness. If she had her stick, the taunting boys would sing differently. Alaina shook the sand out of her mat, rolled it tight, and stacked it on top of Tae's at the base of their palm tree. But it was a new sunrise, in a new land. Abul would make his way.

What might she find here? Certainly they had the most wonderful weavers and colors of thread. Huen's carved feet stuck out of the end of Tae's mat and Alaina pushed them from sight, her fingers lingering on the tiny toes. Tae was up early; he always was. He remained a man—a man determined to keep his promises, a man who loved Huen.

She rubbed her nose. She was a lowborn slave, now a woman thought spoiled. Even if she went home with Kyrin she could never marry. How Sister Ethelbert would clap for joy. Alaina sighed.

She could be a scribe and win acclaim for her poems and tales. People liked them during the long winters. She could hire a scop to read her verses in Kyrin's stronghold. Maybe the caliph, who was the king in this land, would read her works. Tae was teaching her to scribe and to read the letters Sister Ethelbert had begun to help her form. Ali needed slaves who knew letters, who had a perfect hand.

Alaina smiled. The skill would safeguard her since she would lack sons. If the Master of the stars willed she would help Tae translate John's book into her tongue, for her people, like to the Book of Armagh. Not in Bede's Latin, though his work was worthy, but the Lord's word in her own tongue. Owin would laugh long, to see Ali further such a purpose. Alaina nodded. She would become a scribe with a hand to wonder at, and the caliph would notice.

She drew the word *jewel* in the sand with her toe, and next to it the swirling Araby letters. The Master of the stars enjoyed turning sureties on their heads. She had been so certain she was alone. But he gave her a father *and* a sister. She would willingly scribe for Kyrin, and divide her life between Kyrin's stronghold and the nearest abbess's scriptorium. Tae would go back to Huen, become a general, and perhaps save his land from the fierce lords of the horse and—. A wiry Arab among the string of ragged youths around Abul shoved a thick thorn branch between Abul's feet. Alaina gasped. "Kyrin, look!"

Abul staggered to a knee. He got up, his shin bleeding, and turned warily to keep his chanting tormentors from his back. The Arab with the stick shook it in triumph, laughing. Beyond the bottom of the hill with the camels, Umar grinned, his teeth white. Abul put his hand on his dagger.

Alaina's stomach burned. It could not come to daggers or some of them would die, and then Abul. Ali or the townspeople would execute him. Tae was not near. There were seven Arabs. And blades—and Kyrin's fear. *There is only me, and I do not have my stick.* Alaina shook her head—and burst into a run toward Abul.

There came the dull thud of feet on sand. Kyrin matched her, her mouth set, her brown gaze following the Arabs that circled Abul like crows.

Alaina blinked. Her sister would fight with her despite her fear. A fluttering prickle rose in her throat. She drew a deep breath and plunged through the ring of boys. She grabbed one side of Abul's sack and Kyrin the other. Abul straightened with a grunt.

Amid a rise of shrill protests, the wiry Arab grabbed Alaina's arm. His eyes were narrowed under his wide brow above his long nose. She drove her elbow toward him, levered his fingers from her wrist, and twisted around him. She reached to lift Abul's rough sack again. Her tunic tangled in her fingers and rose to brush her bare knees.

Burn the thing! She didn't have time to shake it down.

The Arab kicked at Abul's ankles, and Abul barely evaded him. Kyrin dropped her side of the sack and moved in front of them. The rest of their tormentors gathered behind the Arab, voices high, indignant, calling for blood.

"Go, Alaina!" Kyrin shifted her feet lightly over the sand in the beginning of the martial dance. She did not raise her hands, just stood between them and the Arabs, small and straight.

Abul broke into a stumbling run for the camels. Alaina followed, catching up the slippery sack again every few lengths, panting. She heard nothing behind her and could not turn. Was the Arab drawing his blade? "Go *on*, Abul!"

They dropped the sack at Umar's feet. Alaina spun.

At the base of the sand hill the Arab crouched before her sister. A blue turban perched atop his curly dust and sun-streaked hair. Barefoot, he had a cat's slim build. The ragged pieces of robe about his middle were a sun-bleached muddle, and a torn scrap of blue held the thick blade of a curved dagger close to his side.

Alaina's throat closed, dry. The other Arabs, tall and short, crowded in. Bodies bony and thin, their brown eyes glistened, their mouths a little open. Kyrin glanced over her shoulder, her eyes wide amber. Alaina raised her chin, willing her thought across the open sand. *You can fight the fear, see past the pain. Put the jackal down, Kyrin!*

§

Tae's words echoed in Kyrin's mind. "Run if you can. Submit, distract, attack—do what is needed." She could not run; they would have her down in a moment. So it was distract and attack.

His mouth quirking, the Arab moved forward. He grabbed at her.

Kyrin skipped to the side, half seeing a bloody sword in his long thin fingers. Under her tunic in its soft fur sheath the falcon dagger pressed against her. She left it there.

Doubtless the Arab knew his blade like his fingers knew how to tear roasted quail. His dark skin held beads of sweat, like the plummy kind of cake her mother had made. *He will not touch us again. No, Mother, he will not.* She blinked. There was no sword in his open hand.

He lunged in and flicked her ear and the black earring. "Nasrany!" His other hand brushed his dagger.

Kyrin stumbled.

His mouth tightened, and he reached for her shoulder. Her palm met his with stinging force as she drove his arm up, slid her other hand under it and whirled behind him, locking his arm against his shoulder. He rose on his toes with a sharp cry.

She shoved him toward the other Arabs, forcing him forward by the pressure on his shoulder blade. He turned his head and spit at her face. Grabbing his opposite ear, she pulled his head back. He stamped for her toes.

Kyrin levered his arm farther; he bent forward and hissed, kicking back at her knees.

She shifted and her hold slipped. The Arab jerked free. She broke from him before he could turn and strike. He circled her, breathing hard, rolling his shoulder.

Kyrin turned with him, her breath shuddering in and out. Scalding sand pooled around her ankles, and her rucked tunic pulled at her. Her trousers stuck to her legs.

He was no longer smiling, and his nostrils flared. His thin lips promised pain.

Yipping, the other Arabs closed in, shaking fists and sticks. The Arab yelled, and they stopped.

Kyrin backed toward the camels foot by foot. Where were Abul and Alaina? She could not spare time to find them.

The Arab's jaw flexed. He raised his hands, hunching his shoulders. She heard his teeth grit on sand. He did not seem to feel it.

Kyrin shivered, and backed again. A large hand shoved her between the shoulders, near toppling her to the sand. Market-goers blocked her retreat, grinning and calling cheerfully to each other.

Her heart sank. She slid around the inside of the growing circle, not turning from the Arab. He smiled at her and sprang in a swirl of sand.

She caught the first stir of his shoulder as he drove his fist toward her throat. The blade-edge of her foot found his front knee. His leg buckled. His other knee hit the sand. He bounced back, wove around the knee she drove for his middle, and sank his fist in her side.

Her legs buckled. His third strike grazed her neck. Kyrin's chest was a bellows blown out; she could not get air past the spreading ache in her middle.

He knocked her warding arms aside with two blows, and his kick to the side of her head was quick. Her ears rang, the ground beneath her clutching fingers blurred. Kyrin shoved out her trapped breath. Her sight cleared a little.

"Kyrin! Get up!" From the camel line, Alaina screamed over the noise of the crowd, tearing at Umar's grip in the front of her tunic. Umar cuffed her, and her head snapped back. Beside them one of Umar's men held Abul with his hands behind his back. Abul's scowl was savage, his nose bleeding.

Kyrin curled her fingers. The hot grains dug into her hands and knees, she smelled sweet and sharp camel dung, sweat and hot earth. *Do not break faith.*

The Arab stepped back with a grin and a twitch of his shoulders.

Falcon. She glared up at him.

The Arab leaped, his handful of thrown sand stinging her face. His kick struck her arms and knocked her sideways. Kyrin rolled. Surging up with a scream, she blocked his next kick. He struck at her with his fist.

She captured his wrist with shaky strength. And jerked him toward her. He pulled back, his sweaty skin slipping. She slammed her palm into his elbow as she yanked back on his wrist. Before her ears recorded the *crunch,* she had whipped her elbow into his neck.

He fell, and she let him roll away. His forced-out breath was a groan. His dagger arm flopped by his side.

The Arab boys' chant stopped. The heat beat down. Kyrin's smile pulled at her face painfully.

I beat him! Tae said it—I am not helpless. The crowd stared, from her face to her earring and back. The bettors moved forward, quiet as cobras, their swords and daggers at their sides, untouched. Kyrin staggered back from them, ground and sky tilting.

§

Umar's laugh rang out, and he loosed Alaina. She ran past heated voices and fierce gestures, her heart in her throat. "Stand up, Kyrin! Don't fall!" She held Kyrin with one arm about her waist, leaving the other free to defend her, how—she didn't know.

Kyrin shivered, and Alaina pulled her close, watching the frowning faces of the Arab boys and the crowd.

One man stood, an island in the midst of the flow. He drew a thumb and finger around his mouth and clipped beard, his faint smile approving. His balding head made Alaina think of a holy monk. He was tall, not stocky, but somewhere in between, with the strength of a wolf. His brown tunic bore a blood-red sash.

With an almost audible sigh, the onlookers dispersed toward the town and nearby booths in muttering knots. With a last shrill yell at Kyrin, the young Arabs likewise moved away from the man's challenging stare toward the black tents, leaving their companion on the sand in a disheveled, moaning heap. The tale of the female Nasrany with the power of the evil eye would be told many times before night fell.

The man lifted his hand, almost a benediction, his dark eyes bright. Alaina's heart lurched. Not a monk. His silk-trimmed robe, dense-woven trousers, and long sword proclaimed him one of the Persian warriors Abul had told her of in poetic verse. Persian. Two men in red robes with white sashes and spears in their hands flanked him silently. He nodded and they turned away, joining more of their fellows on the road to the town.

Alaina let out her breath.

Ali was striding down the hill with the Nubian. Umar stalked to meet them, and Abul limped toward her. Half hanging on her arm, Kyrin breathed fast and shallow. She gently tugged Kyrin forward.

The Nubian was imposing as oak, straight as an ash. His arms crossed over his chest, he dropped one eyelid in a slow, ponderous wink. Alaina tightened her lips. She did not have time to wonder at him, for Ali must open his ears to the truth.

Their master listened to her rushing tale with a crooked smile. Tilting his head back, he mused over the black tents a long moment. She waited. He must see the right.

Ali grunted. "The worthless one learns to defend my goods. My displeasure does not rest on her." Without looking at Kyrin, he kicked a scornful scuff of sand over the Arab, who shielded his head with one awkward arm.

Tae touched Alaina's arm, and moved to grip Kyrin's shoulders.

Ali grinned at him, an unpleasant baring of teeth, pointed at the Arab, and turned on his heel without a word. Umar's mouth turned up at the edges. His eyes on Tae, he flipped the Arab over with his foot. The boy cried out. Umar cocked his head, and when Tae remained motionless, he shrugged and walked toward the drink seller.

Alaina rubbed her neck. At least Ali had believed her.

The Nubian's gaze moved over them to Kyrin. He solemnly dipped his head to her, then to Alaina and last to Tae. He turned and followed Ali up the hill. Alaina frowned. What did the Nubian mean by that solemn nod?

Tae eyed her. "Are you all right, daughter?"

"Yes." Her sore head was nothing to Kyrin's.

Tae turned to Kyrin and began pressing her side gingerly. She bent over and was briefly sick, and sank to the sand on a breath of pain. Tae crouched on his heels beside her, a comforting hand on her back. Abul hovered close at her other shoulder.

"He kicked her." Alaina pointed, and the Arab gave them a grimace of a smile and struggled to his hands and knees, the unwound, ragged end of his blue turban trailing down his cheek, dragging on the sand.

In one leap, Abul planted his feet on either side of his head. The Arab stilled, his glare daring Abul to strike. Abul stared down and did not move. Dried rivulets of blood from his nose raked his chin.

Tae sighed and leaned over Kyrin. "I must feel your bones."

"His arm cracked, but . . ." The bewilderment and breathless anger in Kyrin's voice was not from her hurts alone. Alaina wanted her staff. She would show that beast how to crack bones properly—with wood.

"I know. Lie back, now." Tae guided Kyrin to the ground. She gritted her teeth on huffing breaths of pain as Tae flexed her limbs one by one. When he felt along her ribs Kyrin tried to keep back her sobs.

"I am sorry." Tae released her. "You have bruised ribs. They are painful, but not as dangerous as badly broken ribs are. We will get you some tea and wrap you up. You will be well."

Alaina patted Kyrin's heaving back and wiped at her own eyes, glaring at the Arab. She muttered, "His other arm will break. Jackal." He wanted battle, he had it. Long and lengthy for the scops to sing.

Tae turned. "What?"

"It is nothing."

"Rest here. I'm going to take a look at this one." He moved toward the Arab, who curled on the sand, ignoring Abul above him.

"But—he hurt Kyrin!"

Tae looked over his shoulder, wordless, his lips pressed together. Alaina closed her mouth.

Tae said something in a low voice to Abul, who left at a trot, then he bent over the Arab. Murmuring, Tae touched his arm, and the Arab's back arched. His teeth clicked on a choked cry.

Alaina blew out her cheeks and her lips thinned. The Arab convulsed around his pain.

10

Offense

Be to me a rock of strength. ~Psalm 31:2

Abul arrived with a bundle of cloth and a few sticks. Kyrin watched Tae speak low and insistently to the Arab boy. He stiffened, staring at Tae. At last he nodded. Tae straightened his arm in one swift pull.

The Arab's face went bone white. Below his high brow his eyes glittered, dark coals. Tae and Abul splinted and bound his arm until it looked a sausage, tucking it into a cloth Tae hung about his neck. The Arab sagged, his lips puffing out without sound. Sweat beaded on his face and there was blood on his mouth.

Kyrin tried not to think how she would scream with her arm like that. She breathed slower to lessen the pain stabbing through her middle.

Alaina made her way up the hill and then slogged back to Kyrin, clutching Tae's herb bag. Tae laid his hand on Alaina's shoulder. She shot a sharp glance at the Arab, but gave Tae a tremulous smile.

Kyrin hugged her ribs. Tae made everyone he spoke with feel the sun's warmth. Except for Ali, who ignored his goodwill, and Umar, who smothered it with coldness.

Tae sent Abul to heat water over the fire near the slaves' tent. He left the Arab to rest and turned to Kyrin, wrapping her ribs tight with a long, wide cloth from her armpits to her waist. Kyrin set her teeth.

The Arab's dusty curls waved against the sand, his lashes long against his olive skin, his body curled about itself, the haft of his dagger protruding above one hip. A jackal, as Alaina said—but alone, his pack departed.

Kyrin licked her lips. When he rushed her, the fear did not pierce her with icy claws. But there had been no blades. Would she break that icy grip when she faced a deadly edge again?

Alaina helped her up the hill to a place under the palms near the cook fire. Abul and Tae settled the Arab on a palm log across the fire pit from Kyrin. His back stiff, he kneaded the sand with his toes. A bit of his dirty blue turban, which Tae had rescued from the sand, dangled over one ear.

A fierce smile tugged at Kyrin's mouth.

Tae said behind her, "His name is Faisal."

Faisal. It sounded like a fire sizzle in her mouth, but his wiry frame rippled with hints of skill in violence, and the darkness in his eyes . . . his true name ought to be Abdullah, servant of Allah.

Abul called that the water was ready, and Tae made tea. Kyrin rolled the bitter-sweet hot comfort around her mouth. Faisal sniffed at the unfamiliar herbs.

Tae noticed, and sipped at his own cup. "Drink," he ordered.

"Yes, Hakeem," Faisal said clearly. He drank. Tae nodded, sipped again, and handed the rest of his cup to Kyrin.

Faisal soon slid down beside the log and slept in the palm shade, while Tae left at Ali's summons. Winfrey and the other slaves finished loading the camels, and Umar led them toward town, where he would bargain for caravan supplies.

Over the slaves' noon meal of meat, dates, flat bread, and milk, everyone talked over the fight and eyed Faisal's sleeping form with interest.

The older pirate cocked his eye at Kyrin's black earring. "Hmm. He didn't spit you like a dog. The spirits have blessed you—this time."

Faisal sat up on the far side of the fire, his eyes wide, chest heaving. His first glance was wild, and then he scowled. After a moment, expressionless, Abul went and offered him a cold leg of rabbit and some dates.

Kyrin's mouth twisted. So everyone felt it, as she did. There was a wintry lost air about Faisal even as he stuffed the meat in his mouth, fiercely tearing it from the bone. He caught her gaze and his head came up, his nostrils flaring. If his arm were whole, his blade would be at her throat. She bit her lip and rubbed her cold hands over her tunic.

The sky darkened and the stars came out. She hurt, breath by breath. If she could only sleep. Faisal fell asleep again as easy as shutting his eyes. Kyrin glowered. Alaina's shoulder was comforting under her cheek, and she was glad her sister was beside her.

She woke at nightfall. The other slaves sprawled around the warm flames. Tae came and sank on his heels beside her.

"You did well," he said, "to move and fight. Some do not learn that, not against a great fear. Though you will make your guard stronger and never lose an arm lock again. I thank the Master he didn't use his dagger."

"He is like the one who killed my mother." A bit of hair tapped her cheek. Kyrin twisted it into a thin cord. The Arab lay on his back, his eyes open to the stars. She folded her lips. He could not hear.

"I am glad you know it. His people honor vengeance." Tae's face was grim. "Do not expect peace, though we forgive him. I'm glad he took the guest-peace of the food Abul offered. We have three days before he will test us."

Kyrin snorted. "Faisal called you Hakeem."

"Yes. I told him what I am. If he owes me a debt, he will respect you as mine." Tae looked at her sidelong, a smile lurking about his mouth. "If we do not goad him over-much." He pulled her to him and kissed her cheek. "You did well."

Leaning on his elbow, the old pirate hooted, and Winfrey smiled. Kyrin ducked her head, the heat in her cheeks dissolving her uneasy thought of Faisal standing over her in the dark with his dagger.

§

Some days later, Kyrin spied Faisal peering at her over a sand hill, one of several that guarded Tae and Alaina's Subak practice from curious eyes. Sitting beside the fighting ring drawn in the sand around Tae and Alaina, who sparred with sticks, she touched the bandage around her sore ribs.

Faisal invoked Allah often to annoy her. She understood the Arab word and heard Faisal muttering about "the Nasrany" with Umar as he led the camels to pasture. Faisal seemed to hold no ill will against Umar for kicking him, or did he simply join with Umar against her?

Faisal also followed Tae about camp, working at anything that he could do with one hand. Did his arm keep him from her, or his debt to Tae, or did he think her warrior enough that he would come for her some night with a blade?

Kyrin shifted the falcon dagger in her sash, cupping the haft. Faisal's shoulders were broad, with force to drive a dagger deep. She would keep the falcon close, though Faisal knew Tae would hunt him down if he hurt her.

§

Faisal raised his head and thrust his shoulders back. He dared follow the hakeem out of camp. Abul had told Winfrey that Tae rose every dawn to teach a fighting skill to the golden one, Alaina, and the dark Nasrany, Kyrin. The hakeem treated them as his daughters, not his women. Faisal shrugged. He would not tell their Persian master, who wondered about them. The dark one was his to humble.

The young women stayed close to camp while the hakeem attended Ali about his business, often trailing behind the Nubian, who did not object to him as Umar did. Faisal snorted.

The black giant's voice was not deep but higher than a man's, despite his frame. And Umar was likely the Persian merchant's bastard. He could use that knowledge.

But the hakeem . . . he did not fear, though there was no love between him and Ali, and the merchant could snuff his life like a lamp-flame. Faisal studied the three below, moving his arm as little as he could, keeping a wary eye on the Nasrany.

When he first saw her small form step in front of the one called Abul, he had laughed in his heart. Her slight body had been tight as a thread on a loom. As if she could dare to spoil their game, though she carried the dark ring of the evil eye. Why was the ring dark, not blue? Then she hit him. Him—a man.

Faisal tapped his leg with his camel stick. She hit him with her twisted power. That darkness in her ring swallowed power; it did not reflect the evil as did the blue.

She would suffer much for it. No unbeliever could beat Allah's warrior—such could not be. Unless he had done something to anger Allah that he could not remember.

No, it was a test. And he would not prove faithless. But she was the hakeem's, and he owed him the mending of his arm. Faisal frowned, fingering his sling. He had told Tae he was an orphan, and that was true. *But I fight for my father, and Allah.* His frown smoothed. The way would be shown him.

§

That night, hidden by the shadows, Faisal drew close to Tae and the others around the night fire. Ali had given the hakeem permission to keep his Holy Book, for every night the hakeem read the place where it said slaves ought to obey their masters. Faisal sneered soundlessly.

Ali Ben Aidon never listened long enough to hear Tae talk of the royal law, of treating your neighbor as yourself, of the freedom of Jesu. Faisal tightened his fingers into a fist. He was free in Allah—not chained by a false reading of a prophet's words—and he would follow the Nasrany to the end of the world.

The *Nur-ed-Dam* demanded payment. As did every oath of blood. His father watched him from Allah's palace. As for the Persian, Ali Ben Aidon was of mingled blood, and his spirit was as tangled.

Faisal cocked his head. Tae's deep voice caressed the words of the Book. "My grace is sufficient for you, for power is perfected in weakness."

Power perfected in weakness. Hunh. Words as clouded as the Nasrany's impure tongue. Such a thing cannot be. Such a thought a mad dervish would not follow. Power perfected in weakness. It is a book with a split tongue. Whatever thing of ill it is, this god's "grace" will touch me not.

Tae rolled up the book. Faisal shrugged, and walked to the fire. The hakeem looked up, his eyes dark as a peaceful lake, as if he expected him.

"Will you tell us your tale this night? I will speak it"—Tae indicated Alaina and the rest of the slaves about the flames—"so they will understand."

The Nasrany kept her eyes on the stewpot. They glowed amber in the firelight. Faisal sank down cross-legged and stared into the flames. There he would see no curiosity or pity. He opened his mouth.

"The destiny of my birth was by the will of Allah. Distracted by his joy at my first cry, my father opened his tent flap at an urgent call outside. My father saw who stood in the firelight and stepped back to spit, but swallowed it, as is the law. Any traveler is welcome to three night-fires: to our bread, our salt, and our tents.

A strange warrior ducked in, his smile stiff from long riding, ignoring the curtain and the bustle and noise of new life behind it. My father watched him with a frown, but the stranger was a guest under the bond of salt. The warrior said he rode for his tents in the far sands, but was driven to our refuge by faithless raiders.

The next sun-fall a passing Bedouin found me, a day old, rolled like a rat in a rug beside my father's body. The camp had fallen as sheep before the raiders' faithless swords. My father's tent was looted and broken. My mother and brother were gone, with the strange warrior. They did not find his body."

Faisal paused. "Such a man is a hyena, who does not possess the heart to face Allah for his broken oath." He snapped a stick between his fingers and threw it into the flames.

§

His mother, his father, and his brother, all in one night? But how can he know this tale if he was a babe? He made part of it up, if not all. Kyrin frowned. She said slowly, "I have heard of this law. How can hospitality for three days and death the fourth be a law held with honor?"

Faisal spat into the fire. It hissed. "Anyone who does not rest under the compassionate guest law has the mind of a lizard."

Kyrin splashed her spoon into the stew. The third nightfall of Faisal's guesting had passed.

Faisal lifted his chin and said in clear common, "Such is the way of the people."

Kyrin glared. *It is as I thought. He knows common, but will not often sully his tongue with it. He has no honor who will not keep it in a pinch. A twister of words—he is worthy of Ali. H's thinner than the stone statue of the Eagle conqueror at York. His hair has the browns of a mouse in the wheat. What would he look like on the Eagle's stone horse? He is proud.* She cocked her head, assessing his frame. *He would fit well there, a strong tyrant.*

"How do you live in the desert in the dry time?" Tae pulled Faisal's gaze from her.

Kyrin stirred until a whirlpool grew in the pot. When would Tae teach her the sword? In the pot, the stew bubbled. Kyrin gripped the spoon. Soon she would need a sword. Faisal shot her a glance without worry, without anger, his smile satisfied.

He said, "Until I came to the city by the sea, I lived with the Bedu who found me. We followed the rains across the sands. Our camels store water in their stomachs from one to two hands of days if it is not too hot. If the thorn and salt bushes grow tall, a beast like my good Waleed can live without water until the summer sun. We of the desert live on our herds and their milk. If not"—he shrugged—"thirst visions come. Down in the sand mountains, the water of life is hard to find. Unless you seek death, you must have a guide to the seeps and the wells. Your Persian merchant may have need of me."

Indeed. Thirst visions or not, I will grind my teeth flat before I need him. He fits Esther's list well. Last. Kyrin dropped a spoonful of stew into a wood bowl with a plop, then scrubbed at the hot splashes on her tunic. She hated it being so ragged, and now it had more stains. That meddling Arab.

Tae nodded to Faisal. "I will speak with the Nubian." He tucked the Book inside his tunic, rose, and walked toward Ali's tent.

Winfrey yawned, and everyone crowded around the pot. The talk died down to steady eating. Kyrin served herself last and sat cross-legged, blessing her trousers. And the food. Everything in this land was exotic fare after the ship's fish and unending stale bread, but the goat for the pot had been young and tender. Tae had showed her how to drop raisins in with the rice and saffron.

Finished, she scrubbed the pot and bowls and put them away. She unrolled her mat close to the coals.

A scorpion tumbled out of its nest of sand and into the light. Kyrin jumped back with a startled squeak, and the old pirate flattened the creature with a grinding stamp. The segmented stinging tail was smashed into pieces. The old pirate grinned, and Kyrin noted Faisal's smile. The others shook out their mats carefully when they lay down one by one. Nothing else scurried or scuttled. Alaina slept at her back, but Kyrin lay awake. Faisal did not come.

The following night when she bedded down between Tae and Alaina, she unrolled her mat inch by inch. A great red spider sprang up her hand. Its globular eyes shone jet, and its long legs stirred the hair on her arm. She almost fell backward into the fire, flinging the creature wildly to the sand.

Tae tried to stifle his grin. "It cannot harm you, Kyrin."

"I don't care!" She was not comforted—she hated the hairy-legged thing more than a hundred scorpions. Out of earshot, Faisal watched her, unsmiling. She turned from him and ground her heel into the sand, gritting her teeth. "I'll beg Alaina's stick from her—"

"Why?" Tae frowned when Kyrin told him of Faisal's first gift. "A scorpion would make you very sick." He glanced at Faisal and said low, "But you will not take your staff to him. It would do no good. I will speak to him."

"It is well," she gritted out, near to tears.

Abul looked from her glare to Faisal's impassive face. Kyrin wished Abul could help. But it was not his fight. This fight was hers and the falcon's. To be free they must conquer the tiger. Kyrin glanced at Umar, a statue before Ali's tent. The tiger yet hid within.

§

Kyrin learned all she could of the land and their road. She listened to everything and everyone. One day she waited on Ali's pleasure in his tent, beside Tae. Their master bargained with an Arab merchant and a steward. The Arab merchant's round face and heavy eyebrows animated in a most amusing way as he gave Ali news of rival caravans and goods, and possible thieves on the road. Waiting courteously, the steward with the long nose wished to buy slaves for his master, an Egyptian ambassador.

Ali glared at Kyrin until she tore her fascinated gaze from the Egyptian's kohl-lined eyes and white cotton headdress that framed his thin face and swept to his shoulders. A thick gold band graced his arm, and a strange, thick gold torque his neck. Kyrin touched her throat—she rather thought that cold metal might choke her.

"A rich man indeed, though one like us," Tae whispered in her ear. Kyrin swallowed. If she held such a torque in her hands . . . this land would not hold her, storms and frail ships or no.

Over his steaming cup of tea the merchant said, "You know the caravan road skirts the Empty Quarter, the Al Ramlah?" He wiped sweat from his chin, shiny with oil. "It is never crossed without cost. Al Ramlah is a bowl of doom in summer." He nodded sadly.

"It is so. But I need camel drivers to cross the great interior, and a *dalil* to guide us." Ali motioned for Kyrin to offer his guest the platter of dates she held. The merchant took one and gabbled on.

Tae understood enough of his rapid tongue to whisper a translation. Kyrin listened, interested in the road around the great inland desert. The ocean of sand was a savage barrier between north and south, east and west. It sounded large enough to lose herself in, where myriad shades and shapes of gold, purple, and orange dunes ever-changed. The hardiest nomads took their herds there only in winter. The sands' edge touched the undulating Hadhramaut, a plateau that stretched its long arm east to the Oman mountains of Ali's home, then dropped sharp to the Araby Sea and Dhofar on the west side. The west, and the coast.

"I desire to reach my house before orange harvest and deep winter."

The merchant bowed over Ali's gift of a thick, soft wolf pelt, his round face beaming. "Allah give peace to your road, and may you reach your house before snow."

After the merchant left, the Egyptian steward began his bargaining.

His voice was soft but deep. He shot glances at Kyrin, fingering his ear, a slight frown between his eyes. Kyrin rather liked him, though she wanted to laugh. The sight of her seemed to worry him. He shook his head, regret in the tension of his mouth.

Ali scowled and waved Kyrin out. "Fetch Abul, worthless one."

Kyrin laid down the platter and ducked out of the tent, walking fast. Tied near the tent door, the steward's camel nipped at her. She spun away, and its teeth clicked on her sleeve. She swatted at it, and it sneered at her, then lipped at a tent rope lazily.

Faisal said some camels were raised in the sands by the Bedu, and had rough skin on their wide footpads. Elsewhere the rocks of this land wore the beasts' feet smooth. So, the sands defeated them unless they were bred to it, as a falcon was bred to fly the forest and the heather? She stepped over the last tent rope and stuck out her tongue at the camel. It pulled back its rabbit lips and small ears. Its teeth were saffron yellow. Kyrin snorted. She supposed she'd have to learn to ride the beast. Faisal was a son of the sand. She was sure he rode well. That jackal's heart *knew* the desert. Was riding a camel like riding a horse?

She did not look forward to it, or to more Bedu. Faisal was enough. Well to look upon, ready to speak sweet at a feast, and then to slip some deadly thing under his words.

§

Ali sold Abul and Winfrey to the Egyptian for paper and rice. Kyrin stood at the slaves' fire beside the other slaves, numb. Faisal would not stop grinning. Kyrin stared at her toes and turned from him. He must not see her tears.

While Abul walked freely beside the steward, Winfrey struggled, and the steward fastened her wrists to a loop he tied around her neck. He made sure the rope did not cut. Winfrey cursed him, and he tugged at her neck rope.

Kyrin called, "Blessings go with you!" and raised her arm. Emptiness grew in her middle. Winfrey and Abul were going where no one knew their names, no one except the one who ruled the stars.

"And his blessing remain with you!" Abul grinned. Kyrin wiped her face and smiled shakily.

"He *will* keep you!" Tae's voice rose beside Kyrin, and Winfrey caught sight of him and quit fighting the rope, her face smoothing into an almost smile, though her tears still glistened on her cheeks. Kyrin glanced at Tae's dark face and upraised arm. Confidence welled from him, a rope he threw to Abul and Winfrey. The woman sniffed wetly.

Would they miss Tae reading the Book? Abul had listened these last nights, as a summer desert to the whisper of first rain. Kyrin sighed. She had beaten him at practice for the last seven-day, taking the wood blade and "killing" him. She would miss his teasing grin when he dumped her to the ground with a swift leg across her ankles. When she crossed Ali's threshold would she step as lightly as Abul walked toward his new life?

Thank the one above, Tae kept his figurine of Huen standing tall. Surely Ali would not give up his wager against Tae and sell them apart? If she had another master, Alaina would not smile at her in the morning and talk her out of wanting to pound sense into Faisal. She would have no warm back to lie against, and Tae would never teach her to wield a blade. The falcon would die with her in chains.

11

Blood Call

For . . . to Him are all things. ~Romans 11:34

Ali's caravan stretched ahead of Kyrin and Alaina, who packed a last forgotten pot and Ali's dropped slipper on a beast close to their master. Near the middle of the caravan, Ali reclined on cushions under the cloth-covered framework of a litter strapped to his white Batina camel. The curtained sides were open. Faisal strode by.

Kyrin took a bite of the apple in her hand, the last of breakfast, and pretended not to see him, shoving Ali's slipper to the bottom of the pack camel's saddlebag in a wad. Faisal sniffed.

She turned, and her gaze followed his pointing arm. Ali's other slipper lay on the sand on the far side of the pack camel. Kyrin scowled. The driver who packed her master's tent had been careless. Faisal shifted his feet, and his lips quirked.

Why, you little—. He'd taken the slippers, and dropped the last one where she must draw her master's eyes when she picked it up.

Ali leaned over. "You!" Faisal's head swung around, and he trotted to the side of Ali's beast. "My Munira requires sweeter grazing. She grows thin. Are your ears open?"

"I hear. And obey." The date Faisal had been munching dropped into the sand before Ali's camel. Munira snuffed at it and raised her head, demanding. Faisal reluctantly opened his hand, exposing a heap of the sticky fruits. The camel slobbered over his fingers, devouring the gift, crunching down the rock-hard pits. Faisal managed to look disdainful. But he patted Munira's neck on the side Ali could not see.

"It is well, then." Ali gave a short nod, dismissing him.

Alaina giggled beside Kyrin. Concealed from Faisal by the pack camel, she held her hands against her head, her fingers sticking up in a crown around her red-gold hair, and stared down her nose. Kyrin choked back her laugh and ducked under the camel's neck to get their master's slipper.

The sand was bare, the sea bright blue below the caravan on the hill in the early morning. Fifty camels shifted under their loads of sand-cast pigs of tin, lead, and iron, with sacks of silver brooches and bales of furs traded from the North men or seized from her land. The camels carried an ample supply of dried figs, first ripe dates, barley meal, and waterskins, besides an array of local goods. The lead pigs in the near camel's sagging hide bag had been her godfather's. Kyrin's bite of sweet apple turned to meal on her tongue. She wanted to spit, but she would miss the apple before long. She shoved Ali's slipper into the saddlebag with its fellow.

Faisal joined Kentar, the slight dalil standing beside the lead camel. The caravan leader's face was smooth as a barkless ironwood tree. Ali had hired seventeen drivers under Kentar, all thin, strong, and weathered as black walnuts. Kyrin slapped away her camel's nipping nose, tracing their route in her mind yet again.

Kentar would take them inland a hundred-odd miles to the wadi trade corridor, then hundreds more south through wilderness toward the Akaba, an arm of the Red Sea. Ali would stop at Kheybar, Yathrib, and Makkah in the Hejaz mountains. The Hejaz divided the fertile west coast from a thousand Eagle-miles of rock, plains, and sand dunes in the heart of Araby, the Al Ramlah. She was glad Ali had decided not to cross it. Then they would climb south to Saa'na, the Hejaz's highest point. And wend east, down to the Hadhramaut plateau, then Dhofar on the coast, and a short dog-leg inland toward the mountains. And there, in the Oman mountains in a green wadi, lived her mistress. Kyrin rubbed the black earring. No one would rule her long.

Kentar swung his camel stick, disturbing a wave of flies from his camel, then returned to motionlessness. In loose earth-colored trousers and the short tunic of the northern Arab, the dalil had tucked his white kaffiyeh up into a skull-hugging turban. His almond eyes were never still, checking man and beast along the caravan line. He tipped his head toward Faisal, who leaned in to speak with him. Faisal glanced back at her. Kyrin raised her chin.

Ali lifted his arm impatiently. Umar nodded to the Nubian with a small, unpleasant smile, and the Nubian relayed the command to Kentar, his voice rising to a brief high note. Sweat layered his thick bull neck, and he cleared his throat. Kyrin glowered at Umar's back, bit off the last of her apple, and threw away the stem.

The dalil tapped his beast with his stick. The caravan lurched forward, accompanied by scampering children from the black tents, drivers' calls, and camels' grumbles and groans. Kyrin did not see any of Abul's tormentors among the youngsters from the black tents.

The caravan seemed to crawl over the plain toward the gateway to the mountains—the Akaba descent and the wadi Musa.

Gradually falling back with Alaina, Kyrin coughed on billowing dust at the rear. Ali did not give camels to slaves, except to Tae, for he was his hakeem. She would kiss the grumpiest camel this moment if it would carry her.

The day was long. Harsh cold crushed the day's heat the moment the sun loosed its last gleam. Umar handed out blankets in place of the worn mats, which he ordered Faisal to burn. The camel drivers used them to kindle a great fire, and handed cups of camel's milk and tea around the blaze. She and Alaina drank from the small handle-less bronze cups and laughed at each other's grimaces. The strong cardamom drink cleaned her gritty throat and took her mind from her rubbery legs.

She wondered if Faisal was disappointed Ali did not let him guide the caravan, or if he thanked his Allah at his prayers that Umar set him in charge of scouting for pasture instead. Faisal always watched them. She thought he noted when Tae set Huen out every evening, never touching her or Alaina. His eyes were on them when they rolled Huen into Tae's empty blanket in the mornings.

How long and how far would his debt to Tae protect her? He had not touched her. Maybe he stooped only to spiders. He did not bother Alaina, despite her whispered threats those first days to break his other arm. Now she tolerated him.

Fire tongues danced before Kyrin in the skin-tingling breeze, and sparks drifted, shadowing the men's faces around the fire, floating in the purple dark. She leaned back on her elbows behind the men on the still-warm ground and hugged her blanket, staring at the white stars. If only the tiger would not come tonight.

"Alaina . . ."

"What?"

"What do you know about dreams?"

"Dreams? Many of mine make no sense. Sometimes they scare me. I asked Tae once—"

"Have you ever had a true dream?"

"You mean one that happens?"

"Yes."

"No, and I'm glad. If I did, I'd have to think about every dream I had, and if it meant something. I did ask Tae about yours—"

"You told him about the tiger—?!"

"No, no! Only the part about your mother and Ali. Tae said the Master of the stars holds all our dreams, but sometimes he sends special ones. But he always makes clear who they are for, and why. Your bad dreams should get less." Her voice sharpened. "Your dreams haven't happened, have they?"

"No." Kyrin rolled onto her side. Alaina's face was dim. "I just wish I would not see her falling every night, and the tiger—his breath stinks—"

"Yes, and your feet are stuck in glue or mud, and you can't run . . ."

"Yes," Kyrin whispered. Father would make her hot milk and sit with her in his chair before the great hearth and hold her till she fell asleep again. She shivered against the desert chill.

Did he look often at his bow on the wall near Cierheld's door, did he miss shooting with her in the morning? Had he found out from the signs he read so well what happened to her and her mother? Until he knew, he would never quit searching. In the dark, for a moment, Kyrin could feel his arms around her.

Alaina was silent under the pop and rustle of the fire. Kyrin wiped her wet cheek and laid her palm on the sandy ground. A dry sweetness rose from the earth. Her sister would soothe her if the raider or the tiger woke her, ready to give her a warm back. She sighed. The empty dark spread around them. Bits of her were vanishing, some with the dreams and some with her new tunic, or *thawb* as Ali called it.

This evening she had put on the desert clothes that Alaina had made at their master's order. Men's thawbs, not blue as most women's were, so that no Bedouin would be tempted to steal Ali's slave girls and spoil his wager against Tae. Girls with hair the color of the most precious metal were valuable.

The ankle length thawb, a kind of long airy tunic, was comfortable and something Aunt Medaen would not be caught dead in. The cloak, or *bisht* in Arabic, was warm enough, of dyed camel hair. The rough material drew the sense of strangeness closer around her. Her own green wool cloak was warmer, but Ali insisted it was "too fine for a Nasrany."

So her cloak joined her key and girdle-pouch somewhere in Ali's things, and her ragged, dirty tunic and trousers from Tae ended in the fire. She would make another pouch, one to hang around her neck. It would be harder to take from her.

Ali had not looked at her necklace since he pierced her ear. Wood and seashell, however beautiful, held no value against pearls, gold, or silver, and he seemed to find the sigil of the fish distasteful. Did it remind him of loyalty and goodness?

Kyrin traced the shell's silky edge then tugged her kaffiyeh closer around her ears. It still wanted to fall off at odd times, for she had not learned to coil her hair just so beneath it. The square cotton cloth was folded in twain and a bit of cord bound it to her head. It was very like the linen hair wrap she wore for feast days at home.

But in a sandstorm she would drape the cloth over her head, longer on one side, pull it across her mouth under her nose, and tie it the way the men did here, drawing the longer end around the back of her neck. Then that bit rolled up and tied across the top of her head to the shorter tail of the kaffiyeh, to be tucked into neatness. It left only her eyes visible.

Kyrin touched the earth again with one finger. She would get her key and cloak before she left Ali. By all she heard, travel by ship was best. There were ports along the Araby coast. Ali, coward that he was, would stay in every great walled caravan-serai that gave food and water for a fee to traveler and beast. Tomorrow they would reach the first deserted lands.

It was afternoon when they passed the last village, the fields plowed for sowing. Vague, grey-green humps of pale shrubs and islands of thin grasses clung to the ground. Heat rose from the baked earth. The sun beat down between scattered white clouds with heavy, living hands. She found it difficult to believe the first rains began next moon cycle.

Kyrin grew used to the stony footing, walking beside the plodding camels for mile after mile. She escaped Ali's notice for hours at a time among the wending line of beasts. Between her duties early and late in Ali's tent, there were strange animals to glimpse, the meaning of a new Araby word to trick from Faisal, or a landmark to fasten in her mind.

At last they came to the Aqaba. The gateway to the interior descended between sand-rock walls, crusted high up with shale. Rock glittered in darkling piles at the guarding walls' feet. The way opened onto a flat plain of dark sand, then a region of high canyons or wadis.

Kentar called, "The Hisma!" His men took up the cry along the caravan.

Kyrin stepped closer to Alaina. Kentar had told Ali he knew a way to get to Kheybar and avoid a part of the road that robbers had attacked in the last moon. Now Kentar spoke to his beast gently and led the caravan aside into the mountainous maze.

They went over a small dam. The trickling water behind it diverted into a tunnel, and they descended into another dry, shaded wadi, white pebbles gleaming cool welcome under Kyrin's hot feet. She followed the camels under a spanning rock arch into echoing depths of stone. She looked up, wondering at layers of pearl, red, and earth hues flowing like water across walls that reared far above her head. Sometimes thin cracks choked with rubble split the walls. Many of these wadis smelled of damp and plants.

Sandals crunching on the pebbles, Tae came up beside her, his voice hushed. "We are coming to an old city the Roman Eagles conquered but did not change. Merchants come here less since the main trade route switched to Aleppo and Makkah. But I have heard of things here that I wish to see."

"What kinds of things?" A camel ahead switched its tail. All seemed shadowed beyond the noise of their feet: white path, darker wall, endless echoes against stillness.

"Places where journeying spirits fought for their path." He bowed his head, his mouth sober.

The air echoed with a whisper of falling pebbles, and a lizard scurried across Kyrin's foot, its four limbs a blur, eyes glittering black and gold. If it would slow, she could lean down and stroke its grey-scaled back. But what creature slowed for a slave?

She slipped after the last camel through a cleft that met overhead and squeezed out the sky. And came into a wide, flat place before an unending wall of carved, peach-tinted rock.

Pillars taller than any stronghold hall loomed around a shallow door, the rock carved thick with robed figures and beautiful shapes. Kyrin stared up at the evening-lit stone, her skin prickling in the cool shadow stretching around her.

Who could make such a place? And for who, or what? No sight or smell of animals, smoke, or voices. No one lived here.

She had come from a crack in the mountain. Was it a temple, this thing Tae sought?

She looked ahead where the wadi widened. Flies buzzed around ranks of towering facades carved in pink or yellow-grey sandstone over dark doorways. Slabs of native rock, set without hands, made a rippling ceiling for a lower row of dwellings and a simultaneous walkway for the topmost. The usual hum of the caravan drivers' voices ceased. They craned their necks, staring .

A distant voice called and broke the silence, followed by others. Farther along the walkway, women ground meal in stone bowls, sitting before them cross-legged, while their children played on the dusty rocks. Robed and veil-less, more women called to each other from high and low along the walls, pointing at the passing caravan. The youngsters cried out in excitement or tugged at their mothers' sleeves.

Tae grunted. He eyed the walls and all between for danger. Kyrin grinned at the children dancing fearless on the rock shelf above her head, and sneezed.

Faisal glanced back and snorted. "Nasrany! Djinn." He gestured at her and poured out a string of Arabic to the children.

Her ears burned. Djinn—he called her devil. She touched the ring in her ear. So the pot called the kettle black!

A boy with a bit of cloth around his middle backed away from her. His toddling sister held his hand, staring, her finger in her mouth. A woman scolded them, her wrinkled visage watchful, and they ran to her skirts. She hovered over them, her dark eyes on Kyrin.

They left the stone-dwellers at last and turned about a shoulder of rock, the wadi widening, dividing.

Faisal stroked his camel, Waleed, and did not see Kyrin stick out her tongue at his back. A rock rattled under Waleed, and

Faisal jumped. Kyrin restrained her smile. His face red, Faisal swatted at a fly on his camel's rump. Only there was no fly.

She could smack Waleed for him, much harder. Waleed would run. A smile crept over her face.

Tae seemed to know her mind. He shook his head in warning and quickened his pace, up a hill toward rings of rock like seats, carved into the hill.

Kyrin scowled. Who said Tae was fair? He did not think Faisal would be at peace with her until the Nur-ed-Dam was satisfied, the desert law, the Light of Blood that cried, "Blood for blood!" Lie down and bleed for an Arab? Not her. Faisal would never be content with a few drops. She stuck out her tongue at him as far as she could, then turned and hurried after Tae, ignoring Faisal's angry "Nasrany!"

They climbed up the wadi side to a circular pavement in the side of the mountain. Stone benches spread away from them, like rising stair-step rings of an onion. One quarter side of the ring was cut away. Kyrin climbed among the seats.

"It used to have three walls at the top and one great open side looking on the arena," Tae said. The flat stone beneath his feet cast his voice upward. He paused. "This is an ancient place of dying and living." He turned and gazed down the wadi at a wall spanning its width far below. Square house tops behind the wall shimmered mauve under the setting sun. A few lights twinkled.

Kyrin crept to his side. "Tae?" She whispered. This place was so empty . . . though it had been made for so many.

"What." His voice came out flat and he wiped his eyes.

"What happened here?"

"They killed us, with men and beasts, because they hated our Master. Here we died, and conquered."

Kyrin's skin prickled. Her mother had told her the Eagles killed people who followed the mark of the fish, executed them in bestial ways. They died, and conquered. As her mother rose from her shell into that place among the living oaks, her hand healed, all fear consumed. Kyrin's eyes stung.

The tail of Ali's caravan dwindled into the purple evening haze below, wending toward the wall and the town. Kyrin picked her way from the arena after Tae.

"What did you see?" Faisal asked Tae when they passed. Tae only grunted, and Kyrin did not look at him, her throat thick. She would hit him. *You are alive, jackal. Take your freedom and go.*

Near the looming wall across the wadi, carvings clung to the arches of the scattered ruins, intricate leaves and graceful shapes on dusky stone. Kyrin stared at a building of delicate pink columns as she walked, until it was out of sight. How could these beauties be, so many colors of stone in one place?

Kentar got them past the wall's guarded gate quickly. Kyrin heard the sound of gurgling. Water. The camels broke into a trot. Tall houses drew close over the thin street and court walls blocked them in. Following, Kyrin came to a long, wide square before buildings soaring many times her height.

Across the stone flags on her left ran a raised water trough long enough for a multitude of camels, wide and deep enough for her to bathe in. The water rushed beneath a statue of a woman. Wind tugged her marble tunic and curly hair. She mused over the trough at her feet as if she sped with the sparkling water over the yellow stone.

A camel dropped its head and sucked water noisily up its long throat, and the men let more animals shove in and drink. The Bedouin drivers dunked their heads and came up spluttering. Kyrin dipped her arms in the crystal clear coolness and smiled.

At home this place of stone would be almost holy. It was good Esther did not see this. She would pester her father to make her such a watering place. But Kyrin doubted such a stone or stone-worker existed in her land. It was old, by the cracks in the woman's stone sandals. Kyrin gripped the edge of the trough and cupped her hand. The water did not taste like leather water-skins but of light, pleasant minerals. At the end of the trough it rushed through a pipe and disappeared into the stone. There was no stream or pool in sight to feed the water-way, only more buildings, larger and higher than any hall she had seen. The Eagles knew how to build.

The great paved square held a few other caravans seeking to escape high taxes or robbers. Camels and drivers lounged on the near side of the large square or disappeared through a doorway in the opposite brick wall. A few merchants sat on the ground at its foot before their wares, while locals enjoyed the insurge of customers in the scattered shops inside the ancient metropolis buildings. The men and women gossiped of bygone days. Lamps glowed in some windows. Another flickered into being as Kyrin watched, sending the evening shifting away. Cooling sandstone and camel dung scented the air.

"Couch the camels!" Kentar ordered.

Ali found nothing he deemed of worth among the merchant's wares. When night fell he retired in the smallest building for a coin, the Nubian guarding his door, and Umar just inside. Kyrin brought the Nubian his bowl, on the edge of Ali's tray. She indicated it, a large leg of rabbit perched on a mound of rice. He tipped his huge black head, eyed her, took it and dug in hungrily. Kyrin bowed her head to hide her smile, and slipped inside the door with Umar and Ali's bowls. She wondered if the Nubian slept in his saddle.

That night she and the others made do with a warm camel for a back-rest, while Kentar muttered with his Bedouin drivers about heathens, magic, and the evil Haroun, and set the guard. Kyrin listened to the mournful wind in the dark street.

12

Wager

...The Lord my God illumines my darkness. ~Psalm 18:28

A rooster crowed, joining its voice to the bustle of the rousing caravanserai. The city had not lost its jewel-tone mystery in the early light. Kyrin sniffed deep of the dry, sandy chill. She would like to stay and search the branching wadis. It would be an easy place to lose oneself in. But Ali ordered them on into the Hisma, and the Nubian did not let her out of his sight.

Over the aqueduct, the woman of the Eagles dreamed on. Kyrin took a last drink of the clear water beside a camel, which raised its dripping nose. She would remember the rock city.

§

Her feet sore, she walked after Kentar as the dalil settled the camels for night camp, driving them before him. Rimth salt-bushes and flowering herbs that Faisal called *rabia* softened the stony land. It had rained here maybe hours ago.

Small yellow, blue, and pink flowers bloomed about her ankles, and on shrub and herb. Drops of water hung on the tip of leaf and petal, the water drops painted rose and orange by receding clouds and the blue sky. The air was nectar.

A rabbit burst away from the lead camel's thumping pads when he lurched to kneel on the ground. Kentar called out, laughing, to one of his men, and the man brought him a strung bow and a quiver.

With a small weary grin, Kyrin rubbed her face. Her father taught her how to draw such a string. How she had thrilled to her first arrow speeding after Lord Dain's long black shaft, striking through a shock of harvest grain. He had looked at her arrow sunk to its green-dyed fletching, and then hugged her to his side in delight, his warm brown eyes lighting up with his smile.

Two more rabbits broke cover, setting flowers swaying, earth flying from their paws. One doubled back and froze.

"There!" Kyrin pointed, and Kentar raised his bow. He aimed and loosed, and the arrow sped over the rabbit's back and skipped merrily over the stones. Kyrin looked at the ground, lips twitching. The rabbit was twenty paces off.

Kentar growled and sighted on the second rabbit, a good eighty paces if it was one. He took a long moment to aim while the camels grumbled behind him. He missed. The rabbit stretched tall on its back legs, turned seeking ears toward him, and settled to wash its face. Kyrin smothered her laugh in the crook of her arm.

Kentar glared. "You shoot."

"No, no, the rabbit—it was just that it washed, despite the arrow." He did not understand.

Faisal stood on one side, his dark face unsmiling. Kentar motioned him over. "You speak her words to me."

Faisal did so in a delighted rush, glancing at her and raising his chin in scorn, his jaw tight, eyes narrow.

Kentar broke in, turning to her, "You disrespect a dalil? You shoot. You miss, you walk the caravan tail one hand of days."

With dust in her teeth, besides her aching feet. She did not mean to make him angry; he must understand. "My lord, the rabbit was so funny, washing—"

Faisal said something, with a sideways look at her. Kentar's face hardened. The other Bedouin drivers gathered, a listening crowd, the breeze playing with their kaffiyehs. The Nubian raised his head where he pounded in Ali's tent stakes, and his long strides carried him to Kyrin's side.

She stared past Faisal's shoulder. The Nubian said something to Kentar in his own tongue, and the dalil answered.

In stern common, the Nubian said to Kyrin, "You shoot."

She straightened. "And if I hit it?" They looked at her.

"Yes, you hit. You *askar,* yes?" Kentar chuckled then roared, his thin frame shaking.

Askar? She scowled at Faisal.

"He means soldier, fighter." Faisal stared at her, his head cocked, measuring something, something he was sure to find wanting.

Far off, the rabbit nibbled at a plant, head bobbing.

"Yes, askar," she whispered, "like my father." She crossed her arms. "If I hit it, you give me a camel." Her ribs would handle riding, she would make them.

Silence. Then the Nubian broke in. "Yes, Ali will give you a camel. Old one."

It was all they would give. She stretched out her hand. Kentar laid the bow in it and held out an arrow.

She took it, smoothed the feathers, praying. She drew the string back three times, tested the full draw. The hunting bow was heavier than her own, which slept in its corner beside her bed at home. But she could draw it. Smooth, cool horn bound the back of its wood limbs.

Kyrin placed her front foot carefully, raised the bow, and took a deep breath, let part out. No wind; aim a little higher, near that rock. Steady the arm—let the little bird go—the arrow leapt away and the string whipped her arm. The rabbit jumped like a gazelle and tumbled.

The Nubian whooped and walked to pick it up. Kentar's jaw knotted. Kyrin heard indrawn grunts from the watching Bedouins. She rubbed her stinging, bruised arm and said in a rush, "It was a blessed shot, you know. I could not do it again. I laughed at the rabbit, washing bravely in the face of death. Forgive me. I would not offend my dalil."

Kentar stared at her. "A Nasrany with skill, and yet generous; I will tell this to my daughters." He walked away, shaking his head, a faint smile on his face.

The Nubian picked a camel from seven bedded down at the end of the caravan and laid the lead in Kyrin's hand without a word. It was not the oldest. Kyrin bowed her head in thanks. Umar would have hurt her for showing her skill.

Behind her Faisal said, "You will need a saddle. I will bring one."

"My thanks." She could not refuse his stiff offer. Might he forget?

She should have found reason to refuse. In the morning her camel roared in protest when the saddle touched its hump. Kyrin tightened the girth with difficulty, then swung onto the sidling beast. It reached around and bit her foot. When she drew her toes out of reach, it pitched like a ship to unseat her, its tail straight out.

Kentar told her to get off, his eyes streaming with tears of laughter. He found two wicked burrs nestled in the camel's scruffy hair under the saddle pad. One thing consoled Kyrin.

Faisal had not seen her humiliation, the result of his work. Kentar had sent him at first light to pasture the camels. She calmed her new mount with a handful of dates. The camel lipped her shoulder hopefully, anger forgotten.

"Lilith. Your name is Lilith." Lilith sniffed at her kaffiyeh. Kyrin giggled at her tickling touch.

Alaina stroked Lilith's neck. "Her teeth prove she is not as old as her staring hide hints. It must be worms."

Kyrin nodded. Lilith's hide had not fooled the Nubian. At dinner, she fed Lilith garlic from her sash, from her portion of the cloves that Tae handed out. He agreed with the Eagle surgeons' writings that garlic helped cure sickness in any creature. It was his task to keep Ali's living wealth healthy.

That evening a footsore half-grown Saluki pup limped out of the blossoming desert to skirt the fire where Alaina steeped Tae's herbs into tea. Kentar thought him lost, and Alaina took him under her protection.

Kyrin rubbed the pup's soft grey ears. He licked her hand. He had long legs, a lean body, and a high flank that made her think of her godfather's sight hounds. "Good dog."

Faisal snapped, "Bedu may not keep any cursed dog! Salukis are *not* dogs; he is a beast of high favor!"

Kyrin looked into the pup's eyes of ginger-tea and tannin, molten with devotion. *Let Faisal think what he wishes.* She ignored his hard stare and fed the pup scraps from her dinner. The pup licked her fingers carefully and sighed, leaned his head against her knee. *He likes me, and he's lost.*

Cicero, as Alaina dubbed him, soon followed Kyrin everywhere. She was surprised to find he ate dates as eagerly as meat.

Cicero grew fast, Lilith's coat regained its luster, and Kyrin's ribs hardly pinched. The caravan passed Aila and moved toward Kheybar. The moon waxed over the passing nights.

Kyrin tried to draw the majesty of the days and the quiet nights into her soul with the wandering winds; to leave no room in her dreams for the tiger, but the falcon's ankle ring shackled her often. Her wings, weak with fear, would not lift her heavy body from his back. She would wake, falling; yanked to earth by the chain, plummeting into his mouth, the tiger's heavy jaws around her body, his teeth prickling.

The tale of her long shot and the fallen rabbit became common fire talk. Tae got her a bow and five arrows for game. He traded a fever-cure to a merchant for it, who said he got the weapon from a nomad from the land-of-short-grass, the Steppes. The merchant gave the bow for a good price since it was smaller than most. Many layers of thin wood made the polished limbs strong for the bow's weight. The ends were tipped with black horn.

All that day, smiles tugged at Kyrin's mouth. She shot at bits of brush until her arms shook and her left forearm bruised under the leather guard she had made against the whipping string. Rocks made easy targets, but they would shatter her precious arrow points. She felt nearer to her father, with the bow's firm grip in her hand. At the night fire she tied a twisted bit of camel hair around the bowstring so she could find the nocking place for her arrow in the worst light, or no light at all. As her father and Tae said, it was best to be ready.

The Nubian sat in Ali's door, his bare blade between his knees. Kyrin pursed her lips. He cared for that blade like a child—oiling and sharpening, wiping it down—every dusk.

She found there were more rabbits and sand grouse about when the sun rose and when it fell. One day she was sliding a fat, plucked bird into the slaves' boiling pot when a huge black hand closed on her wrist. Kyrin dropped the bird with a hiss of alarm and spun to free herself, driving an elbow toward a muscular arm. She stopped with a sick jolt—a dagger lay cold and hard and flat across her throat.

"Know who you strike—and where they strike—before they reach you." The Nubian twisted the flat of his blade away from her skin and dropped his dagger hand. He leaned over to peer into the pot and frowned. "Bring two birds for the master with the rising sun."

Kyrin nodded and swallowed back tears, hating herself. She had not been aware as Tae taught her. To fight with a child's unthinking, ignorant fear—she was yet a coward. The Nubian's sandaled feet dwarfed her toes. He rocked back on his heels. She looked up.

He smiled, and his thick features lifted into gentle amusement. "Fear not, little one. You learn." He walked easily away, his bare sword shifting at his side. Kyrin wiped her eyes.

So, Ali liked one thing better than rich clothes and fair slaves—his meat. And now she had a reason to ride about the land. She frowned.

A riding camel could cover ninety miles between sunrise and sunset, like Ali's white Munira, of Batina stock. Though a worthy beast, Lilith had been bred to carry baggage. Lilith would keep her close to the caravan; Lilith, and the bewildering landscape.

§

"Come!" Ali rapped.

Kyrin stepped inside the tent and silently held out her sand hen by the neck. Her breath steamed. The Nubian had ordered her out early this morn, and it was as well. She had been curled up on the ground away from the others, watching the growing light snuff the last star, thinking she did not want to see Faisal ever again. But it might be better to keep the jackal in sight—he proved more dangerous unseen.

Ali's eyes raked her. "Keep your hair under that kaffiyeh."

Kyrin blinked, holding back the urge to bite her lip. Faisal was far worse a plague than Umar and the Nubian, even now probably laughing at her outside.

She had woken to Faisal's black-on-black shadow looming over her, a pale gleaming length in his hand. She had exploded out of her blanket, dislodging Cicero from his warm nest between her arm and hip. She struck at Faisal's leg with a wild swipe of her falcon dagger as she whirled away, flinging the blanket between them. And missed. He was expecting her, and she muzzy with sleep.

Cicero landed, spun, and growled, showing all his teeth. That was when Faisal flipped the shining length of his camel stick up in the air and caught it. His amusement was a short, sharp bark. He ignored Tae, up and wary, and Alaina sitting in her blankets, watching him.

"Wretched Arab!" Kyrin bit out, shaking. Faisal's shoulders heaved quietly. Other heads popped up around the sleeping fires. Rolled in their cloaks, men chuckled. Kentar's rumble had carried widely.

Umar must have told Ali long since. Askar, indeed. Kyrin ducked her head, her cheeks hot, and held out the bird.

"Put it by the door."

She laid it down and twisted her hair hastily from sight.

"Do not forget your veil when you come to my table. In my house you will wear the half-veil, for I will see the eyes of all who serve me. Here, the kaffiyeh must keep you from unlawful men; and the bee will keep his flower." Her master grinned sourly.

Kyrin nodded and went out, glaring at the sand. Ali was in a foul humor. After Faisal it was too much, that her master also believed her a dolt. She looked both ways—no Faisal—and mounted Lilith, who waited before the tent.

Alaina slipped around the corner, wiping her face, her damp curls springing from her tucked up kaffiyeh. Cicero left Lilith's heels to put his nose in Alaina's hand, and she leaned down, speaking to him in her low, warm voice. He licked her chin and whined.

Kyrin patted Lilith's neck. Alaina often followed Tae on his camel leech rounds, watching him dress galled spots, pull the burden off a beast to rest it, or shift loads. Kyrin frowned. Her sister should not have to embroider Ali's thawb collars and sashes over smoky oil lamps at night till her head ached. Mother would have helped her with her flashing needle.

Kyrin rubbed the callus from the bow string growing on her fingers. She, it seemed, could not do even that. She traced the embroidery on her date-colored sash. The lumpy stitches sat in front, crafted in sweat and tears on material hand washed and dyed. It had been scorned.

"That color of mud is for your country, and what destruction of thread is this?" Ali pointed at the awkward flowering vine. "Keep your hands from my robes, O my slave." So Alaina labored over Ali's things. Kyrin lifted her face to the sun. It moved slowly this morn.

"What do you think of?" Alaina peered up at her.

"Nothing," Kyrin mumbled.

"A large nothing, that makes you frown so."

"My embroidery is worse than a spider who tries to weave with your thread, and you—you have to do all of Ali's robes yourself. I am sent hunting and riding and—"

Alaina's grin quirked. "You think of me, while our master sends you out before the sun rises? You could think of how hard your lot is, or of your comfort, as Ali does. But you think of me."

"I should be able to use my needle better," Kyrin said in surprise. Not to mention her dagger—Faisal proved that.

Alaina set her hands on her hips and tried to arrange her face into stern lines. "Your abilities are strong; that bow you carry and your hate of injustice. Each to his gift." She smiled gently. "I take joy in my needle. And more than Ali behold the beauty of my designs with an appreciative eye."

With a grateful twitch of a smile, Kyrin gave up. Alaina said nothing of what the entire caravan had witnessed before the sun raised its disk over the lip of the world. Would they ever cease laughing at her?

Her sister gave Cicero a last pat and stroked Lilith's shoulder. She noted the camel's flinch and clucked her tongue, opening a leather bag at her hip. Digging her fingers in, Alaina rubbed salve generously on Lilith's galled shoulder, avoiding her flailing foot, and reached for the long neck, soothing. Lilith leaned into her hand, grunting her thanks for the cessation of pain.

Kyrin shook her head. She preferred horses. Lilith hadn't tried to bite since her first madcap, dry-mouthed ride, but camels were good at exacting their debts.

Like Faisal—that jackal of the sands. He had promised Tae he would not put burrs on Lilith; instead, he put them on the saddle pad and humbled her before them all. But she would teach him. Her opportunity would come.

Alaina ran her hand along Lilith's hump. "Did you give the Nubian your rabbits?"

Kyrin slid from the saddle. Her sister worked too hard, smoothing things between her and their master. She made herself smile. "Yes. Ali has his bird. Come, it's your turn to ride." Alaina's face lit up, and Kyrin held her hands for her sandy foot. "I'll get another rabbit for us. No one cooks them like you."

The corners of Alaina's mouth turned up in pleasure.

Soon the caravan set off to the protesting cries of camels and the shouting of drivers. Kyrin helped Alaina down from Lilith before Ali passed them, swaying in his litter toward the head of the caravan and Kentar. Ali's slaves did not ride without reason.

Kyrin mounted again and nudged Lilith on, glancing aside at Kentar's brown mount. She dared not meet the dalil's eyes and the amusement she would find. Kentar's lead female strode over the expanse of the desert, equal to the bright land—and Arab jackals. Kyrin sighed, hot wrath rising in her stomach again. She let Lilith drift away from the caravan.

Did any grain of sand feel like she did—a trapped, unmoving speck in a vibrant world in a vast universe? She stared at the soft pink edging the sky and breathed in the vanishing coolness. Despite Faisal, the desert's fierce beauty and power made a quiet place inside her, a sense of him who made this land for the wind to play in. The silence beyond the scritch of camel pads seemed eternal.

I miss you, Father. Lord Dain would have given Faisal a lesson he would not forget. When she mastered Subak, when she knew the sword, the land, and the twisting Arab language, when the birds built nests again . . . Surely then the Master of the stars would let her know she had enough courage, enough strength to escape to her father. On her saddle, her falcon dagger tilted in its sheath, eyes eager, always ready. Kyrin studied it. What had the blade seen in its days under the sun besides her mother's fall? What lingering glances, a wordless touch of lover's hearts before a coming attack? What cowards, what spirits leaving earth, what brave blows given with the last strength and heart's blood? Her mother had done so.

Kyrin ran her fingers over the falcon's jet eyes. Better the blade seen than the one in the dark. She grimaced and settled the weapon firmly in her sash. To fight Faisal this night would be a relief. Tae had but one word concerning Faisal's perfidy. "If he comes again, leave him his life." She would show the jackal a true djinn.

Kyrin rode parallel to the caravan. The morning drew away over the sand. Many arrow flights beyond the dalil, brush grew thick around an outcrop of reddish rocks, the beginning of spreading, broken ground. There would be good hunting there. Cicero trailed at Lilith's heels, tired from romping among camels and men and poking his black nose into everything in snorting excitement. Kyrin patted her leg.

Cicero trotted to her, brown eyes worshipful, his long mouth laughing. She patted his silky head. "Good dog, Cicero." His pale fur was short, even to the tips of his ears. He padded in Lilith's shadow, his lean body supple, narrow head high. Her anger easing, she smiled. *There* was a being created for swift, joyful running. Soon he would course after gazelle.

Kentar and the line of camels skirted the broken granite outcrops, and Faisal gathered the pack camels near Ali's white beast, ready to lead them to pasture in the broken land. The horses that Ali had traded many furs and the last of the pirates for in Aila, stamped and whuffled beside Faisal's Waleed, their lead ropes in Faisal's hand.

The two drivers ordered to watch over the precious horses slumped on the last camel before Kyrin, holding their stomachs. One of them slid down and made a dash behind a nearby rock, returning little relieved, his face drawn as a wilting olive. Kyrin hoped Tae had something that cured purges. She did not doubt Faisal worked his will again.

Faisal did not seem to mind that he held the lead ropes of thrice his worth of gold in his hand. He lowered the tip of his borrowed lance in salute to Ali, one knee hooked around Waleed's saddle. His faded blue kaffiyeh draped rakish down the back of the bisht Tae had found for him somewhere. Kyrin scowled.

Tae would not approve of her following Faisal and the herd without Kentar's men there. She shuddered to think of pitting her falcon dagger, no matter how keen, against a lance. She would head for the outcroppings of rock.

Faisal tapped Waleed with his stick. "Hai!" He chivvied his charges toward the outcrops. Her glare burned his back. The hunting hour was wearing away, and he was taking her direction. Where there was game, there was grazing.

She sighed. If she stayed in sight of the caravan . . . She gathered Lilith's rein.

"Worthless one!" Ali called. She pulled Lilith up. And Faisal kicked Waleed past her, his lips twitching with buried laughter. Kyrin's breath came hard and her knuckles whitened. The jackal gloated over his triumph, he meant to spoil her hunt.

But if Ali demanded she get more game she must go out of sight of the caravan and follow Faisal or risk losing herself in the vast loneliness—but she could hardly lose the herd's broad track. As long as they did not hit another pebble plain. She turned Lilith toward Ali with more heel than necessary. Lilith spun her tail and groaned, lifting her long lip.

"I wish two hens and a rabbit by this even, slothful one. Or Umar will see that your aim improves. He spares his whip for man nor slave."

Riding ahead of Munira, Umar turned and grinned back at Kyrin. Next in line, the Nubian studied the air between his mount's ears, his strong black face still.

"Yes, my master." Kyrin bowed to Ali and dug her heels in, spinning Lilith. They rocked away from her master and the caravan.

She bit her lip as they circled the first towering column of red-pink granite. Faisal might think up another nasty trick. But better his tricks than an empty pot for Ali and a sure whipping, with trouble for Tae and Alaina. She settled into the curve of the saddle. She must not fight Faisal unless there were witnesses. It was too dangerous. She must choose her ground. Kyrin shifted. She could not yet ride like Faisal, half-lying at his ease on Waleed's back. While she hunted she wished to keep her feet dangling, her balance ready for any swerve Lilith might make.

The bisht Alaina had made her wrapped her comfortingly, tapping her ankles like a friend. It blended with sand-colored Lilith and the stone below. The odd, clumpily-dyed pattern made her part of the desert, her form melding with Lilith, bush, and stone.

Cicero whined. Kyrin halted Lilith, slid down, and lifted him before her saddle. She stroked his knobby back where he rested before the leather pad, and he turned his head and licked her fingers, for he liked his swaying perch. After his desert journey he had ridden in a saddle sack, only his head sticking out, till his feet healed. She'd have to catch him to make him ride in a sack now. Every day he ran and drew closer to the wind's tail, or so he thought. Kyrin grinned and tugged his petal-soft ear.

They rode across dips and around rocks and up a hill. She squinted across a wide gravel plain on the far side, staring into shadows of rocks and bushes for resting rabbits, glancing down to reassure herself of the herd's tracks. They were wandering widely. Who was herding whom?

She could not see Kentar or the caravan behind her. But she needn't worry, for Faisal could not hide his charges' tracks. The gravel plain was small.

A sand-lark called sweetly, and Cicero raised his head, ears pricking. A cloud roiled over the desert horizon ahead, a flat-topped mushroom. Kyrin straightened.

It didn't smell like rain, and the cloud looked like no storm she had seen. Cicero sat and balanced on his paws, trembling, nose questing. He was quiet, a good sign, but the wind was with them. Kyrin pulled Lilith to a stop. Probably an animal had scared the camels in hope of easy meat and stirred up a dust cloud. Maybe an old lion.

Her mouth tightened and she tensed. Then she grinned. A lion.

Tae's lion call and the bit of hide she was curing for Alaina's needlework might have been made for her—for this moment. It would work.

She nudged Lilith onward. Oh, she would get him. She would bring Faisal to blushing confusion. Her laugh was a half-snort.

By Faisal's count at the night fire he ran off two lions every seven-day. This time they would see who ran, and who fulfilled the hunt, and the fight this night would see it finished.

If there *was* a lion—Kyrin rested her bow across her lap and reached behind her leg for an arrow from the quiver attached to her saddle pad. Her bow was made for smaller beasts. It would kill larger if she put the arrow in a soft spot at close range, but that was a harder shot. She nocked the shaft, fingers anchored around her nocking knot. She would also be ready if hen or rabbit roused from the shade along her way. She squinted at the cloud. Something moved at the bottom, impossible to make out.

When she reached the last dying dust swirls she found several camels grazing about the mouth of a wadi that plunged between walls of basalt and granite. The main herd had veered around the mouth of the wadi, where rocky gullies and scarps and towers spread out. The camels ignored her, their teeth grinding, throats gurgling as they swallowed. Kyrin threaded Lilith between them and down along the sandy wadi bottom.

The shade of the wall felt good on her back. The red-flecked sand beckoned. Her stomach rumbled, eager for dates and milk. She coiled a bit of hair about her finger. After she ate she would raise the lion's scream on the far side of the rocks. Then she would creep away when Faisal came. If he saw her it might mean more than his usual glare. She shivered, with a little laugh.

But she wouldn't care, she wouldn't—not after the drivers' laughter followed her through breakfast. Kentar's chuckles had burst from him when Faisal passed his fire, and again when Kyrin handed him his bowl. The dalil's eyes had twinkled.

I almost hope that jackal's heart tries me. I will tell Cicero to take him down and he will race to do it. This time my hours of training will not fail. At least under Faisal's dagger of shadow she had not frozen in fear. She had not turned to ice. Kyrin smiled grimly. Where was Faisal?

Cicero leaped after her to the ground. Faisal might be chasing the camels among the rocks far from here, or—she warily eyed the forty-foot walls—be about to leap out at her on those soft feet of his. What *was* he about? Faisal would not leave three of his camels behind. Not for any coin.

Kyrin stopped short. On the herd's trail she had seen none of the horses' prints for some time.

Had Faisal run from Ali with a goodly spoil? Was that his mind? She frowned.

At least there would be no more spiders, or laughter, or worse. That Faisal. She struck her saddle with her fist. Or was it something else? She swung up on Lilith, readied her bow, and cast about. No tracks but those of one camel running down the wadi before her. It would take a while for her to circle the outcrop and find the rest of the herd.

Cicero's sharp bark brought her bow arm up.

High at the other end of the wadi he walked stiffly around something she could not see. Many things might lie there. Kyrin urged Lilith forward. Tae would want to know.

13

Hunter

Be not far from me, for trouble is near,

and there is none to help. ~Psalm 22:11

Near the top of the slope only blurred camel tracks met Kyrin's roving eyes. The dry dread growing in her throat eased. But there was something odd about the tracks. She slid off Lilith and knelt.

The single camel had run down the wadi with the weight of a rider. Six other camels faced it here. Camels with riders, for their prints showed the depth and spacing to brace their rider's weight. She traced another print with one hand. Here the fleeing one skidded to a stop and its rider fell, leaving a long hollow.

It might have been a body. Kyrin rose from her knees. But there was no sign of blood, or of the burden being dragged away.

Cicero bounded past her, growling, and stood on his hind legs to sniff the stone wall where a scrape marred it, camel prints below. Probably a sandal. The weight was back on the camel, rider or burden or body?

The camel's prints mingled with the horses' again, soon swallowed by a horde of camel tracks that swerved deeper and higher among the rocks. Kyrin followed, arrow ready, Lilith's rope in her other hand.

She rounded a boulder, jerked aside and fell back, barking her elbow. A man lay on the sand on his back within the circle of towering stones. Blood spread around a hole in his chest and crusted on his blue thawb. A blue the blue of Faisal's kaffiyeh.

Dust dimmed the man's thin black beard, and his motionless hands dug into the earth. The bloody hole filled her vision. Raiders. Faisal might be facing a blade.

She knew the fear and the hope, watching that edge approach . . . her mother's blood ran red. Kyrin turned her head, swallowed hard, and pushed back the vision, filling it with the empty sand below her. There was no sound over the wind, no blue, forlorn body among the bushes. Nothing stirred.

Warm breath blasted the back of her neck. Kyrin squealed, whirling as she leaped, yanking Lilith's rope. Her kick struck Lilith's nose.

Lilith pulled back and snorted again, peppering Kyrin with spit. Shoving her furry head aside, Kyrin wiped her wet face. Laughter wanted to bubble up, but she didn't know if she could stop. Then she wanted to cry. She felt sick. She blew out a few deep breaths. There was nothing near them but the wind.

It whispered to itself, blowing dust among the towers. Thorn branches touched the man's bare, callused foot, rustling against his skin. Cicero sniffed around the man's head then shoved his muzzle under Kyrin's hand, his eyes a little closed, his ears folded back. Knowing there was wrong in the world, he waited, his moist nose touching her palm.

She could tell him that Faisal carried a lance, that it could make such a hole. Ali had sent no one with Faisal—he was alone. And except for the Master of the stars, the Master of all—so was she. Kyrin could not swallow past the thickening in her throat. If she did nothing, Faisal would be gone. He would plague her no more. But raiders . . . and he had not killed her mother.

She must run for Tae. He would know what to do. Kyrin turned.

Her tracks and Lilith's blurred under riffles of whispering sand. In places the wadi looked as if she had not walked there. Beyond the wadi mouth all was blank, dry earth blowing a finger's depth above the ground.

No—she stepped forward—and her foot hit something hard. It tilted out of the sand. A camel stick, a snake etched in coal on the end. Faisal's stick. The shadow that woke her, made her certain her death was near.

She stumbled to the edge of the circle of rocks. Cicero was a wavering heat shadow far out on the open sand, his nose to the scent, gathering what the wind scattered. She could not go back. She could follow him and Faisal.

Kyrin pulled off her kaffiyeh, caught hair, and yanked. She tied Faisal's stick in the cloth and ran back through the wadi to the nearest camel, and fastened the bundle to its neck. Faisal would not leave his stick with her things. Anyone from the caravan would know it meant trouble. She prayed Tae could persuade Ali that she and Faisal had not stolen his horses. But first they must live.

The last two camels followed her back to the rocks, and snorted at the blood-smell. Kyrin gathered their ropes, tugging Lilith's head around after Cicero. She glanced back at the man, sand drifting about him, glad Faisal did not lie there.

Her eyes on the tracks below so she would miss nothing, she caught up to her saluki. Cicero stopped, a faint questioning noise in his throat.

"Go!" Her tight voice startled them both. He lunged forward, a satisfied smile about his slim jaws.

The sun gave a general direction—northwest—and she fastened the landmarks in her mind as she could. She did not know how long they would remain in sight. They left the rocks.

The sandy plain unrolled beneath her, encased in silence. With every step they were more alone. Kyrin searched the horizon under the slate blue sky. Nothing moved.

The sun and silence burned. Winter never touched this land but at night. Her head was on fire. She should have saved her kaffiyeh.

She lifted her hot hair from her neck. She could make a kaffiyeh, but better to keep her bisht whole. The wind had died, and she would not stop to get down.

Kyrin cut a long piece from the bottom of her thawb with her dagger instead. It took frustrating ages, keeping her eyes on the trail enough to make sure no rider left the others, and yet watch that she cut only the material she wished. At last, with fumbling fingers, she arranged the ragged bit she had hacked free over her head. She felt cooler at once, dizzy with it.

Then Cicero began to mince his steps, lifting each paw from the ground. She got him to the saddle, where he sprawled, panting, and licked his hot paws.

A wide hill with a dimple in the middle edged the plain where it embraced the sky. Kyrin had no idea if it was a mirage or how distant it was. Tae or Kentar would know. The raiders' trail curved toward it. Cicero scrabbled at Lilith's side, and Kyrin let him down. He trotted on.

Small noises grew loud in her ears. She muffled a rattling arrow in her quiver. For several hours her dry eyes blinked at grit; she took her hand from the waterskin yet again. The water needed to last.

Hot camel and hot self and hot, empty desert. Pace and sway, pace and sway. Warm, wiggling dog, up in the saddle and down. Heat squiggles in the air.

Kyrin settled into the saddle-pad, into Lilith's stride. The heat struck deeper. The ground softened to her eyes.

She woke sprawled forward over Lilith, a memory of loud noise or danger ringing behind her eyes. The front of the saddle dug a hole in her stomach. She clawed in her sash for the falcon and snatched the blade free.

Lilith groaned. The other camels crowded into her rear. Lilith spun and snapped. Falcon in hand, Kyrin calmed enough to see past her camel's weaving head.

Cicero sat bolt upright in the middle of the trail, his tongue hanging out the side of his mouth. The raiders' tracks were sharp-shadowed, the sun low. Cicero reared, pawing at her leg. She sighed, her fear draining away. He stopped Lilith. He was thirsty.

She needed to stop, too. She had not thought she drank so much this morn, keeping an eye on Faisal over the top of her waterskin as she clutched her bow to her, wishing she could feather him with an arrow.

She ran her dry tongue over dryer lips and clucked to Lilith to kneel. Her eyes were afire. What signs had she missed? She was no fit warrior. She did not move when she ought, did not sense danger, or slept and did not pay mind to tracks. Maybe she *did* bear the evil eye. Or evil watched her.

Well, that was certain. The evil one always wished destruction, death, and stealing of joy. She left the falcon free of its sheath and slid it through her sash, where it bumped comfortably against her ribs. Stamping stiff legs, she worked at the thongs behind her saddle-pad that held her waterskin. After two thirsty gulps she held a third in her mouth. Bliss.

She bent and dripped a few drops in Cicero's wide jaws, who sat at her feet begging, silent, his brown eyes pleading. He did not waste a sparkling gem drop. She had taught him the trick three days ago. It seemed another moon, when she was sure of water and the caravan.

She slid the stopper into the bottle, and her pale sleeve glowed in the evening light. Should she chance a fire? It might not be safe, later. Kyrin worried it over and finally took out the fuel Tae insisted she carry.

When the sticks charred, she smothered the flame with sand and scraped the charcoal into her rabbit skin pouch with some soft cheese she spared from her dinner. She was spoiling her neck pouch, but she had enough rabbit skins to make another. What she did not have was a spare skin of her own.

She ground the sticky mess to paste, eyeing the purple and red dregs of cloud in the sky. Shafts of golden-red shot over the plain, gilding the shadowed prints before her. The raiders might not stop before dawn.

Kyrin urged Lilith up again. Grey swallowed the ground ahead, dimming the hill on the horizon, a darkening, uneven mound.

When she could not see Cicero seventy paces ahead, Kyrin called him and got down. With a hand on his wiry neck, and Lilith beside them, she trotted on, evening pressing close. The mound would be shelter of a sort. She thought the raiders might also seek it. If they did not, and the wind came up in the night or they crossed a large gravel plain between, she would lose the trail.

They drew nearer. The hill mound was large and strangely shaped. Kyrin's feet slowed. Still, she felt better for the solid mound with the creeping shadows and raiders about. Her feet shushed on solid rock and a sifting of sand. In places Cicero's nails clicked where the sand thinned.

Soon the raiders' tracks dissipated. Gravel and boulders lay scattered across a hard, bubbled surface that skirted the steep-sided foot of the mound.

Its rock wall curved in front of her, two camels high. Where had the raiders gone? Kyrin walked cautiously, a hand on the wall's sloping, sandpaper surface. Rocks caught at her feet. She kicked a small one, and it sailed away as if it were a bit of empty honeycomb, landing with a dry rustle. What was this place, where rocks were light as air?

Staring up at the mound, she tripped over another rock. She rubbed her shin, which stung fiercely. Enough. Kyrin climbed a broken section of wall and peered over. Into a channel of stone.

The channel's inner walls were rippled lengthwise from top to bottom, as if the stone were a hollow candle, where the wax had melted and hardened repeatedly. It had a sandy floor and roughly followed the edge of the desert. There were more walls and channels beyond, a confusing maze roughly circling the heart of the mound.

She could walk easier inside the channel. Seven camels wide, it would protect her from unfriendly eyes. But camels and horses could not climb, and where did the maze lead? The sands lay behind her and the channel. The raiders must be ahead, and the light was going.

"No," she whispered, as if to keep the last spark of sun-fire in the sky. She stared at the darkening land until the first star winked in the purple above. She heard not a falling stone, a clicking insect, or the wind. The cooling air smelled of bitter herbs. She shivered. Frost would come soon.

She slid down and sank to her knees, gathering Cicero to her. He licked her chin with his warm tongue. Sun-hot rock smell tickled her nose. She'd burn here when her water ran out, like a caravan they passed once. The men and beasts lay alone, skins black and shrunk to their bones, cracked lips drawn back over their skulls.

But she had known the danger of death before she began. If she found Faisal . . . He could not fall—she would not let him. Not because of her would he lie on the sand, his blood drying. He deserved a beating—but not death. At least not the one a raider would deal. She snorted and rubbed her nose. A tear ran down her cheek. Was Tae trying to find her this moment? No doubt he was.

Cicero nuzzled her. He whuffed through his nose and walked a few steps and came back and pressed against her knees, staring into the dark. Eager. She must do something.

Kyrin sighed and released a frayed curl of hair. Faisal knew this desert. And the raiders might camp close; the abrasive rock would be bad for camels' feet.

"All right." She hugged Cicero. "But we have to eat." She made her way back to the camels in the starlight and rolled a rock onto their ropes. When she returned there would be no time to loose hobbles.

She dug her midday meal out of her saddlebag and sat at Lilith's feet, listening to the wind explore the channel behind them, chuckle, and trail into mournful cries. Lilith and Cicero whuffled over her shoulder for tidbits. "No, later." Faisal might need the bread and dates.

The wind died. Kyrin packed her food and fire-stones in her flattened sash and gathered it into a bag. If something happened, she would need fire first. Water she could do nothing about—unless some of the raiders' came handy.

She laid her thawb on the rock, took her charcoal paste and rubbed it in until the thawb blended with the dark stone. The last of the charcoal she smeared on her face, arms, and legs. She sniffed and paused. The cheese was strong after the day's sun. Another detail a warrior would not get wrong. She bit her lip. She could but hope the raiders ate cheese in their night camp. Or days old milk.

Kyrin looped her pouch back around her neck, slipped out of her bisht, and wrapped it about her middle to free her limbs. She looked down herself, satisfied. The darkened shadows of color in the cloak confused the eye. She tore her make-shift kaffiyeh and wrapped her feet with the pieces, pulled back her hair and tied it with a stray thread.

She straightened. Her stomach cramped. How many raiders were there? Her father would go if he had no weapon at all. She pulled her shoulders back and her mouth firmed. *Askar, my Father. Warrior.* Daughter of Cierheld she was.

She tightened her hand about the falcon dagger, felt the open beak, heard its sharp cry of defiance. And slung her sash bag around her waist, slid one end through her quiver strap, and tied it in front. It anchored the bag to her hips and her hide quiver to her back. Her bow she hung over her shoulder. She rubbed each camel's nose, with a hug for Lilith. And laid her hand on the falcon's head. *Master of all, help me.*

They set out along the edge of the mound, Kyrin grasping a piece of leather looped around Cicero's neck. Counting her steps, she tried to avoid rocks and holes. The sky was full of stars before a thick shroud of cloud in the west; she wished them brighter, so she could see the holes before her feet. She smiled a little. The raiders could not ride far here even if they tried.

One thousand ninety-two steps, one thousand ninety-three . . .

Cicero snorted. Kyrin jumped, banging her sore shin, and a rock rattled away from them. She hopped on one leg, teeth clenched, straining to hear anything or anyone the noise might have alerted. A faint tearing sound came to her ears. She froze.

After a long motionless moment she laid her bow on the ground. Grasping the rock wall, she inched upward, Cicero's nails scraping faint against the pitted surface beside her. She reached the top. Her elbow bumped a section of wall that jutted over her head. The wind tugged at her, colder, and the clouds unsheathed a half moon.

A bowshot below, pale light blanketed silver sand, spotted with stark shrubs covering the channel bottom. Near the far wall something moved. A man knelt by a bed of coals in the moonlight. Seven sleeping shapes lay behind him in the shadow of the wall. He scooped ash over the fire, dimming its heart.

Kyrin bit her tongue and reached slow to grab Cicero's muzzle. She was perched on the outer wall, her head fully visible. But movement gave one away more than the light of day. If she held still . . .

Cicero was mercifully motionless, as if he sensed the need. Another cloud, outrider of the advancing host, crept toward the moon. It would hide her.

Lack wit—where was Faisal?

One bundle lay near the fire, a little apart from the others. It could be Faisal, lying on his side. He would be bound. The raiders' belongings lay scattered up and down the channel. No animals.

She frowned. Bedu slept with their mounts, their most valuable property, both for warmth and safekeeping. The coals blinked out under more ash, the clouds closed in, and the night made the bundle by the fire its own.

First, get down. Quiet and slow. Kyrin reached for a handhold. Again the faint tearing sound. It drew her gaze to the far wall.

Behind the raiders a second wall of pocked stone swooped lower than the wall she clung too. It seemed to border an open place beyond, where she caught the dim shadow of a third wall. Judging by the expanse of curving rim, the inner crater might be two hundred paces across.

Camels moved in the moon-gleam among grass clumps, their teeth tearing the stillness and grass and camel-thorn. A few were lame. There were no horses among those she could see.

Back at the bottom of the outer wall, Kyrin wiggled her sore toes and laid her head against the stone wearily. She might shoot at the raiders once or thrice before they caught her—the closer she crept before they noticed her the sooner she would fall. That would not help Faisal.

The stars wheeled for an age across the sky, cut by the hardened guts of the earth. She fingered her neck, tracing the sword scar. She must wait for them to sleep, and think. A bead rolled between her fingers. Her necklace would be safe in her pouch that smelled of cheese and char. But the dancing fish . . . she felt bare without it covering her scar. She gripped the falcon's chill haft. The fish would stay to face the moon, and all else.

The shadows grew. They seemed to move with life of their own. Did the tiger stalk her? But no tiger lived here. No, it would be a lion instead. But wouldn't the raiders hunt a beast with a valuable hide? Kyrin sucked in a sudden breath.

There might be time. . . . It must be after matins, how long till the sun rose? The clouds fled too swift across the moon as she rummaged in her sash. At last she bit her lip against a noise of triumph. The fresh scrap of lion skin for Ali's pouch dangled from her hand.

She rolled it up quickly and crouched, listening. All seemed quiet beyond. She pattered away several hundred feet and stopped. The wall crumbled here, blocked by brush. Reaching to push a branch aside, she yanked back her hand and sucked it. Thorn bushes filled the broken place and the channel beyond.

The moon shone out again. Kyrin picked her way through the dim tangle with her eyes. Then the clouds hid her. And she crept along the path she had laid in her mind, gathering generous scratches. Her hands and feet ached on the cold stone.

After the thorns the crater wall rose before her, steep and hungry for skin. She was careful not to knock her bow or quiver against the wall as she followed it broad circular base warily. One "thunk" could give her away. But she must find a place to see.

Just opposite the raiders' camp she found a crack in the crater wall. Her lashes fluttered against the rough surface as she peered through. There must be a guard, there was always a guard. Had not Tae said so?

Across a stretch of grass and shrubs she found him. Like a rock among the others, he sat near a split in the crater wall behind the raiders' camp. Wide enough for a camel, the opening lay roughly midway along the outer wall between the raiders' fire and the plug of thorns. They would use that.

The guard turned his head. His eyes grabbed at her, stripping the concealing rock, and she willed herself not to move. His gaze passed on.

Cold kissed her with goose bumps. She edged back from the crack, laying her hand on Cicero's head. She took a deep breath; she must go on.

Drawing Tae's carved lion-call from her sash, she set it on a nearby stone. Ali's piece of lion skin was stiff. She spit on both sides and rubbed.

Strong, wild muskiness rose. She knelt, and with her hands asked Cicero to sit. He obeyed, willing but puzzled. She tied the skin to his back with her pouch thong. He twisted and licked her fingers, stinging with the cold. She nudged his muzzle away with a gentle elbow and raised a numbing finger to the wind. It blew southeast, across the inner crater.

Picking up the lion-call, she lifted her hand above Cicero in silent signal. *Lie down,* and crept away. Her breath came fast. She looked over her shoulder—nothing but rocks and shadows. He was staying.

The clouds thickened. Step, and step faster, back around the crater. *Please, let no rock rattle. Clouds stay fast.*

When she judged she was closer to the guard than to Cicero, she climbed the second wall at the edge of the thorns. She must be closer to Faisal, now, yet further down and out of sight.

She was not far from the jutting rock on the outside of the mound that she must keep near, to find the camels again. It would have to do.

The guard was concealed, but she had a good sight of the grazing in the crater and the farthest wall where Cicero waited. She lifted her hand, and blew. A coughing roar vibrated around her.

Kyrin whistled low for Cicero then gave the lion call another deep rumble under the clouded moon.

Cicero scrambled over the wall. And down. A flash of moon-shadow, he came across the grazing on a straight course, the lion hide flipping across his back. He cleaved the raiders' herd like a streak of moonlight.

Horses screamed and camels bellowed. Pandemonium of hooves and camel pads thudded over grass and stone. Cicero disappeared into the darkness below. Clinging with her head just above the edge of the wall, Kyrin stood on her toes. Where was he?

The guard near the cleft shouted and pointed under the moon, it seemed at her.

She shrank back down. They would catch her, and Faisal's Nur-ed-Dam would be paid. A pity he would not know. She called another lion's shaky challenge.

The herd hit the far side of the crater—a thundering, broken wave. On her left more shouts rose from the channel. The raiders. She could not wait for Cicero.

Kyrin half-fell to the bottom of the wall, grabbed up her bow, and ran for her path through the thorns. They tore at her, then she was out.

Below the jutting rock of the first wall she stopped, gasping. Voices echoed within the channel that circled as a maze, leading the hunters to the crater, eager for their prize.

She thought of their blades in her flesh. Her hand rose to the slight ridge of skin under her necklace. So—the tiger hunted the falcon. But he was only a bad dream. Her hand dropped.

She set her bow across her back and climbed, pushing through the spots that swirled before her eyes and threatened to drown her. Under the high rock she dropped flat on top of the wall and wiggled her bow over her head to lay it beside her.

A long shadow erupted from the dark. Throwing her arm across her neck, Kyrin yanked up her legs, biting back a scream. It was far too late for the falcon blade.

Whining snorts against her face and a cold nose that sought her arm stopped her violent backward roll off the wall. Trembling, Kyrin pressed closer to the stone with Cicero. His body quivered.

Sharp rock and high walls did not slow *him* when she called— even when lions hunted. She drew a breath and looked down. The last raider trotted toward the cleft into the crater, his head up, lance poised, searching the walls.

He tripped in the edge of the fire, and his ripe curse rose.

14

Prey

God is my stronghold, the God who shows me lovingkindness. ~Psalm 59:17

Faisal woke, his spine tingling, every muscle rigid. A coughing roar died on the air. Men scrambled around him with bare swords and ready lances. The coals glowed in their bed beside him. The beast's hoarse cry rose again and ended on a high note. The slowest raider stumbled in the fire-edge and cursed, following the others toward the crater and the lion.

Faisal grinned and went limp. He should rest, save his strength. A rock skittered in the channel behind him.

Faisal squirmed over, pushing against the ground with his bound hands. A long body flowed down the wall, mingling with the fire-shadows. It paused, turned. Moved from rock to bush to rock. Short ears swiveled.

The moon hid. Faisal struggled against his bonds. They only tightened. The beast growled.

He stilled, prayed the lion would ignore the dried blood on his head. *The fire!* Like a worm, Faisal lunged for the silvered pile where orange eyes of coals winked.

A lithe shape struck the ground between him and hope of safety, a silhouette of pyramid ears and a fluidly humped back. Rank cat-smell smote his nose.

The beast swelled and stretched toward him on six legs. A human torso arose. Its hands let down a four-legged thing.

A djinn-demon, cursed creature from Shetan's pit. Faisal shut his eyes. He could bear any end but this.

A hard muzzle nudged his foot and he gasped. His eyes flew open. Unwilling sight burst in.

The black human part of the djinn drew a blade. A wink of light slid along the edge. It neared his throat.

He was going to Allah. This messenger was to take him for his transgression. He had only teased the Nasrany. He cleansed his father's name of cowardice, but not of his defeat. He merited a damp corner of Allah's palace, eating scraps to give him strength to tend Ali and his father's virgins.

Faisal gritted his teeth. A dark braid swung over the djinn's black arm. Braided hair. As the Nasrany's was when she hunted quarry that took climbing. Hot breath blasted in his ear. He flinched. A saluki crooned and nosed his chin, tongue rasping, rasping, enough to take his skin. It did not smell of the pit. He blinked. He tasted blood.

"Faisal?"

He knew that low, clear voice. And he wanted the djinn. He could fight djinn—without questions. Why the noble one ran with his nemesis was more than he knew. Her—with her heart more blackened than her skin—she had him alone.

None of his brothers were nearby. She would give him back his gifts with a blade, the blade she feared, and so would be all the more cruel. She gloated, by Allah!

He braced for the edge, the quick pain. He would not prove his brothers' taunts true. His father would see him and know his name.

Faisal thought his scornful smile might shake. He thrust his chin out in defiance instead. She eased the blade under the leather thong about his throat.

Cat. He didn't breathe, fastened his gaze on the frown between her dark eyes. *May Allah burn your skin from you while you live, take each nail, light each hair to melt and curl, and repay you a thousandfold.* His throat-bond parted with a snap. Her dagger sliced down toward his ankles. He swallowed reflexively, and the Nasrany scowled.

She grabbed his arm and yanked him to his feet. Legs tingling, Faisal wavered. Forcing his legs to still, he held out his wrists. She cut his last bond. Never did the unbelieving hakeem plague him as this one!

Wincing, he swung blood into his hands. In the moonlight her faithless eyes were dark. The moon sparked off the black ring in her ear. When he stepped toward the wall she twitched violently.

He grinned. She feared him, unarmed as he was. Whatever came to him in Allah's palace, her fear held the savor of his father's arm around his shoulders. But he did not mean to see that palace yet. "Come!" he demanded. She followed. She *did* understand simple words of the holy tongue. His strength returned with every reach upward. Faisal threw back his head. *Allah! I will be worthy!*

They climbed the wall, leaving a growing, questioning hubbub within the crater. The Nasrany shoved at his leg from below, urging him up. He could kick her down after she reached the top, but it would be better if he did not have to drag her with him. At the right time he would make her see her dog soul and wallow in the knowing before her just death. *No God but one. In-shah-Allah!*

At the highest part of the wall he glanced back. Clustering around a blazing torch in the crater, his captors searched every shadow for the lion. A lion hide marked a courageous man.

Beside him the hakeem's Nasrany was neither courageous nor strong. Her arms quivered when she turned to slide down the stone wall. A true dog, cursed—weak. Before she slid over the edge she reached to one side and picked up her bow from the top of the wall.

A raider in the crater cleft shouted. In the quiet he turned his head, searching. He'd heard her. Faisal dropped down after the Nasrany. She recovered from her awkward landing and stumbled toward the desert, muttering under her breath. He heard a nearby hiss and a thunk, and reached out and yanked her flat. Another arrow skittered and shattered on rock, spattering him with fragments. He jerked her up by her arm, ignoring her gasp. Her arm for his. Blood for blood. Faisal broke into a stumbling run.

Behind him, the light dwindled; the archer seemed to have lost them. Was he waiting for a better shot? Had he seen the shadow of a lion or his escaping prey?

The Nasrany faltered, reached out and gripped his hand. He snorted. She only began to pay the Nur-ed-Dam. Why did she follow him and his captors? She could have shot him and been pleased, by the look in her eyes when he savored his triumph among Ali's amused caravan drivers. She chanced her life, following the raiders. If an unspoiled woman were taken she would be sold, but with the evil eye the Nasrany bore—it might raise the raiders' cry for every drop of her blood.

He pulled free of her with a curse, his fingers sticky with wet warmth. Her blood. He flexed his hand and rubbed it over his neck. A djinn he could kill. He wiped his hand on his robe.

This one had shamed him, his father, and Allah; the unbeliever must die. He could do it now, in the dark. But the hakeem—he could not bear to look in his face after. To see the light in those eyes on him go out. Tae expected something from him, he was not sure what.

There was a collective yell behind. They'd found him gone. Faisal lunged forward. Despite his swifter pace the Nasrany got her feet under her and followed him at a staggering run. Darker blots against the sand, camels crouched ahead, and he ran on, disregarding the rocks that clattered about his feet.

Ali's second-best camel rose to meet them. "O swift one with wings, carry us quickly!" Faisal whispered.

The Nasrany raised her hand to the saddle. Her legs gave and she slumped. Faisal grabbed her and heaved her up, still clinging to her bow. How light she was in his hands, her soft body turning to hard muscle under his fingers as she scrambled astride with a low breath of pain. Foolish Nasrany—she had not thought to change the saddle to a fresh camel. He threw her saluki with its outland name on the third camel, and yanked loose the beasts' tethers.

He struck Ali's beast with his hand, "Hai! Hai!" It lowered its neck for his springing foot. He leaped up and swung to the saddle behind the Nasrany. He could not leave her to talk. They reached the open sand without seeing their pursuers. Laughing low and ragged, Faisal tightened his hands on the rein and his arms about her. The hakeem's Nasrany crumpled against him. Faisal snorted.

§

Kyrin heard his disgust. Weary beyond caring, she let him remove her quiver and bow. After a moment, she wrapped the kaffiyeh he offered around her shoulders and hugged it against the night.

She had paid his Nur-ed-Dam, blood for blood. Yet she was enemy to his Allah. Her sticky tongue was hard to move. Her voice came out a crow's. "I do not know the way back. You will have to find the caravan, the wind took them . . ." He grunted, and her eyes closed. Lack-wit, she thought muzzily, the wind took the tracks, not the caravan. Three camels paced away in the starlight. They swayed through the still land under the glittering sky, pursued by the whispering wind.

Faisal's thoughts bit him. The Nasrany, warm in his arms, stole Ali's camel, risking her hand that stole—and her head—for him. Her enemy. It was not possible.

And if she had not come for him, then what did she seek? Her mind was strange and twisting. As twisted as her words *strength made perfect in weakness.* It did not change her judgment before Allah. But did not the prophet say, 'Allah is the most generous, who has taught by the pen, taught man what he did not know?'

Faisal grunted. What could she be if she began to believe? She was a book of mind-numbing equations, this fighter and coward. She made his stomach uneasy. He could not close his eyes while hers were open, lest she bring dire change. And the hakeem would reward him for her return. He could wait for justice. It was a debt he must pay, for his arm's healing. The Nasrany shifted, and Faisal tightened his grip. She relaxed against him. The stars faded, and the east lightened. Faisal bowed his head. *What will be, will be.*

§

Kyrin woke, curled as much as she could curl in a saddle. Her neck was stiff and her ear bounced against a dusty, muscular shoulder. Arms fenced her in.

Faisal. His movement woke her. He held her falcon dagger to the sunrise, and it was a creature of blazing bronze, the blade a line of molten fire. She stiffened. He flipped the weapon, his brown fingers quick. The dagger rose, spun, and thumped into his palm.

She knew the comfortable feel of its perfect weight. The falcon readied itself to fly into the dawn, crying loud and clear—victory! She and Faisal were alive. Kyrin smiled. And frowned.

Near the tip of the dagger a deep scratch marred the bronze, revealing smoky ripples of forged, folded metal. It must have happened when Faisal yanked her away from the raider's arrow. The rocks scraped her and marred the dagger in her sash. That was steel under the brazen coating. She reached out, unthinking. And Faisal laid the falcon in her hand. She grasped it stiffly.

The finely crafted haft of the falcon *was* too good for a bronze blade. Why had someone tried to hide the falcon dagger's worth? She'd heard a tale or two of Damascus steel; blades woven with dire struggles and help from above. Faisal did not seem to mind Allah's law against animal images—since he touched the dagger. She handed it to him. "Keep it this day."

Faisal's lean arms tightened. Suddenly warm, she sat straight up. She'd been sleeping in the jackal's arms. Kyrin bit her lip. Maybe she should not have offered him the falcon. But he had no other weapon, and she still had her bow. Yes, there, he had put it on Lilith sometime in the night. If he planned to harm her, last night was a gifted moment. Now he eyed her and pulled back, his lip curled a little. He could yet return to the caravan with ten believable stories of how he lost her in the sands.

Kyrin looked away, stiff against the camel's sway. Soon he halted Ali's beast and slid off. Kyrin dropped down the other side by unspoken agreement.

Faisal walked ahead, scanning the grey-black gravel plain. What did he look for? Where were they?

The undulating expanse was still and empty, a few sparse shrubs clinging to life.

Kyrin quickly loosened her thawb from her scratched, scabbed legs with a moistened corner of her cloak while he attended to business, and she to hers. She was glad of the camel between, though its shielding legs were thin.

In a moment she walked after Faisal, one hand on Cicero's head. Cicero nudged her wrist, his nose damp. "Prince of the wind, you are. Lion hunter." She smiled, and he wagged his tail, solemn, his brown eyes molten with devotion.

When she came up beside him, Faisal stared at her as if she was an unknown animal and he was unsure whether she was worth hunting. She crossed her arms and lifted her chin. She missed the falcon dagger—and a blade in her other hand. "What do we do now? The Nur-ed-Dam is paid." Best to know if he thought so. He reached out and touched her bronze earring. Kyrin gritted her teeth and forced herself to stay steady, to keep her gaze on his. He owned her not.

"The Light of Blood is paid, Nasrany," he said, grudging. His eyes narrowed. "For now, it is peace."

After the scorpion, the spider, the djinn—the terror when he stood over her in the dawn? Not a word of thanks for his life? Kyrin snorted. She should not have untied him. But now, he knew the way back. She forced the words between them. "Then let it be peace."

The stony ground welcomed her more than his disdainful silence and short nod. He switched the saddle from Lilith to the spare camel, leaving Lilith barebacked for her. Kyrin glared at his turban, robin's egg blue, the end swaying across his shoulder, untidy as usual. It would be good if the saddle galled him.

The day brightened from a streaked sheet of orange to full, blue fire. It roasted the first scent of green salt-bushes and the dewy earth into oblivion. They rode slowly to spare the camels, heading toward Ali's trade stop south of Makkah. They were not going back. Faisal thought Ali would flee to find the nearest caravanserai. Kyrin could only agree.

Her strung bow slid across her thighs, her quiver close to hand. She picked a thread from the hem of her char-blackened bisht and sewed up the holes the rocks had torn in her thawb. She would drape the bisht whole over her head until she got another kaffiyeh; she was not going to tear more from her thawb. Every few moments she glanced up at Faisal and around them at the hot emptiness. There was no sign of the raiders.

Lilith's shoulders hitched and slid, hitched and slid. Kyrin finished mending her bisht and said little over the afternoon. Faisal said nothing, nodding or grunting to her inquiries. The sun rose, burned them, and set.

In early light the next morn they crossed a caravan trail, the prints nearly filled with sand. Faisal turned to follow it. Kyrin's eyes watered from sun glare, and her skin chafed with dirt and heat. These old tracks were useless.

Faisal got off Ali's camel and stooped over a pile of rock to one side, staring at it. "Do you know this?"

"Should I?" Her voice cracked. She coughed against her dry throat. Could they not have a drink from the waterskin? But Faisal hoarded it.

"Will you look?" His back was stiff.

She slid her foot across Lilith's shoulder and thumped to the ground, limping over.

"This is not of my brothers." His lashes were dusty, his thin face for once almost human with weariness.

"No." She had never seen anything like the precise pyramid of black rock that rose as high as her knees. Clearly a sign of some sort. Hope soared. Might it be . . . it must be. . . Tae—and water. "Our caravan was here!"

A smile tugged at Faisal's mouth, chased by a frown. "Why do you say so?"

She hesitated. "I don't know. I think Tae made it. Could it be any other?"

"Yes." He tapped his new camel stick against his leg. This time the tracery of a sword graced its pale length, waiting for henna or charcoal to color it at their next camp. She thought it would be blood-red henna. Dust gritted between her teeth, her legs ached, and her cracked lips hurt.

He said, "Many merchants cross the desert edge here toward the Asir, the highlands."

Her heart dropped to her toes. "Then why did you ask me?"

"I wanted to know if you knew the shape of it. Why do you frown like a djinn? Your sister smiles as one of the bright ones."

He set her up beside Alaina? Kyrin stamped the sand, her eyes stinging. "You are stone! You care for nothing and no one!" She had reason to frown as a djinn, did she not? She was hot and thirsty and she hurt. But so did he, and he only asked a question. She stared at his feet and blinked hard. She had not thought to quarrel; if only he would tell her his mind. "I am sorry." She licked her lips.

"I have forgotten your words." He bent over the way-sign, giving her his quiet back, and began to take the cairn apart to the sand. After a moment she moved around him to the other side. Stones thumped to the ground.

"Hai!" He held up a twist of cloth. Two grey-blue embroidered falcons winged across the undyed material. Kyrin knew those tiny, beautiful stitches as well as she did her awkward ones.

"Alaina!" She could not keep back her smile. Her grin faded as she peered closer. Two birds—two days? Ali was flying for his eyrie, indeed. The empty, water-sucking desert under her feet mocked her. Their waterskin was almost empty.

Faisal stared at the red beads on Lilith's lead rope in his hand, rolling them, frowning. He looked small against the desert.

She touched the edge of his sleeve. "The Master of all knows we need water."

He pulled away, head up, his nostrils flaring. "If Allah wills it, we will find water." He loosed the waterskin from his mount with quick jerks at the thongs and shoved it in her arms. She clutched the hot leather bag to her chest. He mounted and kicked his beast to a trot. She gazed after him with a growing frow. A little later she trailed up behind him on Lilith.

He turned, the end of his dirty blue kaffiyeh rippling like a live thing over his shoulder. "You are a *fool*, Nasrany."

"The Master of all—"

"Be still!" He laid his hand on the falcon blade in his sash. "You blaspheme, and my brothers let you live, Nasrany of the Book! *Allah* will judge if we are worthy! What will be, will be." His eyes were slits.

She sat back, pulling on Lilith's rein, and savagely tugged at a bit of hair caught in her bisht at the back of her neck. It came free with burst of pain, and she grimaced.

Not if she lived a thousand years could they be worthy, or purify themselves. The true Nur-ed-Dam worked only if the blood shed was pure—and given in freewill. The falcon by rights should turn in Faisal's hand and drink his blood—but the Master of mercy said not. He paid the Nur–ed–Dam on behalf of all. Only one had been pure since the creation of the world— after the forbidden was taken by men. She sighed, and left the tired silence undisturbed.

The fourth day they found no water at all. Faisal seemed used to the throbbing quiet. Kyrin counted passing thornbush skeletons and camel strides. Foam dotted Lilith's swaying neck as she walked after Faisal's beast toward another tall stone outcrop.

There was a little shade at the base. Kyrin gave Lilith a pat and dismounted. She leaned against her, too tired to move for the moment, scratching around Lilith's small ears, joining her dreams of water-pools in her long-lashed eyes.

They stayed in the rock shadow through the afternoon, the camels chewing cud. In the westering sun the wind shivered through a clump of bleached grass. The blade tips made thread patterns in the sand. Lying full length, chin on her hands, Kyrin watched the swaying blades and shadows play.

Faisal had spoken often with Umar of the swift gazelle, the *reem,* and how he longed to hunt the oryx. That would be a shot to boast of, with the bow beside her. The oryx, a lordly Wudhaihi, would likely take a stronger bow and a heavier arrow.

She stood to catch Faisal's eye. He glanced under his arm he'd laid across his face, and she motioned at the pack camel in question. He grunted. She took it as agreement and unhooked the waterskin's strap and her sash sack. Laying the slack bottle on the ground, she divided the last dates between them.

She lifted her head. "Faisal, why do you love these empty lands?" His laugh was a scornful bark, and he rolled over to face the other way. She huffed out a breath and scowled. He thought her lacking in wit, or unworthy, did he?

But heat in the heart *was* better than despair. Or was it? Her stomach growled. Kyrin chewed her rock-hard date a long time until it would go past her dry throat. After one gulp from the waterskin she forced her hands away. The wet leather taste relieved her swollen tongue but a moment.

How she dreamed of water, of cold trickling streams, of rain dripping from roofs, the ship's barrel, even of shallow caravan pools murky with slimy plants and other things she did not want to think of. She tapped Faisal's shoulder and handed the skin to him and watched his throat bob. He picked up his date. His mouth was set. Did despair eat at him also?

"Allah the merciful," was but words on his tongue. He had a distant master. The purple evening slipped closer. She guessed the sun drew close to nones, ninth hour after dawn at home.

Without a word, Faisal took the saddle off his camel and gave it to her. She watched his back, tight-lipped. He did not want his beast to bear the burden any longer. The third camel they would use last. She saddled Lilith, and they mounted again.

With dusk they arrived at a wide place of gravel and sand. Faisal approached a bare, trampled place in the midst of the plain, his head turning, as if a thousand enemies hid in plain sight. There was not a spear of green anywhere for a camel to stop for, only a long crack in the earth.

The camels burst into a swaying trot, and Faisal made a wild grab for his beast's neck, almost losing his seat. Dust puffed from his bisht in swirls, making him a dust wraith on a fog-shrouded beast of legend.

Kyrin stifled her hacking laugh. If they were in a tale, they would find some deadly or some beautiful thing at the crack.

The camels pawed and snuffled at the ground, moaning. Faisal untied the water bag and Kyrin dropped off Lilith. She almost tumbled to her knees. When she could, she lowered the ancient haul bag into the well, and it came up bulging with cloudy liquid. Not wanting to offend Faisal, she handed it to him.

Then she took the bag, and ignoring his protest, gulped till her throat and belly protested. Her thirst soothed, her stomach began to complain of its emptiness as they watered the camels with bag after bag.

After dark Kyrin huddled between him and Lilith's broad side, wrapped tight in her bisht. She reached after a wayward edge blown free by the wind. Faisal caught it, stuffed it under her shoulder, and turned over. His back was warm. Cicero curled inside her arm. So they slept under the starlight.

Waking early, they forced all the brackish water they could into their straining stomachs. And left the well. Some time later Kyrin looked over her shoulder.

"Faisal—" it was a croak of dismay. The waterskin behind her saddle flapped against Lilith with every stride. The last gleaming drop leaked to the sand as she watched, leaving a dark trail down Lilith's side.

"By Allah, cursed one, do you not care if we die?" Faisal reined his camel around, drew her falcon blade and fiercely slashed the skin free from Lilith. His camel shifted under him with a groan, and Faisal fingered the hole in the end of the waterskin.

Kyrin tightened her hand on her bow and pulled Lilith away, head bowed in shame. Her eyes burned, without water for relief. How could she not notice their life dripping away?

15

Saviors

Nor is it in a man who walks to direct his steps. ~Jeremiah 10:23

The sixth sunrise since they fled the crater, Kyrin swayed atop Lilith, dreaming of a spring, and of water dribbling down her chin. Cicero lay limp across her thighs.

A low whine escaped him. Kyrin raised her head, blinking swollen, dry eyes, drawing the air of a furnace into her lungs. Among mountain slopes of sand to their left, a camel walked. The far image shivered in the heat. Faisal rode ahead among barren dunes taller than storm waves.

Kyrin gripped Lilith's rope with white knuckled hands and ran a parchment tongue over her crusted lips. The camel's snake head sank below the edge of a dune crest; another camel rose in its place. Their backs were bare, and they walked without rope or watcher.

"Faisal!"

Hunched on his beast, Faisal lifted his head as if it were lead. He turned toward the camel and paused, then nodded.

It was night when they struggled up the thousandth steep dune beside the camel tracks. Four hands of fires twinkled before dark tents spread across a valley below, curving around the base of another hill of sand.

181

Kyrin floundered down the slope after Faisal, leaning against Lilith's shoulder, not sure if Lilith supported her or she Lilith. Her hand cramped about her bow, and she sniffed at the homely smell of smoke, mouth watering.

Faisal could see better than she in the faint light that showed uneven ground. At least he did not stumble or fall. They reached the bottom of the dune, mounted, and breasted a wall of protesting camels that milled between them and the tents resting in the starlight.

Kyrin kept her eyes on the fires before the closest tents, waiting for welcoming voices, ready to laugh in relief. She could drink an entire waterskin herself. Faisal coughed, a dry rasp, and called out to warn of their approach. His voice was thin and cracked.

Kyrin tensed. There was something in the deserted shadows, in the hum of voices within the dwellings, that chilled her like rising mist. She touched his sleeve.

Faisal turned, opening his mouth with a frown. She never heard what he said. A man screamed with rage. There was a loud "phoomp," mingled with the sound of shattering pottery, and the black felt walls of the largest tent at the edge of the camp shook with a struggle of many bodies. The tent sides flared into hungry flame.

Kyrin stared; Lilith raised her drooping head with a snort. Faisal was a lurid shape against the light, his eyes dark pits. He yelled, "Down!"

Kyrin was halfway when Lilith bolted. She dug her fingers into Lilith's curly hide and kicked against the ground, lunging back for the saddle. Not far enough.

The sand fled beneath her. Kyrin strained to keep her grip on the cantle, and wedge her ankle under the saddle-pad. Her bow swung from her arm.

Lilith raced between the tents and the bitter night whipped Kyrin's sunburned cheeks. Screams and wild yells rose from running figures. Someone snatched at Kyrin and missed.

Lilith swerved, and Kyrin struggled astride. The camel circled toward the burning tent. Kyrin urged her away, fumbling for an arrow.

Men with lances ran toward her in a line, yelling—Lilith skidded to a stop. Kyrin pitched over her shoulder. And landed with a stunning shock and a cry of her own, sand spraying wide. She scrambled up, her arms and legs heavy, her bow and arrow somehow still whole. She limped toward the concealing dark, paces away.

Behind her a child screamed in stark terror. Kyrin whirled. A small boy ran from the fiery tent, his brown legs churning, fleeing a man. The Bedouin lunged, his dagger low, seeking the little back.

Her heart thumped once, *No—.* The clamor dimmed into frozen stillness. Nock the arrow—pull—through shaking stars and angular tents. Her vision settled on the dark form behind the bright, swooping blade. Another shriek—the child dodged. The man slowed, turned.

Kyrin loosed.

The arrow struck under his raised arm with a wet thud. He toppled, and a robed figure sprang over him to scoop up the stumbling child. Kyrin reached for another arrow, stopped: Lilith bore her quiver. The figure held the wailing boy and faced Kyrin, long hair flying against the starry sky.

Kyrin lowered her bow. He had his mother, and she had him. A heavy blow from behind spun her. She staggered, looked down. A glistening arrowhead poked through her left arm. Panting, she lifted her head, the air fire in her throat.

Bedouin converged on her, firelight too bright on bow and blade and lance. Voices buzzed, arms rose, pointing at her. She shrank back, catching her breath at the fiery pull of the arrow in her arm.

The men stopped, a circle of faces. *Father always said to get the arrow out*—Kyrin reached for the shaft, could not grip it, and cried tears she thought the sun had sucked dry. Then Faisal was beside her, his lips tight, bringing her warmth with the determined brown heat of his eyes.

His fingers closed around the shaft close to the arrowhead, and his other hand slid behind her shoulder. His knuckles whitened—the shaft snapped. The head dropped to the sand, and her knees went.

She swam out of grey pain, and he held her up with one arm around her middle.

Why? The cool sand would feel good after the burning sun. Then she shivered with a bitter cold as harsh as the pain spreading through her arm. The tent flames beckoned her with the promise of warmth, dying down behind the still figure of the sprawled Bedouin, the black felt almost devoured. Her lips twitched, cracking painfully.

The raider would not harm anyone again—the ice inside did not stop her arrow. *If I only had my bow, mother, for you—but I had my hands. I did not use them. But I did not know you had the falcon.* She was crying.

Faisal's arm tightened, crushing her ribs. Kyrin raised her head, but her protest died. A lance point nudged Faisal's throat.

"Nur-ed-Dam, *Sheyk*," Faisal said, rock still. A shiver rolled through him. She wanted to laugh. Death, death, all was death and cold.

But the lance—it waited. She could help, should—she swayed, and blinked past the edge of the lance, following the painted shaft to a poised arm and a hawk-nose under a white kaffiyeh. The man's face was tight with wrath.

Faisal said something and pulled off her kaffiyeh, shaking her hair free. Tangled, rough strands fell around her face. She must push him away, scream at him to run. Knowing what she was never stopped raiders. Only the falcon could—if it fought. But the falcon was chained, chained by ice to the tiger waiting outside the circle of firelight. A tiger that could kill with a blow.

Death, and cold—the tip of the lance promised loss—it should be her, not him. Kyrin willed her hands to the lance head, to guide it from Faisal's neck, past her body. At her side her fingers did no more than twitch. Her teeth chattered violently.

The man lifted his lance and grounded the butt. In the abrupt silence a breeze fanned the flames behind them in a rising crackle. Faisal let her down to the ground and propped her back against his knees. His hand pressed her shoulder. Holding her up or steadying himself, she could not tell.

The Bedouins surged forward, weapons forgotten, their voices urgent. Kyrin clamped her lips on a scream when they lifted her, jostling. Someone pulled the rest of the arrow out. Then she was inside a tent, lying on something soft. A skin bottle wormed between her teeth and camel milk squirted over her tongue, strong with desert herbs, sweet as Aunt Medaen's mead.

She swallowed once, twice. "Faisal . . ." Someone moved her arm, and the tent and the faces fell away and shattered.

The raider chased the child. Kyrin ran with her bow between never-ending black tents under the stars, her legs weak, losing, losing ground. She must shoot now. She willed her arrow forward, it arced down, and the raider fell. Before the tent poles, trailing smoking cloth, his body dissolved.

A tiger sprang from that haze of smoke. On its back the falcon braced against a loop of heavy chain that dragged under the tiger's chest as it bounded past the tent poles, fluid, muscles rippling. The beast checked. The wide torque about its neck reflected her as it turned its head, ears up. Kyrin struggled to lift her bow.

Too late. She braced as his paws thudded against her shoulders. Her hands slipped in the deep fur of his chest. She flailed at him.

Kyrin's eyes flew open. She gasped in a breath, batting at Cicero's paws that danced on her chest, his nails pricking her skin. He licked her nose and face in a frenzy, whines bursting from his throat, ignoring her choking grip on his neck. With a soft sob, Kyrin let him go and gathered his shivering body close. She cried into his soft coat. Dimly, she knew her arm was afire.

Which was better, fire or ice? Fire, because she could move her fingers now. The bandage about her upper arm was tight. A few spots of blood seeped through.

Over her head swept black tent cloth. The three center poles formed the tent's spine. The thick black felt swooped to shorter poles on either side and dropped to the ground. Three sides of the tent were closed, but the sun shone bright beyond the fourth.

By the heat sliding inside, the sun was hours high. A camel groaned, and someone called, voice faint with distance. The gaily patterned rugs spread on the floor were red or green, with blue, purple, or black leaf-and-line motifs.

A goat hair blanket wrapped her. Faisal lay stretched in another blanket on a rug a few feet away. Kyrin lay back, careful of her arm.

She had stopped the Bedouin chasing the child, but she didn't help Faisal—she paused before the blade. She did not know if it was fear or the haze her head had been in. Tears gathered and slid past her ears. Her heart felt sore, and thin, and wondering.

It had been the man with the lance who let Faisal live. But why did Faisal stand with her? Did he want Tae's goodwill, or her guard down—that he might deal with her himself at a moment of his choosing? She grasped her blanket and stiffened as her left arm throbbed, sinking tiger's claws in her shoulders. Weak as a pup. She closed her eyes.

She was not thirsty, but somewhere she smelled roasting meat. Kyrin slid out of her blanket, with pauses to fend off Cicero. On his back, Faisal was motionless but for his steady breaths. Her falcon dagger was not in his sash, and she did not see her bow and quiver in the corners or among the rugs. She wanted a weapon before she took another step, but Faisal was better than nothing.

Sleep had smoothed his savage frown, leaving his face a blank parchment. She touched his hand and backed away. She didn't want to be close if his waking was anything like hers.

His eyes flicked open. He stared up, and blinked. "Aneza," he said in a harsh whisper, and sat up quickly.

She nodded. "You could have left me to them."

"It was not to be." His lips thinned, not quite a sneer. "I took your defeat in the name of my father, for Allah."

Took my defeat? There was no defeat, and if there had been, she would never give it to him, the jackal. "How is killing a murderer defeat?" She would kick his tail past his ears when she was whole. Kyrin shifted and winced, licking her lips. She was not in a good position to glare. "How is killing a murderer a defeat?" she repeated.

Faisal said slowly, "They thought you were with the lawbreaker. When I chose generosity, to show them your womanhood, I blotted out the shame you brought on me. I purified my name and my father's, and so I defeated you. I am a warrior of Allah." His smile was satisfied. Then his brown gaze shuttered, and he rose to his knees, pulling his bisht about him. "No shame or blood now divides us."

Kyrin resisted the urge to step back. There was more blood between them than Faisal ever dreamed. Blood of a different kind, that spoke better things than Abel's. As for shame—he twisted things. An arm for an arm. He knew her deed at the crater paid any Nur-ed-Dam he might claim.

Tae was right. Faisal believed one deed could overwrite another. She imagined him splitting a camel hair and laying the gossamer threads on a pair of scales, carefully balancing them. He thought she owed him. The words stuck in her throat, but truth was truth. "I do not—see all you say—but for my life I thank you." She rubbed Cicero's ears.

Faisal sank back on his heels with a faint sigh and tucked the end of his kaffiyeh into his turban. Had he been worried she might hit him? She grimaced.

At least there would be no more spiders. And Faisal might keep his word to her, for Tae's sake. The corners of Faisal's mouth turned up, and he reached to stroke Cicero. He might even smile at her some unguarded moment. How Father would laugh. He would say if they were not enemies, they were allies. Captive allies. Were they?

"My dagger and bow are gone. Are we guests here or—" Kyrin stopped short as a woman ducked inside the tent.

Plump and weathered, her wrinkled face was a sun that beamed joy in its own right. She was unveiled, and henna designs graced her thin hands. The woman set bowls of camels' milk and dates before them with a nod, and rested a waterskin as big as a camel haunch beside Kyrin.

Faisal said something in the woman's tongue and her eyes twinkled. She answered, with a low laugh. With a piercing stare at Kyrin she set a bowl of milk down for Cicero. He lapped with a good will.

Kyrin smiled at her. "Faisal—"

"Yes, we are guests. And the noble ones are blessed of Allah and may sleep on our rugs. She honors him as is right. They will not kill us." Faisal picked up his milk bowl, dipped a date, and ate it whole.

Kyrin snorted. He looked at her gravely, but said nothing.

"Why should we trust them?" She twisted at her bandage. If she could only cut off the pain by tightening it.

"They brought us into their tents. Have you forgotten the bond of salt, slow one?" He pinched his mouth shut, studying her a moment, then turned back to his food.

Kyrin took a long drink of her clotted milk. He did not have to be so superior. How did he know the Aneza would keep their word? Or that all of them gave it? The guest-bond *ought* to give her three days.

Who had she killed? She sighed. There was nothing to do but believe the Arabs would keep the desert law. Then Faisal could get a weapon and a spare camel, and she would ask for her falcon blade and her bow. Surely the Aneza would return them, and they could leave.

She held up a soft date. Bits of the brown skin stuck to her fingers, and she shivered with delight to lick them off. Closing her eyes, she let the sweetness melt on her tongue, letting it push her throbbing arm to the edge of awareness. She had not thought to taste such food again. When she looked up, Faisal was grinning.

"You eat the food of kings."

She could not shrug. The clean, sour taste of the curded milk grew on her. With the dates it was very good. She had emptied the bowl when a shadow extended over the rugs and alerted her. She pushed herself to her knees with one awkward arm.

A Bedouin man slipped into the tent with a woman behind him, a child cradled on her hip. Cicero growled low, inquiring. Kyrin laid a hand on his back, and he subsided. She struggled to rise and bow, but the Bedouin waved her back with deference.

His hawk nose proclaimed him the man who had held the lance. Faisal had called him a sheyk. He spoke. She did not understand his spate of Arabic, and turned from his piercing regard to Faisal.

Faisal burst into fluid reply, touching his hand to his forehead in a curious motion of respect. He whipped toward her. "What did you do, who did you shoot?"

"I don't know—what does he say?" She twisted a bit of blanket around her finger.

Faisal pulled in a hard breath. "This is Sheyk Shahin, his wife Mey, and his son Rashid. Shahin, sheyk of the Aneza, lays his arm, his tent, and his camels before you for the life of his son of promise. Tell me—what did you do?"

"The man was going to stab the child." She motioned toward Rashid, nestled in the woman's arms. "So I shot him. Then an arrow hit me." She met Shahin's gaze, and words clogged on her tongue. "My lord, you honor us too greatly. Though I thank you." Her mouth was sore, and she wanted to lie down.

The sheyk nodded, looking from her to Faisal. He had a short beard. Without the rage of the night before, his brown eyes were self-possessed and quiet. His date-colored hair rippled against his cream collar, and his thawb was gathered by an orange sash to his waist. A silver filigreed dagger was thrust under his sash-knot. Beside her husband, Mey did not blink, but watched Kyrin with doe eyes, rocking Rashid on her hip. He crowed—as babies do—and stretched out his arms.

Then somehow he was in Kyrin's lap while Mey gently kissed her cheeks, even her nose. Kyrin felt a blush rising. Rashid grabbed her hair.

He smelled of milk and clean dust. She smiled, untangling his strong fingers. Rashid's delight was sunlight through rain on flowers stirred by a breeze. He gurgled a laugh, and she cooed back. He was alive—because she killed a man.

She swallowed hard, while his father smiled on them both with pride. Mey's husky laugh wove around her son's.

Dizziness struck Kyrin. She tensed and concentrated on the rug under her knees, green and black. Shahin asked something, and Faisal leaned to look intently in her eyes. "Shahin wants to know if your eyes always do that."

"They—darken when I'm glad or angry or hurt. It's my arm."

Faisal nodded. Shahin chuckled and said in common, "Your eyes see with the falcon's spirit. You come on a favorable wind."

Mey whispered something in Shahin's ear. He grunted, his eyes on Kyrin's face, attention flicking from her necklace to her earring. His amused goodwill did not falter. Did the eye of evil hold no meaning for him, or did he disregard it?

Faisal said, "The sheyk believes the falcon sent you to protect his son, despite the mark you bear." He took care not to look at her.

Kyrin shook her head gently, not to jar her arm. "The falcon follows the Master of all. He guided my arrow."

"Say instead, Allah, who sent the camels to guide us."

Kyrin bit her lip and let her words stand. Her good hand curled into a fist. Never had she wanted to hit Faisal so much. Instead she touched Rashid's nose with one finger. He laughed. A tattooed blue falcon on his chest, wings spread, hovered over tiny tents far below. Kyrin cocked her head. Its wings seemed to beat with his breath. Was the tattoo a token that he was destined to be the tribes' protector, or a plea for his protection, or in honor of the spirit of the falcon that these Aneza seemed to revere?

After Shahin and his family left, the afternoon dragged at Kyrin like her aching arm. She could not sleep. Faisal knelt for his prayers outside the tent. No wonder his kaffiyeh was dusty. Out in the desert, with no water to spare, he had often dropped on the ground, always making sure he was in her sight, to cleanse his arms from wrists to elbows in sand in elaborate ritual.

Now his was the only voice she heard without. And Shahin had not greeted her with an invocation to Allah. The sheyk thought the falcon sent her. She pursed her lips. So, the Aneza worshipped the spirits of water, earth, and air. She turned restlessly. They were not spirits but created servants.

Her skin felt oddly hot. Where was Ali's caravan now? Tae would know how to speak to Shahin, and he could ease her arm. As if sensing her need for distraction, after his prayers Faisal entertained her with what he knew of the Aneza.

They were not as closely associated with the towns as Kentar and Ali's northern tribal drivers were. Nomad warriors, the Aneza used lances and bows afoot and on horseback. Their almost-straight swords were for war. Every man and some of the women wore a dagger for cutting meat and for other things. Their dagger blades ranged from slightly to heavily curved.

Kyrin smiled to herself. None of their daggers came close to the falcon's straight bronze length. She must find a smith to melt the brazing from the Damascus steel soon. But then Ali might take it—best keep the steel hidden. Her bow and quiver rested by her head against the wall. Shahin had returned her weapons without her asking.

She reached out to touch the horn tips. What was Tae doing now? And her father? When he hunted for the table, did he

spare a thought for her? Her hand faltered. She would not be
drawing a bow for some little while.

Faisal growled, "Are your ears closing?"

"Yes. I mean, I hear." She crossed her arms over her chest and
turned back to him.

"Shahin's people use peregrine falcons and salukis to find
and catch the reem."

Kyrin nodded. She had caught glimpses. A hooded falcon on
a passing lancer's arm, salukis sniffing at another hunter's heels.
The bird made her think of her hawk, Samson, and Cierheld, and
of her father. She longed for his protecting arms. And for the
live spring of a falcon launching from her glove. Kyrin stroked
Cicero's side, ignoring hot tears, born of pain and loneliness.
The Aneza falcons were Araby birds. Would they know her, or
she them? If the sheyk allowed, she might find their perches in
the coming days, though she could not hunt.

Faisal fell silent. She tried to smile at him, glad he stayed
with her. He nodded.

The sun passed sext bell, by the shadows creeping outside.
Faisal dozed, his mouth open. A fly buzzed around him in the
stuffy tent and looped toward Cicero, who slept against Kyrin's
legs. Cicero flicked his ears with a huffing groan, and Kyrin
waved the fly away. Her thoughts pressed in, driven by pain.

Though Shahin promised them fresh beasts when they
wished, it would be foolish to travel on. The thought of walking
made her cringe, let alone riding. Tae and Alaina were getting
farther away every moment. And she could do nothing.

She yawned with weariness, tears welling, and shifted a bit at
a time until she rested her aching arm on another cushion. The
pain eased, and she melted into her blanket at last.

With evening, the old woman returned and packed a fresh
boiled leaf poultice around Kyrin's wound. With hand motions,

the woman told her the arrowhead had mostly gone between the muscles. Kyrin nodded. Since her arm had been motionless it had torn less when the arrow hit. It would heal fast.

The poultice stung; it must have the proper antiseptic properties. Alaina would know by the sharp, astringent smell. Faisal would know what the tea the woman gave her was called.

He snored behind her. Kyrin's smile twisted wryly, and the wrinkles around the woman's eyes and mouth curved up in answer. Welcome sleepiness pulled at Kyrin again, and she laid her cup down.

She slept, woke, and ate with Faisal, often interrupted by Aneza who stopped to greet them. Faisal eyed her, considering, as yet another man left.

"They say the Twilket you shot was their guest, a trader, a mender of metal. He possessed skill but sold it ill, and came with hard words. An Aneza reproached him with bitterness toward his host, and the Twilket trader attacked him. Shahin went to his tent with the elders to sit in judgment.

"The witnesses spoke for the Aneza, and Shahin's face blackened against the Twilket. The trader saw Rashid playing on the rug and seized him, putting a dagger to his neck. When Shahin drew his sword, the man kicked an oil lamp into the fire. It exploded. During the confusion, Rashid broke away." Faisal scowled. "It is good you killed that djinn's offspring. But be wary, you have a tribe of the best trackers in the sands on your trail."

"What? But—I cannot ride, and we cannot stay here forever." Kyrin's voice went high. Cicero rumbled, head against her thigh, singing his threat.

"You knew the blood law when you shot him," Faisal said, one eyebrow rising, "or is your mind like a river, without memory?"

"No, but—" Her stomach told her she had leaped from a high place.

"The Aneza will fight for us, and for themselves."

The side of the tent stirred. An Aneza girl with an aureole of tiny dark braids peeped around the tent door, pulled back, then peeked in again.

Kyrin motioned her inside. Small and shy, she came. She skirted Faisal widely, but drifted near enough to brush Cicero's head with her hand. Kyrin forced back her smile. This was one moment Faisal would blush to be thought fierce. The girl's breath caught and she stopped, still as stone.

Kyrin followed her riveted gaze. And slid the falcon dagger from her sash and offered the blade with a smile. The girl brushed the falcon's beak with her fingers, and laughed in wondering delight. Then she darted outside. "Rashid, *Shaheen!*" her voice drifted back, light as a goat's bell on the wind. "Rashid, Shaheen!"

Faisal busied himself gathering a cushion. "That is a good blade. Who forged it?"

"I do not know; it was my mother's." Kyrin stared at a passing woman in red and green who led a maaing goat, her udder heavy with milk.

"Your mother's?"

"Yes. I took it after Ali's men killed her." Faisal cursed. Her mouth quirked. In his daydreams he must have cut her own throat often enough. And she saved him from the raiders. But then the arrow hit her, and he saved her from the Aneza. Then at the last, Shahin withdrew his lance. No matter, she would not plague Faisal long.

But would the broken law of bread and salt between the Aneza and the Twilkets mean a great Nur-ed-Dam spreading across the desert? Kyrin's jaw tensed and she shook her head sharply. Death followed her—this time to the Aneza. She must not cry—a pox on those who could not leave others in peace. "I will go," she whispered, "to my father and my home." She lifted her eyes to Faisal's. "In the spring."

His lean face was sober, his lip did not curl as he spoke. "The caravan road is hard and far, but I think you will follow it."

16

Byways

Let us cross over ... perhaps the Lord will work for us ... ~1 Samuel 14:6

Night brought all the Aneza. The men sat under the open side of the tent, around a large fire before the door. Women and children settled beside their men, some in gaily patterned thawbs of tan, brown, green, and red. Sparks fanned over the wide fire pit and the waiting faces. The young ones chattered, and the women whispered. The men greeted each other gravely.

Kyrin wished she knew their tongue.

A black slave poured cups of tea. It smelled of honey and flowers. The pot was a ewer of shining comfort in his stocky, capable hands. Kyrin thought of Alaina, and her first taste of bitter-rich cardamom. Shahin walked into the tent.

"Ahhh." The Anezas' sigh of welcome drowned Kyrin's greeting. Shahin acknowledged them with a gracious dip of his head. After him, two men bore a great platter on their shoulders.

Atop it rode a roast sheep, skin crisp and brown over moist flesh, succulent fat melting into a mound of spiced rice and almonds. Dates and milk followed in silver basins, winking bright above their bearers' heads.

Shahin sat in the tent door, and the platter was eased to the rug before him. More rugs were spread. The tea, which could stand on its own, went round again. Shahin dipped into the mutton and rice, and with a grin, invited his guests to join him.

Faisal bowed, and elbowed Kyrin when she reached for the platter. She frowned, for she knew her manners. If her right arm had been hit, would they have let her eat with her left, the unclean hand, or would Mey have had to feed her? But her right hand was unhurt, no matter the left made it ache in sympathy. She balled a bit of hot, fragrant rice and tossed it inside her mouth without touching her lips, trying not to jar her arm.

§

Faisal grunted and stretched. He was full for the first time since the raider knocked him off Waleed and he drove his lance through him. His enemy had been strong, his eyes full of hate.

Kyrin. Her name held strength, though apparent only to one with wisdom to see it. She bent over her food, hiding her pain, her good hand twisting and pulling at her evil mud-and-moss colored bisht. What father bestowed such a strong name on a girl child? But he could not ask her of her father, for it could not be that she ask after his.

Faisal scrubbed his hands clean in sand and discarded his cushion close to Kyrin's side. After a doubtful glance, she propped her arm on it. He pretended not to see.

Shahin stood. "My people, the Aneza gather now to find wisdom."

Faisal whispered the meaning of the sheyk's words to Kyrin. She bent her head, listening, the dark earring winking darker against her skin.

On the far side of the circle a wrinkled man stood, his black eyes bright, his hair white as his cloak and tunic, his voice a calm river. "The Twilkets will come for the Nur-ed-Dam, though the trader's punishment was most just. They have looked long on our herds and wells with a jealous eye. We must call our people to the mountains to fight. So have I spoken—it may be, with wisdom from the spirit above."

A young man rose, tense, his kaffiyeh quivering with his indignation. "Are the Aneza to run like the reem? We are a lion on our enemy's ground! The Aneza lances are a thicket of protection, our swords, thorns, pricking to the heart! We will fight under the shaheen's wings and win our enemies' herds for our own!"

"Yes!" Another leaped up. "We should seek the mountains, but divide our people so the Twilkets do not know which protects the taker of blood. We can seek peace with them when their anger cools! I will gift five camels to any who need them for the journey."

"No! We should fight now, as one, while we are strong. The blood of our son Rashid, whom they sought, will stain them until the moon fails over the sands!"

Kyrin tightened her good hand on her cushion. She foresaw an endless circle of Nur-ed-Dam—blood sinking into the sand, calling blood after it. *Why?* Her lip parted in brief pain under her teeth. She had done the only thing she could—she could not have let Rashid fall. Why did they not end it in the way that cost the least blood?

"Are you going to cry?" Faisal's eyes were wide.

"No," She gritted, and gripped the falcon hard, blinking swiftly and again. The council ended in favor of the elder speaker. The Aneza would move camp and ready for war.

When she lay down on her rug, Kyrin tossed. At last she fell into uneasy dream, between the tiger's paws. His claws were sheathed. Did he play with her, a sand-cat with a desert mouse?

She woke early to a chill dawn, a thought fuzzy in her mind. Faisal was gone. Kyrin got up awkwardly and walked out of the tent. Her arm did not ache so much. The sky was covered with puffy crimson and apricot clouds against blue. The air was fresh and dry over the mountains of sand.

A few fires crackled, new-fed with dry camel dung. A tent-flap was thrust back here and there, a child cried for food, or for its mother. A man spoke soothingly to his camels. Kyrin picked her way toward the center of camp. None seemed to see her.

Shahin's new tent was the largest. Faisal stroked a stallion tied beside the sheyk's door. The horse tossed its small brown head, ears pricked and regal, soft eyes wide. A group of young warriors murmured together nearby. Kyrin approached Faisal and touched his sleeve.

He leaned close to hear her whisper then shook his head. "I cannot!"

"But I must speak to him!" She kept her voice low.

The warriors paid no mind to her. One of them, the fiery youth from the council, said something and spat sharply toward the tent.

"A way to find swift death without glory!" Faisal snapped back over his shoulder.

Kyrin eyed them curiously. "What did he say?"

"Youbib says they will kill the Twilket dogs on their own ground."

Shahin lifted the side of his tent, and Mey propped it with a pole. The young warriors straightened. Shahin tested their restless glances with his own, then gestured his permission. He listened to the fiery youth from the council, his eyes keen, then nodded. "Youbib, you will fight at my side."

"With the women?" Youbib choked, and thrust out his chin in Kyrin's direction.

Shahin's eyes glinted with steel. "It is not only fear that makes a warrior run; courage does not always bid him fight." A tendon flexed on the back of the sheyk's hand on his sword hilt.

"The Aneza will defend, and attack, when the moment is right."
His stern words left no room for mockery.

Youbib's fists whitened. Frowning thunderously, he turned
and stamped away. Shahin said a short word to the others, and
they dispersed, arguing among themselves.

Shahin turned back toward his tent, caught Kyrin's gaze,
and smiled. "Shaheen! This morn is bright."

"Sheyk Shahin, I think I can help." *Please.* She reached out to
him. They must not die for her.

His smile fell away and his brown gaze sharpened. A lump
blocked Kyrin's throat. He reminded her of her father, looking at her with that regard that would protect her at all cost.
This sheyk's heart was open, looking for good things—like her
father. Ali's heart was an open waste-pool, full of himself. She
rubbed her damp hand over her thawb.

"Yes, Shaheen?" He stepped closer, speaking slowly as if to
make sure she understood.

She took the plunge. "Sheyk Shahin, if I go, and you tell the
Twilkets what happened and give them the camels you gifted
me—except the one I ride—will they leave you in peace?"

"What do you think would happen to you, Shaheen?" He
peered into her face. Faisal's lips thinned, no doubt for his camels that she gifted back to Shahin. What did the sheyk mean,
calling her Shaheen?

"I—I know they might follow me, might catch me, but I cannot stand for you all to die because of me. I know that," she said,
welcoming the pain in her arm that excused her pricking tears.

"We must fight them, if not now, then later," Shahin said
kindly, "and I will not break my word to you and Faisal."

At her feet an ant crawled around a fist-sized rock, as power-
less to move it as she was to help the Aneza. But Tae—he was a
warrior and a leader among men.

"My Lord Shahin, I know a man who can defeat your enemy!"

"Who do you speak of?"

"My teacher—he is a high askar, though also a slave to my master. He defended his land against many." Name Tae her husband, no, that she would not. Tae could tell the sheyk if he wished, after Shahin found the caravan. Faisal's face gave away nothing.

"Hmm. It is well. I would like to meet such a man." Shahin sent his black slave for three messengers who would search out Ali Ben Aidon's caravan. "Now," he said with a grin, "we will have a falcon hunt in the mountains a sun's journey from here— to keep Youbib from rashness. Let our enemies wonder whether we seek the favor of the falcon or whether we have nothing to fear."

§

Around the tents of his people huddled at the foot of the mountains, Shahin set watchers in the tamarisk scrub as night fell. Every Aneza in camp and without kept his weapons close.

Kyrin woke early. Her stomach fluttered. Something had woken her. It was not the tiger. All was still.

Above her head the tent poles met in indistinct angles of the felt, just visible. Turning awkwardly, biting back a groan, she sniffed the damp scent of greenery.

It had rained last night, the fifth since the arrow struck her. There were mountains, dark blue and clear cut, above the slopes just without. The bit of sky parting the tent flap was silver-blue. She rose and tiptoed past Faisal's snoring length.

She saw no living thing but couched camels chewing their cud, and wandered out of camp, up the gentle tree-clad slope. The guards saw her but did not call, doubtless thinking her about the common business of early morning.

Deep in the trees, Kyrin touched a trunk. They grew thick, and greener than in any place she had yet seen in Araby. Shorter than her great oaks of Britannia, they were furred with moss. Stubby evergreen needles graced junipers that towered over her, their invigorating sharp-sweet scent drifting with the coolness. One tree had intricate branches covered with narrow silver-grey and green leaves. An olive.

There were many figs, whose canopy and leaf shape reminded Kyrin of the oaks of Cierheld. Here she saw no leafless skeletons. Here at the edge of the desert the trees lived, as if springs ran beneath.

Grass grew at their feet. Wiry and rough, still it was grass. Not too many Eagle miles from the mountains that reared north and south, the sands began, down in the pastel haze of distance. She could not see the top of the mountain for the trees climbing the slope above her.

A parrot squawked. The air was warm and damp. Some distance off a band of creatures with the furry dog-like face and hunched figure of a dwarf, broke the morning stillness with squalling barks.

One of the baboons crouched in the limbs of a nearby wild fig, busily eating a green fruit. He paused to watch Kyrin, his earthy coat blending with bark and ground better than her bisht. His teeth were dangerous as a wolf-hound's, and his hand-like paws were quick. He studied her, his gaze sand-colored with hints of green, deep with the curious vibrancy of life. The baboon reached over his head for another fruit, his paw sure, then leaped to a branch. His long arms and short bowed legs looked awkward to move so gracefully.

The parrot swooped in on wind-brushed feathers and snatched the baboon's fig, gliding out of reach to a clump of olives. The emerald bird gave the baboon a cheeky glance from a bright eye, one foot clutching sweet spoil. It opened its beak and squawked such a lighthearted string of noise that Kyrin felt her mouth pulling up in a laugh.

The bird jeered and chuckled, its rosy feather collar about its throat pulsing in joyous abandon. The baboon halfheartedly bared its fangs, picked another fig, and ate it in one bite.

"Shaheen!" The call echoed through the trees. Kyrin recognized the name. Mey must have good ears. After the sheyk first called her Shaheen, so did all the rest of his people. Faisal had not offered to tell her what Shaheen meant.

Questioner, over-bold one, meddler, or bringer of change? Did they have tales of old blood among the Aneza, or gifted ones, or djinn? She would ask Mey. Kyrin's brow furrowed as she walked toward the tents, picking her way through the trees. Her changeable amber eyes, the fish necklace, the falcon dagger, Ali's jet earring; they did not seem to bother Shahin. But the falcon dagger had nothing to do with spirits. The Master of the world created the falcon's heart to ride the wind.

Mey met her at the edge of the trees, pushing a low-hanging juniper branch out of her way. With a few words in common she asked Kyrin if she was ready for the falcon hunt.

"Yes, oh yes!" Dates and milk and her questions could wait.

It was not long before the hunting party set out, climbing one of several wadis that descended the mountain. The group included everyone but the Aneza sentries, nursing women, and the old. Kyrin left Cicero with a pat and a promise of a later hunt for rabbits.

They rode between the thick trees, and Kyrin nudged Lilith closer to Mey, staring at the craggy mountainside. It was nothing like the misty, rounded mountains and green valleys of Cierheld.

Cierheld, where she began to learn to care for her stronghold when she was four summers old. She spent hours with the cook, with those cleaning and mending: helping even if it was only stirring the stew, sweeping the flags, or holding the yarn. Father had commanded she inherit Cierheld whether she married or no.

Lord Dain Cieri might be a dangerous, distant figure to some, but never to her. Her father's warmth and strength had no end, enfolding her with the smell of the cinnamon he liked so well. Over the seasons, he took her to watch the guardsmen at their weapons training and showed her how the fields were planted and harvested and which insects harmed or helped.

One harvest-time she told him harvesting seemed a great lark, and he let her come to the fields with the workers. By vespers, hot and tired, they walked down the ruts of the cart track toward Cierheld.

"Do you still think it a lark, daughter?"

She had smiled in proud satisfaction. "It was hard, but I did it. And the lark that sang for us was a true lark."

Lord Dain laughed until he wiped tears from his face, and carried her home on his shoulders. As she grew older and her days grew long, she escaped to the hills for a walk or to the woods for a ride with Samson on her fist. In those years her mother taught her numbers, reading, and writing. She allowed Kyrin's forays so long as she learned. They often picked flowers in the woods and looked at cloud shapes and talked of the ways of plants and trees.

Mother had a soft spot for her brother, or Father Ulf as many called him, Benedictine monk that he was. To Kyrin, he was Uncle Ulf. Did he yet have long conversations with Father, now that she was gone? He had made her smile with his gentle teasing, but she always feared his arguments. He sternly insisted that one's sin must be forgiven by a priest. Lord Dain smiled and said he could not agree. Kyrin leaned forward and rubbed

Lilith's dirty-mustard coat. She did not fear Uncle Ulf's tongue much now, not after Ali. But he would be curious about the Aneza, their worship, their tales, and their tongue. She grinned. He would cool Youbib's hot blood with learning.

Lilith's head bobbed as she climbed. Kyrin picked at her bandage. Her arm was beginning to itch. Accompanied by fragrant juniper, the hunters followed the wadi higher, toward the water-and-wind gouged heights, past clumps of twisted wild plum and persimmon. The slope clambered to stark ledges folded above the mountain's foot. The hunters turned the last rising bend and scrambled out of the wadi onto a lower ledge, Youbib in the lead. Kyrin stared at the nearest crag—almost an elongated, bony head and shoulders of stone—rising above empty air.

Juniper trees filled vertical crevices in the towering neck and gave the melancholy face a tumble of grey-green hair. Around the stone features the sky held a gossamer overcast. The riders paused and squinted up. Wind whistled around the rocks.

"Shaheen!" The call rose, echoing. Many arms pointed to the shelf and the face's jutting chin. From a mounded stick-tangle beard, a falcon dropped into a gliding spiral, screaming at her unwelcome guests.

A grin stretched Kyrin's mouth. "Shaheen" meant falcon. The bird caught a draft and tilted higher. Kyrin watched. How often she had longed to follow Samson's wings into the sky, away from the looks of pity her plain gowns had earned her from Esther.

Did Samson hunt now—for her father? Kyrin closed her eyes and touched her necklace. The pouch dangling below it yet smelled of charcoal and cheese. She fingered the leather and glanced back. Faisal trailed behind, near the end of the caval-cade, head down.

The Aneza shouted as Youbib and another young warrior trotted to the base of the chosen crag. Forearms wrapped in cloth, their kaffiyehs tucked into turbans, they began to climb. Encouraged by jokes and catcalls, the lithe warriors pulled themselves toward the small shelf of the mountain's chin far above. Once Youbib stopped, a lizard spread-eagled on a rock that bulged outward below the vigilant falcon's nest. She swung toward him on the wind—and dived, a blur.

Youbib's companion waved her off vigorously. The men below shook their lances in admiration, and a ululating cry of encouragement rose from the women. The falcon's shrieks rang between the crags. Youbib inched around the bulge and his companion followed. Kyrin shuddered at the eighty feet of air beneath their feet. The waiting Aneza fell silent. Then the two above crawled over the edge of the shelf.

Youbib rose from a crouch, a dim ball of feathers in his cupped hands. He called something that was lost among wild Aneza yells.

The falcon lifted and dived again, her angry cry echoing down the mountainside. Youbib rocked back and ducked, flailing his free arm around his head to keep off the furious mother. She beat her wings for height so she could stoop again. And Youbib and his brother turned to descend.

Could not the falcon keep one of her children? Kyrin looked down, but a gasp from Mey brought her gaze up.

Youbib's foot had slipped. There was a roar of ridicule from the Aneza men, and Kyrin's arm flared at her sudden twitch. She held her breath.

Youbib cast about for a hold, his arms straining. His toes found a dark crack. He hung a moment. His companion continued on, and thumped to the ground. Youbib found another hold, and at last reached the earth.

Sweaty and scratched, the young Aneza shook their daggers in the air, triumphant, and were pushed and patted by the crowd, which opened toward Shahin and Mey. Kyrin felt the laughter and relief around her and in her throat. Lilith crowded into Mey's beast with the Aneza hunters' sudden surge to get a glimpse of their prize.

Youbib's face shone, and he stood taller as he took a cloth-wrapped eyas from inside his thawb and lifted it before Shahin with a wide smile. The young falcon screamed, a stray bit of baby-white feathers ruffling among the plumage on her head. Youbib's companion took a second bird from his sash.

Shahin looked over the eyases carefully. He gave Youbib's to Mey and set the other in a covered container on his saddle. The second bird's screams and hisses quieted.

With a last shriek, the mother falcon flapped back to her nest above the Anezas' heads. Kyrin smiled at the hungry and interrupted shrieks that drifted down. Youbib had not raked the nest of all the young.

She had last set eyes on an eyas at Esther's stronghold, and had dreamed of flying a falcon in her woods. But Esther had said her eyases were not ready. Kyrin sobered. Instead, her Samson had conquered Cierheld's winds, surging up in swift power from her glove, all the world his in storm or calm. It had not mattered that he was a cook's hawk and a tiercel, smaller than his female kin. Her throat tightened.

The bird in Mey's hands cocked her head, her gaze bold and dark, a questioning noise in her throat. She clicked her beak and bobbed her head. Shahin and Mey whispered, their heads almost touching, and the falcon screamed between them.

Kyrin was puzzled. Bedouin said almost nothing in secret. Then Mey dismounted, and smiles bloomed on every face.

Mey met Kyrin's eyes and stretched up her cupped brown hands, the eyas quiet and alert, wings bound to her body by a cloth. Kyrin gulped. It couldn't be.

"A shaheen for you, Shaheen of a true spirit." Mey's words were careful in the hush.

"I-I thank you," Kyrin said, her voice low, and reached out. The falcon's jet eyes changed to amber in the sun as the bird struggled, head bobbing. Kyrin's heart rose—and beat back the memory of blood on her mother's still body.

"You acted truly for my son, from a right spirit." Mey choked, and there were tears in her honey eyes.

Not trusting her tongue, Kyrin nodded—and her smile shook wider as the mottled eyas rested secure in the crook of her arm, cupped under Kyrin's hand, turning her steel-blue and grey head—wisps of feathers sticking out around her yellow beak, her bright eyes blinking, funny and fierce as she attacked the cloth about her with her beak. The height erupted in cheers.

Through the rough material pinning the falcon's wings and sharp talons, a quick heartbeat radiated warmth into Kyrin's palm. The falcon was strong, ready soon for her first flight. She peeped and cocked her head to stare at Kyrin with a round eye, the cheek patch of the peregrine falcon distinctive below, with dark markings also on her wings and breast. Kyrin looked back at her terrible falcon. *Soon you will be a hunter of the air—without malice in your deadly dives—beautiful, adept in your airy paths.*

What could she use for a hood? Kyrin slipped her pouch thong over her head; the pouch would fit the bird. The falcon would not mind the smell of cheese. The eyas struck at the leather bag with her beak but calmed as soon as Mey held her, and Kyrin slipped the pouch on.

On the way back to camp, Kyrin was but dimly aware of their path down the mountainside, every scrap of attention on her eyas, not to let her be unduly frightened or jostled. The Aneza stopped to water the camels at the pools in the wadi, lined with green moss. The water at the bottom of the mountain near camp was sweet, not the mineral-heavy, bitter desert water. Kyrin couldn't get enough. She raised her head, dripping water from her chin.

Though she was ready for a cushion for her arm, it was so good to ride again. She grinned. Faisal must see her falcon. Maybe he would help her get a rabbit or a sand-hen heart to tempt the eyas. She must eat before morning or her feathers would form brittle hunger lines, and break when she tried to fly.

But Faisal was nowhere among the robed men who scratched their beast's necks while they drank, or those unsaddling and couching camels near the tents. Kyrin sighed. Her stomach growled.

Their late meal was interrupted by a galloping messenger, yelling even as his horse skidded to a stop. Most of the Aneza rose to their feet, kaffiyehs and thawbs shifting in the wind.

"What is it?" Kyrin could not understand the messenger's rapid speech.

"Tae is coming!" Faisal whooped, the scowl he'd been wearing at her news of Mey's gift disappearing.

Her heart leapt, then paused. "Only Tae?"

"Do you believe your most generous master would forget to trade the use of all his slaves to a desert sheyk?"

Her smile hitched sideways. "No." Ali was never generous unless it gained him something.

"He will kick us and say, 'I am most merciful, you lost those thrice your worth.'" Faisal imitated Ali's scowl impeccably.

Kyrin laughed, her heart lightening. Faisal had lost the horses but gained his life. And she had found a measure of peace with the jackal.

17

Assassin

Watch over your heart with all diligence,

for from it flow the springs of life. ~Proverbs 4:23

Ali rode at the fore of the caravan on Munira. His litter had been packed out of sight. He saw Kyrin among the throng of Aneza and slid down calling, "My treasured one!"

A hand under her good arm, Faisal helped her kneel to touch the ground then knelt beside her. She rose and endured Ali's embrace. He kissed her cheek, jostling her arm, and his sweating skin was cool as a fish's.

Ali raised Faisal, kissed his cheeks ceremonially, and turned from them to greet Shahin. Kyrin lost herself in the crowd, wiping Ali's kiss from her face. She found Tae guarding the rear of the caravan, covered in dust, a living wraith. She ran toward him.

Kentar shouted and the camels lurched toward their grazing for the night. Tae's hug loosed. He brushed at his eyes and said in a roughened voice, "Run and attend Ali, later we will talk."

On her way to Ali's tent, Kyrin stopped when Shahin motioned her further from Ali's hearing. Ali did not notice, as he was ordering the Nubian to move his tent nearer Shahin's.

The sheyk's fingers bit into her arm. "Is he here?"

211

"Yes, Tae is at the end of the caravan. Ali *would* put him there." She could not stop smiling. Not that Ali's command would deflect Shahin's favor. Tae was himself. Whatever company he was in, he could not be ignored.

Shahin's jaw flexed.

Kyrin's brow furrowed. "What is wrong, my lord?"

He looked at her under heavy brows. "I asked your master for your price. He offered me any other slave, and at a beggaring cost. You are as his daughter, the prop of his old age." Shahin's voice dripped irony.

Kyrin's mouth opened—nothing came out. Shahin had thought to buy her?

Shahin clasped his hands behind him, staring at Ali's back as her master kicked at a tent stake the Nubian had pounded home. "I will ask Tae Chisun to accompany you among our tents, for a husband should protect his master's 'treasured one.'"

Kyrin flushed hot with relief. Ali had told him. Was Shahin angry she had not?

"Your master cannot refuse your rightful lord's protection. Our trade is not yet agreed." Shahin's brown eyes lit, and his lips parted in a dry laugh. "Tonight will instruct us all, Shaheen."

He nodded and walked away. Kyrin stared after him, glad she did not wear Ali's sandals across a trade agreement with the sheyk of the Aneza. But Alaina must be near, and Faisal might be with her. She would ask him to help Tae with the camels—making it clear to everyone, slave and free, that Faisal had guarded her for Tae's sake—and that Tae was satisfied.

That night Kyrin sat with her companions at the edge of the Aneza council.

Shahin made a stirring tale of the Twilket's attack and Kyrin's bow drawing down on his son. Of the fearless shot that brought their enemy down, the Aneza arrow that struck her, and Faisal's unarmed stand against his lance. "This faithful daughter saved us all, coming as a falcon on the wind out of the desert." Shahin smiled at her, and Aneza murmured their approval.

Ali stood and was recognized. His lips parted over his teeth in an eel's grin. "It is so, and my slave will not go without reward. But the house of Ali Ben Aidon has no part in any Nur-ed-Dam of the Aneza, though it pains my heart. Allah, the wise, has not blessed me in the art of war. I will pray to merciful Allah, and he will give your enemies to your lances. Though I may not lift a lance with you, my heart is open to you. My hakeem, Tae Chisun, will carry the name of my house among you. May your ears be open to the wisdom of my mouth. And when Allah blesses your justice, let your hand be generous."

Shahin bowed. "In sha'allah. We will speak further on the morrow. I bid you rest under the bond of salt."

At that, the council circle broke up, the Aneza muttering among themselves.

Kyrin ran a finger along her falcon dagger. Shahin would take more important council this night. Someone poked her ribs.

Startled, she jumped, spun, and batted away Alaina's next touch and then scored a neck blow. She twined her good arm with Alaina's and slid loose. They struck against each other: attacking, seeking, and defending in quiet delight.

At last Alaina captured Kyrin's hand and pulled her close. "I missed you."

Kyrin laughed. Her arm hurt little. It would be whole soon, along with many other things.

Standing with the men, Faisal sniffed in disdain at their martial play. Kyrin sniffed back and laughed again. He could not make her angry this night of bright stars, with the love of Tae and Alaina around her.

Now, even when Faisal appeared as if out of the air and tickled the back of her neck with his stick, which amused him no end, she wanted to shake him instead of beat him senseless. Their war had ended.

Tae had been smiling at them all evening. She did not try to stop her grin and ignored Faisal's scowl. She grabbed Alaina's hand and pulled her toward the falcons' tent. Somehow she could not speak of Faisal yet. He could move quieter without being seen than anyone she had known. He had been doing it a long time in the streets, outwitting his fellow beggars, hunting food, hiding when he must. Kyrin licked her lips.

Watching her with her penetrating green eyes, Alaina said soberly, "These people almost killed you—and those raiders—. Ali would not let Tae look for you, you know. He tried to steal a camel, but Ali had them guarded. The Nubian almost caught him. I cried every night you were gone, even a tear or two for the jackal." She indicated Faisal.

Kyrin wondered how hard the Nubian had tried to catch Tae. And Faisal was not a beast, not now. "It *was* terrible, but my debt with Faisal is paid. He saved me, remember? And I am with you again." She swung their joined hands up, then her smile faded. "Does Ali think we stole the horses?"

"Tae found the dead raider and told Ali you did not. He yelled, 'that worthless slave, she brings the evil eye to destroy my goods, and chases after another worthless one.'"

"Is he angry now?"

"He mutters in his tent. Outside the walls, you are his favorite." Alaina eyed her sidelong. "At least until the Twilkets are not a threat and his trading with the Aneza sheyk is done."

Kyrin stopped short, squeezing Alaina's fingers. "Enough of him, Alaina. I want to show you something. The Aneza gave me a falcon. She is yours, too. She's beautiful—you will treasure her. And—she'll fly from your hand first."

"I? Fly a falcon? *Me?*"

Warmth stole through Kyrin at Alaina's joy. "Yes, you. She'll need us to feed and train her well before she is ready to fly. And she screams a lot, but she is an eyas. The Aneza usually catch grown falcons with a pit and bait; they already know how to hunt. Lord Bergrin, Myrna's brother at home, he always said the grown ones were better hunters. But I am glad we have her young. So she will always fly back to us." Kyrin glanced down.

Long ago at Esther's birthday feast, Esther had snorted in derision. "You always were a moon-eyed one, Kyrin! Falcons cannot love men." She had seated Kyrin next to Bergrin, Myrna's older brother, and with a mocking lift of eyebrow, she turned to him and said, "You will find Kyrin's interest in your hawk breeding instructive, my lord."

Kyrin had blushed and sat stiffly. So Lord Bergrin Jorn was rich, and knew all the dances and the gentle girls. Still, it was true, what she knew. Falcons were loyal to their mates, fed their young tirelessly, and if a bird treated a human well, was that not love on some level? Some humans could learn from that. She eyed Esther's back, then met Bergrin's amused hazel eyes, and her neck heated.

She lifted her chin. "I think raising falcons in the mews does make them worse at hunting, though loyal. But your wild bird has heart, Bergrin, since she escaped. Leaving her to find a mate in the wild and taking a chick that fledges would keep her line in your hands." The strand of hair she twisted violently about her hand made her wince, but she held his gaze. She had no other way to represent her stronghold but with truth.

Lord Bergrin greeted her rush of words with a crooked smile, a smile that leaped out of ambush. Kyrin's heart beat hard.

Crossing one scarlet stockinged leg over the other, Bergrin leaned back on the bench. "I have thought of it. Her mother was a fine huntress, and you are right, I hate to lose her." He quirked a thoughtful blonde brow. "But I would gain her skill in her daughter. And who knows, maybe her daughter's mate, from my mews, would teach her to be a loyal hunter, to love me." He set his feet on the floor. "I think I will do it."

He looked at Kyrin from the corner of his eye. "Esther is more right about you than she knows. For all your blood of the hills, you are someone to watch—at least in the mews." He chuckled at his own wit, and walked away to join a bright threesome about the fire.

Kyrin glared after him. *Lords' sons, they are all the same. Cunning and strong as boars, sometimes as agile as the hart, but led by the nose by their wants, far less loyal than their hounds. And not to be compared to a falcon.*

Kyrin released Alaina's hand. No bride-price had ever been settled on a lord for her. Now her falcon slept, hooded on a high perch in the black tent with the Anezas' birds, her head tucked under her wing. And she loved her already.

§

"Oh, she's beautiful!" Alaina had never seen a falcon so close. Falcons were for stronghold first-daughters, not woodcutter's get. She wished it were lighter in the tent so she could see more than the falcon's slim head and pale cream breast. The falcon squeaked when she rubbed her soft, feathered crest. Alaina jerked her hand back.

Kyrin laughed and sank down next to the perch. "She is not screaming now, and my ears are glad. She ate meat from a stick a while ago; soon she will take bits from you."

Alaina wrapped herself in her cloak and sat too, shivering with wonder, reaching up to stroke their falcon—and her falcon.

It smelled of dust and somehow softness, like her lambs-wool embroidery thread.

She whispered, "I finished the last of Ali's pouches so you won't have to do *that,* but"—she smiled at Kyrin's shadow—"you will have to practice hard to catch up. Tae taught me how to defend against a lance after he found the dead raider. Faisal killed that one?"

"He must have." Kyrin said nothing more.

Alaina held back a sigh. Why did Kyrin avoid speaking of him? Something had changed; they teased instead of killed each other with their glances. But Kyrin would not speak until she was ready. Alaina ran her forefinger from the falcon's head to her tail. "When does she need food, and what does she eat?"

"Rabbit hearts give her strength, and sand-hen keeps her in good flying weight . . ." Alaina let Kyrin's clear voice fill her ears and sank against the post. Her sister was with her again. She was not gone, thank the Master of the stars, though she had come close to dying more than once.

At a soft step inside the door the falcon shifted its feet and screamed sleepily. Alaina laid her hand on the bird, and the falcon quieted.

"Shahin wants you. In our tent," Faisal said, his voice stiff.

They scrambled up, and he led the way. He held up the tent flap, left closed against the night's unpredictable wind, and Alaina ducked inside after Kyrin.

Near the middle poles inside, the sheyk waited cross-legged beside a bright oil lamp. Tae rested on a wide cushion opposite. He leaned into the lamplight and nodded. Alaina smiled at him, and bowed uncertainly in the Eastern way to the sheyk.

Shahin inclined his head, courteous, and Alaina settled on a blue and black rug near the door, glad of the clean softness instead of the rough sand of the hawks' tent. She shoved another cushion toward Kyrin, who settled on Shahin's right in the place he indicated. Her sister might wish the support for her arm.

The sheyk was the only Aneza present, not a warrior, not a servant within. Did he mean to test their intentions? Alaina's forehead rumpled. He would not find them lacking.

Faisal settled himself next to Kyrin, disdaining cushions.

"We meet to consider our path." Shahin slapped his hands against his knees. "I am impatient. Your master has complicated things."

Alaina stared in surprise. He said his mind at once, unlike every other Bedouin she had met, who first inquired after every relative, their well-being, and their doings under the sun. This war must be near.

The sheyk's eyes glittered in his edged face. "Does Ali Ben Aidon think the Aneza fools? But enough. The Twilkets gather on the other side of our mountain. Tae Chisun, you have led your people in battle?"

"Yes." Tae said it simply, with complete confidence.

"You know what Shaheen did for us, and what comes. We ride against three hundred at the least. They fight as we do, in swift attack from camel and horseback with lance and sword."

Alaina's chilled toes were warming. The Twilkets felt as far away as the morning sun. She glanced aside, her lips tightening. They were not hunting her, burn them, but her sister. Kyrin hugged her knees, resting. Faisal's eyes gleamed in the shadows.

Shahin's voice murmured on. The lamp glow dimmed. Alaina's eyes grew heavy, and her head sagged to her knees. She jerked awake.

Tae was saying, "It is all or nothing. Set a trap in the wadi. Your messengers tell me it has high walls, and in the middle are defensible islands that have water. Within two days every man, woman and child must be ready. I—"

"You will lead us? Can you do so?" Shahin leaned forward, watching him, dark as a hawk, dangerous within the shadows of his kaffiyeh, ready to kill to protect his people.

Would Tae show him what he was? Alaina bit her lip.

Tae was gentle. He said softly, "When a man says such words in my land it shames his name, casting doubt on the strength of his heart. But I judge you speak so to find the truth. No, Sheyk Shahin, I am askar, but not sheyk. You know your people, their weaknesses and their strengths. I may direct your Aneza with knowledge, but you lead their hearts.

"To fight unmounted, in a wadi, a trap, is not the Aneza way. But it is the way to overcome the Twilkets. It is a way to live and fight again. Every Aneza warrior to count against their three."

Shahin said nothing, and Tae continued, "Some of us will raid their herds next nightfall. We must control their movements. Make them come to us where we are strong, bunch them together. Cut them down with each arrow, each lance, each blow. You will lead your people, spirit and heart and body. I will show you how to overcome a large body of men with a few. But you must turn their hearts toward the fight." Tae leaned back.

"You are a crafter of words and wills, whatever else you may be." Shahin grinned. "You also have your Shaheen's love, and she is led by the spirit of the falcon." He inclined his head. "Your plan is good. It will be done."

Tae looked him full in the face for a long moment, then dropped his eyes and bowed where he knelt, baring the back of his neck.

Alaina let out her breath. It was a sign of utmost trust, to risk a deathblow by exposing the neck. It was a moment she must remember to record for her grandchildren. If she ever had them. She frowned and picked at the embroidery of her sash. The stitches were not as fine as she would wish.

Tae straightened. He said quietly, "My God bids me fight for those in need of just defense."

"The one the Eagles killed on crossed trees?"

"Yes, and rose afterward."

"I have heard of that God. I am content." Shahin watched Tae, his eyes glinting. What did he wonder?

"My Shaheen follows his true spirit, as do I. The falcon reflects his power."

"We will speak of that when the spirits clear our heads of battle."

"As the Father of all wills." Tae clasped Shahin's wrist and released it.

Shahin hesitated, then with a smile, his fingers closed on Tae's arm in return.

Alaina shifted off her tingling feet. Impassive or reflective as water by turns, Tae's face and Shahin's intentness fit each other like the flat sides and edge of a sword. The Twilkets did not know how strong a flood of Nur-ed-dam they had released.

Faisal stirred. He stared at Tae. His mouth opened. His nostrils flared with his hunting look. He turned his dark eyes on Kyrin, almost with regret.

Alaina's heart constricted. "What—"

And Faisal clamped one hand on Kyrin's leg where she sat beside him and slid her dagger from her sash with the other. Alaina lunged for him. Faisal rose to one knee, flipped his wrist back and threw.

Snapping to face Faisal's quick motion, Tae saw the blade flipping toward him. He dived aside then rolled up to a crouch. The dagger struck the tent wall with a thump, stuck a moment, quivering, then was dragged through.

The wall bulged as a heavy weight slid down. It hit outside with a faint thud. The felt shivered to stillness.

Alaina shot to her feet beside Faisal, the lamp ready in her hand. The heavy base comforted her, a good club if an enemy entered. He would target the light.

Kyrin held her cushion cocked over her shoulder, seeming uncertain whether to hit Faisal with it or not. Her eyes darted from him to Tae and back. Alaina choked a giggle behind her hand. Faisal watched none of them but held his own dagger ready in place of Kyrin's. His eyes were locked on the slit where the falcon dagger disappeared.

§

Tae's heart thundered, lamp-smoke bitter on his tongue. No sound. No shouts from sentries, no attacking yells, no soft step without. It would be a hard-nerved man, to wait for the first move within the tent after his fellow fell. But it could be. He would wait longer. They must be sure.

Everyone had a weapon in hand. Following his lead, they did not move. On the edge of his awareness, Tae knew Faisal had not relaxed. *He was wise. I should not have left my blade off for this first meeting.*

There came a step outside, and someone touched the tent wall near the slit. Shahin barked *"My* warrior!" and grabbed at Faisal's arm. Too late.

The dagger catapulted from Faisal's hand. He looked after it in horror. Kyrin snatched at it and missed. Alaina had not trained to catch one.

Tae exploded forward. He slapped his palms around the spinning blade with a "clop!" and drew his hands toward him, swiftly diverting the weapon's force. He *had* been trained.

Shahin twitched—and lowered his blade from Faisal's side. He inclined his head in respect and breathed out silently. An Aneza voice rose outside, shouting in alarm and question. The camp would be awake soon.

Tae lowered the captured dagger, with a long sigh, glad he was not forced to take blood in payment for one of his own. "Most times you get cut." He considered his unmarked hands. He handed Faisal's dagger to him with a bow, then abruptly gripped his shoulders and hugged him close. "My thanks, warrior, that the falcon struck true. Though my heart is glad your own blade did not."

Faisal reached up and just touched his shoulders, solemn.

The bond of brothers. Tae inclined his head and stepped back. It was good.

Faisal lifted his head, triumphant, his blade beginning to quiver in his hand. Tae smiled and turned to Shahin. And his mouth flattened.

A dagger in the back was the lowest blow of the low. But with the assassin outside might lie a chance to end the war before it started.

18

Consequence

Commit your works ... unto the Lord ... ~Proverbs 16:3

Shahin went to the tent door, opened the flap. Two Aneza slipped inside, wary. They whispered to their sheyk, fast and angry, with sidelong looks at Tae. "No," Shahin said. "Speak plainly. This man is my brother, and these"—he swung his arm to include Kyrin, Alaina, and Faisal—"are within my tent."

The older warrior gave Tae a short dip of his head. "Our enemy moves swiftly. That was a Twilket. He is the only one at this moment."

"Your men search now for his camel?" Ignoring the warriors' first anger, Tae slipped into his place of command with barely an ache.

The older warrior looked to Shahin, and at his nod, turned to Tae. "Yes. They will find his beast, and no Twilkets will get past us again. Guard yourself, my sheyk, though I will stay outside."

"Yes. We need every lance." With a curt gesture, Shahin sent the younger Aneza warrior to assemble the camp.

"I would like to see the Twilket." Tae waved at the tear in the tent wall. A disconsolate wind nosed it, revealing ragged darkness.

Shahin held out his arm toward the tent door. "As you say."

Tae ducked out, dragged the man to the front of the tent, and laid the limp body on its side. Alaina raised the lamp.

For a moment, the dirt-smeared high cheekbones and wrinkled brow turned the Twilket into another. Into Paekche, Huen's father, frowning even in his sleep. Tae blinked, and tightened his fingers on nothing. That night of treachery came long ago. It was not now. The round brown eyes and thin beard of the Twilket man were again strange to him.

Tae bent and ran his hand around the man's ribs. Was this a simple warrior, or one used to assassin's work? Yes, there. He retrieved a thin, heavily etched dagger and set it in Shahin's hand, the well-worn blade of a man who kept his tool with care. The sheyk pursed his lips.

There were other places to look. Tae unwound the assassin's turban and found several small darts wrapped in careful folds. He set the darts aside, their heads rammed harmless in the sand, and searched on. He held up two blown-glass vials to the light and edged the corks free, careful not to jostle the cloudy contents. He sniffed, a bare intake of breath a handspan above each vial, and passed them to Faisal. One was snake venom, the other a deadlier poison he did not know. Faisal handed the vials to Shahin, while Tae rolled the assassin free of his sash.

Nothing. He pulled the man's arm from under him and slid back both long sleeves. In his left fist the assassin clenched a blowpipe the length of his hand. Tae freed it with a twist and laid it beside the darts. Few but an assassin would carry such.

§

Faisal eyed Tae's stony face. It must have been a long-ago head wound that left his hair above his left ear white. He moved without wasted motion, as a man who dealt often with bodies and weapons.

The assassin must have stood close to the felt, listening, waiting for his moment. And he had chosen Tae, not Shahin. The falcon blade had taken the Twilket in the side, through the ribs, to the heart.

Tae withdrew the blade, wiped it on the man's thawb, and handed it to Kyrin. She grasped the end of the haft between thumb and finger. There was still blood on the blade.

Faisal wondered if she would scrub it. The light streaming from the lamp glowed warm on her hair under her kaffiyeh, weaving in reddish lights. In the desert she had bent under fear like a willow; in strength without breaking. What a warrior of Allah she would make. Would she go by his side then?

He had seen her at the edge of one of the pools, scrubbing her arrow shaft she had wedged under her knee, as if she could cleanse the life-blood away with the force of her hands. He grunted. The Nasrany should glory in a rightful death, not wipe it away.

Faisal stooped and touched his enemy's still warm body, reddening his fingers. This one threatened them and paid to his blade. How would a Twilket neck feel under his foot? He rubbed sand between his hands to clean them. Kyrin had yet to be worthy of her Damascus blade. How *had* the falcon come to her? Such steel, in such a shape, he had not seen before.

§

Kyrin's stomach cramped as she stared at the bloody blade. Again she had done nothing, had not known where to strike, and found a cushion in her hand. Again unaware. Though Faisal and Tae kindly acted as if nothing were amiss.

At Tae's side, Faisal studied the dead Twilket. He must not want to witness her shame. He probed the assassin's side and stared at his red fingers. He pressed one red spot to the haft of his dagger, then sat on his heels and washed his hands with sand. He claimed the kill.

Kyrin turned her back.

Shahin suggested they examine the assassin's Batina camel his men had found couched behind a large rock outside camp. "Stay here," Tae said. "With the light. You are well-guarded."

Then the men left them to find what sleep they could. Kyrin wished Faisal stayed. Would he ever stand by her again, quiet and fiery, with a smile in his eyes?

Much later, the men wandered back to their beds, and the last child was soothed to silence. Alaina breathed gently, an arm flung over her pillow, her fingers touching Kyrin's. Tae slept within the tent facing theirs. Kyrin waited.

She had left the lamp alight in the door of the tent. Faisal stepped outside Tae's tent opposite, and turned. His eyes caught the glare. Except for the sentries, he went to his rug last. He nodded somberly, and dropped her tent flap.

It hung between them, stitched in dark thread, stitched in strong, uneven, struggling marks. Kyrin twisted her hair painfully around her finger. Sleep did not take her for a long time.

She woke, clutching her pillow, claws of pain tearing at her arm. She had slept on it, and the tiger had come. It was yet dark.

A beast cried outside. In loneliness, in anger, in fear or hunger, she could not tell. She huddled around her sweat-damp cushion, biting at her hand to make sure the tiger's black nose did not lift the tent flap. She did not wish to watch the black felt slide away from his hungry gaze, over his pricking ears, until he spied her in her blanket and sank his jaws in her throat. Kyrin bit down harder.

Foolish fool, there were no tigers in this land, only lions. Yet she watched the shadows until sleep caught her away.

Alaina rose with the sun, whistling her sand-lark melody. Kyrin groaned, wishing no one knew where she slept. Her thick head clamored it was not the moment to get up. *The assassin.*

She bolted upright. Any or all of them in the tent could have ended on the sand. Tae almost did, and Faisal would have followed if his second dagger had flown true, his life owed to a Aneza's oath of blood. Nur-ed-Dam. One was enough.

How quick did the darts dipped in those vials work? She thought of Faisal twisted in agony, or sprawled, his throat cut, and of what it would mean for him. Eternity, with djinn.

She rubbed her arms. The morning was cold. Meat and dates waited in dishes by the crackling fire Alaina fed. The fat was congealed, the fruit a too-sweet lump. Maybe later, when her middle did not cramp so and she did not feel sick.

§

Tae found her in the hawks' tent, the sides raised for air and light. Kyrin did not turn but kept coaxing her falcon with a bit of rabbit liver. The bird turned her beak from Kyrin's hand, her feathers ruffled, and leaped with a stubborn shriek off the perch. She caught short against her jesses and swung back against the base, wings flapping furiously.

Avoiding Tae's gaze, Kyrin got the upside-down falcon on her feet, calmer. She wished she could so well calm herself. In the night the invisible veil of her girlhood had fallen from her, in a rush of blood. Ali must not know. No one must know.

She pushed the liver against the falcon's beak again. The falcon refused it.

Tae wrapped the tail of his black bisht around his arm, slow and steady, and nudged the bird's feet. She stepped onto her new perch, her talons dainty and steel strong.

Kyrin bit her trembling lip, nodded her thanks, and settled a new hood over the bird's head. Mey had showed Alaina how to make the eye covering part of the hood, comfortable for a bird, and had given her a bell and two feathers, which bounced gaily on top.

Tae whistled softly to the falcon. Kyrin fingered the raw liver in her hand and pried her tongue from her teeth. She said in a rush, "Why can't the Twilkets leave us alone?"

"Because they want something." Tae stroked the bird's breast with a brown finger and regarded Kyrin, his head cocked, his brows drawn down. "I will give you a brew for the dreams, daughter. They will fade."

Her mouth twitched. He knew of the raider and her mother in her nightmares, and she had told him of the tiger, but not of his captive . . . She scuffed the ground with her foot.

He lifted her chin with one callused hand, a hand that had saved Faisal from blood-feud. His dark gaze was searching, intent, earnest. "When you take a life like you did to save Rashid, your heart may rise against you. You must not believe it. It is wrong."

She turned her head aside. When she turned back, he was staring into a dark place of his own.

"Last night filled you with fear, didn't it?" His voice was soft. "It would be easier to die than to see others fall, especially Alaina or Faisal or I. And anyone can fall.

"You think of fighting the Twilkets, and you fear your fear and the confusion.

"Every fight is confused. *I* am full of fear; against one or fifty. The good we fight for happens within the confusion, or not at all. You did right to save Rashid, and you will find your courage when you must, as Faisal fought for me." He set the falcon back on her perch. "You need seasons to learn and to grow, like this one." He eased off the falcon's hood, and she bobbed her head.

He was proud of Faisal—it warmed even as it pricked Kyrin. "Why, Tae? Why didn't I take Faisal down when he threw my dagger—at you? I should not have trusted him so far. The Nur-ed Dam is forgiven, but . . . can he change his heart so fast? I do not think so." She chewed her lip.

Tae smiled. "You do not want to think evil of him, for you see the battle inside him, but you doubt. You are right, for he follows Allah. And until he knows Allah's falseness, he is part of that deception. Deception creates hardness. Worshipping Allah creates a wrong pattern of heart, twists the thoughts, as all untrue things do."

Kyrin looked at her toes. Faisal followed a twisted pattern—strong and torn and heart-lost.

Tae's smile slowly left him. "I am sorry, daughter. Does he see you in his heart?"

That was the worst thing. How could he? Faisal hated cowards and weakness such as hers—and she must find her father—and she was not free. She stroked the falcon's back. Her blood had come. "I am yours . . . "

Tae laughed, long and loud. "Only in name—and that stretched by intent—and quite broken by faithfulness to the Master of all and to my Huen!"

Heat in her face, Kyrin ducked her head. His words were true. She was free, and would be doubly free when she escaped Ali. But where *did* her heart lie? It tugged her so many ways: toward home and her father, and Tae and Alaina, and yet she could not stop thinking of Faisal.

His smile is like no other's. As is his anger toward the Master of all. She stared at her feet. "Allah divides the springs of our hearts," she said low, and scowled. That Faisal and the thorns he brought. He was closed to the Master's truth. If he did think of her in his heart, she would break his other arm. "I can say nothing to him."

"I think you are wise. Wait until the Twilket threat is gone, my daughter, unless the Master of the stars makes a right moment."

The right moment. Kyrin bit her lip. Faisal killed a man and almost destroyed a friend by mistake. What had it done to him? She had never been good at finding the right moment. She would blush and make a pudding of speaking to him.

Tae rubbed his chin, eyeing her. "Trust our Father. Give yourself and Faisal to him, with anything else that might happen. But you do as he commands."

Kyrin reached out and touched the falcon's foot, the yellow skin scaly and cool, her talons sharp. Faisal, Tae, and Alaina must stay safe. They held her heart. Master of all. . . .

"I have an errand to the Twilkets."

Kyrin lifted her head. "You will raid them with Shahin's men?"

"No. I go to their camp this evening, as a traveler who asks shelter. I must find a way to secure a day for council between Shahin and their sheyk, Gershem."

"You alone?"

"Faisal will wait outside camp for me—none else. Any Twilket would know an Aneza by his kaffiyeh, his saddle, and his voice. I am a stranger to them, and so is Faisal."

"No, Tae! You cannot! They will—"

"It may stop the war."

"But I loosed the first blood, I started it." Her tears came fast. *My heart and body both wake in the midst of death.*

Tae pulled her close. But he could not drive back the cold growing within her.

His voice was steady. "In truth, you did *not* begin it. And you may not end it. The Master of the stars sent you to save Rashid, and he sent Faisal for me. We do not often know what we are to do before it comes, but he made us for this time." He dropped his arms. "Shahin has given me a camel, one of yours"—Tae grinned—"and Alaina is packing me a feast. I will watch the stars rise this night. You will see them from here, and our thoughts will meet in the Master of the stars. Do not fear; I will not walk into ambush without care."

He meant to make her laugh, but thought of the assassin's darts strangled it in her throat. He left her with a kiss on the forehead. She did not look, wanting to run after him and hold him back.

Camel pads thudded. Alaina called something to Faisal. Shahin raised his voice. "Go with the blessing of the Aneza and all good spirits."

Kyrin did not turn. She could not watch them leave. "Stay alive, my father," she whispered.

The rabbit liver squished between her fingers, her throat ached, and her nose ran. Peering through a watery blur with a sniff, she nudged her falcon's beak again. It smeared the mess over her hand. She stroked the falcon's feathers and growing wings and whispered to her, to God's bird. His creature, as she was. Kyrin drew a deep breath. All was not lost.

The falcon cocked her head, eyeing her, and rubbed Kyrin's wrist with a gentle razor beak. Kyrin held her breath.

With a lunge, the falcon snagged a bit of liver and flipped it down her throat. Kyrin gave her bird a wavery grin. She had risked a torn hand, not wearing a glove, but the falcon had eaten again. Her flight feathers would not break when she lifted into the sky, rising free.

The camels' footfalls faded. Kyrin left the falcon resting under her hood. Such blindness kept her from leaping from the perch and hurting herself, kept her unafraid and calm, taught her to know friendly voices.

Usually one master trained any one falcon, but all creatures instinctively trusted Alaina. She would feed the falcon and fly her. Shahin had assured Kyrin that eating from the fist came first, then a short flight to eat there, then longer flights to pounce on a lure, and then—wings surging into the boundless sky.

Kyrin followed her thoughts toward her tent. She ought to have waved farewell to Tae. If he could have spoken to Faisal for her, Tae could have told him—what?

Did Faisal's dream beasts laugh at him or hunt him, as the tiger hunted her? She should have said good-bye. But enough.

The falcon would fly between the clouds, wings shining. She must have a name. Willow?

Her mother would favor that. No, it did not fit. Deathfall? That did not quite fit either. Kyrin wiped her hand across her wet face. She would *not* cry more. *Master of the stars, give grace to their errand.*

19

Daggers

See the goodness of the Lord . . . ~Psalm 27:13

Tae rode with five Aneza down a small wadi, toward the base of the mountain between them and the Twilkets. He would circle wide, out over the desert, pass the Twilket's mountain camp, and approach from the far northeast, not the southwest where the Twilkets expected the Aneza. Craggy hills and outcrops about the mountain's foot slowed them. Then Tae left his escort and rode into a concealing huddle of low-limbed juniper.

Before first light he had sent Faisal ahead to scout their path, and as he instructed, Faisal had left one of Ali's camels tied among them. He dismounted, untied two saddlebags and a large sack of goat hair. Swiftly he took off his thawb and slipped on a worn kaffiyeh and the shorter tunic and trousers of the northern tribesmen. Tae mounted the fresh beast, swatting its sides lightly with the rope.

Any tribesman of the sand could tell camels apart by their tracks. They would know the Aneza beasts. But they would not have seen the pad prints of Ali's second best camel. There was one thing more, to finish the illusion. Moments later, a stiff man-shape rode out of the trees on Tae's camel, strapped upright in an Aneza saddle.

Tae squinted. The stiff sack of goat hair garbed in his thawb would fool the eyes of any watcher on the mountain. His Aneza companions swept close around the camel in a thicket of lances and dust, and escorted it back toward Shahin's camp.

Tae waited, motionless in the juniper shade. Thinking and resting. At midday Faisal joined him. They rode north, Faisal unquestioning, his dark eyes alert. He told Tae he had seen nothing during his scout but creatures of mountain and desert and the worn crags.

Tae studied him. "You have done well. You have my thanks."

Faisal nodded. "It lightens my debt."

Tae hid the twitch of his mouth. Didn't he know he'd paid all debt by guarding Kyrin? They lapsed into silence. Far beyond the mountain they rode, taking pains to remain hidden in the wadis. The day passed without sight or sound of camel or man.

Tae peered at the sky. He had about a finger-length of sun remaining; he would arrive before dusk to quiet suspicion. It was good the Twilkets camped close to the caravan road on the way to Taif and Makkah. There was more cover. But it was too quiet.

He ran his thumb around the grip of the sword Shahin had lent him. A silver blossom of five petals etched both ends of the cross-guard, with a double-petaled flower gracing the haft butt. The sharp, well-balanced blade had no jewel. Its worth was in the folded, resilient blade: strong steel, light and quick. Tae's mouth flattened.

He could have worn the assassin's robes and returned his venomous gifts. What he attempted instead was more dangerous still. Yet there was a chance of lasting peace.

Near the crest of the ridge above the Twilkets' wadi, Tae said, "We stop here." Faisal tethered his camel to a tamarisk, and Tae dismounted. Did he remember? "How long do you wait?"

"Till the dew dries in the morn, Hakeem. Insha—" Faisal bit his lip.

"I accept your good will with thanks." Tae grinned. "I go with the Father of us all. Though he is better than the one you believe him to be." He sobered. He could not ask Faisal to care for Alaina and Kyrin if he did not return, with a husband's duties inherent in the asking. He settled his sword. It was not pleasant to think on, the lightning blow through skin under the ribs' midpoint, the feel of a man's insides around his fingers as he struggled to end his life. The other death-strikes were quicker. It was why he carried weapons, to deal merciful death. Kyrin and Alaina needed three years before they learned the touch of death. If he was given the time to teach them.

Tae swallowed. He had not relaxed his before-dawn training, for Kentar's men had given him the solitude he asked. His camel carried his lance, and his dagger and sword slept at his side. Faisal wore a dagger as befit a lost slave—so he would say he was—if a Twilket chanced upon him before Tae returned. Tae grimaced. If he brought death to the Twilket tents, it was to keep life for many more.

Life. He took a slow breath and faced Faisal. "If I do not meet you in the dawn, know that you are a son of my heart. And the One who died on crossed trees loves you more than I. He made you for joy. Do not forget."

"No, Hakeem." Faisal regarded him, his mouth tight, frowning. Tae grasped his shoulder, and Faisal grinned a little and touched his arm.

It was time to finish what the assassin began. Tae mounted his beast. The camel picked her way down the ridge. The sun hit the earth's edge behind him and bathed the juniper and olive trees along the wadi in soft gold.

In the steep-sided bottom a few pools lingered. Two hundred tents lay beyond, pitched along the wide valley. The fires were lit, and men's calls mingled with the lighter voices of women and children.

A Twilket man before a black tent rose from his fire and called cheerfully to Tae, "Ahlan wa sahlan! Welcome!"

Tae dismounted, bent, and stood, trailing the sand of peace from his hands into the wind. He glanced at the darkening sky. If peace was with the Twilkets, peace would stay upon them. In common he cried, "And to you be peace!"

Other men gathered to greet him, some older, carrying lances, their dark hands and faces weathered, the younger men talking excitedly among themselves. Feet kicked up dust, kaffiyehs and turbans gathered around the fires. The smell of roasted goat, cumin, and curry hung on the air.

The man who had called to Tae gripped his shoulders and kissed his cheeks. He stepped back. "You are not of the people." His tone inquired.

"I hunt a lost slave." Camels and horses shifted and stamped before every dwelling in sight, tethered, ready to ride. They had not gone—he had come in time.

"Ahh. We have seen no stranger during this sun but you." The others nodded agreement.

Tae shrugged. "My slave is cunning, but worth much to me." He did not see the sheyk he sought. Was he ill? The Twilket before him was long-boned and gaunt. When he spoke, his slight stomach swayed, reminding Tae of a camel.

"Slaves are ever so. One must bind them by the will of Allah."

"I thank you for your kind words, my brothers." Tae bowed his head and turned his camel toward the water.

The Twilket who had first spoken to him grasped his sleeve. "Stay, my friend! My wife would throw her stew to the sand-lizards if you did not taste it."

The rest of the Twilkets grinned, and hands patted Tae's back. A horn blew. The men scattered to their fires. Their faces were tense.

Tae looked after them. No stranger, a carrier of news, was left unheard without cause. He followed the man to his tent, and tethered his camel beside his host's. If the Twilket inviting him to his fire knew his errand, he would not be so welcome.

Abdeel was his name. His quiet, gracious wife served a heavy platter and disappeared back into the tent, and they sat down to meat. Abdeel twisted off a rabbit leg and gave it to Tae. "Eat, my friend, eat!"

Tae savored every bit of juicy meat and hot rice, leaning back on his elbow, gazing up. The stars were in the sky. Kyrin would be thinking of him.

His host tipped back his head and drew a deep breath of content, smiling at the stars. "The night is quiet and full."

"Yes," Tae agreed. "The day was good, and this night is made better by your welcome."

"It gladdens my heart." There was a pause.

The expanse of the moonless heavens was wide, as vast as the moment. *Ah, Huen, pray for me this night.* He would leave more children to see the glory of the stars. Even if they were not his own, in the world.

"My journey is long. May I rest this night in your tent, Abdeel?" His bones were full of lead. *My Huen, do you sleep safe behind Paekche's walls with a child of mine, of ours?*

Abdeel smiled faintly. "Again, stranger, you are welcome. I also have an errand. If I am not here when the sun rises, do not think ill of me. If it is your pleasure to await me, and your journey permits, we may feast together when I return."

Tae bowed. "You are most gracious. Do you have children?"

"Yes, Yazid and Sahar, ten and five winters." Abdeel beamed, his bearded face revealing bright teeth. "Does my guest have children?"

"Alas, not yet. My family waits for me, as God wills."

"Ah, as Allah wills." Abdeel nodded wisely.

"I see your sheyk knows camels of good blood. My camel is of that line, I think. Do you see the likeness? In the line of brow and nose?"

Abdeel looked critically at Tae's camel couched at the edge of the firelight, chewing its cud, sniffing at the ground. "Ah, yes!" His face lit, then fell. "Sheyk Gershem has a long eye for the strongest females for his bull." He waved at his camel. "This is one of his daughters, and I think yours is also."

"My heart is glad." The fire snapped. Tae sighed. "It must be good to live with a leader of wisdom, who garners wealth."

"Allah has been generous." Abdeel's words were quiet and he looked at the ground.

Tae raised his brows. "Such a sheyk would not overlook the son of your youth, about to become a man. There is no camel out of the sheyk's bull and your good beast for your Yazid? "

"The sheyk's camels are his to do with as Allah wills, though our glorious arm of Allah has more horses than camels." Abdeel's face was tired and lined.

"It is good," Tae said mildly, "for a sheyk of the people to lead with generosity."

His host smiled wryly. "As Allah says." He stirred the fire with a stick and lifted his head. "I see your heart is weary. The mountain way to the holy city is long. Would you rest?"

"You are generous—" The man assumed their steps bent toward Makkah.

"No, no, it is nothing. This way."

Tae followed Abdeel inside his tent. The Twilket's white thawb rippled around his strong legs. His wife had retired behind the curtain.

Tae took off his bisht and lay down in his thawb beside Abdeel, waiting for the Twilket's breath to even. He fingered his dagger. If this courteous man had been the tinker who came to the Aneza, the war would never have started.

He woke some time later as he had been trained and slipped out. From a corner between two tents a saluki raised its head, lifting its lip with a low growl. Tae threw it a bit of meat he had slipped from Abdeel's platter. The dog circled the offering, sniffed, flipped it into the air, and gulped. The meat was gone.

Tae's amusement strangled in his throat. Tears came to his eyes. *Huen, your father was right. Paekche said I regard too much the lives of those under me. Unwilling to sacrifice, he said. But it is not right that you suffer because in his eyes I killed the wrong man, my love. The Aneza will not suffer the same. Nor another pay for it, as I did.*

The saluki followed him. Others watched. Tae crept by camel after camel, but the beasts made no complaint. The tent with the most horses about it was smaller than he expected, though it lay near the middle of camp. He regretted it was not closer to the edge. But he did not mean to leave. Yet.

My heart, our enemy took the chance I paid for peace in our land. Paid for you and our brothers. If only your father had wrested peace from what he thought a wrongful death, I would wake to see the morning beside you, and Paekche would see our children. He sighed. *That death at my hands was not wrong. The Master of the stars keep you—and make my strike straight this night. I would see you under the stars again . . .*

He moved slowly to the windless side of sheyk Gershem's tent. He pressed his ear close to the felt. His skin was tight, waiting for a blade or an arrow between his shoulders. A light snore came from within. Tae made a scratching noise on the ground, and laid down the rest of the meat he'd saved.

He eased up the side of the tent. The night wind wandered across the fragments of roast goat and beneath. Ageless moments passed. No breath within but the lonely snore.

No saluki, no slaves, no wife or children? But many horses. A prickle crept up Tae's neck. What kind of a grasping man was this sheyk? He might spell doom. To both tribes.

Tae closed his eyes a long moment. Inside, there would be no starlight. He took three deep breaths and loosened every muscle. Knelt. Lifted the side of the tent and rolled under.

In the dark he stopped, ready to roll back if someone held a sword above him. His eyes swept over a floor-spanning rug, shadows of saddles—and a sleeper in a mound of rugs. The rest of the tent was bare but for a few cushions and an unlit lamp. He checked again, glancing at the roof. No one in ambush. This Gershem had not much in his heart but his herds. There was no guard for his heartbeat.

A bare moment later, Tae clamped his hand over the sheyk's mouth and set his dagger where it might sever his spine with a single downward thrust. Gershem gave a choked snort. His body spasmed, then he lay still, staring up into Tae's face.

§

Every time Kyrin closed her eyes, the tiger sprang away from her. His mouth opened and he dropped a bow and a sword. She snatched up the bow. There was no arrow.

But the beast would not let her step over the blade. He laid his ears back and bared his teeth. His claws threatened the falcon, which screamed and struggled under his crushing forepaw.

The etched wings on the torque about his neck seemed to move, to strain in the shadows under flamelight, the amber eyes of the falcons darting here and there.

The blade was heavier than a horse. She could not lift it. Gasping, she tried again. The tiger sat, tail lashing, gaze steady. He lifted his paw, staring straight at her.

The falcon flopped over on her back, flapped upright, then flew to land beside Kyrin, her chain chinking on Kyrin's foot. She cocked her head, studying Kyrin with a bright eye.

They waited for her to grasp the sword. She must take it up. She reached.

And woke, staring into the darkness of her tent, breathing hard. There was no tiger's panting rasp in her face, no sword at her feet. She plucked up the welcome edge of the felt wall by her head to let the night cool the heat of her dreams. The long day had not made the tiger sleep.

Shahin had moved his people to the top of the island by compline. Everyone but the sheyk, the elders, and those who watched above the deep wadi walls that split around the island went wearily to their tents and rugs. Shahin sat by the fire with the elders, where they committed Tae's instructions to memory.

Across from the island, on the other side of the wadi, Ali slept with Kentar and his caravan. Her mouth curled. She knew Ali Ben Aidon would bargain with the victor of the battle. The air chilled Kyrin's bare neck and arm. The stars were still out. Did her master sleep peacefully, knowing that Umar stood within his door and the Nubian without, and Kentar and his men around him? But he was not out of Tae's reach. Tae walked under those stars—if he yet lived.

When Kyrin could see her hand before her nose, she left her bed and crept out to feed the falcon. Cicero followed, and she tied him outside so he would not frighten the birds. The falcon cocked her head at her first sight of Kyrin's gloved hand. She lunged for the offered rabbit heart. Her paler eyas feathers were awkward and wispy among the darker feathers of adulthood on her head.

"Good bird, good bird," Kyrin whispered while the falcon gulped the morsel. She tilted her head, whistled at Kyrin, and stretched out her wings, shaking herself vigorously. She did not resemble the grey and silver queen chained to Kyrin's nemesis.

Kyrin wrapped a piece of camel hide hanging on an empty perch around her arm and guided the falcon onto it. The bird felt strange clinging tight to her right arm, when she should rest on her left. The falcon stood quivering, then settled.

Kyrin stroked her: long calming strokes from head to tail. Samson had feared her as the falcon did, until he grew to love her. Did he yet live in Cierheld in the oak outside her window?

On her wrist, the falcon stretched her tallest and extended her wings, flapping hard. She clacked her beak and screamed softly. "Ugh, shall I call you . . . Stench? No, there is a deep spot of dust near the path to the bottom of our island." Kyrin stroked her again. "I will get you a dust bath, and a water bath when I can."

She sighed. Alaina would fly their sky-hunter and find her name in moments. Words flowed to Alaina. Would she choose a name to evoke a queen of the air, soaring above all she surveyed, wind rippling her flight feathers on a warm day?

Kyrin eased the falcon's hood back on and set her on her perch. She ruffled and settled. Were Tae and Faisal creeping from the Twilket camp even now, or did they flee their hunters while her bird bent her head to clean her beak with a talon?

Outside the last stars faded. Kyrin walked to the island edge. Birdcalls hovered high over the still wadi below. Behind her, women began to move among the tents, silent wraiths.

Kyrin loosed Cicero, his strong neck wiry under her hand. He danced around her and dashed about to nose the Aneza women kneeling on the flat south edge of the island. They let down skin bags from the rocky height, dipping them into a crack at the island's base where water pooled, then brought dripping burdens up from the bottom. Kyrin rubbed her nose wearily. Tae had chosen well. Their water supply was protected by the same height that guarded them from their enemies.

After a few dates and a cold drink from Mey's waterskin, Kyrin walked to the north end of the island. There granite towers nestled about the single path downward. The tallest rock, which leaned out over the wadi, was higher than Samson's oak. The powdery dust of the path lapped Kyrin's toes with the icy softness of morning. Against the echoing expanse of night-cold air and the purple-blue of the wadi, she felt small. Her father could barely get a shaft across that shaded depth with his long yew bow. The top edge of the wadi gleamed under the first fingers of the sun.

She followed the thin path that crept back and forth down the rocky drop. Toes numbing, Cicero at her heels, she picked her way across the uneven wadi bed and up to where Alaina sat atop the south-eastern wall under a sprawling juniper. Fragrant and twisted, the tree grew apart from its fellows. At home the bell for prime would be ringing.

"Our falcon ate some liver, Alaina. You'll feed her at mid-day."

Alaina set Tae's Holy Book down in her lap. "Yes," she said, sober. She gazed over the wadi. "In quietness and trust is your strength . . . ." Kyrin edged closer to her. Did Tae lie cold somewhere, earth clogging his ears? A lark called, and wind sighed in the branches. *Bring Tae and Faisal back to us.*

Alaina released the Book, and the scroll rolled closed in her lap. Kyrin opened her mouth, and stopped. Her sister's sash was blue—old and torn and mended. It was well that she remembered Faisal by wearing his sash.

Kyrin rested her chin on her knees, forlorn.

Faisal had avoided her. He had not run his hand over Cicero's head or stroked Lilith or spoken to her before he went. But she had not sought him out, either. His words had been short after the assassin fell to his blade. And he'd scowled the day Shahin and Mey gave her the falcon. Kyrin sighed. She had faced the raiders' lances and Shahin for him.

Beside her, Alaina leaned over her knees, a few blue-green juniper needles in her hair, staring across the wadi as if she could pierce the mountains and see the Twilket camp.

Kyrin scooted close until her shoulder touched Alaina's. In the medicine tent her sister had hovered over a stock of salves, poultices, and brews, picking up one and setting it back down in the same place. She'd avoided Tae's herb bag that stood against the center pole. As if his bag could bring him back to open it.

Had the line between Alaina's brows been for fear of the war and whether she could bind the wounds that would come? Kyrin cleared her throat and nudged Alaina's shoulder. "Your hands have healed every one of Ali's camels—they have not complained. You will not do less for us, it is not in you."

"I know it well. See?" With a wry smile, Alaina pointed. "My medicine is better than that." On the far side of the wadi, the Nubian carried Ali's wash water out of his tent to set before his camel. The beast lowered its head and drank. "Your medicine never poisons anyone, even if it does taste like Ali's camel water." Kyrin grinned. Alaina's laugh warmed her.

Ali flipped up the side of his tent, and Kentar rose from a group of drivers sitting on their heels near the lead camel. Kyrin's smile faded.

Ali had not let his animals go with Shahin's men to safer pasture. Kentar and his drivers had not been pleased. One had muttered, "Does he trust none of his brothers?"

"Shahin does not trust Ali, either," Kyrin whispered.

"What?"

"There, see them, Alaina?" Kyrin held out her arm. Three Aneza archers rested on the north rim where the junipers grew shaggy, clinging to the mountainside. And more Aneza were concealed in a great circle out of sight of the island, watching all that moved over sand, wadi, and mountain about them.

Alaina shaded her eyes with her hand. "Yes, I can see them."

Tae should come soon if his errand had succeeded. Kyrin bit her lip. How she wished the waiting were over.

Far down the dry watercourse the wadi walls towered sharply above a water-carved rock of pale limestone, a giant falcon's egg nestled deep in the rocky bed. Twenty of Shahin's warriors waited in the brush and low trees about it for Tae, who must pass the stone on his way to the island. Did they gather to honor their war leader, or did they feel like lambs staked out for Twilket wolves?

Below the giant egg, the wadi descended an Eagle mile before disappearing into the gravel plain. The wadi was the easiest way to approach the island. But if Tae's plans went awry, he and Faisal might flee down from the mountain or come up from the desert side.

Shahin walked among them all. He bent over a child and laid a hand on his head in assurance, and explained paling placements to Youbib, gesturing above and below at the camp, indicating the height of the defenses with his hands. Youbib nodded.

Kyrin let the hair coiled around her finger spring undone. Below her, women busily sharpened the long juniper poles and fastened them with cords into sections of paling. Children dragged juniper branches that the men had cut into the wadi, and fetched and carried oddments. Older men sat about the tents above; repairing weapons, making arrows and lances; and sharpening daggers and swords till the blades would shave hair.

Kyrin smiled in farewell to Alaina and walked down to join the women. She hoped Youbib learned war was not glory before it was too late. The smell of blood and the emptiness of her mother's eyes returned.

Working alongside the women, Kyrin flipped the fish at her throat up and down, up and down. Tae had not come. Mid-day slipped toward evening. The tightness in the women's faces grew. Fear closed in with slicing claws.

§

What time I am afraid I will trust in you. The first shadow crept into the wadi. Alaina waited for Kyrin's attack between two lines of Aneza women.

Kyrin raised the falcon dagger over her head and sprang. Alaina deflected her strike with crossed forearms and twisted Kyrin's blade toward her shoulder. Her sister crashed to the ground and Alaina mock-slashed her throat on the way down. The women murmured. Some gasped.

"Again! Watch." This time Alaina deflected Kyrin's overhead stab into her leg. She stole the falcon blade from Kyrin, and holding it reversed along her forearm, drove in low and swift. "Slash in and out like a whirling wolf. Don't stab, even if your enemy does. You don't want to lose your blade in a Twilket's ribs. You want to make them bleed out from many cuts."

The line of defending women gripped their daggers. Their bishts wrapped their lead arms, fat as wasp's nests swollen about apple limbs in an orchard. The opposite line of attackers lunged as one, eagerly hacking at their "enemies" with sticks. Pale thawbs and dark bishts whirled as the defending women countered, taking the stick blows to their shielded arms. Their daggers flashed up and under, to stop a handbreadth from each attacker's belly or throat.

The Aneza women seemed to know where their blades were in relation to themselves and their attackers at all times. Alaina shook her head. It was what came of using blades since childhood for all sorts of things, not to mention killing goats for the pot.

The women disengaged smoothly. Alaina called for the slashing drill, and the women sprang toward each other again—with the will to kill. They needed no one to teach them that. If their men's defensive line broke, they fought for their lives and their children.

Alaina met Kyrin's gaze. Her sister nodded, and Alaina smiled, grim but satisfied. She had been right to fight their rising fear with something they could do. At times, a single blade in determined hands could turn a battle. As in Tae's land, where women often trained as bodyguards. Where if a leader fell, others took up the fight.

Alaina's throat dried. When a falcon fought, it fought to the end, and many died. She handed the falcon dagger to Kyrin, releasing it as if it stung her.

Kyrin slid the blade into her sash, tapping its head lightly, a small smile lurking around her mouth, a contented smile.

Alaina swallowed. The falcon dagger did bring death—but it was also beautiful—and it could save.

Sweat glinted on the skirmishers' faces, and Kyrin called the halt. Alaina nodded. Warm and ready was good, tired was not. Tae said so often enough.

The women laughed, patted each other's arms, and scrambled up to the island, hope in their voices. They set out cold food for the men, then ate and fed the children.

Alaina scuffed the ground with her foot. Without doubt the Twilkets knew their position, but there would be no fires. The sun was setting.

20

Unravelings

Waters...break forth in the wilderness...~Isaiah 35:6

Kyrin told herself for the twentieth time to pay attention to the camel butter she churned, rocking the skin bottle with her stiff left arm to strengthen it. Her bow close beside her, she kept her eyes on the wadi rim. "What time I am afraid . . . I trust in thee." A child crouched over the dust before her tent, playing with a stone, and she looked up at her whisper. Kyrin smiled.

On the rim, gilded by the evening, an Aneza archer raised his arm. Someone was coming. Kyrin left the bottle of butter to rock in diminishing lonely arcs and ran to the edge.

The wadi opened below, cavernous and quiet. She knelt, licking dry lips. The smooth, cool wood of her bow under her fingers felt dreamlike in the heavy silence. The falcon blade lay equally heavy in her other hand.

Tae picked his way up the wadi past the giant egg of limestone, head bowed. He was alone. An Aneza moved around the curving limestone behind Tae—and stopped. He looked back and forth quickly. A reverberating hum shivered through the air. It filled the wadi to the brim. Then the earth itself swayed.

Kyrin clung to the ground. Aneza poured out of the shrubs behind Tae, staggering toward him. They huddled near, staring upward. Dust drifted high and thin. Was it over? Kyrin drew a cautious breath, loosening her tight grip. Was that bit of blue behind them possibly Faisal's kaffiyeh?

The wadi jolted—a stiff-legged camel with a grudge. Man-size boulders and huge slabs crashed and slid down the wadi sides. A splitting juniper shrieked. Gravel trickled past the edge, tumbled down a ledge below Kyrin, and spun over tenacious shrubs into free-fall. Rock groaned.

Kryin scrambled back from the wadi edge, could not stand on the heaving earth, and rolled. Booms and thuds of colliding boulders mingled with the scream of tortured rock. Plumes of dust shot up all along the wadi. The earth surged again—and quieted.

Behind Kyrin, Alaina hugged the tent flap around her, wide-eyed. Cicero peeped out between her legs, his ears pinned, his jaws a frozen snarl. Kyrin's ears buzzed.

All sound seemed muffled. She put down her bow and slid her dagger into her sash. Other Aneza, as dazed and shaky as she, moved here and there to help those on the ground and the crying children.

One of the archers on watch above the other side called, anxious and questioning. He raised his lance when Shahin shouted back, and returned to his post. Shaking, Kyrin walked closer to the edge. Golden dust billowed and drifted, revealing crushed trees and piles of shattered rock. The haze hid the place where Tae had been.

"Tae! Tae!" She yelled, her voice tight and strange. Cicero bounded over to press himself against her leg, and Alaina ran to grip her arm on the other side.

"We are here!" Tae called, his voice echoing up. "Do not fear!" The round dome of the egg gleamed through the dust.

Kyrin turned to Alaina, weak-kneed. "He is all right, they are all right." They hugged, the tension broke, and tears came in a quick flood until Cicero wormed his head between their knees. They patted him, laughing a little, and Kyrin dried her face.

Near the medicine tent someone cried out, high and shrill in pain. A small girl curled on the ground, clutching her thigh. A long gash bled under her hands, blood sheeting down her leg. Alaina gripped Kyrin's arm. "She's hurt!"

Kyrin followed Alaina and helped her lift the girl into the tent and onto a rug.

Alaina grabbed bandages from a nearby stack and pressed them against the wound under the girl's fingers. "I will start on her, but I need Tae!" The girl twitched and leaned forward when Alaina clamped both hands on her leg, her hair falling in a curtain around the girl's pain. Kyrin whirled toward the door.

The dust was thinning and some tents were down. Aneza were lifting the poles to shake clean the felt. Kyrin sprinted past, and met Tae at the bottom of the path. She gasped out her news, and he ran up after her.

Mey had a fire going outside her tent. They passed her at a trot, and Tae asked her to boil as much water as her pot would hold. "I will need more soon." Mey nodded.

Avoiding the press about the medicine tent door, Kyrin pulled up a loose side of the felt. Tae ducked under and she followed.

Strong herbs on a wave of steam made her cough. Alaina bent over the girl's leg in the light of a lamp, wiping around the wound with a steaming cloth. The girl gripped her rug in rigid hands, panting and fearful with pain. Alaina dropped the cloth and reached out a bloodied hand, her gaze on her needle and thread in her fingers. "Hand me that cup."

"I'll do it." Kyrin lifted a vessel of hot dark liquid from the floor beside the girl, who rolled her head restlessly. Kyrin froze. It was the little Aneza who had admired her falcon blade.

"Kyrin," Alaina said.

Kyrin blinked and held the cup to the girl's lips. She drank, her pleading gaze never leaving Kyrin's. She gagged a moment then quieted. Kyrin set the cup down, drew her falcon dagger, and put it in the girl's hands. "What is your name?"

"Neddra."

"Be brave, Neddra." Neddra touched one jet eye of the falcon and smiled, clasping the haft close. Her eyes flickered shut. But there were others hurt.

Kyrin rolled cut bandages from the nearby stack. Alaina glanced at her. "Did you wash?"

Blushing, Kyrin went to scrub her hands in the basin at the end of the tent where Tae was already elbow deep. She finished and returned, gulping down her stomach as Alaina's needle wove Neddra's flesh together over white tendons.

Tae took the girl's wrist, counting the beats of her heart. He laid her arm down gently and wiped his forehead. He looked at Alaina. "How do you say she is?"

Alaina tied off the bandage ends around the girl's leg. "She is good, now. The blood has stopped and her skin is pink. She breathes well, and you know her blood-beat is steady, though a little fast from the pain. If we can keep the green swelling away, bathe it in myrrh every day . . ."

"Yes. The myrrh heals. As your hands heal." Tae touched Alaina's shoulder in approval. "Now we must see who else needs help. I will ask outside." Alaina looked after him, cheeks reddening, and glanced aside at Kyrin. Kyrin grinned, and nodded approval.

The Aneza moved camp down from the top of the island to the middle of the wadi, out of reach of rocks falling from the sides of both. If the earth quaked again the island might collapse. There was more danger from the gaping cracks spidered across the top of the island than from the Twilkets. At least the sentries would send warning of their enemies' attack. The earth gave none.

Faisal lurked near Kyrin's back as she worked, still silent, and Tac went to take council with the elders.

§

Kyrin waited outside Shahin's door. A bed of coals cast shadows across her. She twisted a long piece of grass around her finger up to its bristly head then let it go; over and over until the grass was a ragged cord. Tae strode out. She scrambled to her feet.

"Tae, what did the Twilkets say to your errand? Will their sheyk speak with Shahin?"

Tae stopped short but did not turn. Shoulders bowed, he said, "The Twilkets want half the Aneza herds and everyone's right little finger in tribute, down to the last child."

Kyrin bit her lip.

Tae raised his head, his face bleak. "It is not certain yet, for the sheyks *will* talk. I have done that much. Go back to your tent, you need what sleep you may have. I must speak with the Master of the stars and see what he would have me do."

Back in her tent, Kyrin's arm ached savagely, and the ghost of burning settled in her scar at her throat. Alaina opened some salve and began to work on her arm. She whispered to Kyrin, "The Aneza know that *someone* looked out for us in the earthquake, it is just—they are not sure who he is. The women say their spirit of the air, of the falcon, cannot move the earth like that." Her strong fingers slid under Kyrin's necklace and down her shoulder and arm, rubbing in warmth and salve, chasing away the pain and lonliness.

Kyrin worked her throat. "The Twilkets will come in the morning for Shahin's answer."

"Yes. But the one who rules our destinies is also here."

Kyrin wished she could be so sure their destiny would be good.

Alaina sang softly, "Giver of all good gifts, all things work for good. Council me with Thine eye upon me, give me courage, be a strong tower unto me. For by Thee I can run upon a troop . . ." Kyrin lay back on her blanket. After a bit, she took a turn rubbing Alaina's feet. Alaina's breathing soon evened. She never slept ill.

Kyrin's throat ached with Neddra's pain and the sorrow of the many hearts besides hers that might cease to beat in the morn. Her hands tightened. The tiger stalked this land. Shahin posted watchers near and far, but they were little use against what hunted this night. She covered Alaina's feet gently and rolled up in her rug, her heart torn by a great cry. *Why must so many fall?*

§

Tae woke in the late watch. He rose and circled the camp, restless. His brow furrowed at the faint echo of running water, and he questioned the Aneza watching near the island.

The warrior shrugged. "There has been no rain, but it may be the wadi changed course, underneath." He pointed at the rocks near their feet.

Tae followed his ears southward, casting about. The chattering chuckle whispered to him, not from the island cisterns. It came from the great limestone rock, rounded by countless floods. At the bottom of the south-sweeping curve, a spring bubbled up in a pool, a rill running out from it.

Tae knelt beside the wayfarer, his knees sinking into good brown earth. He tasted the water. It was sweet. He shook the cool drops from his hand, suffused in the spring's peaceful song of heart-breaking power. He knew what he must do. "I am hwarang; Paekche cannot change that." Unnoticed, formless morning passed over him. He raised his head at last when birds twittered to greet the grey dawn.

Laying aside Shahin's sword, he took his horse from the two set aside for him, and fastened his ironwood stick to his saddle. He let the beast pick a cautious way past the tents and the waking Aneza, and stopped where Shahin and his men had gathered near the pool with the excited sentry after the earthquake.

He glanced up at the wadi rim. Ali Ben Aidon had stayed in his tent. Tae clenched his fist. He wanted to kill Ali. Was there not enough pain and greed in the world but one must circle it like a hyena, waiting for the weakest to fall? And the Twilket sheyk was as like Paekche as brother.

Neither of them could see generosity nor offer it. Even as Paekche lusted for power, for a name; to the ruin of all, and himself, and Huen. Tae forced his fingers straight. Battles of the past must stay there. Anger was his enemy. This day he outwitted a sheyk driven by blood and power. This day, the right man must die.

§

Kyrin ate her portion of dates, camel milk, and cold mutton. The sun rose, warming the air. News passed among the Aneza over their dead fires. She waited, shifting uneasily. Tae rode by.

"Tae!" Did he hesitate?

Glancing aside, he said, "Shahin told me to offer the Twilkets the spring."

What spring? Tae's laugh was soft but his voice held the sharpness of glass as he turned to her. "Have you been to the limestone rock? No? You might go—and take a waterskin."

Kyrin twisted her necklace. This was not the time to ask news.

He looked at her. "I will bring Shahin to the sheyk before the sun sets. The Twilkets will not attack before the sheyks speak, for Gershem enjoys us thinking about our fingers blackening on the sand." He stared down the wadi, his face tense. "The Master of water and men's hearts must mend this—if I and Gershem are willing." He closed his eyes, his mouth flattened, and he shook his head. "Forgive me."

Kyrin ducked her head in a nod. Something ate at him, a sadness and an anger.

They rode to meet the Twilket sheyk near sunset. Kyrin urged Lilith up beside Faisal and Tae. Her plea that she was a part of the blood debt had at last persuaded Tae to let her come. Lilith followed so close that Tae's horse side-stepped. Kyrin glimpsed his stick on his saddle. His thawb molded to his rigid shoulders. She glanced at Faisal.

Straight and easy on his horse, he held a limber lance, and his dagger shone in a rich blue sash, Shahin's gift for his part in Tae's errand. Head up, kaffiyeh in perfect place, Faisal leaned forward. A hunting falcon, his dark eyes missed nothing. He had still not said a word to her.

He rode as a desert lord, good to the eye. Though he would never make it onto Esther's list of lords. She would say he needed land and gold. Kyrin could just see their first meeting, Esther mincing and bold, Faisal tossing his head in scorn, proud as an Arabian stallion. Esther's mouth would drop open—she was not used to scorn.

Kyrin released a curl of hair. Celine now, she would follow Faisal. He had the drawing power and aloofness of a tiger, but he could be warm when he chose. She stared at the rein in her hand, then at Faisal's back. Did *she* follow him?

Tae shot her a distracted frown as Lilith jigged into Faisal's horse. Fire rose in Kyrin's face. Faisal did not look around, as if it were of no moment. She wanted to retreat to her tent—but she must hear Gershem's reply to the offered terms.

Ahead of Tae, the wadi mouth opened broad and shallow onto the gravel plain. There Shahin waited, flanked by Youbib.

Gershem Ben Salin met them eight arrow flights from the giant falcon's egg of limestone. His body was lean and strong, and his brown hair beneath his kaffiyeh was grizzled. A scar crossed his high, thin nose. He stared at them, his cinnamon eyes wily with years.

21

Revelations

Those who sow in tears shall reap . . . ~Psalm 126:5

Riding behind Sheyk Gershem, seven warriors wore winter bishts of earth colors: sandstone, tawny grass, and basalt. Drawn up in a crescent behind their sheyk, they rode horses, muscled beasts with delicate heads, glistening coats, and intelligent eyes.

Sheyk Shahin walked his brown stallion forward to face Gershem. His horse whuffled, tossing its black mane, and stopped. Everyone else halted as one. Tae's horse was stone, as were the warriors' eyes on him.

Gershem's thin, wrinkled face was still, his eyes alert as a bird's, tense as a coiled cobra.

Tae's shoulders contracted the least bit.

Shahin's voice rose—deep, rich honey with the warning sting of a sword beneath. "Before us there is laid death, and more death. Or the water of life to offer for the blood of your warrior. The water of life for a death, and peace for our generations."

"Water?" Gershem's voice held no inflection.

"Come." Shahin reined his horse around and led the divided parties up the wadi toward the pale limestone rock visible above the junipers. Tae dropped back with Kyrin and Faisal, his knee even with the Twilket sheyk's across from him.

Gershem eyed the likely ambushes along the way.

"Do not fear. Shahin's word is his law." Tae clamped his mouth shut after those few words, his jaw iron hard, staring straight ahead. Gershem glanced at him with distaste.

Kyrin nudged Lilith up beside Tae, through a last screen of juniper between them and the limestone egg. The rock rose over her head.

Gershem halted his dancing horse midstep. Kyrin knew his amazement. The quaking earth had opened its mouth to give life.

Tufts of tender green herbs and a profusion of yellow, purple, and blue flowers waved above grass in a great swathe around a spring. At the stone's foot the sheet of water rippled, throwing shafts of light over every warrior who gaped around it. Beneath the silken surface, pebbles tumbled over the sandy floor. The water rushed from the pool in a clean channel among the dusty stones. It laughed, rushing toward the south wall of the wadi in a gurgling bed, edged with stone, fragrant grass and flowers, and disappeared beneath the ground a bowshot further on.

Gershem stared at the wide pool. It would come to a man's shoulders. The channel had room for many thirsty camels.

Tae said softly, as if he feared to break the water's peace or sour the sweetness of the flowers in the air, "This is the work of the Master of the stars. You felt him shake the land, I think. If the peace is accepted, Sheyk Shahin offers you twenty horses and the use of this water for all your generations. You will be welcome in the tents of the Aneza, to trade and profit and grow. Here we are close to the caravan road to Taif, and the road to the East. A caravanserai here would bring gold, silver, spices, and every rich thing."

Gershem grunted and turned his head. "We are three to your one. What if I take the horses and the spring and give the murderer justice?"

Kyrin looked at Tae.

"It would not be just, and you would die, and many of your men."

"Not all?" Gershem laughed, his gaze sharpening.

"As many as we can kill, and you first," Tae said gently, as a man tells his host his choice of meat at dinner. "I call on the closest brother to your slain warrior to seize the blood debt from me. If he cannot, you will withdraw the Nur-ed-Dam. Kyrin," Tae said, without turning his head.

Kyrin's throat was too dry to speak. This was the part she hated. She nudged Lilith forward and stopped beside him. Tae reached over. He pulled her hair loose beneath her kaffiyeh, his eyes never leaving Gershem. "My wife in name shot your warrior when he tried to kill Shahin's first-born son, a child. As you say, blood is thicker than water. Blood for blood will never end. With a caravanserai here"—Tae swung his arm wide—"you will rule the desert and this oasis, as you please."

Gershem rested his hands on his bay's crest, considering. His dark gaze flicked over them all, then he straightened. "Only if *he* comes with us." He pointed past Kyrin.

Tae stiffened. Faisal moved up until his sandaled foot touched Kyrin's ankle. She glanced at him.

"Why?" Faisal said, his voice thin and clear, as he grounded his lance beside his horse.

"What is your name?" Gershem lifted his chin, an old warrior, proud as poison, his thin neck stretching.

"I am Faisal." Faisal's nostrils flared and his eyes were hot. Red darkened his cheeks.

So that was why he had never told them his tribe. He did not know it, or he would surely give it now. A father's name was a precious possession. Kyrin shifted, and Faisal's hand tightened on his lance.

Gershem said scornfully, "You submit to Allah, yet go with unbelievers?"

"I am bound. How does it concern *you?*" Faisal's voice was brittle. Shahin and his men watched, still, waiting.

Gershem rode closer, lip curled. Tae did not move, and Kyrin held her breath.

"I saw you meet this one"—Gershem jerked his head at Tae— "after he left my tent. He held a dagger to my neck and asked much. I let him have his life. Allah is generous."Gershem smiled, wrinkles deep around his mouth. His goodwill did not touch his onyx eyes. "My men followed him to make sure he spoke true." He stroked his chin. "You remind me of someone. Who is your father?"

"My father is dead. His name is great, though I know it not." Faisal's scowl was black as Kyrin had ever seen it.

Gershem reached for his rein. "Ah yes, a man in a tent, his brow as angry as yours, falling over his wife to save her, who would not let me have a common rug—"

"You—murderer!" Faisal whipped his lance down like a cobra. Kyrin swung an arm around his neck, half unseating him. Tae guided the end of Faisal's thrusting lance under his horse's neck into the sand. Faisal dropped the lance and grabbed his dagger.

"No!" Tae shouted, gripping his arm. In a low voice he said, "There is more."

Faisal paused, breathing hard.

Warriors had closed in.

"Stop—peace." Tae lifted his palms to the Twilket lances hedging them in. "Let us speak together." Horses shuffled and grunted, snorting under uneasy riders. Shahin and Youbib held their blades to Gershem's ribs. "Be easy." Tae motioned and they let the sheyk go. The Twilkets relaxed.

Gershem bristled. Faisal leaned forward, hands whitening in his horse's mane. *"What* do you know of my family?" he demanded.

"Stupid boy!" Gershem clenched his hands about his reins and glared. "Alud Ben Salin was my son." His head bobbed. "Yes, and by the decree of Allah, I lost him."

Faisal jolted back, a shying colt. "I am no blood of yours!"

"It is as Allah wills." He shrugged. "Would you bring your friends here to death?"

Faisal shut his mouth with a snap. His eyes were hard.

"Faisal, don't . . ." Kyrin whispered.

And his jagged consternation smoothed from his face. He gritted out, "I accept your peace. Blood is thicker than water." He glanced at Kyrin and Tae and extended his dagger, haft first, to Gershem.

The sheyk took the blade and said solemnly to Shahin, "I accept your spring. Though this one"—he motioned at Tae— "could have lost his life among my tents, except that Allah made me wonder what manner of jackal dared beard me in my den."

Faisal opened his mouth, then his teeth clicked together. Tae pressed his thumb hard into Faisal's near thigh, the movement hidden from Gershem, who rested Faisal's blade before him.

§

Faisal winced. *This sheyk must be blood of my blood, to bait a lion like Tae in* his *den. Did Tae tell him I killed his assassin? But it was war . . .* there was no lawful Nur-ed-Dam for him to hold.

Tae slid from his saddle and walked around Faisal to Gershem, and stopped at his knee. He looked up in his face. "No, honored

Sheyk of the Twilkets. I let *your* men live. The warrior in the brown kaffiyeh behind you holds his breath when he stalks men with a long sword in his hands. And the one in white, the feathers of his arrows rustle." Gershem's warriors stirred. "I could have killed them all." The silence was thick.

"How?" Gershem's voice was a derisive bark.

Tae shook back his sleeves. A band around his wrist held the butts of the assassin's darts, their black heads buried in a second leather band about his forearm. The blowpipe lay snug against his other side in his belt. His ironwood stick was a dark viper in his hand.

Numbness crept into Faisal's fingertips as if the darts' poison worked there. He let out his breath. Among the Twilket tents one uncertain move would have been agony and creeping grey for Tae, dragging him down to blackness—death to him, or to any number of the Twilkets. Warriors who were Faisal's tribe now, if the sheyk who claimed him spoke with a straight tongue.

"A warrior with sticks claims this?" Gershem looked around with a smile. He tilted the dagger in his hand and stabbed swift as thought at Tae.

Faisal opened his mouth to shout. Tae's hands blurred, struck Gershem's wrist. The dagger flew from his grip to arc over Faisal's head.

Thrusting the sheyk's ankle above the horse's withers as he pulled down on his arm, Tae whirled Gershem out of the saddle. In the space of a breath he tapped the sheyk's temple with his stick, spun behind him, and held the weapon across the sheyk's throat. The ironwood could as easily break his head as his neck. Gershem gagged. The dark wood eased away, to quiver before his face. Eager.

Faisal looked at Tae. Tae's mouth was tight, and his dark eyes flashed. It was effort to hold himself back. Yes, he knew much of death—or death knew of him. Faisal swallowed.

Gershem's men held their lances high, ready to thrust. Startled, wary, angry—they faced a thicket of Aneza weapons. Their sheyk, his sheyk, swayed then gained his balance. Shahin merely waited.

Gershem choked, eyes bulging. And Tae released him. The sheyk turned slowly, breathing carefully, his chin high. Tae stepped back and dropped his robe of readiness.

Gershem nodded. The sheyk's blood-beat jumped in his wrinkled throat like a rabbit's, but his voice held the new-forged iron of respect. "What tribe reared such a warrior? Djinn might call you brother."

"I was reared hwarang, beyond the land of spices." Tae bowed, waited a moment as before an equal, then turned his back to mount his horse. There was an uncertain moment, then the soft noise of swords sliding through sashes and lances grounding. Gershem stared after him and nodded again, mouth puckered as if he thoughtfully sucked a lemon. He acknowledged the game to Shahin with a bow.

Tae had done it. Faisal grinned. *I have a name.* His grandfather glared at him, and Faisal wiped his face clear. *Alud Ben Salin, I am your son.* He was a son of the Twilkets.

§

The feast of peace between the Aneza and the Twilkets would begin with the fall of night.

"Ruthlessness requires ruthlessness, or the appearance of it." Tae smiled.

Sweat trickled down Kyrin's neck. There was not enough boiling air to breathe in the tent. For once in its lifetime, the closed walls refused all breezes. In the heat of the day, all rested but the flies—and those with hard words to say.

Faisal said low, "It was your right to test my sheyk's blade and his rash words."

"Why was it my right?" Tae's voice was equally quiet.

Faisal held up his hands with a shrug, "You had the strength, and you are a man."

Unsatisfied, Tae turned to Kyrin. "Why did I possess the right?"

She knew. It came now, the difference between her and Faisal. She could taste it, bitter on her tongue. Tae waited, and Faisal frowned.

Her throat tightened. "Power does not give a man any right. The Father of All says to do justice, to love mercy. *He* gave Tae the right, the command, to challenge Gershem."

Faisal shrugged. "Allah says to convince unbelievers with whatever must be. If they do not come willingly, the sword shepherds them to knowledge."

"Yes, Allah says so." Kyrin forced her thick tongue around the words. "Our Father says not. A sword convinces no one's heart, but his body alone. Our Father's power comes from his love—he will have the best for us. Though he lets those who wish choose their own way."

Faisal's brow wrinkled. "Why do you speak of love? Love is for women. Loving is a part of their nature, for children. The joy of the sword is for men." He tapped his stick against his knee and smiled, a quick quirk. "Let us rest this hot hour, and in the morning Cicero will chase us rabbits to shoot."

Kyrin wished her lips could lock closed over what lay in her heart as a burning, heavy stone. She whispered, "Faisal, falcons must fly with the same wind to fly together. We do not. My

Father opposes Allah. Allah, who feeds you other peoples' blood and takes you where the wind of mercy is not."

Faisal's brows slammed together.

Kyrin slid the falcon dagger from her sash and touched the point, forcing her tears back with the prick. She held up the blade and looked at him over the edge. "If this threatened to draw your life away, would *you* believe my Father?"

His mouth flattened and he looked aside. Then he took the falcon, tugging it free of her fingers with a wry smile. "Will you wait to see if we might enjoy the journey together, and fly to the same eyrie in the end?"

That Faisal. "You do not hear. Our path divides." *You smiled for me the first time yesterday. Oh, I hope you see the Master of the stars. See his care in the crater, and his love when you stood under Shahin's lance. Oh, why must my heart wake? I feel more a child than a woman. How Esther would laugh.*

"It is not that you wish to be the hakeem's." Faisal looked from her to Tae in doubt, and Tae shook his head.

Faisal continued hopefully, "You are his only in name. I will speak with Gershem."

Tae stood wearily, as if he felt old. "It will change nothing. Your heart is not whole, my son, though you may yet be mended. She cannot join you now."

"Or ever?" Faisal's lip curled, and he got to his feet, the falcon tight in his hand. "Is it that I have but few camels, no tent, and no weapons, hakeem? And my blood is Twilket? What of her, a slave who shrinks from blood, and shivers before a blade. She knows more of the warrior's art than of painting henna flowers and rearing children. And what of the blood between us?"

Kyrin rose; her chest hurt. She lifted her chin. "Yes, I know the art of war; I will never fall again to someone such as Ali. And I do not love the needle and the loom. I left the cooking fire to shoot beside my father and walk with my mother in the hills. My horse and my hawk made my heart beat fast. I dreaded my alliance with another stronghold."

There did not seem enough air. Her words came fast and her breath harder. "You stirred me, with the anger and blood between us, and then our peace bound our paths together. But blood also separates us. My creator gave his life for me, his very blood, and I cannot deny it. I think you will understand this—my heavenly Father paid the Nur-ed-Dam I owed him. I owe him my life."

Tae said evenly, gently, "My son, she tells you her heart."

"You—refuse me?" Faisal leaned forward, a pleading, lost look in his face. "Together we will ride the desert; we will hunt. I will take you to Gaza, a treasured woman of the Twilkets, and you will sail across the sea to find your father."

He did not wish to hear the truth that lay between them. Kyrin held herself tight, every muscle. He knew pearls and gold and perfume would not sway her; he knew what would. Tears rushed up with the hope of seeing her father. When she set the hope down, they spilled. "It cannot be, Faisal. It cannot be." Her throat closed, aching.

He dropped the falcon blade at her feet. It bounced on the rug. Kyrin flinched.

"You are not worthy." His dark face was grim. "A falcon makes its own way."

"Makes its own way on what—a shriveled, sun-eaten heart—without our creator's wind?" Her voice went high, and she turned away; she could not bear to see his stubbornness flower. Kyrin nodded to Tae and hurried out of the tent.

§

Before the feast Faisal walked past her tent on his way up from the Twilket camp below. His grandfather's tents spread from the spring down along the wadi, a black flood out into the desert. He saw her, lying awake beside Alaina. His eyes were hot coals. Then he averted his stony face and went inside Tae's tent, yanking the flap closed.

Kyrin rolled over, burying her face in her cushion. So Gershem Salin agreed with her and Tae. It was not a fit handfasting.

What might it have been like to walk with Faisal in the majesty of the desert, unbound, on her way home. To go before her father as a bride; to hunt rabbits and Wudhaihi, laughing at each other's shots; to drink sweet tea and paint her hands with bright henna flowers? What would she give to see Faisal's smile light his face, to feel his kiss like the desert wind over her skin? Faisal would come to see their Father, he had goodness in him— then when his anger at the one who made her Nasrany forged him to a brittle blade, they would destroy each other.

He must let love in, before he can love me. I wish I had never seen him. Truth hurt. *No, no I don't.*

She tossed and turned, and at last rose. Her bloom of womanhood had passed till the next moon. Best to find Ali and get the question of the Aneza's gift of the falcon settled. Her falcon would take feeding and training. Ali would have a worthy prize. She might even raise other birds for him if he thought well of how she handled this one. Maybe then she could nap, despite the heat. Her heart lightened.

Umar admitted her to Ali's tent, unsmiling and watchful. Ali turned with a grimace from examining a fur laid on the table. Moths had chewed the edges over the long voyage.

Kyrin knelt, touched her forehead to the rug, and told him of the Aneza and the capture of the falcon. She gathered her tired will. "The falcon will hunt much game for you." She looked up in hope.

Ali avoided her gaze, his voice tight. "No. You moon-gaze enough without a falcon to draw your feet after it. A gift of gold would have better fit your worth to the Aneza and to me."

Kyrin could not help her puzzled frown. The gift of a falcon honored him, and he disdained it. Was it because Shahin honored Tae and consulted him openly? Or did her master know of her womanhood? But Alaina would say nothing, and she was the only one who knew. "My master—"

"No falcon will be yours, worthless one," Ali said. "Is it not enough for a slave to be as her master?" His smile gave nothing.

Kyrin's mouth trembled. She would never be like Ali. And no matter this master's words, to reflect in any measure her Master of the stars—that was an honor.

"Out."

"Yes, my master." She bowed to the rug, a hot ball in her middle. At least Cicero was hers.

Umar held the door flap aside, his palm on his sword, his mouth satisfied. He stretched out his leg. Kyrin stopped short. "Do not think you cannot be touched." His whisper turned the heat in her stomach to a shard of ice, and he slid the falcon dagger from her sash. She grabbed for it—too late. *Fool!* She lived as an equal beside the Aneza and forgot to hide her blade.

Umar tossed the sheathed dagger to Ali, who raised his eyebrow. Kyrin wet her lips. He turned the haft in his hand, rubbed one of the falcon's eyes with distaste, grunting at a glimpse of bronze. "It is an uncommon creature, even for an askar."

So he'd heard Kentar and the drivers call her askar, a little serious. Now he mocked, his voice smooth as chilled wine. Kyrin saw him in a falcon's blink.

He writhed on the ground, the falcon dagger sheathed in his middle. She walked unafraid in his blood, stooping to trail her fingers in it, and left the print of her hand on his forehead like a benediction.

Kyrin dropped her burning stare to Ali's sandals. Umar tapped his foot, meditating on the tent poles. "Allah forbids it. The haft is much like the Eagles' standard, the creature the Eagles worshipped. "

He will take my mother's falcon. No, he must not!

Ali rubbed his chin and leaned back. He shrugged. "It is of poor worth, and it fits your unbelieving blood, Nasrany." He tossed the sheathed weapon at Kyrin's feet. She fumbled for it, her heart rising. She could wear the falcon at her side. He did not know it was her mother's. He must never know.

Umar dropped his brown gaze to hers. If he wanted to put her in a slave's place, he had. Or to fill her with fear, he did that, too.

Walking away from the tent, Kyrin considered darkly. Umar would have watched her mother fall with a smile. Someday, not from her seeking, she might watch him over a blade. She crossed her arms. The coldness inside would swallow her. She had thought Umar's anger might lessen with his fading scars. But it had not.

She shook herself. Ali would get an extra rabbit in the morn. She must keep his favor as she could, brief though it might be. As she rubbed her face wearily she could still see Faisal's glare across the falcon dagger he threw at her feet. Tomorrow she would hunt alone, with Cicero. Maybe the Nubian would be at Ali's door to take her catch, and she would not have to watch Umar caress his sword hilt, his gaze lingering.

§

At dusk, every Aneza and Twilket sat or lolled around the many fires. Shahin and Gershem had five camels and many more goats roasting over great beds of juniper coals. No delicacy was spared.

Kyrin nibbled nuts and rice, and late, frost-kissed persimmons. Tea with cardamom, honeyed milk with cinnamon, and rich, spiced dates were wonderfully sweet. She ate until she could eat no more. In her lap, Rashid gurgled over his cup of milk with cinnamon and date syrup. His warmth had kept the chill desert night at bay. He wriggled to be free. Kyrin let him go. Had she lost the chance for such a warm bundle of her own, a little form breathing against her, heart thumping counterpoint? But would he ever know the one who made him? She wiped her cheek and sniffed. No matter what hid the chasm for a time, Faisal would always be divided from her, .

The evening air up and down the wadi rippled with laughing voices, old and young. Endless stories and jokes passed from one shadowed kaffiyeh to a gleaming face under another. The goodwill grated at Kyrin's sore heart. Her master sickened her, smiling widely at all who passed Shahin's fire, where he ate.

The Aneza and Twilkets had traded much with Ali Ben Aidon. His goods were increased five-fold, with hope of more. He added Bedouin rugs and rich blue, purple, and red dyes to his packs of spices, ivory, and silver, and bartered for ten loads of crushed date pits for his camels' journey. Kyrin sighed.

On the morrow, they would leave.

When the last pleading child was firmly ordered to his rug, and fires were banked, Kyrin walked to her tent with Alaina, who chattered happily about their falcon.

"What will we call her, Kyrin? We must find a good name."

"I do not know. May we speak of it in the morn? I'm tired. " It would be soon enough to tell Alaina of the falcon and of Faisal when the sun rose.

While Alaina slept, Kyrin lay quiet. Ali took what was hers by right, and the falcon remained captive. Tears leaked into her pillow.

22

Division

Faithful is He who calls you . . . ~1 Thessalonians 5:24

Arrangements had been made. Only bitter parting was left. Stars hung in a cobalt sky above a grey horizon; at home the bells of lauds gave way to prime.

The cold stung Kyrin's nose despite her thin veil. Ali's litter waited near her, and Tae held Munira's rein for their master. Alaina rubbed her arms, shivering. The Aneza and Twilket tribes were mounted, their tents packed on their baggage beasts, the tribes arrayed in two long lines behind their sheyks.

Shahin stood before Ali. A sword lay across his hands. He raised it, silver inlay winding about the pommel, the blade bright and clean. "I give you this gift in parting, Ali Ben Aidon. You have served us well." Shahin smiled. "If your dalil ceases to bring us thrice-yearly news of our Shaheen with your trade, we will seek you out, and the desert will know your end. May prosperity be yours and increase."

Ali grinned, took the weapon, and kissed Shahin on both cheeks in the manner of the desert. "Such a two-edged seal is fitting to our bargain." He handed the gift sword to Umar, who sheathed it and slid it in Ali's pack. "Your blade will guard me well, second to my father's." He patted the sword in his sash.

"And to you and your people be peace and prosperous trade. *Allah yisullmak*, God protect you."

"*Wa alaykum as-salaam*, and on you be peace."

Kyrin's jaw knotted. Ali thickened her chains with his refusal of Shahin's offer to buy her and Alaina and Tae.

Ali climbed to his litter. Shahin turned from him to grip Tae's shoulder briefly, then lifting his arm, he raised his voice. "This warrior, Tae Chisun, was brought to us by the Master of the stars." The Aneza raised a shout.

Tae grinned, dropped Munira's rein, and bowed. He clasped the sheyk's arms in farewell. "He who seeks finds what his heart treasures." His mouth was solemn, but his eyes held joy.

Shahin leaned close to Tae and whispered, "Is that warning or encouragement to a brother?"

"Both, my friend. The falcon serves the true king."

Shahin raised an eyebrow. "We have seen he is not a strengthless king."

"No."

"He enjoys hiding burrs under your saddle."

"Rather, truth bears a rough stride until I learn where I fit between it and the world," Tae said.

Shahin ritually kissed Tae's nose and cheeks, with a chuckle. "For riding that uncomfortable beast which is your lot, I give you this." He took a sword from a servant behind him and laid it across Tae's hands. "And"—he extended an arm toward the Twilkets—"my brothers give you these, in token of farewell."

Tae slid Shahin's sword through his sash slowly, with reverence. Then he accepted a lance tufted with bright parrot feathers and the curved bow of a horse nomad, and raised the weapons in his fist with a broad smile. A great, glad yell rose from every Twilket and Aneza throat.

Shahin moved to Kyrin. He kissed her in the three places of honor, not touching her skin, as was the ritual. A blush crept up her neck. He smelled of myrrh.

Shahin laid a bundle with a black bisht folded around it in her arms. Kyrin shook the bisht over her arm. An embroidered falcon on the sleeve of a black thawb arrowed toward the wearer's heart. Kyrin stroked the widespread wings. Folded beneath the thawb were Persian style trousers, tight at the ankle and roomy in the leg. The soft gifts warmed Kyrin's cold, clutching fingers. Mey had woven them of her most expensive cotton from Egypt, dyed black. The bisht of dark wool had a thick hood.

The trousers and thawb were perfect for Subak practice, and the scarlet sash wound within all would hold the falcon's sheath in elegant grace. Except for the sash, they would be most useful for blending with shadows.

Kyrin's mouth tipped up on one side. Ali could not refuse to let her wear this, his ancestors' garb, gifted to her by a sheyk before all. She bowed. "I thank you, O most honorable Sheyk. I will walk the sand and think of your generosity and your might— that you brought justice and peace from war." She bowed again to Shahin, and turned to Mey, who sat on her loaded camel, first in the Aneza line, with Rashid before her. "I thank you," she said in a soft voice, and Mey smiled warmly.

While Shahin moved toward Alaina, Kyrin gathered herself. The hardest parting came close. She needed strength to give the gift she must.

Alaina stretched her arms wide to reach around a fat bolt of wool. Shahin gifted her enough to furnish every slave in Ali's house with a fine winter bisht. The sheyk reached back to take something from Mey, and laid on top of the material a hank of indigo thread the blue of Rashid's tattoo.

Alaina's eyes sparkled like the spring, and she bowed. "I give
you all my thanks." She sobered and disappeared among the
camel lines to pack her gifts. Everywhere, all was ready. But
the last tent to come down was the hawks' tent. Kyrin's breath
came faster. She smoothed her damp palms against her thawb
and breathed deep to steady her heart's race. *Alaina, be quick.*

Shahin stopped before Faisal. Kyrin clenched her hands. If
Faisal could but see her face behind the veil, he might accept her
gift—which bore her heart for him. She would never forget him,
the flash in his eyes when he flung his head back, ready to fight
all who came. Would he accept her peace? Faisal would marry
another, his blood would go on. But what of his spirit? Would
he love killing and find despair, or seek justice and discover the
wideness of mercy?

Shahin beckoned, and Youbib led a good racing camel up,
with a tent and weapons tied in their places. Shahin laid the
beast's neck rope in Faisal's hand. And Faisal glanced at Kyrin,
and kissed Shahin with full honor, his face grave.

"Sheen! Sheen!" Rashid crowed, jumping in Mey's arms,
pointing with a gurgling laugh. Faisal spun. Kyrin swallowed
and turned slowly, knowing what she would see.

Like a queen, Alaina carried their falcon on her arm between
the lines of wondering Twilkets and Aneza. Head up, without
a glance aside, she stepped between Ali litter and Umar, and
strode to Kyrin.

Kyrin handed her thawb and trousers to Alaina, and wound
the tail of her new bisht around her left arm. The falcon shuffled
onto it, full of promise of swift strength—if nothing hindered
her growth. Ali opened his mouth, thought better of it, and gave
Umar a withering stare. Umar glided to Ali's side, his narrowed
eyes on Kyrin.

"Sheen!" Rashid crowed.

Kyrin licked her lips. Ali told her to leave the falcon behind. She obeyed—in her own way.

Somehow she forced her legs the last few feet to Faisal, keeping her arm steady under the falcon. The veil whiffled against her mouth. *At least that can go.*

She pulled down the veil slowly and heard gasps. Though the Aneza women did not wear it, they knew the meaning for those who did. Kyrin dared not look at Ali; Faisal must see her face. "Let there be peace between us. Let us part brother and sister, as we rode in the desert." Her voice was clear, without treacherous huskiness. Caught by Faisal's stony gaze, for a moment she thought he would spit. The falcon peeped. Faisal glanced at the ground and back up, expressionless.

Don't make me touch you. Please. He did not move. Mouth dry, Kyrin lifted his wide, unresisting wrist beside hers. He held stiffly still. Every man and woman was utterly silent, craning to see.

She had not thought so far; he had no guard against the bird's talons. Hoping he did not take it amiss—*it is all I have*—she wound her veil around his arm. His wrist was warm and strong under her flinching fingers, and she did not want to let go. His glance went from her to the falcon, stepping onto the tight-wound cloth. The bird shook her head and clacked her beak, ruffled her wings, and settled.

"You will teach my sky hunter well?" Kyrin's voice cracked. "Her name is Truthseeker." She could not look at him, staring at the falcon's jesses she had carved from leather, embossed with the leaves of her beloved beeches, now hanging over the corded muscles of his wrist.

Faisal said nothing. He was not going to speak. She closed her eyes, turning away.

"Can Truthseeker ever fly ill?"

Against the sunlight behind her, his eyes were shadowed, his mouth tired, and the fire of his anger was bleakened ash. "I wanted such a bird, Nasrany—as an honored gift from these good Aneza, not taken from you by—necessity."

Ah, necessity. So he protected her from Ali's wrath, and accepted her peace. Her smile grew strong. It was the last thing Faisal would have of her. "I do give you my falcon, warrior, with all the honor I possess, and my thanks." She bowed her head and turned to the sheyks.

"May this falcon, my lords, be a token of my esteem and desire for the peace you have forged. I have nothing else to give, and may not take the shaheen on such a journey as lies before me, lest it affect my service to my master."

Shahin did not look displeased. He and Gershem bowed. Kyrin returned the gesture, warmth blooming inside her. They used Tae's custom to honor her. When she turned toward her camel, the Nubian's face was split with his wide smile.

Kyrin took Alaina's hand. Tears threatened; what did Faisal think of her bold tongue? Aunt Medaen would be proud of her most lordly speech. Gershem stepped close to Kyrin, staring down his fierce nose. "I will not forget your deeds for my blood, son of my son."

"As I will remember his for me." *That jackal's son.* She dared not look at Faisal—her smile would shake.

"It is well."

Shahin interrupted the whispers that ran up and down the lines of men and women by pulling Faisal to his side. "Here is the one who sealed our tribes together. He defended our Shaheen, who saved the son of *my* blood. And our brothers have found him, their lost son! To every son found, every son saved, to all our sons among us!

The women raised a ululating call, and the men shook their lances or beat them against their shields. And Kyrin blinked hard, and smiled at Shahin. He had begun to bind the tribes by blood. He released Faisal to Gershem's right hand, and Faisal went to take his place, face flushed.

Tae stepped quickly forward and stopped him. He stared into his eyes. Loss pinched Faisal's face. Tae slipped his ironwood stick from his sash and set it in Faisal's hand. "Remember the right of strength." He laid one hand over Faisal's heart. Then he walked away.

Faisal stared after him until he mounted, and raised the weapon to his forehead in salute. The Twilket warriors murmured. Gershem scowled, so like Faisal that Kyrin wanted to laugh past the prickle in her eyes.

Gershem strode with his grandson to their horses. Faisal stroked Truthseeker's back and looked up to hear something Gershem said. The sheyk had his grandson, and Faisal had his grandfather. He was no longer nameless.

Ready to ride, Gershem raised his arm and let out a whoop. He clamped his heels to his horse, and it sprang into a gallop. With a long shout the Twilkets streamed after him in a thunder of hooves and camel pads, lances high, the baggage camels pacing after them through the dust.

Faisal paused, glancing over his shoulder at Kyrin. Trying to imprint her in his mind, or did he remember her lack of womanliness?

Alaina whispered in her ear, "I gave him some words that Tae translated from John's Book. I hope he reads them."

"So do I." Truthseeker was a good name.

Faisal nodded, dipped his head to Alaina, and turned his horse after his people. He did not look back again, his beast kicking up fat puffs to join the haze. The dust was cold and pale in the morning. Kyrin made herself breathe again. *May your heart live.*

23

Paths

Thou hast taken account of my wanderings.... Are they not in Thy book?
~Psalm 56:8

Ali waved, and Kentar called the caravan out. The Nubian laid a great hand on Kyrin's arm and escorted her to Lilith, and Alaina to a camel behind her. Kyrin told herself that was one thing she had gained: Alaina rode now. It would not do for one beloved of the Aneza to have no mount.

Nudging his camel after Ali, Umar looked back, and his gaze bored into Kyrin. Ali had been angry with him because he had not warned him of what was in the wind with Truthseeker. Religious though Umar was, he knew she never wore her veil but at Ali's table. No, he was not upset at her loosing her veil before Twilket and Aneza men.

His gaze was on the Nubian, his lips flattening. Did he despise the black giant's kindness? Kyrin sighed. Umar was Arab from the heart out. She gripped Lilith's rein, about to mount, and stopped. Tae had sheathed Shahin's sword on his saddle. With it, he carried the Aneza's favor.

She could leave Ali tonight with Tae and Alaina and follow the Aneza, then go to her father. He would make Tae his weapons master. And Tae would make Lord Dain Cieri the most powerful man but the king. Alaina would be her sister in truth. And for herself—she need never fear again. Cierheld's walls would be of her godfather's thick Eagles' stone—and no one got past her father's arm. Tae would teach her the sword until no man could best her.

White Munira walked to the front of the caravan, jostling Ali's litter, the red tassels on her headstall feathering in the wind. Tae would not bring danger to the Aneza. She was back to leaping to Ali's whim, like those tassels. Kyrin wiped her wet face and kicked the ground savagely.

Faisal was gone. The wadi spread up the mountain, lonely and clean but for the scars of fire pits that would fade under the next rain. The spring chuckled merrily, far away and to itself. The Oasis of Oaths, as Alaina called it, cared nothing for her troubles. Shahin and the last of his people wended toward the desert. Mey called over the dust and noise, "I will see you, Shaheen!"

At the call, Kyrin looked up, wordless, her throat thick. She raised her arm to Mey. Struggling onto Lilith's back, she stroked the embroidered falcon on the black bisht, then buried her face in the clean wool. She could not stay, and left behind those she would not find again.

§

At Ali's command, Kentar did not lead them to Makkah. They camped beside a Persian trader in the mountains near Taif. The oasis had many trees. Date palms leaned above pools of water, and ditches fed life to nearby melons and grain growing in the fertile soil.

Ali drank tea with the Persian merchant while the stars swung overhead. He traded a fur and some pigs of lead for a bolt of silk for Shema. Her mistress.

Kyrin wound a curl of hair about her finger. Would Shema be as bitter hot as Umar, or as cold as Ali? Indifferent, or ceaselessly biting about this task or that?

Ali had said his worthless one would be a living warning to his Shema. Marriage to him would be chains enough for any woman. Kyrin shook her head with a twist of her mouth. Neither she nor Shema were beloved of Ali. Maybe they would find common ground.

The following days were full: hauling water for the camels, packing and unpacking loads in starlight and dawnlight, walking until her legs buckled and then riding Lilith until her bones felt ready to shatter. Frost coated everything in the mornings. Kyrin yearned for a roof and warmth at night, not to slog onward at every sunrise. She thought of rest, and watching sun and shadows chase each other under the trees, through the grass.

Maybe then a smile instead of an ache would linger in her heart. The tiger stalked her grey thoughts; Faisal would never escape Allah, and her father would never know she lived. In every fight her heart failed, another piece broken, with the falcon as witness.

The caravan clambered along the feet of the mountains for many miles around the edge of Faisal's great sands. Torturous wadis descended from the rocky heights to disappear into the sand, hiding in their depths splashes of lacy green abal bushes that waited for winter's rain to hang their pink flowers over white carpets of chamomile. In the sands, dunes of pink, mauve, and tan grains moved ceaselessly under the plucking fingers of the wind. It hissed, moaned, wailed, and laughed. Clouds of grit whipped into the air from the tops of far ridges, like dry ocean spume.

Near Saa'na they turned east to the Hadramawt plateau. At the end of the first day of travel over the sharp stones, Alaina held a hide bucket of butter for Tae, who dipped Lilith's torn feet. He sewed leather pads to Lilith's soles where she lay, while Kyrin crouched over her head, covering her eyes with her bisht, hanging on to her neck with both arms to squelch Lilith's wild wrenches. Watching Kyrin's grim hold, Tae grinned. "That arm is healed."

Kyrin grinned back. It was. Her heart, not yet.

At the well of Shishur near the border of Oman, tradesmen, common people, and merchants mixed in the great traders' *souk* to barter and buy. Pearls, fish, frankincense, slaves, and myrrh resin for incense were common competitors in the great market. Ali traded the last of her godfather's tin and his other slaves for goods from across the Indian sea.

The old pirate shrugged and stepped to his new master's side. Kyrin nodded to him. He would find a good position as a guard with the martial knowledge Tae had taught him. Ali accepted the first of his payment, a sack of seed pearls from the old pirate's buyer. The buyer growled, "Take care of those pearls, they are the best out of Salala. You are blessed of Allah that my ship stopped here this morn instead of next sunrise in Makkah."

So shipping ran from here to Makkah, on the Red Sea? It was good. A good place to lose herself—if she was running. Looking at the old pirate's back left Kyrin with a strange feeling. She was the last strand of a knot of three: she and Tae and Alaina. And without the other slaves to distract Umar she must doubly conceal her growing womanhood.

Four days from Shishur, Kentar shepherded the caravan around a grey-white expanse that extended beyond Kyrin's sight. Dry mud curled at the edges of glittering sheets of salt. Tae's face crinkled as he squinted against the sun. "Kentar says the liquid earth under that crust swallowed a hunting party last spring. There is less danger now, at the end of the dry season." Umar looked over his shoulder. Tae grinned at him.

Umar snorted. "Only one such as you might dare this place of devils."

Tae shrugged. "If the need was great." He was cheerful the rest of the afternoon.

Beyond the salt flats, the Oman mountains rose, more rugged than any Kyrin had seen. Their western roots struck sheer, their heads soared sharp. Some purpled in the shadows of their brethren, while other bare heights blazed with fire under the falling sun. All were seamed by water and wind.

Tae glanced at Kyrin. "Those mountains cradle hills and deep, fruitful wadis. Ali has his house in one of them, away from the wet, hot summer shore. We are a day or so from there."

She nodded and nibbled on a finger. The mountains were cooler, then. And they and the hills at their feet could hide her.

The seventh dawn out from Shishur, Ali sent a messenger ahead to prepare his household. The sun beat at the caravan by terce bell, the third hour. Kentar called a halt to rest, and the Nubian and Umar escorted Ali's litter underneath some nearby palms. They took their stand at either end, arms crossed, swords bare, still as statues.

Kyrin's lips twitched. Ali and his ceremony, even when there were none to see. When he did not feel the need to impress anyone with naked swords, the Nubian and Umar wore their scabbards. Walking about with a naked blade knocking against rock, wood, and leather dulled the edge. They must tire of sharpening them.

"Water!" Ali called querulously from behind the litter's closed curtains, and Umar sprang for the waterskin. But the Nubian was ahead of him. He grinned and lifted a thick arm, raising the waterskin in triumph.

Kyrin smothered her laugh and let Lilith wander toward the water, where the drivers tended their grateful charges. She never tired of watching the water slide down their gullets. Lilith could drink near as much as six oxen. She snuffled at the water and drank deep of the bubbling spring that wound around the palm trees' roots. When she finished, Kyrin urged her up the side of the ridge before them. They wouldn't stray too far ahead, for there might be raiders. But the ridge-top was near and she wanted to see the lay of the land. Walking the last slight incline with Lilith's rein looped over her arm, Kyrin topped the ridge and stopped in delight.

A wave of warmth undulated across scattered grass clumps, smelling of damp. The bittersweet tang lifted her kaffiyeh. Her thawb flapped about her ankles. Kyrin tilted her head back and walked under a thick-leaved tree, creaking under the warm rush, bright leaves rustling. Here the desert ended. Here was land that could be farmed.

In Cierheld's fields she had crumbled a spring clod, chill and dark on her toes, while her father followed the oxen with a bag of seed on his hip. Kyrin rubbed sweat from her nose. Her father would want to know how these people grew fruitful crops with so little rainfall. She would use her forced stay well, and bring him all she could learn.

Alaina's faint voice called Kyrin, and she turned back to watch the caravan struggle up the rocky hillside. At last Ali's litter swayed across the ridge-top, and Alaina joined her.

Peeping under clouds, afternoon spread rosy over the hills ahead, giving depth to tree-bark and every shrub and stone, lengthening shadows. The clouds piled higher as the caravan wended on.

They passed a village of mud huts high on the side of a terraced wadi. The people stared, the women pulling heavy black veils across their faces. The men inclined their heads when Ali lifted a hand as they passed. The Nubian watched the villagers, while Umar ignored everyone, watching ahead. Kyrin rubbed her throat, where her skin itched under the necklace. She noted that no one's eyes quite met Umar's.

Melons and grain and trees of many kinds grew about the village in patches of green, bounded by short walls of stone. Her mouth watered at the variety: peaches, pomegranates, apples, and dates; millet, oats, and barley. There were trees she could not distinguish, for branch and leaf blent with the land.

On the far side of the village the dusty path broadened into a track and climbed out of the wadi, along the ridge, down and up again. Camels lifted their heads and men quickened their steps; a ripple passed down from the head of the caravan to Tae.

He drew a quiet breath and patted his camel's neck, instantly watchful. Kyrin's smile faltered. Umar and the Nubian closed up on Ali, tightening their sashes, checking that sword and dagger angled just so. The drivers beat dust from their thawbs and straightened their kaffiyehs.

At Tae's nod, Kyrin eased Lilith back beside Alaina. She tucked her unwashed hair under her dusty kaffiyeh, wishing they were not so grimy, and that she carried Truthseeker on her arm. Cicero trailed at Lilith's heels, tongue hanging out.

At the front, Ali's litter dropped out of sight. Kyrin came to the edge of the wadi descent.

Below the switchback that descended to cut through the middle, the valley ran roughly north-south. After a rocky drop high at the south end, the wadi descended in a few terraces. Everywhere was green, gold-touched and rich in the lowering sun. At the wadi bottom, a ribbon of water wound through grass and lonely shrubs.

An arrow-shot beyond the water, Ali's house lay high above on a wide bench of land safe from flood on the west side of the wadi. There, red tiles roofed a single-story dwelling of many parts. Enclosed by a gate, the open end of the U shaped house faced south. An inner court divided the long east and west wings. An extensive low building joined them at the north end, with two small courts nestled behind it.

It was nothing like home, the strongholds Kyrin knew. Instead of the Eagle towers of her godfather's stronghold, trees raised proud heads inside the stone walls around the house and the main court in the center. There was a curious configuration about the west wing: part of it stuck out in a way unlike the symmetrical east wing. It seemed out of place. As out of place as herself. Was that how Shema would see her? Kyrin's hand shook.

Lilith know nothing of looming fears, and so followed the road. The house disappeared behind the north wall as it rose toward them. The road had become a track of packed earth, imbedded with leaves and grass. Harvested grain fields extended on either side. Date palms marked an orchard boundary, running away from the house in a straight line west.

From the inner court, orange fruits flashed among the tops of the trees, and the perfume of apples tickled Kyrin's nose. No watering ditches led to the house or fields from the upper wadi stream that she could trace. The irrigation system was underground, or Ali had extensive springs.

Alaina sighed beside her. There were tears in her eyes. Kyrin smiled, short and weak.

Cicero dropped his nose and sniffed the prints of his own kind among horse droppings that beaded a path to a door in the wall, the back of the second smaller court she'd seen.

Ali said something to Umar with a laugh, and Umar dismounted. "Dalil!" he cried. "Take them in." Salukis barked high and sharp, echoing from the kennel on the other side of the wall, and Cicero perked up his ears.

Kentar gathered the drivers and pack camels, who followed him through the door to the stables. Kyrin began to cry after Kentar that she wished him and his daughters well, but Umar's face forbade her. She closed her mouth. She would find Kentar later. If he did not hire immediately with another caravan, she would make him a gift.

Ali switched Munira's hide, urging her to along the east wall and down round toward the south gate. Kyrin dismounted with the others, holding Lilith's rope tightly. Shrubs and vines almost buried the pale stone of the arch on either side.

Few doors in Araby opened to the outside world, but there would be many opening inward on the beauty of the main court. Shema's court. There was the life of the house. Kyrin's hand tightened on the haft of the falcon dagger.

There was bird-chatter, and the warning call of a parrot within. A voice carried faint from the stables, but nothing else before Ali nodded. The gate opened silently ahead of her master.

Kyrin glimpsed greenery and trickling water behind a boy who stood with his hand on the wood portal. There might be a bath for her and Alaina this night, and a rug. Shema might have a soft touch and a softer voice. Or there might be hard stone to sleep on and an empty belly.

Ali clapped his hands, with an expansive smile. Kyrin jumped. "Come, leave the beasts." He nudged Munira through the gate. Behind her master's litter, Tae and the Nubian lifted their heads from a low conversation, and the Nubian beckoned to Kyrin and Alaina. Tae dismounted to follow Ali within.

Kyrin looked back at the gate. Three beasts such as Munira would fit through the heavy portal side by side. If it were shut and guarded, there would be no entrance or exit. These walls would shut out the stars.

Kyrin forced her chin up and called after the Nubian, "Lilith, where does she go?"

"I take her, you find later." He pointed toward the gate. "You go in, now."

The Nubian would keep his word. She did not have to fear for Lilith. Why did she feel alone and cold? Cicero whined. With a farewell rub on his warm, comforting head, Kyrin urged him toward the Nubian. "Go, Cicero, follow!" and hurried after Tae to help Alaina with Ali's things. If she was not swift to obey, Ali would be even quicker with a blow. And Shema would be watching.

Kyrin stepped under the pale stone of the gate arch—and almost forgot Ali's hard hand.

Flowers such as she had never seen, huge blooms of vibrant color, climbed and nodded and stood guard around a wide pave of crimson flags. The red flags enclosed a pool. A fig tree towered from an island in the midst. Six slaves lying across the water could touch the bulrushes growing at the far edge, attended by lilies. The water smelled sweet and good, she could smell it where she stood. A frog sprang from a lily pad, down into shifting shades of mossy green, his body a blaze of yellow flame.

Kyrin let out her breath. It was Eden after the desert, but Ali must not catch her moon-gazing. Nor must Shema. She looked up, and her throat closed.

Offerings

Enter the house, give it your greeting. . . . ~ Matthew 10:12

The slaves of the house had gathered at the end of the colonnade along the west wing. Silent men in one line, and women in the other, ready to greet Ali Ben Aidon with peace on his way to his door. Shema was not there, at least, no lady such as those Kyrin had seen richly dressed and vested.

The deep blue thawb of the closest household man hung on his gaunt, stooped frame, bound with a red sash, but the rest of the men and women wore earth colors: cream, white, ocher, burnt orange, and brown. They were clean, even those slaves called from the fields, their callused feet, hands, and hair wet from washing. Most of the men were bareheaded, some with oiled beards.

Flower scents drifted from the veiled women. All wore veils of light material but for one in the middle of the line. By her bulk and stained brown thawb she was the cook. Her bowl-cropped pepper and salt hair hung to her shoulders. The skin of her heart-shaped face reminded Kyrin of spice cake with cloves. Her raisin-dark eyes were elongated by kohl above a strong nose. One of her ear lobes had been sliced away. She eyed Kyrin and her companions, her eyebrows drawn heavily together, her generous mouth tight.

What did she look for, a slave to haul wood for her hot oven? A cropped ear like hers meant accident or shame. Her short hair made shame a better guess, an old shame, since she had advanced to the place of cook. Those around her gave her room. Kyrin moved closer to Tae, and the Nubian passed them on his way to their master.

Ali's trembling peacock feather in his white turban completed his blue-robed splendor. He pulled himself up in his litter, and the Nubian linked his hands for his descent, his muscled arms gnarled as dark oaken roots. Ali stepped to the flags. After a glance around for Umar, who had not returned, he motioned the Nubian to lead the way to the house. His bodyguard straightened, smiling a little. He inclined his head toward Kyrin briefly, and she smiled back, uncertain. Why did the Nubian look like he'd won a prize?

Sandals whispered. Umar was at her side. Kyrin moved to step away but he seized her arm, his dark stare ordering her to stand still. Kyrin held as motionless as Tae on her other side while Umar glared at the Nubian, who preceded Ali with his back straight, his head high.

Ali grinned as Umar's challenging glance caught every slave in the court and they straightened one by one. Except for the very old and the very young, the women bowed their veiled heads and the men's eyes slid away from Umar's. The cook sighed.

The gaunt older man bowed to Umar, whose red sash was twin to his. Kyrin's brow furrowed. No one else wore the color of blood.

Tae stared ahead, expressionless. With a satisfied curve about his mouth, Umar gripped Kyrin's arm tighter. She winced, and stilled her instinct to pull away. The burn scar had not weakened his hand.

The cook sniffed. Attentive to his master's wish, the Nubian waited for Ali who examined his slaves closely as he passed, and both ignored Umar.

Kyrin gritted her teeth. Umar used her in some matter of the house, in a struggle for position, the son of a hyena. Tae did nothing—so it was as well she did not. Her arm hurt, but no movement would betray her. She fingered the edge of her kaffiyeh with her free hand, wishing she could pull it across her dust-coated face and conceal herself from the household eyes fastened on them.

Ali ended Umar's skirmish of wills. "As salaam alaykum," he cried with a broad smile, beaming around the court. His household chorused, "And with you be peace!"

In the following burst of movement and chattering voices, Ali raised his brows at Umar, smooth as a snake uncoiling, and Umar bowed and said, "Your lady Shema awaits your pleasure."

"Aahh, your words are honeyed milk to one weary from the desert." Ali's shoulders relaxed. He indicated Kyrin. "Let the worthless one bring in what is mine." With a wave for the Nubian to preceed him, Ali turned toward the colonnade and the door.

The Nubian raised his arm and led the shout that rang from every throat, "The House of Ben Aidon is merciful and great!" and strode before Ali, his muscles rippling. Umar's smile at the Nubian's back did not go beyond his bared teeth, and he released Kyrin's arm with a sharp twist. She refused to rub it.

The cook frowned, sharp eyes going over Kyrin again from head to toe. Kyrin met her gaze, raising her chin. She could not help the cook—she had often burned her mother's plum cakes. The cook's eyes widened then abruptly narrowed. She glanced at Ali, and then at Umar, lips thinning.

Kyrin clenched her fist against the ice of fear spreading within. What did the cook guess her kaffiyeh hid? Rigid, Kyrin walked toward Ali's bags, her jaw tight. Someday Umar would not dare touch her. Nor any who loved blood. She would conquer the ice, and she would not forget the Nubian's kindness. She stared after him as he opened the double-leaved wood door for their master and followed him inside. A sigh passed over the court.

Kyrin glanced back. The south gate behind her was shut. The building at the north end and along the east side shared a wall. No colonnade there. A door and two windows graced the north end, where kitched platters clattered. A man lounged in a stark doorway in the east wing, his bisht over his arm, hair wet. So, those were the men's quarters. After that, the wall ran south to the barred gate.

Kyrin reached for two of Ali's rolled rugs in his heap of baggage and paused.

Before the first pillar of the colonnade, a young man grinned and poked his sister. Dusky hair curled against her graceful neck. She dropped her veil and wrinkled her nose at him with a grin of her own. He laughed and darted down the colonnade, across the breezeway between the house and kitchen, and strutted out of sight around the corner.

Where he disappeared beyond the breezeway, two smaller gates rose. One must lead to the stable court. The other surely did not lead to escape.

The girl's mother reached after her, with a worried glance at Umar. The girl stuck out her tongue after her brother then smoothed her veil back over her face. Umar pretended not to notice. Kyrin squashed her grin.

Here were two near her years who were not at all afraid of Umar. Her smile fell away. The courtyard was a small, beautiful cage. Her legs ached to run—she hungered abruptly for the sky. Behind her in the southeast corner of the men's quarters and the wall, a young olive with silver-shadowed leaves grew below a vibrant orange tree. A carved horse head poured a stream of water into a blue-tiled basin between their mossy roots. But the great gate—a man stood in the sun-shaft between the trees near the gate; the boy who had opened it was gone.

Umar nodded to the gate guard, who looked at her. The man rested his hand on his dagger and inclined his head. There would be no place for riding or her nomad bow here.

Ali would send a hunter who knew these hills for his meat. Maybe the brother who teased his sister had snares for rabbits, and Ali would hire him and others to catch his fleet mountain reem. Kyrin seized one of Ali's dusty bags and opened it with a yank, as if it were an enemy she gutted, then set out her master's slippers in a neat row.

Whispers rose behind the women's veils. Kyrin shrugged. The cook watched her thoughtfully. Kyrin's back stiffened. A slight woman in black with a blue veil whisked forward to pick up a bundle of Ali's thawbs Kyrin set out next. Her thin, wrinkled arms held her load firmly. A sapphire glinted on her bony hand. A slave, with such a ring? Kyrin snapped her awed mouth shut.

At Umar's order the other slaves dispersed in various directions, and a man escorted Munira to grazing, while others hauled Ali trade goods through the breezeway and the storeroom door opposite the kitchens. The women descended on Ali's bags, chattering among themselves. Kyrin looked at them. Would they even listen to one strange to them, or understand?

Umar pointed, and Kyrin rose and followed the old woman with the ring toward the door. She gave the girl who chased away her brother a wry smile.

A leggy rosebush with yellowing, toothed leaves snagged Kyrin from the edge of the court. Limping up the steps under the colonnade, she reached down to rub her stinging ankle. Someone bumped her from behind. When she turned, the girl leaped back and bowed her head in apology. Kyrin nodded, with a reassuring smile, and stumbled inside Ali's house. The girl feared her.

The old woman slid her feet out of her sandals and dropped them at the end of a row along the wall. Kyrin brushed off her dusty feet with one hand. She liked her sandals off when she rode Lilith, at this moment they were in her bags. The old woman shook her head with a snort.

Kyrin lifted her chin. A favored concubine's disdain could not compel her. Only her master's word. Her mouth twisted, and she looked away from the woman. Lamps lit the stone room.

It was rather like Cierheld's entryway except there were no murder holes over her head or in the walls, nothing but a long approach that would narrow an attack to two doorways, one at a right angle to the other, some distance apart. Tae would approve.

On her right the plain lintel gave onto a broad passage and many lamp-lit doorways. In front of her a heavy bas-relief arch was framed by high blue curtains. Did the blue conceal a curious west room, out of place under the tiled roof she had seen from the road?

She directed her feet toward the passage after the woman, her eyes still on the thick arch. Carved reapers, gathering sheaves from a field of pale stone, shouted to her that the Eagles had been here. Or that Ali had hired an artisan to copy their work. Were there no places but men's hearts that the Eagles' had not conquered? No doubt Ali thought himself great beside those ancient masters of the known world.

The fourth doorway down on the left, the concubine stalked into a sleeping room off the passage. She laid her load of thawbs on a bed. Ali's bed sat on a wood frame with a motif of crossed swords carved on the sides. The old woman smoothed the elegant embroidery around the neck of the top thawb, her fingers lingering in wonder.

Kyrin caught her lip between her teeth. Alaina would never rest once the women learned she had embroidered most of Ali's thawbs. Kyrin half-smiled, but her hands suddenly trembled. There were too many people in this place. She wanted to be somewhere—anywhere—alone. Without stifling stone shutting her up with weary fears and desperate hopes. Her throat thickened. She could not get out, she would never get out. Kyrin bowed her head and breathed deep, shuddering.

The woman looked at her sharply, and Kyrin stumbled back a step. "I am Qadira." The old woman spun her about. "What torments you? This is no moment to rest. Go, go, our master's task must be finished." With a flowing torrent of chatter, she shooed Kyrin out, past Ali's wood paneled door, for more of his things. Kyrin found she could breathe again. The sweetness of rosewater was less heavy here. Her thoughts must go to the Master of the stars, her fears to be bound, her hopes to rise with a falcon's strength.

Most of the other rooms along the passage had curtains across their doorways, but there was one solid door near the entryroom, and another across from Ali's paneled door. Was that one Shema's?

Kyrin shivered. Her mistress must not take her from Alaina. Would Shema let them keep Cicero? And Lilith? Kyrin hugged her middle. *Walk, breathe, just a few more steps. You will get out. Ali will feast soon. Surely he will let us rest a little before he gifts me to Shema.*

She paused. A mosaic spiraled down the passage under her feet, a blue-green vine with a bird of prey at each end. More of the Eagles' work.

Alaina approached with her arms full, and frowned at Kyrin.

Kyrin mumbled, "I must go finish," and fled. In the paved court she retrieved a glazed red bottle of Ali's frankincense and his last bag. She straightened with a grunt. It was heavy, a bag of foodstuffs, maybe. Outside the gate with his back to it, the guard held a torch, yet unlit. The clouds closed in around the setting sun.

Someone tugged at the bag in Kyrin's hand, and she spun. The cook lifted it, her eyes snapping. Kyrin sighed and released the bag, grateful not to carry the leaden weight. She inclined her head in cautious thanks.

The woman bore a necklet, a pair of wings with an eye between them. The eye of Horus. Without a word, the Egyptian slung the bag over her shoulder and bore it toward the kitchen.

Kyrin lagged behind the rest of the women who pressed through Ali's door in a flocking gaggle, eyes bright above their half-veils.

The blue curtains at the end of the long entry room pulled at Kyrin. She stopped, her fingers tight on the bottle of frankincense. The women's voices echoed in the passage.

Arab women, spineless creatures. Kyrin grimaced and slipped between the undulating curtains. The panels of silk rustled together behind her.

Under her toes was a huge blue petal of a mosaic flower. The other four petals gently cupped the floor around her. Kyrin stepped off the petal hurriedly. Surely such beauty was not meant for stepping on?

Blue water-stones set close together formed the graceful petals, with stamens of glittering black gravel, forever still. But there was more. On each side of the flower a row of empty rugs and cushions stretched far to her right across the grey floor that shone with a slight sheen. Ten pillars supported the arched roof, while four at each end enclosed the temple of quiet that began at her feet. The pillars made a walk that encircled all.

Water murmured. Very near, just beyond the first seat of the double row of cushions running up the room, a marble hunter poised beside a small tree with lacy leaves. His bow sank in his hand as a fountain sang in his ears, the water sparkling as it left the shadows.

The stalking hunter's brows pulled over his eyes as if he listened for an elusive call. He never moved, crouched above the sweet, low speech of water about his feet, intent. What he hunted must be worth listening for.

Gold and silver light touched the cataract as it poured over his sandals. Kyrin wanted to trail her fingers in it, touch his feet, but dared not. But for the water, all was quiet and still. The tree raised its branches as high as the hunter's head, reaching for the last tracery of sun-glow streaming through high, fretted windows above. The hunter's pale body glistened, patterned with fretwork shadows that made his mouth seem to smile. Mottled green, red, and orange leaves drifted on the water. Kyrin shivered. The air from the windows was storm cold, cold as snow. But this place was far from dead. It was full of peace.

Was this a place for counsel? Did Ali sit here often? The light in the windows faded, leaving the hunter a statue. Kyrin turned away. It was but well-formed rock. Why then did she sigh?

She sighed again and shrugged. Her day had been long. Ali's perfume warmed in her hands; she could smell it. She must go soon, in one moment more. What *did* Ali do here? She tiptoed past the silken cushions toward the farthest four pillars, leaving the hunter.

At the end of the row of bright-dyed cushions, a low table rose even with her knees, opposite a great chair of black wood. Two of the four pillars flanked its carved sides and two guarded the back. Her master did not leave himself unprotected. Wise of him. But the pillars could hide an enemy or his guards.

Laughter came from beyond the blue curtains. Kyrin darted to a pillar. It was gritty under her fingers, and the bottle tinked against the stone. The curtains did not move. Blood beat in Kyrin's hand against the pillar. It was gritty and cold under her fingers.

A warm breath fluttered in her ear.

Kyrin spun, cracking her hand painfully on the stone.

"Beautiful." Alaina stood on tiptoes, staring past her at the statue in the dimness.

"Alaina!" Kyrin rubbed her stinging knuckles.

"Ali wants us."

Kyrin blinked. "Does he?"

But the hunter never gave up. Yet could he mistake the truth? Did the call he heard ever whisper of things not true? Would she ever see Cierheld? Her father was so far away . . . there were so many things between.

She followed Alaina back past the table, stepped around the blue flower, and slid through the curtains—to collide with a white-robed body. She jerked her head up, holding the bottle before her helplessly—she must not break it.

Umar's jaw knotted. He cuffed her, a lightning blow to the ear. "Put that away and find the cook! You will serve our master's table."

Kyrin fell back and steadied herself against the wall, her ears ringing. Umar had a thin, rolled tapestry under his arm. Orange and black, and a blazing eye. The tiger.

"You will be . . . a costly gift of the house of Ali Ben Aidon to its mistress. See that you show your worth." He strode through the blue curtains.

Kyrin let out her breath in a hard rush and scowled. It was a threat, with a thread of something else—but she had yet to see a murdering Arab who could *ask* for anything. Rubbing her ear, she hurried down the passage behind Alaina, who skittered ahead.

Past Ali's room and the other wooden door, the passage ended in a storeroom. On the far side another door beckoned. They went through it—and found the open breezeway and the kitchen on the other side, filled with echoes, good smells, and busy slaves.

Beyond the circle of light in the breezeway the court was dark. Ceaseless voices, laughing and demanding, clattered in Kyrin's ears. She followed Alaina uncertainly and looked inside the kitchen. The girl who pinched her brother stood just inside the door, next to a shelf of oil lamps, reaching for a lamp she wanted.

Kyrin kept her voice low. "What is your name?"

The girl startled, but her surprise rippled into delight. No sign of fear now. "I'm Nimah. You just came; are you like me or like my brother? You both wear clothes like Zoltan, but cook says you are like me." Nimah took in their dirt-caked toes, streaked thawbs, and the lank hair slipping from Alaina's kaffiyeh. "You'll get whipped, you're dirty." Her eyes caught again on Alaina's tangled gold hair, and the force of her thinking curiosity made a wrinkle between her eyes.

Alaina smiled at Nimah. "Umar sent us to find the cook. Can you tell us where to wash? Do we use the horse fountain near the gate? And where is our room? "

"You know nothing, do you? You are so *brown*. You will be whipped many times," Nimah said. Alaina's smile faltered and heat crept over Kyrin's face.

"Come, I will show you your room *and* the pool." As if she had not just insulted them, Nimah took a lamp from the shelf, smiling, and grabbing Kyrin's hand, pulled her outside. Laughter welled in Kyrin's throat. Their small informer was not so young as she seemed.

Their room was the one with the wooden door at the south end of the passage. It was square, big enough for two withe beds of the kind her father made. There were no beds, but three thick rugs with blankets for each of them. Kyrin saw Tae's bag, his stick and sword leaning against the wall.

"Are you married to the hakeem?" Nimah's eyes were big with question.

Kyrin looked sideways at Alaina. "Yes—"

"No." Alaina pulled off her kaffiyeh. "Or our Master says we are, but we're too young. I might tell you more sometime." Kyrin was sure Alaina blushed, though her cheeks were so golden in the lamp-light it was impossible to tell.

Nimah nodded. "Nara says the hakeem is the only man in the house, besides Umar and our master." She turned to their saddle-bags that had been left on their rugs.

Ali tested Tae on all sides. Kyrin's chest tightened. "Where does the Nubian sleep?"

Nimah gaped at her. "He is not all of a man. He guards us at night, and sleeps across the doorway on his rug, near our master's room." She brightened. "Could—could I see your robes? The ones our master gives you to serve in are so blue they glisten. And your veil—my mother's does not show her eyes when she goes out. She says it makes her hot. I cannot go out. I may only help Nara cook and serve tea." Nimah looked down and her voice was wistful.

From her bag Alaina pulled the half-veil and pale serving robes that she had fashioned at Ali's word. "If you find the cloth I can make you some like mine—if I am allowed, after we are accustomed to things here."

"Oh, will you?" Worship glowed in Nimah's face. "My master will let me wear them soon, if they are as beautiful as yours."

"We will *never* get 'accustomed to things here,'" Kyrin muttered, jerking her robes out of her own bag and knotting her half-veil around them. She slipped the falcon dagger under her rug then slung her veil and robe bundle over her shoulder, ignoring her skinned hand. "Where now?"

They crossed the breezeway and cold pavement and slipped through the unknown gate. Into a shadowed garden. In what Nimah called the women's pool, Kyrin and Alaina took a hasty dip. The water was warm. Kyrin had no moment to look around, for Nimah covered her lamp while they bathed, and then they went back to the kitchen.

Nimah skipped through the swirling women and the other girls to the large ovens looming against the back wall on either side of the fireplace. The cook turned, hands on her hips, her short hair sliding from behind her misshapen ear. She glanced at Kyrin and Alaina and raised her spoon, gazing across the end at them with a frown. Making up her mind, she pointed the scepter of her domain toward a counter laden with trays. "Take those to our master in the blue room."

Nimah walked back to them with a platter of rice and lamb and one of almond cakes. She gave them to Kyrin. They were heavy.

"The room with the blue curtains, that is the Blue Flower room?"

"Yes. You noticed the flower? Wait inside the door until Umar lifts his hand for you to come. He gets angry if you do not see his first call, so keep him in your eye. Our master has a guest, Sirius Abdasir. Don't look in his eyes."

"I won't make him angry—I mean, I will watch." Kyrin bit her lip. What a fool she sounded.

"There's a platter for you, too," Nimah said to Alaina, and darted back to the counter. Kyrin eyed the steaming, spiced rice with succulent meat underneath that she held. She could eat it all, and the cakes—what did they taste like? Her nose tickled awake. Vanilla, almonds, honey, cloves—and cinnamon.

Her father had liked to suck bits of the bark. Her mother used the warm spice for her best apple tarts. It cost much, but she always managed to have a bit about the kitchen for father. The lamps affixed to the kitchen walls wavered into orange blots. Kyrin wiped her eyes against her shoulder. The platters would not get warmer. And Ali waited. Was Shema with him?

25

Ploys

If the house is worthy, let your ... peace come upon it. ~Matthew 10:13

Kyrin jumped at the swish of another slave's feet, gripping her platter hard, and peered behind her. There was nothing under the passage lamps. She sternly told herself falcons were not taken unaware by echoes or anything else. Their keen eyes, hearing, and sense of smell told them of enemies before they drew near. She came to the Blue Flower room and slipped inside the curtains, stepping to the side of the door.

At the end of the room and left of Ali in his great chair, a woman sat at the knee-high table, her feet curled under her. Beneath a black veil, Shema sat silent and still, her form slight in a grey robe. Kyrin gaped. On a wadi hillside she would resemble one of the rocks. But maybe that was her purpose, to avoid notice.

Umar sat on Ali's right hand. Beside him sat a guest with a long face, blander than the stone pillars but for his mouth upturned in slightest amusement. His dark eyes saw everything and everyone. His lips curved, and he watched under the cover of his smile. His fine black bisht was trimmed in gold and draped a green-robed shoulder brushed by dark hair, straight as an arrow. It was clipped, with a well-oiled thick curl at the ends that

305

contradicted a small bald spot. His smooth, sure movements re-minded Kyrin of lords she had known.

His indifference was that of a wolf, a sated wolf at present. Sirius Abdasir. From his name and features, he carried Greek blood in his ancestry, and his long form hinted at the fleetness of the desert Arab. There was nothing weak about him. She must not look at him. A golden hunter.

Kyrin raised her head and her breath froze in her throat. The tapestry of the tiger had been fastened on the wall above Ali's chair. Within the shadow of the pillars, seeming to pace behind her master, the beast waited its chance.

May it not hunt me tonight. I will wake screaming. That will not gain my mistress's favor. She would not think of it—and there would be no dreams. Her stomach growled.

Ali or Umar would call her soon, for the rice and lamb she held in front of the thinner dish of almond cakes in her tiring arms, cooled. Though she would be happy to eat any of it con-gealed, hot, or dug from under a handspan of snow. But it was too warm for snow in this land. And there was so much food on the low table.

Fruit was piled before Ali in a lacquered Persian bowl. Closer to Kyrin, dishes of goat, roast chicken, and soup steamed. Alaina and Nimah joined her, taking up places on the other side of the arch. Umar motioned them forward, but waved Kyrin back when she moved to follow.

Her face burned. Was her veil not straight, or had she missed a bit of dirt or mussed her hair?

Alaina presented her bowl of dates to Ali, while Nimah set a jug of tea near the fruit bowl. Kyrin shifted her feet. Her plat-ters were lead, her arms on fire. At last Umar lifted his hand imperiously, and she walked to kneel carefully between him and

Ali. Her gaze shifted between them, for she was not used to looking for Umar's command rather than Ali's.

On her blue rug on the far side of the fruit bowl, Shema reached for a date, her hand and wrist delicate, her veil hiding her face. Kyrin extended her dish of almond cakes a little further, but Shema made no move toward it.

Ali nudged his wife with his foot. "If you are well, O moon of my desert, eat. It is the hour to rejoice and savor the fruit of our labors." His voice was quiet acid.

Shema's head lowered and she shrank into her grey robes. Ali lifted fragrant rice and meat to his plate from Kyrin's dish, rolled it in a ball, and tossed it in his mouth, chewing with relish.

The Nubian was not in the room. Ali must feel safe enough with Umar alone to guard. Though Umar sat without a visible weapon he would have a dagger or two on him, under his bisht perhaps. He ignored Kyrin. On Umar's other side, Ali's guest held a date, nibbling, still with that amused smile.

Kyrin eased the meat platter onto the table with one hand, careful she did not bump the pitcher of tea Umar had shoved toward her, or the cup near the guest's plate. The man left his date in his mouth and reached. He touched the back of her hand with one finger. Kyrin stifled the impulse to hit him. He was a guest—who touched the female slave of another. His rich robes, his daring, stank of power.

She blinked, and glanced at Ali. His eyes hooded, giving nothing. Running prey drew the hunter. She must attack. Kyrin reached for the pitcher of tea, but the man waggled his cup. No more. Kyrin set the jug down, disengaging, and slid silently back from the table.

Ali's cheeks wore dusky red, but before he could open his mouth the raven-haired man said softly, "Forgive me, my host. It was but a little sport." His eyes were satisfied, the lamp-light reflecting in them in bright points. His lips curved in perfect self-reproach.

After a sharp glance at him, Ali's face smoothed. At length he nodded. "There is nothing to forgive."

Kyrin's hands tightened again on her platter of cakes. Men often glanced at her, whether they saw the uneven white scar beneath her necklace or not. And they stared always at Ali's black earring in her ear, a dark contrast to her bronze slave ring. Sirius looked at neither.

Ali leaned back with a belch and wiped his mouth with a cloth. "As you can see, my slaves are free born. I train them to have correct manners and the finest minds. When I break a slave, I train a hissing, screaming eyas. It learns who feasts it, and then it comes to possess a warmth of affection, even a kind of love, for its master. This worthless one"—he indicated Kyrin—"looked to my hand when you regarded her."

The unyielding silver hurt Kyrin's fingers. There was warning for her in Ali's voice, in his flattened mouth and flushed face. Feel warmth for *him*, that pale eel who stole her life—never.

"Her sister is a golden flower from the north, but this one contains the spirit of the desert, despite her scarred throat. She holds a rare skill. My hakeem teaches her and the golden one. They will be the talk of Baghdad, trained in the fighting art of the East."

Ali raised his hand to meditate on his tea in his cup. He stared past it at his guest. "My hakeem is a slave with healing in his hands, but he holds that most rare jewel in a warrior's body. You will have the pleasure of seeing him perform, O guardsman of the caliph, since you savor the intricate art of war." Ali sipped at his tea.

From the doorway came a muffled clunk. Shema's veiled head turned, and Kyrin followed her gaze. The curtain billowed where Alaina had knocked her platter against the door in her swift retreat.

The caliph's guardsman regarded his host with a pleasant smile, not indicating he noticed. Kyrin shifted. Sirius Abdasir was one to be careful of. Alaina was well out of the room.

"Ah yes, slaves." The guardsman waved his hand, dismissive. "My Kef guided you on your task, and bore you on my ship until your feet could not stay from home, from the apple of your eye." He indicated Shema without looking at her, and stroked his chin with thumb and finger. "And yet have you found a man in the far north with the knowledge to change silver for the caliph? No? My eyes darken. No news of the traveler?"

Ali said nothing, his mouth screwed up in pained regret. Kyrin grinned behind her veil. He looked like her father's purser when her father asked money of him.

"My soul sighs for you, my brother. A merchant so skilled ought not to return without equal trade. It cannot be that the disfavor of Allah rests on you, not on one whose excellence is so often proven." Sirius smiled. "When might we see this slave's dazzling skill?" His ironic voice sent ants up Kyrin's back. What did the guardsman play at, with his interest?

Ali said, aggrieved, "I beg you, O most estimable Sirius, to honor my house when your days permit. Your words are gems of truth, but the hakeem must deem this one and her sister ready. It is a most rare fighting art. Their readiness will repay you thrice."

"Ahh," Sirius said, "I wait on your wisdom with impatience."

Ali smiled. "I will not disappoint our worthy master—or your most virtuous trust."

Ali touched Shema's shoulder. She twitched away, and he chuckled. "My quiet one is a desert mouse, soft and busy, un-usual among women. She seeks glorious fruit for my house."

Shema bent her veiled head, her breath sucking the cloth in and out rapidly. Kyrin curled her fist at her side. Umar crooked his finger at her, and indicated Shema's empty plate. Kyrin slid a honey almond cake onto it.

Strange that Umar considered Ali's wife. Stranger still, Ali took no notice.

Shema ate while Ali talked with the men. Her hands moved in short darts, as if they feared to be caught, and drew her food behind her veil. Dark lines wound about her fingers. When her plate was empty, Ali motioned for Kyrin to come and kneel before them. Kyrin bowed to the floor. Heavy with minute flower designs of dark henna, Shema's thin, child-like fingers retreated to her lap.

Over Kyrin's head Ali pronounced, "This is my wife, Shema. Flawed as you are, worthless one, you will be worthy of my generosity when you bear us a son of a warrior."

Kyrin lifted her face enough to see Shema. His generosity? Shema wanted a gift he would never give. And no woman wanted another woman's son.

Cradling a pearl, the silver circles of a double ring bit deep into Shema's white finger. Her hands clenched on her knees. In the quiet room, water trickled around the hunter: touching, giving, its offered treasure unnoticed.

Shema said no word. She smelled of mint, not flowers. Reaching out, she touched Kyrin's forehead with one finger. It was so cold it burned. Kyrin slithered on her knees in retreat, so low she bumped her nose.

"So it is done. Do not keep your nectar too late from the bee." Ali dipped his hands in a bowl of fragrant water Nimah held for him. He rose, and turned to Sirius. "On my journey I learned much of trade—and of winds of change across the desert. My bargains were blessed. I will speak further in your ear."

Sirius nodded gravely. Umar stood with him.

There was a whisper of cloth at the door. A large black arm pulled aside the blue curtains. The Nubian entered and stood at attention.

There was blue at his collar, and a white sash bound his black trousers. His sword and dagger gleamed. Kentar slipped inside past him. His thawb yet bore traces of the desert.

Sirius raised an eyebrow and walked down the room to greet him. Umar and Ali followed. Eying Sirius, Kentar bowed to the floor.

From her prostrate position, Kyrin stared. The dalil was a free man. Just who was this Sirius Abdasir?

A stinging slap out of nowhere rocked Kyrin to her heels. On her knees, Shema glowered at her, clutching her thick veil beneath her chin. Kohl was a heavy smear about her eyes. With a quiet sob, she drew her hand back again.

Treacherous Arab! Kyrin warded the blow, gripped to twist Shema's hand and drive her to the floor. She paused.

In Shema's eyes lay the broken shimmer of a torn soul—a slave's anger and despair.

Holding her mistress' hand harmless, Kyrin rolled beneath Shema, dragging her own veil aside, and lifted her chin to bare her throat. She stared up into Shema's face. *Understand—please.*

Surely the Nubian saw them, but Kyrin heard nothing but her master and the guardsman's quiet voices. Beside Ali's chair, Nimah shrank against the pillar. Her eyes darted from one to the other. Braced, Kyrin held Shema, yet leaving her throat open. *We bear the same chain.*

Shema shoved her veil impatiently behind her shoulder. Kyrin turned her head, waiting for the blow, the kick, the call for the whip. She could yet pull this Arab dog down and run. But she could not leave Tae and Alaina to suffer for her escape. And Ali crushed Shema before the caliph's guardsman, despising her in one fell stroke—*she seeks glorious fruit for my house*—while flaunting a slave who would bear a son she could not.

Crying silently, Shema yanked against her, panting. Kyrin dared lift her necklace, pull it aside in a last bid for common ground. Her throat worked as she remembered the blade. *Please.*

Shema sank to her heels, staring at Kyrin's throat, the back of her hand to her mouth in wild pain. Then her hands dropped in her lap, abandoned birds.

The Nubian's sword hilt clicked twice against the wall. Ali, deep in conversation with Sirius, was turning back up the long room toward the table.

Kyrin rolled onto her stomach and clasped Shema's wrist in abject supplication, and bit her lip on a wild, wry laugh. It was Shema's word, whether she was whipped. Kyrin swallowed hard.Her mistress' veil was in place, and she had not seen her move. Here was another woman born graceful as Myrna. With the thought her grip tightened on her mistress's wrist, and she forced her fingers to loosen. Shema squeezed back, gentle. Kyrin dared hope.

Sirius said, "Remember, the caliph has a wide hand toward his faithful servants. As salaam alayakum, my friend." And he kissed Ali on both cheeks.

"The pieces on the board must move, for the good of our master. In this, I am your servant, Sirius Abdasir."

Sirius went out, and Kentar followed. Ali stalked back to sink down in his cushioned chair. He eyed Shema and Kyrin wryly. Did he see ought, or suspect what had passed?

Kyrin bit her lip. Shema waved her hand over Kyrin in a gesture worthy of Ali. Her voice was low and smoky. "We need you no longer. You may go. Nimah will clear this." She flicked a hand at the table. "Come to me at dawn."

"Yes, my mistress." Kyrin did not dare ask which room.

Ali stared down at the table, his chin in his hand, allowing her dismissal. Kyrin bowed, slid backward on the floor a few paces, and rose, glad Umar had not seen her humiliation. She paused before the curtains. The Nubian remained motionless. Kyrin tilted her hand, hoping he knew sign and that her heart beat fast with thanks.

In their quarters, Kyrin pulled the half-veil from her face and collapsed on her rug. She pulled the blanket over her and scooted back against Alaina, who stirred uneasily.

It was warmer in the house than the desert nights, but the air was dead. Kyrin ran her fingers over the falcon under the edge of her rug, and stared into the shadows below the window at the tiny figure of Huen. Silent, still, moonlit, the dove springing from her hands. Kyrin remembered Shema and her pain. Did she study her revenge?

Then the shivers came. There had been many possibilities and intents in the Blue Flower room. Her head spun, and she felt tears coming. What game did she stumble into between the caliph's guardsman, Ali, and Umar, even the dalil? How did Ali serve Sirius Abdasir, who served the caliph?

Ali wanted something from the guardsman, and the guardsman demanded something Ali did not possess. As for Ali, he wanted Alaina, Tae, and herself for more than sons. A son was only the first face of his revenge.

Would she face the whip tomorrow and Shema's wrath, or would her mistress toy with her at leisure? She had looked quite out of her head. Was she the queen on Ali's board, his courtly chess piece, or his destroyer? *I would not be her enemy. Oh Father, I would not.*

Kyrin wiped her face. Her falcon dagger would not leave her side again. She would find Cicero and Lilith when the sun rose.

Surely the stables would be warm, with friendly faces. Tae's breathing was even on the other side of Huen, who seemed to smile at her. Kyrin's blanket warmed.

§

Something heavy landed on Kyrin's legs and bounced off. Her comforting cover vanished, and cold air washed around her. She rolled off her rug, scrabbling under the edge, and her fingers closed on the falcon. She blinked at a large figure before her.

The cook cried in a cheerful voice, "What a pair!" and tossed Kyrin and Alaina's wadded blankets from her large hand. Kyrin released the dagger and rubbed her face. Tae's neat place was empty.

"Wake up, girl!" The cook leaned over. In the grey light before the window she was large-boned as an elephant. She threw them each a blue thawb. Kyrin fingered hers. Such a sapphire hue would not last long in the kitchen.

"Call Master Ali 'Master' when he speaks, do not go near him unless you are clean, do not speak to anyone older than you are unless they question you, and do come get a bath and something to eat. I am Nara. I will show you about the kitchen, the garden, and the court. You will learn quickly. Come, ready yourselves! There are things to do!" Nara smiled, not at all out of breath.

Kyrin's mouth twitched. She kept back a laugh at Alaina's awed stare. Her sister seldom stood at the bottom of such a waterfall of words as Nara's deluge.

Kyrin straightened her rug and pulled her blanket smooth, her back to Nara, and slid the falcon into the folds of her bisht. Their quarters smelled of washed stone, sweet flowers, and Tae's herbs; not a trace of dust or smoke or sweat of dreams.

Nara led them down the passage, across the breezeway, and through the gate into the court of the women. A high wall enclosed it. Abundant vines sought the top of the walls, jade tendrils laden with a veil of white buds. Inside the wooden gate Alaina ran her fingers over the soft, new leaves with a smile.

The round pebbles lining the path were warm under Kyrin's feet. On her right, water splashed at knee level from a chipped ceramic spout into the large pool she had bathed in but seen little of on her first visit. There were flat sunning rocks along one oval edge. The last tension leaked out of Kyrin. Here were riches. Water, more precious then gold, living green rather than sand, and food, and others like herself. Here was life.

Water flowed from the pool into stone channels that bordered the court walls. One channel divided into runnels that nurtured the vegetables and herbs growing beside the west wall.

Nara ordered them to strip. Kyrin shifted the falcon to her serving thawb, praying Nara did not pick up the garment to scold her for its wrinkles like Aunt Medaen would. Kyrin splashed and spluttered in the morning chill of the pool, and at last Nara nodded her satisfaction at her scrubbing.

Kyrin stepped out quickly. Her blue thawb clinging to her with damp, she bundled her old thawb under her arm. Then she held still while Nara examined her head for biters. The cook cleaned and cut Kyrin's nails and trimmed her hair, evening the wisps about her face, broken by heat and cold and numberless tucks behind her ears. Nara's curt, darting way reminded Kyrin of a mother hen. The cook finished at last and cocked her head, her hands on her hips. At her urging, Kyrin stood beside the pool with Alaina, who had undergone the same treatment, and stared into the water. Her reflection stared back.

A ripple waved Kyrin's sleek, wet hair around her tanned face. Her chin remained sharp, her eyes wide-set. Her mouth was thinner than she remembered, and she lifted a finger to her black earring. The water twisted her face into a gargoyle's, left her serious and dark beside Alaina's pleased smile.

The blue thawb fell graceful to Alaina's ankles, and she filled it with beauty. But the serving blue sheathed Kyrin quite straight from shoulder to toe. The ridges of the pale star at the base of her throat rose where the skin puckered.

Kyrin centered the fish over it. A boy's slenderness made a good fighter. It did. At least she would not be sold.

Alaina twisted her hair, and the falling drops scattered their images, mingling them in oblivion. Kyrin slipped behind her and fingered her sister's bright wet curls over her shoulder, blinking back the sting in her eyes. Her sister's hair was glorious, like her smile, and swept down her back to the darker blue of her sash. Alaina deserved a young lord to cherish her, not slavery. Alaina twirled, as if she could not help herself, and the clean blue flared around her. Kyrin smiled. For her, this morning was not marred.

"The Master does favor that hair," Nara said. "Come now, that's enough, there is something for your stomachs inside." The cook turned toward the gate, but Kyrin clutched her thawb in sudden horror.

"Oh, Shema wanted me at dawn!"

Nara clucked, frowning. "Easy, girl. She never rises before the sun reaches the middle of the sky, when the master is about the fields."

Kyrin slumped and Nara reached for her bundle. Kyrin stepped back, holding it tight to her side. The falcon was not for all eyes.

"What is in that, girl?" Nara asked sharply. "Not a snake, I hope."

"It was my mother's." Kyrin lifted her chin. "Ali said I could keep it."

"Show me."

Reluctant, Kyrin peeled away the thawb to reveal the falcon dagger. Nara sniffed, but then she looked in Kyrin's face and said not another word. She tucked a fold of the thawb back over the blade and led them to the kitchen, talking at a furious pace.

Female slaves served Ali on assigned nights at table and worked the rest of their days around the house and in the gardens. If they displeased Ali they would be banished to the fields for a time. The threat of a day there made the most disobedient slave girl beg at Umar's feet.

"The sun spoils the girls' skin, you know, not like around the Nile, where we bathed in the bright morning, and rested during the sun's strength." Nara eyed them with a smile. "But I can see you have tasted the sun and know he harms you not, if you respect his strength."

At the kitchen door Nara lowered her voice. "Umar is the men's overseer, and things are different here than in the caravan. Seek wisdom, watch and learn." She shoved Alaina inside ahead of her, and Kyrin followed.

Men and women sat on the floor before the ovens, eating from large, separate platters. Every head turned toward them. Nimah's smile was almost worshipful, where she sat among the other women, near Alaina's feet.

"You protect them from their first lesson, Nara." Umar leaned against a cold oven in the back wall, beside the largest dish, surrounded by men. "Slaves cannot sleep as they please in our Master's house, they must be faithful to serve, rising with the sun." He disapproved.

Kyrin stiffened against Umar's lingering stare. Did her blue thawb anger him? She and Alaina were the only ones in the kitchen wearing the midday shade, but they wore sashes of darkest blue, not red like his.

Nara's mouth thinned. "Young lilies they are, but not too young for a husband it seems." The look she shot Umar would burn a hole through stone. "There is less uproar in my kitchen when *I* show them how we women work, and *you* teach them golden obedience."

Umar snorted. Nara smiled grimly and went to stir her pots over the fire with a vigorous arm.

Alaina nudged Kyrin. She shut her mouth. Nara could be more than one woman. Watch and learn indeed.

"Eat." Umar tapped the stick in his hand against the floor. "You must not faint the first day, if our Master regards you so high as the blue."

Kyrin rested on her knees like the rest around the platter. She would far rather wear Nara's brown than bear the glances and whispers of the others. Nimah's mother was silent. Kyrin felt awkward after so many hours around friendly fires and open faces. She ate beside Nimah, fumbling to form her balls of raisins, rice, and cinnamon. Alaina's lips twitched, her somber eyes on a perfect ball of rice in her hand.

Nara returned to sit with them. She whispered, "Everyone knows Umar carries a poison spirit in him, but the women's overseer, Jachin, is kind. He watches out for us. And since I am our Master's only cook . . ." She nodded, her straight hair bouncing. "All give me their favor, or suffer."

"And who is Jachin?"

Nara stared at Kyrin. "He came in caravan with you, the Nubian."

"Oh." She could not say she had always thought of him as "the Nubian." He, of all men, deserved a name.

26

Longing

I will lift up my eyes to the mountains, from whence shall my help come?
~Psalm 121:1

Nara paired Kyrin and Alaina to work in the garden. She gave them each a bisht of earth brown and they put them over their thawbs, drank a ladle of water, and began their first task.

While Kyrin weeded the long beds of herbs and vegetables near the pool she stretched her stiff back. Sleeping on stone on a rug was much different than on sand. Sand at least made the right hollows.

Before the noon meal Nara sent Kyrin to Shema with a platter of good things. Outside her mistress's door Kyrin set her shoulders. The wood panel was cracked open.

She pulled her thawb higher toward her neck—as if it could cover her necklace and her scar. She had left her veil in her quarters. That she would wear only to Ali's table unless he commanded otherwise. "Let them stare," she said to Alaina half defiantly, "These women are tame flowers who do not know the free air."

Kyrin sighed. She suspected her sister rather liked the silky veil and the sense of mystery it lent the wearer. It was wasted on her.

"Come." Shema's voice had a breathless quality. Kyrin stepped inside her mistress's room. Without her outer robe, Shema was as slender as a peeled wand in a sleeveless white thawb. Henna clasped her hands and arms in delicate, curling vines, and her eyes were ancient oak hollows full of rain-water; under them her skin was pale as goat milk. She raised a listless arm, tinkling with bracelets, and pointed at her bed. Kyrin laid her platter down on the red silk cover and waited, as Nara had instructed.

The floor was polished brown tile, with small blue, red, and white flowers around the edges of the squares. Her mistress' slippers were scuffed, dainty, poppy-red silk. Shema cleared her throat. She moved to the bed and sat, fingered a date and set it down, took a sip of milk and shoved back her cup with a squeak on the platter. "How are you as strong as an oryx?" She did not look at Kyrin.

"Oh," Kyrin breathed, and licked her lips. "My mistress . . . I have kept my stronghold in many ways since I was small, and my master set me to learn the warrior's way that my—my husband follows." Heat spread across her face.

"Mmm."

Nara had said to be silent until her mistress asked for something, but Shema had made such a face at the dry date and winced at the warm milk.

"Would—would you like an orange?" Kyrin slipped it from her sash and held it out.

Shema looked at her and drew back, then her gaze wandered to the orange. Her swan throat bobbed.

It was one of the first fruits from Ali's trees. He had thrown it to Jachin as too green for his taste. Jachin had gifted it to Nara.

The cook said Kyrin had need of it after the desert, and to share it with Alaina. Its delicate scent had teased her since Nara put it in her hand. But Alaina would not mind if she gave it.

Kyrin approached and laid the orange on the platter. "Please, let me get you more? There are greens too, with vinegar and oil; and the garlic, the way we do it in my country, it is good."

Shema stopped, her thumb under the first curl of peel, her brows furrowed. She said with the force of every fiber in her body, her eyes hard agate, "Did Ali gift this to you?"

He had, in a way, but that was not what Shema asked. "No, mistress."

"Who, then? One who admires you besides your husband?"

Kyrin's throat dried. If she named anyone, and the tale got to Ali . . . "Many friends gave this gift of the sun until it came to me, mistress." There, she could be a poet, if an anxious one.

Shema giggled and set the orange in her lap, her eyes dark and deep. "You protect these 'friends.' I could tell my husband." She leaned forward, her delicate lips curling to fierceness.

Kyrin said nothing and did not drop her eyes from Shema's. Thieving could take her hand if the full measure of justice was taken, but Ali's whipping could take Jachin's life.

Shema reached out to stroke Kyrin's hair and wrapped a strand around her finger. Kyrin bit her tongue and forced herself still. Shema said, "I will not deliver you to him. I hate him, the light of my eyes. He took my life from me, what life I had."

She wound and wound Kyrin's hair, watching it slip away through her fingers, as if she did not truly see what she did.

"I did not steal the orange."

"I know. You can get me whatever is in season next sunrise." Shema paused. "My father the *wazir* is weak in body, may he live long. Now the wazir's daughter and a strong merchant house have been joined. Joy breathes not in our union." She dropped her hand and gathered herself on the bed, her thin shoulders hunching, fingers tightening across her stomach. "I will not give him a son! A son, who will learn to use the weak, to raise his sword for death, for gold, and for a name, who will despise the righteous on their knees!

"A son who will scorn me," she whispered, her hair sliding down to curtain her face. It hung limp and oily, and did not smell of lavender. "Umar—he is Nara's son, he knows."

Surprise choked Kyrin, and pity. Her mistress was indeed as much a captive as the falcon. She said low, "My father was not able to defend his house." She coughed.

Shema's gaze did not move; she seemed to hold her breath.

"Ali killed my mother, and—he gave me this." Kyrin lifted the necklace from her throat. Shema frowned. "And this." Kyrin touched the jet in her ear. "In my land, I inherit at my father's command. You would say that I am the heir of house Cieri. He has no sons."

Shema bent her head and laughed, short and bitter. "It is hard for one who has walked on rose petals to step onto a slave's path of burning sand. Yet you have given me but a handful of grains from your tale to judge."

Kyrin took a deep breath. "If it would please you, I will tell more."

Shema brightened. "It is good, tell on."

At last Kyrin finished and rubbed her face. She felt as if she had walked all day behind Waleed, with Faisal jeering at her. Her throat was paper-dry with old anger and pain.

Shema yawned. "Have you met Qadira?" At Kyrin's questioning look Shema said, "She is my husband's oldest concubine, save Nara, who now orders the kitchen. Qadira rules the women under Jachin, and around him when she can. She wears a blue veil and a ring with a sapphire. She is a jackal who will follow this wazir's daughter into the desert, waiting for her death. But I have a sword to my hand yet," she muttered, eyeing Kyrin.

Qadira had led her to Ali's room last night. Kyrin lifted her chin and stared back at Shema, letting her mistress take her measure.

Shema nodded. "You will come to me when the sun rises. I am awake then, though none know it." Staring out into the warm afternoon, she waved her hand in restless dismissal. Kyrin hesitated at the door. But the time for hesitation was past. Standing in the passage, she bowed. Deeply. "My mistress."

Shema nodded, a formal dip of her head. They understood one another, and understood what the rest of the house needed to see. Kyrin's lips curved in a smile. It had been far too long, and it felt right. She arranged her frown back in place.

Soon she carried Tae's healing brew to Shema thrice a day, at terce, sext and vespers bell.

Their master wanted sons, and a strong wife. Shema wanted strength but no children. Tae ordered Shema to drink what he gave her for the evil humors in her blood, but said only the Master of the stars could do aught about her children.

Shema gave Kyrin an exasperated, fearful look when Kyrin told her, but she drank the tea—and afterward threw the cup down and ordered Kyrin to pick up the shattered pieces. Was the mistress not used to being commanded by a hakeem who expected obedience?

Kyrin grinned, taking any sting of condemnation from the last of her tale related to the kitchen women. "The Hakeem's word is strong, as I well know. When he says run, I run." She mimed with her hands along the table, with a wide-eyed, wary glance over her shoulder.

Nara's lips twitched, and Nimah and the others working in the kitchen laughed.

During her forays on Shema's errands, Kyrin found that Nara was the first to rise in the house and the last to bed. Her work began before dawn, in lauds, though here no bell sounded the hour. It was hard for Kyrin to think of Umar as Nara's blood. He was not of her heart.

And Kyrin found the other women pitied her, and followed Nara's lead in their own ways. They stared at her thawb that she could not keep from garden and stable dirt. And Qadira clucked when she caught Kyrin in the passage one evening after serving Ali, tossing her tangled veil over her shoulder, limp and torn as a slain rabbit. Kyrin had jerked away from Qadira's insistent, untangling fingers, and the old Jezebel snorted and stalked away.

People, more people, and walls, wherever she turned. Nowhere to escape the whispering voices and cautious tread of her sister slaves, who, except for Nara, Nimah, and Nimah's mother, most often looked at Kyrin out of the corners of kohl-slitted eyes or clutched their veils as if afraid of catching her evil eye.

Kyrin grimaced where she sat on the garden wall and traced the edges of her dagger in her lap.

The women of Ali's house did not go out. Shema might have taken some of them with her if she wished, but when Kyrin asked, she said it was either too hot or she was tired or the road was too rocky or muddy. The court with its flowers and trees were enough if she wanted a walk.

Kyrin thought Shema did not want to think of what she could not have. The women were guarded from both danger and joy, shut in by Jachin, protected even from the night sky. Her mistress might endure it, but she could not bear to live caged.

She often crept out to walk under the stars, with no one the wiser but Tae, who would look when she rose, and nod and roll over. Jachin never noticed her when she left or returned, always in his place on his rug across the women's door, his breathing even, his sword under his hand, his eyes closed whether the lamp above burned high or low.

Kyrin longed for the desert. There she had hunted under a sometimes serene, sometimes blazing sky, but always she roved over clean sand without the stink of man; the sound of unkind whispers and the scent of hidden meanings. The women's frankincense and costly rosewater and jasmine made Kyrin sneeze, and she avoided their quarters.

She sought the stables often, bringing a bit of meat or a bone for Cicero, and dates or an apple for Lilith. Cicero's brown gaze held reproach and yearning when she left the stables without giving him even a short run. She had not hunted since she entered Ali's house. Ever she looked for a way to roam the hills with her bow. To keep her promise to her mother—she *would* learn to hit a mark at two hundred paces. It was possible with the nomad's bow. But it was impossible to get by the guards.

Ali posted men at both the great gate and the side gate to the stables. The west gate, after the women's court, led to the fields behind the house and lay under many slaves' eyes. All the gates were locked after the sun fell. And the men under Umar kept a close eye on Kentar and Tae's late comings and goings.

Zoltan bought food that the slaves did not grow in Ali's gardens from the wadi villages for the household, and Kentar or Tae procured any other goods from towns or the Aneza at Umar's orders. Kyrin envied Zoltan.

He ran beside Ali's salukis in the hills after gazelle and hare and fed and trained the long-haired dogs. Ali favored his fawn beasts, for they were good hunters. Their cast-off litter mates who had shorter hair, or heavier heads, or mottled black, brown, or white coats had become Umar's pack. He trained his salukis in the manner of the renowned hunting bloodlines of Egypt.

But he taught them to trail men. His Hand of obedience, he called them. They growled at Kyrin savagely whenever she passed by.

Ali's salukis ate like kings, succulent meat and rice with vegetables, cooked on Nara's fire. To share the noble ones' dinner was worth Zoltan's tongue or his head. Worse, Umar's swift Hand might be loosed, to bring him down like a gazelle. But Zoltan was not so careless.

Kyrin smiled to herself and tested the point of the falcon blade. Still sharp. Zoltan had brought her a rabbit skin for another soft neck pouch. He had plucked the hair from it in the shape of a cross. His talk about stable doings was not the poetic conversation the women of the house savored, but she relished his bald words. There was no double tongue with him.

Even Shema confessed at times that she tired of searching her head for a fitting word in reply to house banter, and Kyrin heartily agreed. But Alaina thrived on the back and forth word-building, quick to think of a pleasing line.

Kyrin sighed. With a little guidance, her sister would have made a better lady than she or Shema. She frowned. Alaina seemed never to hear the women's jabbing tongues. She passed through the kitchen, the Blue Flower room, the women's court, and even so far as the women's quarters followed by joyful clapping of hands before unveiled faces and eager interest in the poetry she learned from Tae and shared with all. It was rare when she did not stand in the middle of a circle of women, a smile on her face.

Did it mean nothing to Alaina that she was bound to her by ties deeper than blood? Kyrin wiped wiped at an errant tear. Were the women suspicious of her because she allied with Shema, or because of her scar, or did she look so evil? Ali's mark *was* fodder for their weaving tongues.

Kyrin stared at the falcon's amber eyes. She had one thing Zoltan and the women of the house did not. The garden.

Jachin had told Tae of an old, unused garden close outside the wall. He had convinced Ali it was a good place for Tae to raise his herbs and teach his women his martial mysteries. Ali grinned when Tae asked permission to seclude their *dojang,* or place of learning—doubtless hoping that they learned more from him than their martial art. Kyrin's mouth flattened in satisfaction despite the taste of salty tears. Huen yet stood, holding Tae's honor faithfully between them every night.

Kyrin gripped her hands. She had helped Alaina root out every weed, stick, and stone in their practice ring. They left an old fig at one end of the garden and a gnarled olive in the middle.

Tae had said the thirty paces of bare earth near the olive tree should rightly be a ring of sand, but there was less need since it seldom rained. He extended a water pipe from the women's court and through the tumbledown garden wall for his herbs, and they planted seeds thickly on both sides of the gateway and about the sere garden, the patches guarded by rings of sticks stuck in the dusty earth. Kyrin wiped her face on her arm and sniffed deeply of the scent of Tae's half-grown oregano and mint.

As was her habit, she'd hooked her legs over the wall and curled up and back down till her stomach ached, then jumped from a knee-high stone to the ground and up again until sweat ran down her burning calves and her thawb stuck to her back. She had thrown herself into Subak in the only place where she could be alone, practicing every spare moment. A strong stomach, strong legs, and sure feet gave a warrior speed and power. She needed that power. She ran around and around the garden after Cicero—all for that power.

The sweat of her last practice cooled on Kyrin. Daily, she shot her bow the short distance the garden allowed, and sparred with Alaina in the pool the rare moments they had it to themselves. Sponge in hand, she would hunch her shoulders and lift her arms to protect her head. Then shuffle around Alaina, darting the sponge at her sister, covering her face with her other arm. She'd grin at the rewarding "thush" of the sponge at every hit, and take Alaina's blows in return.

Kyrin's shoulders drooped. She needed the power of the warrior.

But that power meant nothing if she only saw Alaina when they ate, at the pool, and when they lay down to sleep. Her sister was closeted with Tae much of the rest of the time, learning scrolls or practicing the words he set her to copy on a wax tablet, while he left on Ali's errands, sometimes for days.

While she could only wait on Shema, carry her mistress' messages and food, chat with Nimah and Zoltan, and practice until she was too tired to think. Never after that first night did Shema let her know that she swayed her decisions. Kyrin understood. She was a friend—and yet a slave.

In the sun dying across the west, the falcon's eyes gleamed almost orange. Her sweat made her shiver. Kyrin slid the dagger through her sash, got down from the garden wall, and walked toward the west gate. She gently shut the door of the women's court. Umar frowned on her using the stable entrance where she might impede a messenger, his salukis, or any man about his business. And she did not want to meet Umar's Hand if Zoltan was not there.

Behind her, a hedge of olives concealed the garden walls. She was late leaving her refuge for the safety of the house. At Ali's word, all must be inside by dusk. She slipped through the field gate with a sheepish nod to the guard, who grinned.

Kyrin envied the wadi water; it ran where it would. She was not ready to leave the evening where she was not crowded by the echo of many voices. Rooting noises and a snort under the vines against the wall made her pause. Another rustle and silence. Only a hedgehog after insects.

She shrugged and pulled herself up the vines that matted the north wall until she could see over the top. The hills were blue beneath the purpling sky. The desert lay beyond them, at the feet of the jagged mountains.

Somewhere across two seas far north and west of them, Cierheld and her father waited. The hedgehog rustled the dead leaves. Kyrin's arms tired. The gate scraped, and feet crunched gravel. Kyrin dropped back to earth.

"There you are. I thought you might come here." Alaina hugged herself against the cold in the dusk, a smile in her excited voice. "My scribing went well today. Tae said my pen is passing Umar's, and I will not disgrace Ali. Umar says a singing teacher is coming from Baghdad. He says I will need my needle, my pen, *and* my voice to be worthy of the great city. I will work with some of the greatest translators and scribes for the caliph." Alaina paused. "Umar says the caliph has more women than can be counted, and I am married, so I am safe. I wish you could see the round city. It is magnificent."

"I don't know, Alaina. Safe from the caliph's eye, maybe, but from his sword? What of that?"

Umar wanted Alaina fit to serve in that high, fearful place, the caliph's court, where fortunes were made and lives lost, but Ali had said nothing. Would he send Alaina and Tae to the caliph and keep her behind with Shema? Could not Tae teach Alaina to sing well enough?

But it was different for Alaina. She had nothing to hide. Not yet. Nara and Shema made excuse for Kyrin when she had need at each moon.

Nara had smiled and stroked Kyrin's hair. "It is good you are small, though you will have to wrap your chest soon. It takes time for a seedling to become a tree, for a mustard seed to ripen, for a falcon to grow into her wings, for a girl to become a woman."

Kyrin snorted. So long as she made Shema congenial to Ali, giving him greater chance of an heir, and she herself grew in the way of the warrior, her master remained pleased. But if Alaina went to Baghdad, she would be alone again—and Umar might see his way open for vengeance. His scar was a pale bar across his palm that reddened at the least touch. But he had not discovered her womanhood, or Ali would have known it between one moment and the next.

Alaina said, "It means more to me that I scribe for our Lord, and my people, who will read the works I translate. Kyrin, words can steal so much. And give so much."

Words. The shadows were thick under Kyrin's feet. She suddenly wanted Alaina and Tae running beside her, the whisper of camel pads over moonlit sand, and Cicero's lean form ghosting before them into the dunes. Or home—with the sweet-dry-musty smell of the oaks. The vined wall loomed before Kyrin. She shut her eyes. "I was looking at the hills. I am going to the garden when the sun rises." She forced her voice to evenness. "Will you come, Alaina?"

§

Alaina heard the hope in Kyrin's voice and felt her heart lighten. Maybe if she could talk to Kyrin, she would understand why she must pursue Baghdad. "Oh, yes! It has been too long since I practiced. I will also bring the part of God's Book that I am finding Arabic and English words for. I do not think Father Bede's translation of the Book exists here for me to copy, and I want our Lord's word written for us, in our tongue. He makes my heart climb swift into the sky—like your falcons, Kyrin. He holds the truth of everything." Alaina held back her sigh. The Baghdad school gave official scribe status only on their terms, under their tests. Her works she'd translated under Tae would be useless to prove her skill to them. She must go to Baghdad. *I cannot go home a beggar, I will not.*

Kyrin sighed. "No, I do not think the Arabs love our Bede's Book and Latin. But why do you want so much to go to the translator's school? Is Arabic so beautiful?"

Alaina smiled. "They make the facets of words glitter with truth. They paint ugliness, and evil, beauty, and kindness. And yes, their script has a kind of beauty."

Kyrin snorted again, and Alaina pulled back her veil. Why could her sister never understand? "There is no harm in serving our master, Kyrin, and praying the Master of the stars to rise over him with healing for his heart. Our master also serves the caliph. If I serve them well, either he or Ali will reward me." She said softly, "If we were free to go home, Tae could go back to Huen. He is so sad, sometimes."

Kyrin said nothing. Alaina spoke as Nimah's mother and the others, hopeful of their master's generosity. Even Faisal said so. She should know from Ali's dealings that Arabs used a vessel and broke it when it was of no more use.

.

Heart Studies

He trains my hands for battle. ~Psalm 18:34

Tae bowed, and Nara inclined her head. The cook walked through the garden gate after Kyrin, who strode ahead in Mey's black thawb and trousers. The late sun edged Nara's brown thawb with red-gold, making caverns of her eyes, highlighting the loss of her earlobe. Tae waved her past him, indicating the east wall with his stick. "Watch there." Her steps could not hurt the seedling herbs still in their coats beneath the earth.

He smoothed the solid ironwood in his hand. If injustice could only be overcome by such weapons it would make his heart glad. Ali had bought Nara from an Egyptian slaver and took her for his concubine, though he did not acknowledge Umar as his son. And Nara loved Umar fiercely. She had given him her mother's heart with her milk—and watched him follow Ali. Tae shook his head. Then Ali married Shema, daughter of the wazir, and made Nara his head cook. If Ali fell to poison, all eyes would look to her. To Nara, who shielded Kyrin.

"Make ready!" Tae called after Alaina and Kyrin as they ran around the inside of the garden to warm their limbs. They skirted the sticks marking the plots of his life-giving herbs at full speed, dust spurting from under their feet. It smelled of this

sere land and forgotten days of green life, nothing like the leaf
mold of the many-fingered maples of Huen's gardens, blazing in
red glory. She used to wait for him there, after his practice with
his hwarang brothers, and they would walk among the trees,
where his skill and his heart had grown.

Kyrin's skill in the way of his fathers grew as his had. She
took joy in the warrior's way, exulting in her strength. She was
determined to overcome the sword and purge her shame over
her fear of a blade and her mother's fall. Tae sighed.

All men feared. And fear did not leave on its own; it was ignored and walled in to fester, or wielded into anger, or cast upon
the Master of the stars, who gave courage and mercy in its stead.
And Kyrin's heart had not healed of its wounds.

She was not ready for the touch of death. That carried the
power of life giving and life taking; he did not give that power
to any without trusting their heart's mettle. Her fear and anger
and pain might fashion her into a dreadful weapon. Kind firm-
ness was needed to bring any rangdo to the height of a master's skill. The seeds of obedience and knowing began here. Tae
rapped in his own tongue, "Jun be!"

Alaina and Kyrin grinned at Nara and halted before him, two
warrior at ready rest.

Kyrin stood yet straighter, her hands in fists before her as re-
quired, chin up, eager. She bowed, and Tae inclined his head and
gestured toward Alaina. Kyrin bowed to her drill companion.

"Seajok!"

Kyrin drove a round kick to Alaina's ribs and switched feet
rapidly—switching and kicking, faster and faster—until she
gasped for breath. Alaina did the same to her, their kicks landing as one, pounding grunts from each other despite their leather body shielding. But they no longer knocked each the other's
breath away or hunched in sudden pain. They had toughened,

though in a few moments sweat gleamed on their faces. Tae nodded. They were warm and ready. "Poomse!"

Without a pause they slid apart and leaped into the stylized forms that linked the tried fighting moves of his teachers.

Pursuing an invisible attacker, Kyrin pivoted into a low strike to protect her lead leg and grabbed her opponent's arm, pulled him into an open tiger-mouth between rigid fingers and thumb and crushed his windpipe. She elbowed, threw him, dropped a knee into his gut, rammed another elbow to his throat. Her thawb snapped with power and speed, the faces of her pale-robed enemies visible only to her.

Tae glanced at Nara, who sat on the wall and watched Kyrin's fierce movements with wonder.

A rider, created out of an old thawb stuffed with palm fronds and rocks, perched astride the wall. Kyrin and Alaina sent him flying from his mount a hundred times by turns. The one not kicking vaulted the wall to catch the falling target and reset him. One kick, vault over, catch the rider and replace him for her partner's kick, and vault back to kick again. Tae swung his stick against his leg, suppressing his smile. His rangdo had struck a rhythm and made a game of it.

Kyrin rubbed a scraped knee and called to Alaina, "You'll burn too if you miss again: kick him off!" Alaina's heel thumped the rider's sternum, and Kyrin caught him and heaved him back up with a groan. They vaulted past each other: one on this side of the rider, and another on that. Good. They remembered they must evenly strengthen their bodies by switching sides.

Kyrin kicked next but her foot swung wide, batting aside the rider's arm and striking air.

Tae let his mouth flatten in displeasure. "Close only works when you cast Greek fire! Strike the precise point!" He waved her and Alaina away in disgust. "Off with you. Run!"

They swung over the wall and sprinted about the garden. Panting and dripping with sweat, they returned, each trying to catch the advancing shade of the olive. Alaina cried, "The rider moved! It's your burn this time, Kyrin!"

Tae held back his amusement. It was hot near the wall. They eyed him, panting, wondering if their torture would end if they collapsed. They must learn they could go on. Tae raised his arm. "Ap bal chagi!"

A hundred snapping front-kicks to the target's throat, turn by turn. A pause for water and back to the rider, whose stuffing began to come out. His rangdo missed more often, circled the garden slower, and kicked desperately. And missed. At times they gulped down tears, but the uneven thwack, thwack of their feet against their opponent went on. Legs wavered. Again they limped away under his watchful eye. Tae grinned, knowing his face was mirthless. After the testing, the further forging.

Nara made a small sound of protest. Tae tapped his stick against his leg. "Pil sung!"

His rangdo chorused together, "Certain victory through courage, strength, and indomitable spirit!" Shaking, breathing in deep gasps, Kyrin eyed Alaina beyond her raised fists and drew her body up into position.

Alaina too lifted her right foot to her knee, a stalking water bird, slender and golden haired. Tae paused while Kyrin found her balance. Last practice she had vowed it was Alaina's turn to run the circuit fifty times around the top of the wall for losing.

"Ap bal chagi!" he snapped. Kyrin thrust her knee up and her foot snapped into the air high over her head. "Barow!" he barked. She drew her foot back to her knee without touching the ground, her body straight as an arrow. Alaina also brought her leg back on command, but leaned to the side, losing her balance, her arms weaving. Kyrin smiled.

Tae tapped Kyrin's ankle with his stick. Her leg wobbled. Panic pulled her twitching mouth straight. Tae crossed his arms, rocking on his heels, and forbade his laugh. Two cranes stalked the same frog. "Yeop chagi!"

Kyrin lashed out with a side kick. Her leg reached extension a span from Alaina, or her foot would have broken ribs. Kyrin eyed her sister's equally straining, dirt-dark toes inches from her face. Alaina grinned, her leg a quivering leaf. "I burned your nose!"

"Burn yours!"

"Dwi chagi!" Tae cried. Kyrin leaned forward and struck backward with her heel. Her foot struck through the air with body-shaking force. Their lives might depend on their strength of will, of limb, of spirit: on souls joined by sweat and blood, bound by love in the will of the Master.

Tae walked toward the massive olive trunk to set up the next target. A good back kick would stop an incoming enemy in his tracks, breaking ribs, shocking lungs and heart. The skill Nara saw in Kyrin was a pebble on the mountain of knowledge she had yet to gain. The next target was harder.

"Naryu chagi!" He grabbed the olive branch, pulling it down to a handspan above Kyrin's head.

Wiping her eyes, she focused, shuffled forward, and jumped. Her knee knifed up, she loosed her foot, and her instep struck the tip of the waving branch above. The clump of leaves exploded. She struck the recoiling branch with her forearm on her way back to the ground and landed, ready to run or strike.

Tae nodded. Soon that axe-kick would break bones and knock an enemy from his mount without his senses—or dead.

"Switch legs, and again! Harder!" Olive leaves fluttered. He grunted. Kyrin's stolen moments jump-kicking at the vines in the women's court paid her in gold coin.

Alaina struck at the olive leaves. Her foot passed through the air fingers away and she jigged in a circle to keep from straining her leg with the empty force of the blow. Tae waved her toward the wall and a long run with amusement. "Go! You write too many letters!"

Kyrin leveled her hand at Alaina with a hoot, her palm down, pointing in the eastern way with her whole hand. "Your turn to burn, Alaina!"

Alaina gasped a breath and waved at her with a merry, dismissive smile. Kyrin sprang at her, and Alaina fell back in mock fear, tumbling to the ground. She rolled over her shoulder to her feet with a grin, dusted herself off and spun, sprinting away, watching her footing.

"Good!" Tae called after her, and to Kyrin, "Enough killing the olive for this day. You have done well. See, Nara smiles for you." The cook was smiling indeed. Tae rubbed his hand over his stick. His rangdo could pass as a man.

She was lean enough as she walked behind the gnarled olive's thick trunk, her black trousers and short thawb stuck to her back and legs. Kyrin returned after a moment in her serving thawb again, smoothing a wrinkle from one blue sleeve. She looked up at Nara on the wall. "So, do you think our skill enough for the court, Nara?"

Tae frowned. Ali had bestowed the blue on Kyrin and Alaina, making them second to Qadira in the house. But as a scribe Alaina had no place to wield her authority, and Kyrin had not tested her rank among the household. Instead she befriended unloved Shema. Kyrin had been wise not to antagonize the household until she found who held the lines of power. It seemed Qadira ordered the house, while Nara exerted a compassionate rein on her rule.

Nara glanced over her shoulder and dropped her voice. "This way of the warrior can do many things: bring life or death, I think." She stared at Tae, shrewd. "I have heard tales of your land."

Tae kept his face still. "You may come when you wish and judge the straight from the twisted."

Nara raised her brows. "I will."

Tae met her gaze steadily. Words. Some meant nothing. Others, danger and death. Or safety and life.

Alaina would assist him to heal the wazir when they journeyed to Baghdad—for Shema feared for her father, who had the same blood plague as she—might his white hairs see years of wisdom. They might be kept close, that was the danger. Ali sought the wazir's favor—yet he ordered his hakeem to record everything he heard in the wazir's passages, room, and court. And then the caliph's guardsman would also ask Ali for his news. That double task could lead to death.

Tae's mouth flattened. The guardsman who pursued something, what, he was not sure.

Within the courtly talk of silks, perfumes, and jewelry that the women of the caliph desired, and the men's long debates of what a merchant might gain for his goods or what ploys might catch the caliph's eye, lurked buried perceptions of the esteemed caliph's court—the most gracious, most blessed of Allah—and the players for power positioned in it. But there was more than news in the wind, as there had been before. Some words should not be loosed.

Standing once again in the torchlight of his command quarters long ago, Tae watched his rangdo bend his head and step into the warm rain to carry his message in a sealed bamboo case to an enemy. And then word for word to Paekche Kim, their *kuk-sun*. Tae's proposed peaceful surrender to the enemy commander had sparked banishment from his Huen and nearly the parting of his head from his body.

Once in Baghdad he must judge whether to drop a bit of paper, scrubbed pure, to blow on the wind, or to give all news into Ali's hand. Other lives than his rested on his judgment. He could not be betrayed again by words, true or untrue, going where they should not.

Nor could Nara. That knowing was in her eyes, in the struggle of her love for Kyrin and her son, which strove to push back her fear of him. Tae drew a long breath.

If it came to their master's death, it would not be poison. He did despise one who could not look his enemy in the face. He smiled. He did not think they would be enemies. "Mistress of the roast and rice, I say I will not soil your hearth with fire from mine. There is wisdom in this."

Nara nodded, short and sharp. She turned her smile on Kyrin. "That was well done. A caliph would give much to command such artistry at the lift of his finger. But my pot boils away." She called to Alaina, yet running on the wall—"Run well!"—and then the gateway swallowed her.

Tae's mouth twisted. Nara accepted his word.

The night was quiet except for Alaina's dragging feet atop the stone wall around the garden. Kyrin stared at him, quiet and wondering. He turned toward Alaina. "Enough!" He vaulted up to sit. Water trickled in the wadi below. Dusk stretched to the surrounding hills.

Kyrin climbed up beside him, then Alaina sat on his other side, breathing hard. Tae snorted softly and put an arm around each of them. Not yet masters of the way of the warrior, their warmth and the smell of sweat comforted him. None here schemed for power.

Nara would not betray them. She knew nothing to betray. And love was strong in her. He smiled, a bare curve of his mouth. The death touches would come to his rangdo in time. And to him, the wisdom he needed. The olives outside the wall whispered of it.

§

Kyrin felt alive, quivery and good, her hands braced on the cooling stone. She grinned. Alaina ran the wall this time. And Tae's arm was warm approval about her shoulders. Nara had left them with a smile. The sky before them had no boundaries, only bright stars in clear depth upon depth. He who made this vast moment had no limit of power to find.

Her smile faded. She had learned the deadly ways of the warrior in the desert, where Tae showed her and Alaina how to bring an enemy down with a few blows. Yes, she knew the muscles must learn with every fiber what the head grasped, and that such knowledge would be seasons building. But she did not have seasons. She must learn the sword.

Soon, Tae said, soon. Not soon enough for her.

§

Winter came cold and wet. Rain thundered on the roof tiles, baring the hills of color and leaf. A brief snow fell once. On one winter day at first light, Kyrin accompanied Tae and Kentar to the stables. Ice-blades grew out of patches of frost, and the sun twinkled iridescent among their ranks, more beautiful than jewels, daggers of glass. The carpet of crystals upon Ali's house, field, and limb graced the wadi with beauty. The hills and the mountains above were silvered.

In the stables Kyrin gave Lilith's rein into Kentar's hand. She was old, and Ali and Umar were not kind. "Lilith is thick with fat. Take her on your errand. When I ride again I would have her ready to run."

With a smile that recalled their days in caravan, Kentar took the rein in his weathered hand. "She will remember the rabbit that won her, in the hills of the Aneza."

Kyrin bowed her head. "My bow has forgotten such a distance."

"But your heart has not. All may change at an unforeseen moment." Kentar touched her shoulder with his camel stick. "Then—"

Tae broke in, "Do not forget the amounts of poppy, myrrh, and astragulus that I need for mistress Shema. They must be exact."

"I will dream of them," Kentar said dryly.

Tae's body shook with his silent laugh. "See that you do, O my messenger."

Kentar raised his arm, "As salaam alaykum!"

"And peace to you!" Tae and Kyrin returned his farewell. Kyrin hoped Kentar turned Lilith out to pasture with his herd for his daughters' pleasure. Lilith had forgotten how to run. With a groan, she trotted out of the frozen courtyard between the stable and the kennels, past the square-built privy against the wall. Kyrin rubbed her cold nose. The frost pricked fiercely this morning. Poor Nimah.

She had to put ashes down the privy holes before every sunrise, though she protested she was glad to be their master's most faithful ash strewer. For then she could steal moments with Kyrin and Zoltan, and pet Cicero and ride Lilith about the court in the early morn, their breath steaming—with Ali none the wiser.

Kyrin snorted. If she had put one foot across Lilith's back the whole house would have whispered of it before the stars gleamed in the sky. Cicero licked her hand as she watched Kentar ride away, and she stroked his knobby back. Even in the depths of

winter Ali forbade her the hills, but Tae had added horn strips
to her bow, and it spat arrows with viperish speed. If she could
run with Cicero on the sand he might come close to catching the
feather fletching. "Wind-runner."

She pulled his ears in gentle love. His wise almond eyes had
found her the moment she entered the stable door. His tongue
peeked between his teeth, bliss half-closed his eyes, and he
leaned against her with a groan of content. Kyrin smiled.

Her clean-limbed Cicero walked among his shaggy brethren
in the kennels as if he was born their king, with Zoltan his guard.
Holding his head high, he ignored the other dogs that circled
and sniffed with raised hackles. His solemn manner said he had
weighty matters to pursue in the world—he could not behave
like a pup. He suffered Zoltan and Nimah to pet him, deigning
to eat from their fingers after Kyrin put her hand under theirs
to offer the first bone. And hearing Arabic gave her practice in
the tricky, twisting tongue. She made progress, though not as
fast as Alaina.

Even after Kentar left, the winter ice did not reach the fountain and the marble hunter. Though the blocked windows were
drafty, the Blue Flower room kept warm, the mosaic floor heated
by fire beneath. That was one thing the Eagles did well. Hot
baths, running water, warm floors. Kyrin's quarters kept warm
by association.

When the hoarfrost melted, it left her with an empty feeling.
She remembered snow in the woods, warm fur, and steam from
the smiles of her people as they carried a great king-oak home
for the midwinter fire in Cierheld hearth. Her mother had sat
as queen before the last bright blaze amid gathered green holly.
Her black hair shining loose around her, she had sung with the
rest of them of the King's star in the heavens. Then she had
fallen. Because of a stronghold daughter's fear.

Kyrin rubbed her eyes wearily. When would she be strong enough to drop over the wall in the night and ride for the coast? She knew enough Arabic to pass, and slave boys were common. But she could not go until she could face a sword.

Spring burst from the deep-breathing earth: sap rose in the orchard, shoving fragrant clouds of white and pink blossoms out to air, and spikes of downy grass were green-smelling and feathery under her feet. Warmth crept over Ali's fields and gardens, bringing birds with their important, tiny doings and chirps close to speech. The underground irrigation channels of fired clay pipe rushed precious brown water from the wadi to Ali's orchard and gardens, while Tae's herbs poked their green heads above ground; thin or thick, curly or sharp, busily pushing aside the soil.

Merchants and their messengers visited Ali's house often. Since his agreement with the Aneza, he dealt widely in the latest goods and news, the changing dangers of the camel road and client demand. Kentar brought it all from Sheyk Shahin, and Tae sifted Kentar's news for his own use.

Kentar arrived late one evening with a cloth-wrapped bundle and a message that he handed to Tae in the entry room on his way to an audience in the Blue Flower room with Ali. "From the prince of the Twilkets," he said, with a grin at Kyrin.

Something from Faisal? Kyrin peered over Tae's shoulder while he unrolled the pale parchment. "What is it?" Alaina stood at Tae's other side, curious.

Tae said, "Truthseeker flies well. And Faisal learns Twilket lore while his tribe roves—tracking, writing, history." He grinned. "The prince says he pursues peace and wealth with a ready hand and tongue. Gershem Ben Salin leaves the Aneza to keep the caravanseri, and Shahin and Mey live with no one to shake a spear over their tent. Rashid eats of the fat, with milk and honey. The caravans bring them riches—all for a taste of the spring that sealed the Nur-ed-Dam between the Twilket and Aneza that brought them into brotherhood, the Oasis of Oaths." Tae's voice softened. "Faisal says, 'I have not forgotten, my father. I keep the rights of power before me.'" Tae tucked the finished message carefully inside his thawb, then opened the bundle. He paused, stared at what he held, and then laid something hard and small in Kyrin's hand.

It was a jet pin of a long-winged falcon.

Kyrin blinked back sudden tears and held her breath against a widening space inside her. Faisal had forgiven her. Strangely, she did not ache for his smile, but for Truthseeker's solid weight and her father's strong arms, the hum of his voice in her ear. The falcon brooch would set off the dark bisht Mey had gifted her. Kyrin frowned. She ought to feel something for Faisal besides relief. Her heart needed to speak. She must find Cicero, for he would not mind if she whispered in his ear.

A handful of quill pens dropped out of the thin roll of paper that Tae lifted from the bundle. With a gasp, Alaina caught them and smoothed the feathers, running a finger over them gently. Kyrin eyed the paper. So different from wax tablets or skin or scraped vellum. Faisal was generous.

Kentar slipped back out of the Blue Flower room on a waft of incense and camel sweat. He gave them a tired smile. "Our master wishes your service, Kyrin."

She nodded soberly. "Nara will send food for you." Tae would bring it to Kentar's quarters and gather his news. She walked through the blue curtains, her hand clenched about Faisal's pin. He had forgiven her, at last. She wanted to smile and cry and hug Cicero, but Cicero must wait.

Ali's thin smile split his face when his gaze lit on her, and he paused in his pacing before his chair. "Bring Shema to me."

Kyrin bowed and hurried out. Her master's news must have been a good return for the gift of swords and spears he sent with Kentar to the Aneza.

Challenge

A fool's lips bring strife. ~Proverbs 18:6

A seven-day after Kentar departed again for the Oasis of Oaths, Kyrin walked toward the women's pool, smeared with black spring mud from head to toe. The water would feel good. She had been out since dawn behind the plows, sowing the field, covering the grain kernels with warm earth. She had gotten into a clod war with the men following the other plow, started by Tae. She grinned. Field work was not torturous, though as hard as the warrior's way.

She had been careful to more than fill her quota of sown earth. Watching the slaves laugh and enjoy the planting, Umar had tapped his sword hilt. Kyrin's smile faded. Once she had caught him rubbing his scarred hand, his unreadable eyes on her.

She had not made him reach for the brazier, and he had enjoyed her pain under Ali's lash. She had a feeling in the field that Umar thought of Ali's whip. Those of his blood, of Araby blood, owed her people her mother's life. Kyrin rubbed her throat. She would not drop Shema's tea in front of Ali again for a taste of freedom. She slipped through the women's gate.

But the sun had warmed her back in the field. There had been no Qadira to scold her, no kohl-ringed eyes to turn from her with whispers behind veils or hennaed hands. The men laughed with her while she dodged dark clods and strength surged inside her. Apple blossoms sweetened the air. It was a good thing, the planting.

Paul spoke of it when he spoke of the creator of all. The seed of barley swelled with water, left its hull to death, and thrust out roots into the dark, to raise green spears of fruit.

Ali's voice cut across the front courtyard, distant beyond the gate. Kyrin paused as she shook dirt from her hair beside the women's pool. The lilies again, it must be. She could almost make out Ali's complaint and the comforting bass mumble of his guest.

Her master hovered more over his rare plants more than he did over Alaina when he ordered a new collar design for his best bisht. Over his gardener's objection, Ali showed his precious roses and lilies from the mountains to every interested guest.

The gardener was a king in his own right, to Kyrin's mind. Relieved of his red sash since Umar's return, the ancient overseer had been relegated to rule Ali's flowers. He praised Kyrin's efforts with the pot herbs in the women's court. In a waspish voice, he had told her she was fast on the way to knowing every herb and its uses in Tae's garden, though she trampled them so often. Querulous and demanding as Ali, he was kind beneath.

Kyrin tugged her fingers through a stiff hair snarl. So she might yet surpass Alaina in one thing, herbs. She dropped her hand. Was Ali's guest the Baghdad teacher, come to train Alaina's voice?

"You! Worthless one. Clean yourself and tell Nara I want her," Ali barked.

Kyrin spun, one foot splashing into the pool, and almost tumbled in. Ali peered around the gatepost, frowning. Kyrin blushed and averted her gaze, and he withdrew with a frown. She shut her mouth tight, glad she had not begun taking off her thawb.

No man came here except Jachin and Ali—and never when any of the women bathed. And Ali had come less and less since Shema began to please him. Her mistress had gathered Ali's attention now that her bones had flesh. Now that she took care, since Kyrin urged her to be the mistress she was, and let no one take that respect from her. Her hair was lustrous and her garments sweet with the mint she loved, and a hint of jasmine. Kyrin had suggested yarrow and sage blossom for their wild richness.

Kyrin snorted and kept her ears pricked for any step outside the gate, scrubbing hard and fast.

What did Ali want besides news, that he would send Alaina and Tae to court to tend the wazir? They must not let themselves become too valuable to Shema's father. Serving the caliph they would lack nothing except freedom, and maybe, sometime, their heads. And what unpleasant tasks would Qadira and Umar find for her after they left? Qadira had a tongue sharp as a brooch, though she hid her wrinkles well under veils and scents and creams from lands near and far. Nara could only do so much. And Alaina—Kyrin's throat tightened.

She would miss the Alaina who had whispered with her in the caravan, who slept at her back, who loved Cicero. The last three days she had not seen Alaina but for meals, for she learned court ways under Umar.

Kyrin shrugged her serving thawb over her damp arms. Ali would have *her* head if she did not hurry. She went to the kitchen, where Nara scolded Nimah, who held a scorched rice pot before her as if to hold off the cook's anger. Nara paused for breath, her bosom heaving, and Nimah rubbed tears on her sleeve. Kyrin gave the cook Ali's message.

"Very well, I will come. But could you not tell me before?" Nara frowned and rushed across the breezeway into the storeroom, muttering about spring air and worthless heads of feathers.

Kyrin bit her lip harder, a hot spark growing inside her. She did not know Ali wanted Nara, how could she tell her earlier?

Nara huffed back into the kitchen. "Should your feet be forever heavy? Take this to Zoltan." She shoved a dish of rice and meat scraps into Kyrin's hands.

Kyrin's breath came fast, and she bit her lip. It took all her will not to throw the dish on the floor. It was spring. She ought not to be here.

To serve another Arab with an oily smile, fat-faced or thin, greedy merchant or heartless slaver, even a messenger: she could not bear it. Cruel, they but pursued gold and power. Their corruption touched even Nara.

She could almost catch the rank scent of red-and-black fur and hear the rumble of the tiger's pleasure. Those of Araby bound one with chains forever. There was no escape. She could not breathe. Kyrin raised her hand to her neck pouch, whirled and stamped outside.

The outside air was freer. She drew a deep breath. If she hurried she would have time to feed Cicero before she must carry Ali's first dishes to his table. Then she would drive the tiger from her by feathering her stuffed enemy with arrows and practicing the warrior's way until her muscles shook. The closer she drew to mastering the first rank of the warrior's way, the closer she was to studying the sword. And after the sword—home. *If you may be made free....*

In the stable court Umar and Ali's salukis crowded against the two woven pen walls, whining and licking their chops.

Zoltan had gutted an oryx destined for Ali's table. He waved the beast's bloody guts on the end of his long dagger towards Alaina, laughing. Arabs.

Alaina skipped back with a startled noise.

That smell. Of death and darkness.

Daring, Zoltan slid the mess off with a flick and lunged at Alaina. Alaina stepped back, her eyes wide, sucking in her stomach, and the blade whispered past the breast of her thawb.

Blood and metal. Kyrin burst through the ice that held her even as Alaina took Zoltan's dagger from him with a quick twist and a laugh.

"Witless—dog!" Kyrin grasped Zoltan's throat, her other hand buried in his hair, yanking back and down, bowing him over her hip as she poised to take his legs from under him. "Do that again and I'll break your legs!"

Zoltan's mouth was slack with shock, his eyes wide.

"You will not run so easy with your noble ones then!" She spun him upright and shoved him toward the dead oryx.

He staggered back and glanced at Alaina, pulling his thawb into order. Alaina shrugged, shot a look of reproach at Kyrin, and wiped his dagger and gave it back. His hand closed around the haft, white-knuckled. His mouth was tight.

"Zoltan was only teasing," Alaina protested, "he will soon wear the blade as a man."

"Teasing?" Kyrin clenched her hands. "Do you want to tease death? To play with word-spinners in the house and be so worthy a scribe that Ali sends you to Baghdad to set the board to play for your life?"

"Why do you fear?" Zoltan cocked his head.

"I don't mean so, Kyrin!" Alaina's defense fell on the heels of his words.

"No! You don't. Your wits sleep." Kyrin's voice was hoarse. She would never overcome the ice of a blade that was too near those she loved. If Zoltan had wanted Alaina's life he could have taken it. "You don't see the hard words and the sword that waits: you see lines of beautiful ink and soft tongues and herbs that flower where they are planted."

Alaina's chin quivered. She lifted her head despite her filling eyes. "Kyrin, I do see! I mean—I mean to gain a skill, to make something of myself! Why is that so wrong?"

"Do you remember Ali's whip, when he gave me this gift?" Kyrin touched the black ring in her ear, heavy and smooth.

"Yes, but Shema is gentling him."

"Oh, yes, when you give him gold or add worth to the house of Ali Ben Aidon, the master favors you. If not, who but the Master of the stars knows what he will do!"

Zoltan glanced back and forth between them. Her hand over her mouth, Alaina turned away, her head bowed. Kyrin shoved the bowl of saluki food into Zoltan's stinking hands. "Feed Cicero!" She had tangled Alaina's tongue for once, but it gave her no joy. She whirled away.

"I am not blind!" Alaina cried after her.

In the house Kyrin slid her falcon through her blue sash and settled her veil with shaking fingers. She ought not to have said that to Alaina. Zoltan's eyes had flickered from Kyrin's stricken face to his blade, which her eyes could not leave. He knew.

Her mouth flattened again, grim. He had best not ask her of it. She rubbed at her sore shoulder and glided with measured steps into the Blue Flower room, carrying Ali's roast sand hens overlaid with split almonds in honeyed curry sauce.

At the table, her master's frown was sharp. The dark haired guest on his right turned his head. Sirius Abdasir, the caliph's wolfish guardsman.

Kyrin fought not to stumble. She straightened and felt to be sure her hair wrap hid her black ring.

His shoulders wider than some, Sirius wore black with blue trim and a white sash this night. He passed pleasantries with Ali and snapped at his slave who stood at his elbow. The slave moved back, his mouth sullen, his hair the color of sunburned corn tassels.

Sirius had not yet noticed her, but she had her thin half-veil and her hair covering. She had not liked his teasing touch her first night in her master's house, as if he owned her. And Ali had spoken of their martial skill pleasing the caliph. If she kept her eyes down, the caliph's guardsman might forget he'd ever seen her.

It was no secret the caliph favored Ali through Sirius, though Ali's neighbors counted her master less than a believer because he kept a shamed cook who went bare faced and allowed foreign slaves and customs to flourish in his house. But the neighbors' curiosity, Ali's lavish table, and the presence of the Caliph's guardsman compelled them to accept Ali's invitations.

Ali beckoned to Kyrin, and she knelt and offered the sand hen, extending her arms, head down. The guardsman paid her no mind, frowning at the table while Ali cut him a choice leg. Sirius's slave watched her under thick brows.

He had a lighter complexion, but somehow his intent gaze reminded her of Faisal. Kyrin felt her lips curve and lowered her eyes. The edge of the veil itched across her nose. She rubbed at it and risked a glance at Alaina, waiting inside the curtains with a fluted platter of rice. Alaina met her eyes, calm, and smiled.

Kyrin swallowed, and some of the tightness left her shoulders. When Alaina passed her on the way to the table the rice did not smell burnt. It lay smothered in peppery gravy on a bed of mint. Nara, always ready—but poor Nimah.

Sirius Abdasir's slave moved closer to his master's back, ignoring Alaina, forcing her to walk around him as she served. Alaina did so with the barest shrug. The small quirk of the slave's lips dissolved his sullen look.

Kyrin cocked her head. It had been a long time since she saw someone with such pale skin. He would not quite pass for a wind-browned shepherd on her father's moors, though he was as silent. Was it possible? Did he come from Britannia's shore?

When Ali and Sirius finished with the last dish and washed their hands, Ali ordered the table cleared and dismissed Alaina. He sent Kyrin for sweet cakes and tea, and she returned, eyes down, her feet quiet on rug and mosaic flower.

"A slave is but a slave—"

"But I must say in your ear, O my guest, a slave wears the subtle mark of his master's hand to any with eyes to see! As one who commands many, surely you have seen the greatest jewels and those who are less worthy than a grain of sand." Ali gestured widely.

Kyrin grimaced under her veil. With the pitcher of tea, she stepped back beside the pillar on Ali's right hand. She might have a long wait.

The pitcher was warm and heavy, the rug welcome to her sore feet. A length behind her a green enameled vase of brilliant peacock feathers rested on the stone. On the other side, Sirius's slave extended his foot, idly dragging his toes on the floor, back and forth, back and forth. Gracing the air between them, the feathers sprang over the wide lip of the vase, crowning his hair with blue-green splendor.

Sirius touched his near empty cup, and Kyrin moved to the table to pour for him. The guardsman made no other sign and with relief she turned toward her place.

The sole of the guardsman's foot faced Ali below the table edge. He wiggled and stretched his slippered toes a long, luxurious moment—and slid his foot into courteous position again beneath him. Sirius's dark eyes on her were purposeful. He knew her and cared little to honor her master.

Kyrin lifted her pitcher and put her back to the pillar, cool through her robe. Sirius could insult her master all he wanted.

"O my host," Sirius's smooth, interested voice continued the debate. "How do you value your slaves so highly? I have given less for a girl of more worth than yours." He indicated Kyrin. "My slave's voice is a dove's in the morning, her walk graceful as a gazelle. Her skin is smooth, pure as camel's milk."

Through her veil Kyrin touched her throat and the leaping fish. The scar. She shivered.

"You compare *my* slaves, taught at my table, to the muck bartered in the stalls of the souk, beside baskets of lentils and the crushed pits of dates?" Ali straightened, his mouth turning down. "How does a jewel compare to dung!" He threw out his hands.

Sirius leaned forward. "How does a jewel compare to gold?"

Behind the debaters, the guardsman's slave began to play the fool. He mimicked Ali, shaking his head in silent mourning that one could so misjudge a slave. Kyrin stared at him. He dared beard Ali?

The slave fell into soundless laughter, perfect resemblance to Ali's loud, empty pleasure. The slave grinned, and his eyes sparkled. Kyrin covered her laugh. He examined her from veil to toes and looked so long in her eyes she shifted her pitcher, glanced into it and sniffed. A cap with bells would not become this jester.

Then he turned to darker things, miming drawing his finger as a blade across his throat, and tied a strangling cord about his neck, tilting his head to one side, his eyes rolling up. He forced his tongue between his lips, turning blue with his held breath. He gave her grisly executions: hands cut off, hot pokers in the back, the live skinning, and the blood-seeking, glazed eyes of panting salukis. Their hot mouths closed and their teeth tore, with no one to call them off.

Kyrin asked him to stop with a small gesture. Though light-skinned, he could not be of Britainnia. No, he could—even a lord's son—mayhap fitly of Esther or Jorn's house. The slave tossed his hair back from his face, ignoring her, and began over again.

Ali sniffed. "It is the path of wisdom to instruct oxen with a stick *and* a gift. So I train my slaves, of ten times an ox's knowledge!"

Training oxen. At least that did not make her skin crawl, though her Master of the stars was the one who gave her the heart to serve Ali his meat. Tae was right, and she would serve, and wait. She would not look aside and give *this* Arab the satisfaction of fear. Kyrin glared at Sirius's slave.

Sirius smiled slightly. "My praise and fitting gifts have rewarded my patience with those who serve me a thousand times over. My oxen, my men and women would pull the moon to the stars' end at my word."

Kyrin scratched one ankle with her foot.

If Sirius would only get to the news. If he said nothing of Britannia, would she dare ask his slave? Tae or Zoltan would get more news from such a one than she. They would.

Her hands were damp against the pitcher, and she wiped them on her thawb. The steam smelled light and flowery. If some were left, Nara might give her a sip; she had never tasted such tea, famous from the western sea to its growing place in the East. It smelled of a new land.

Something pulled on her feet. The rug jerked away, and Kyrin sprawled on her back, just missing the vase with one wild, flailing arm. Honeyed tea flooded her. The vase rocked then crashed to the floor, shattered glass pattering across her.

Sirius turned and stared, and Ali gaped like an angry eel.

Gasping, Kyrin scrambled to her knees with her empty pitcher. It, at least, was whole. She wrapped her arms around it, waiting for Ali's blow.

His glance scorched her and slid beyond, to the slave. Ali's mouth tightened. He turned to Sirius with a lift of his chin. "There! It is as I said, O illuminated one, oxen and slaves do not recognize a pure hand! Beast-like, they understand only a gift or swift mastery."

"It was the laugh," Sirius said lightly. "What man or slave can bear a woman's laugh?"

Kyrin gripped the pitcher, her heart thundering. Sirius's slave stared at the floor. His mouth twitched.

So. The rug did not grow legs on its own. Treacherous Arab!

Ali's eyes smoldered. The slave ducked his head. Ali said, "My worthless one is not a gazelle's tender fawn. My guest, take a most lowly merchant's knowledge bought by torturous years. Seek devoted slaves, shape and use their milk-white flesh against them: so they will become jeweled blades to fit your hand. Your Seliam has less temper than her steel."

"She? Stronger than Seli?" Sirius said in astonishment, raising his brows. "Not if she crossed a hundred deserts!" His tone hardened. "When I raise my hand to instruct, the sword falls. My slaves know that. Does this hakeem of yours know your sword?" He smiled.

Ali glanced aside, his lips thinning. "He has known my displeasure, and tastes the sword of his loves. A spirit pierced by shame dies slowly, with more pain."

The grey mouth of the pitcher was sticky. Heat spread from the warm clay to Kyrin's chill hands, bringing the beat of her blood to a prowling beast of the night.

"That is truth, my host. But it has come to my ears the hakeem has a shield."

Shahin of the Aneza. Kyrin hardly breathed. Ali slammed his cup on the table. "More tea, slow one! This is cooled!"

Holding her pitcher carefully in front of her, Kyrin glanced over her shoulder at Seliam's smug mouth. *I could beat you into a sack pudding. If you bring trouble to us, Arab—I will. Tiger or no.*

When she slipped back through the curtains with the fresh tea it was not wanted. Ali and Sirius faced each other before the listening marble hunter.

"It is a match, O my friend." Ali's voice was deep with satisfaction. Kyrin gritted her teeth. Another of her master's wagers.

"As you will," Sirius said with a shrug. And eyed her.

Ali held up his hand. "Let us prove our methods, O my guest, with something gained." Head bent in thought, he rocked on his heels. His hungry smile spread over his face. He said to Kyrin with amusement, "Leave me. Bring Nimah."

Sirius's face gave her nothing.

§

In the long entry room Kyrin met Alaina with a basket of clothes on her hip. After one glance at her face, Alaina pulled her down the passage. In their room she brushed pieces of pottery from Kyrin's hair in the light of a lamp. She gripped Kyrin's arms. "What happened?"

Kyrin poured it all out, her tears coming with her words. Alaina dropped her hands, shaking her head. "Burn the treacherous fool! What was the wager?" She searched Kyrin's face.

Kyrin sobbed. It was as if her sister did not remember her hurtful words in the stable court. "I am sorry. Alaina, forgive me, I should not have shouted at you and Zoltan . . ."

"It is nothing." Alaina pushed the insults aside with her hand.

Kyrin sniffed. "I don't know who will be in the match, or what Ali wagered. He might make use of Umar's salukis or an ox. They spoke of oxen." She wiped her face. "Sirius goaded him—and the way Ali looked at him . . ."

Alaina's eyes narrowed. "I might have to stitch Thunderbolt again, and he almost took one of my fingers last time."

"He clawed you, and Tae had to sew *you* twice." Kyrin picked out Mey's short thawb from her bag at the head of her rug and began to struggle into it. "I forgot my supper," she muttered, "if Nara will give me any. She yelled at me—and Nimah burned the rice. Why did he do it, the Arab pig!" He was Arab to the heart. She gritted her teeth and hopped, trying to get into her trousers. And stopped in alarm. "Oh! I was to send Nimah to Ali!"

"I'll get your dinner, and Nimah. If you go you will be plagued with questions. You need to bathe before you dress."

Kyrin sighed. She was a sticky mess. "My thanks, Alaina."

Alaina pattered out, and tears welled in Kyrin's eyes again. She dashed them away. Her sister was a jewel indeed.

§

Kyrin sank toward sleep after a comforting dinner, into a dream of grey shadows. The deep "chuff, chuff" of an approaching animal's breath in the dimness was broken by the soft whispers of women. The whispers grew, threading around the sound of heavy paws padding about her rug. Kyrin could not move.

The dark shape of fear swung above her: the heavy head, the pricked ears, the short ruff. There was a rustle. The shape whisked away, and air swept across Kyrin's face. Voices hushed.

Her door slammed open. Kyrin broke her icy cocoon and rolled over—and stared up at a furious Nara with a lamp in her hand.

The room was empty but for her and Alaina and Nara. Kyrin sat up and Nara stalked to Alaina, who watched wide-eyed. The cook whispered in her ear. Alaina slipped out the door.

Kyrin got to her feet, swallowing to wet her dry throat. Surely Nara's anger could not be for her threat to Zoltan, if Nara knew of it.

The cook managed the five paces to her side without exploding. "You are in the stew-pot, girl." She snorted gustily, but not at Kyrin.

Kyrin blinked. "Did Ali blame you for the vase?"

"You did not bring shame," Nara said gently, "but—I heard of it from Umar." Her arms quivered with distress.

"I ruined the rug, and—the vase?"

"The guardsman rebuked Ali for his lack of mastery over his household." Nara paused. "You and Sirius's slave Seliam will fight in the morn, two marks before the sun's height."

Kyrin stared—and gulped. If only Sirius Abdasir was not the judge of who won. None would say the caliph's guardsman nay.

"What is our master's wager?" It did not matter. It would give her pleasure to instruct Seliam in Tae's way of the warrior. He would learn courtesy.

There was shuffling about the door, and some of the women peered in, eyes big and wondering, some of them in tears. Jachin growled outside. Qadira's shrill voice answered.

Nara snorted. "I know not the wager. Our master says his rod makes better slaves than Sirius's gifts. And Sirius demands proof. Blade against blade. Fools."

A shiver swept through Kyrin. So it was to be a blade. Daggers. "Where is Tae?" And why had Ali not told her of the stakes?

"Alaina will find him." Nara hugged her. "You . . ."

Kyrin did not hear the rest. Did Umar hide something of Ali's wager from Nara? Tae would protest to Ali. He would find out. She must prepare, she must show Tae by her skill with the dagger that she was ready to learn the sword. *Prepare to be beaten, Arab.*

A light touch on Kyrin's back made her stiffen and turn. Nimah's mother squeezed her shoulder, tears in her eyes. Another woman reached toward Kyrin with a sad smile and a touch like a farewell. Kyrin gaped.

Nara slapped their hands away. "What do you do? I know this one, she is no fragile flower of thyme. She is not chopped yet, this one does not belong in the stew. She eats it." Nara smiled at Kyrin with a slow wink. "She has tricks you have never seen. Be fearful for that idiot slave."

Nimah rushed to hug Kyrin's waist, looking up, "Is this true, your tricks?"

"Yes." Kyrin made her stiff mouth smile. When she broke his arm Faisal had not known she was trained to fight. Surely Sirius would tell Seliam to be cautious, since the guardsman was so interested in seeing her martial skill. Or he might dismiss her training. What skill did Seliam have? He looked strong enough.

The women gathered around her, their kohl painted eyes wide, full of questions and encouragement. Flushed, Kyrin gave them short, soft answers, uncertain how to answer. They had been her enemies. Qadira hushed them when Tae came to the door.

Kyrin made herself smile at him. Nara waved the others out, and Qadira led the way. Tae nodded at Nara as she passed last and said to Alaina, "Bring my herb bag. We have need of tea."

Entrapped

They have set an ambush for my life. ~Psalm 59:3

In the kitchen Tae set Nara to pounding and crushing and steeping. He sat cross-legged on the floor, his back to the still warm ovens, while the cook twisted tough leaves in her strong hands.

"Are there dates and milk?"

Nara nodded. "Nimah," she raised her voice, "we need a clear place and the platter prepared for Kentar." She cocked an eyebrow at Tae, and he inclined his head.

"My thanks."

Nimah scrambled to put a rug on the floor. Her mother brought Kentar's fare and set it before Tae. Alaina settled beside Kyrin.

Qadira sorted spices on a nearby shelf, Nimah's mother swept the floor with the barest rasp of the broom, and the other slaves found something to busy their hands. Kyrin bit back her grin. Nara never had so much help making up a second platter for Kentar.

Tae offered up thanks, and they ate. Over the food, he leaned forward. "Umar says Seliam has been told to mark you till first blood."

Kyrin nibbled on her bread and set it down.

Tae sat back. "He is not self controlled. Do not trust him. You will disarm him. If you must, take a cut and clear the way for your strike. Make any killing blow with the spine of your blade so it does not harm, but see that you draw blood."

"Yes." That would show her skill. Kyrin chewed a date and washed it down with milk. The sweetness almost made her sick. *He will try to cut me, maybe more. He deserves to bleed.*

"Use what you know. Stay back from his blade until you can get inside or outside his blade arm." He reached across the platter. "I know you. You will do well, daughter."

He made Kyrin a cup of bitter tea, and she drank while he entertained all in the kitchen with tales. They returned to their quarters. Tae sat outside the door under the lamplight, his back to the wall, busily shaping four handspan-long sticks. With Kyrin's falcon dagger.

Kyrin went to her rug, dreading the tiger. Alaina put her arms around her. She dreamed, though she did not remember the flaming beast, for sweat dampened her rug when she rose. Alaina busied herself about the room without comment. Kyrin was glad.

Her sister bound her hair into a braid that swung to her waist, and Kyrin flicked it over her shoulder, wishing she could toss thoughts of Seliam's dagger away so easily. One slip . . .

She would have no veil in the fight, and no necklace her enemy might use to choke her. The sign of evil in her ear and her scar would be bared to all.

§

Outside the door, Tae rose, thrusting his whetstone and the sticks under his sash at his back. The night had been long while he spoke silently into the darkness, beseeching, pleading, listening. He handed the falcon dagger to Kyrin when she opened the door, and led the way to the kitchen.

The falcon dagger's balance and edge was perfect. Kyrin stared straight ahead while they crossed the breezeway. Tae could not fault her. In spite of cheerful birds and leafing shrubs, the court flags glowed as blood under the new sun. They would hide well any that was spilled.

Prowling outside at first light, he had inspected the court-yard for offset stones that might catch a foot. He had found Ali among his roses at the end of the colonnade, his arms crossed. He had not liked their master's stare. Ali's wide, unpleasant mouth was turned up as if he laughed to himself.

Tae took Kyrin early from the kitchen and the palpable excitement there to the garden. He ran her through dagger drills beside Alaina, giving them quiet words of praise.

When Seliam's blade whistles in, she will fight. Her training will return fifty-fold. Yet within the space of the first blow, all is uncertain. Faisal would give her the fire she needs besides my trust.

Stepping aside, Kyrin retched up her rice and milk beside the wall and wiped her mouth. Tae dipped a cloth in the water flowing from the pipe for his herbs and offered it, catching her miserable eyes with his gaze.

"A little fear sharpens you." He held her hands, so much stronger than they had been the first time he cupped them in his. "Your way is through this fight. The Master of all has given you the warrior's way. He is growing what you need within." He touched her over the heart. There was so much more to to give her, to warn her of, to teach.

§

Alaina thought of Seliam's blade marking Kyrin's chest where Tae's fingers had rested, and her hand tightened on her dagger as she tried to still her quivering anger. What right did

Seliam have to terrify her sister with his blade, what right did the Arab raider have to take her mother from the world? None.

Tae's words seemed to comfort her sister, for she rinsed her mouth and nodded. She seemed to feel Alaina's anger, for she knocked the breath from her in the practice ring under the fig, turning the wood point and striking with the haft at the last instant. Tae rapped, "Enough!"

Alaina groaned over her stomach where the haft had sunk deep and gulped for air. *Save such blows for your enemy—the fear will not slow you. It won't.* A frown balled tight between her brows.

There were rapid steps at the gate. Zoltan cried, "Our master calls you to the Blue Flower room." He did not meet their eyes, and spun to leave. Alaina chewed her lip.

He goes to summon the others to the pavement. Burn him, he could offer her a smile. This match should give him enough revenge. She will surely take a thump or two. Alaina rubbed her sore stomach and followed Tae and Kyrin to the house.

Umar ushered them between the Blue Flower room curtains, his eyes bright. Incense lingered in the air, and sun-shafts slanting through the windows bathed the hunter in white gold. The light touched the armrests of Ali's chair, lit his neat-trimmed nails to pink as he drummed his fingers on Shahin's sword across his lap. His face was in shadow.

Ali settled his shoulders against his chair. The tiger leaped over his head above. Alaina firmed her mouth. *Don't let your fancy run with you.* His hands fell still. Alaina did not like his smile. Cultured, with something else lurking within.

"Well, well, the master of thousands brings his rangdo before me. Two askars—and no child to honor me. Umar speaks in my ear of a carving, a beautiful woman." He waved his hand sharply. "Remove your veils." He tapped the hilt of his sword, his eyes on Tae. "Let there be truth. The truth you claim to seek."

Head up, Kyrin tugged her veil free, and Alaina pulled her veil down, her skin cold. *He knows of Huen.*

"This one"—Ali pointed at Kyrin—"will struggle for my house." He mused softly, gently, "she brought the shame, and so she will cleanse the stain. She would not fight if she bore more children than the doll wife in your room, Hakeem." He raised his hands and his shrug was eloquent. "The Sheyk of the Aneza understands I am but a merchant, I cannot deny the most exalted guardsman of the caliph, who wishes to prove his slave. Though all wisdom does not reside in him."

Ali abruptly pointed his blade at Kyrin. His face was dark with anger. "My Hakeem is a fox, and daughter with an evil eye that you are, you know his secrets."

Kyrin's jaw tightened, and Alaina drew in a breath. They did *not* know the death touches—their master was mistaken—though they were close to that learning.

"You know well it is a delicate matter to shed blood," Ali continued. He arched a brow in playful, deadly levity at Tae. "Your askar, O my Hakeem, will prove against my guest's slave our differing minds on the teaching of a slave. *If* your training is sufficient."

Why did he call Kyrin askar and not rangdo? Soldier—not student? Does he mean to take her from us in some way? Alaina laid her hand over Kyrin's cold fingers on her arm. *He planned this—because we chose not to have sons—for the Master we obey.*

Rage shook her. Kyrin was right, she had been blind, wanting her companions' admiring glances, desiring Ali to change. Blind with yearning for a place of peace and friends.

Ali fingered the tip of his sword.

Alaina wanted to rip it away, to show him he was not secure in his power. Her master shrugged. "It is not to death—but to proof of blood. Or a limb. Arm, leg, ankle, it matters not."

Crippling, he means Seliam has leave to cripple her. Alaina folded her arms over her stomach, abruptly sick herself.

Ali turned his anger on Tae again. "If you or anyone steps between them, Hakeem, she dies. An askar more or less is a grain of sand in my slipper. Your knowledge of the warrior—and the rings in her ears—lend her what small worth she holds. If the worst befalls, my Shema will have any other in the house that she desires to serve her." Ali let his sword-tip drop. "It is not a fight to the death but the first disabling blow. Your askar *can* use her falcon dagger?" He raised his eyebrows. "That is more than her empty hands against Seliam's sword."

Sword? Alaina flinched with Kyrin and gripped her hard. *No. Dagger against sword?* He was mad.

"If she falls, she falls, O Hakeem, because her evil eye taints what she touches, and your Master of the stars is no master at all. She will die a virgin, as you have said." His smile dared them to speak. "Or did my binding word fail?"

Tae's jaw flexed. Alaina's harsh breath stung her nose.

Crippled. Death was a moment of pain and then life. Begging as a cripple in this land of poets meant dying by fingerbreadths of heat and hunger in a dusty corner, faltering under shame heaped on by women and children, cowering under the blows of men.

But Kyrin did not cower. Head up, her cheeks burned, her eyes fever-bright. The passive slave had gone with her veil, as if she had never been.

Ali stretched out his sword and lifted the limp veil from Kyrin's neck with the tip. It slid down his blade to his hand. He rose, laid the woven, gauzy blue across the arm of his chair, and trailed a finger along Kyrin's bared scar. His smile spread.

He spanned Kyrin's throat with his palm and stared into her face, his forehead almost touching hers, his voice sweet, soft poison. "If you do not cleanse my name, your sister, whom the hakeem does not desire for a wife, will divorce him and marry Seliam. At court she will hear the voice of the most Illustrious, and her hands will record. Seliam Abdeel swears by Allah that he will keep her as the light of his eyes."

Alaina shook, and thought of ways he could die. A blade in his eye, his heart, his liver. Her staff-blow would crush his throat, his temple.

Kyrin trembled under Alaina's hand. Alaina's knees went weak. *I said he would have to go through me to get to her. He has.* Her throat closed, dry as dust, and she coughed, a strangled sound.

Ali glanced at Alaina and amusement tilted his lips. "O most fortunate, you will live and die in the exalted court. Your excellent scribing will shield the caliph, blessed be he of Allah." There was licorice and mint on his breath. *His revenge comes above gold . . .* How had she ever thought he might care for anyone?

Her master slowly dropped his hand from Kyrin's neck. "If victory finds you worthy, worthless one, and you cleanse my name, you and your sister may not darken my door again." Ali sat and rested his sword against his chair.

Kyrin was white about the mouth.

He is keeping Tae—and banishing us. Kyrin! Even if you beat Seliam, Umar's Hand can find a dropped lily a hundred miles inside the desert, and we do not have the coin to make hands willing to aid us, to seal spying eyes and mouths.

If Ali keeps his word and if we reach the coast, many of the ships will be gone on the spring trade winds. But if you fall, I lose you and Tae and my body. I will be lost from land, hearth, and salt—all that I am. You will be lost from life. Alaina opened her mouth. She must speak.

Her master's form wavered through her tears, his mouth pursed in pleasure. It was but a first taste of revenge. Words would not sway him.

Tae said, "The guardsman raises his slaves as those of India nurture their bulls. If a mere staff overcame his slave's sword it would instruct him."

Alaina looked up from her despair. She must choose her words well. And take Kyrin's place. *My staff will have to do—it can defeat any dagger ever forged.*

Ali laughed. His belly shook until he wheezed. "I admire you, O mine enemy, alert to advantage even under the breath of death." He sighed and dried his eyes. "My esteemed guest has sealed the wager and the weapons used." He chuckled still, turning to Kyrin. "Do you hear, O my askar?"

"Yes, I hear and obey, my master." Kyrin drew herself straight, her arm sliding from Alaina's, and bowed in the way of the warrior.

Alaina stared sightless at the hunter's feet. The moment for speaking was past. Even Shahin would never get word in time. And the Aneza had little strength to pit against the caliph's askars.

§

Tae could not look at Kyrin. He said too much, had waited too long. Would it have been so evil to protect them with his body and his name? But it was not right. *My Huen! Lift your hands to Heaven for us.* Possibilities swirled, battering him against the hands of the Master. Those hands that held every bird and speck of dust. Tae willed his heart to slow, his breath to deepen.

Ali smiled with all his teeth. "You have taught them well, Hakeem."

It was a slap that bore more than one edge. Tae took a step forward. A shadow behind the near pillar shifted. Jachin.

Tae bowed, an ill taste in the back of his throat. There would be less chance on the court flags, but he needed time.

At the door, Umar stood back for them to pass, smiling broadly. "Stand on the pavement, O mighty Hakeem, to see her fall and the other divorced, or the decree that they go from this house, alone."

Tae stared at him. Yes, he could almost pray Seliam's sword went too far . . . Kyrin would not suffer, or be hunted in the desert by such as Umar.

Kyrin paused beside Tae. Her voice was low. "Umar. I do this for my father"—she laid her hand on Tae's arm—"and for my sister." Her eyes burned dark. "Whatever happens, I *will* see you no more."

"Hah!" Umar arched his brows. "You speak true, worthless one, I will see your face no more. A blade turns your bowels to water." With a thin smile, he drew his sword a fingers breadth.

Her eyes went to it and to his face, and then she turned away and went out, unmoved as stone. It was her oath.

Tae allowed his inner grin. The scent of Ali's burning incense no longer smelled of deceit and webs. A crystal drop of celebration slid along every entangling strand, encasing it in sparkling beauty. She named him father.

§

The sun washed around Kyrin, replacing the stuffiness of the Blue Flower room as Umar escorted them down the passage to the court. He stepped aside under the colonnade. Kyrin did not feel the air's warmth, only the falcon in its sheath, eager to taste the blood of justice.

But to what purpose? *Alaina, Alaina—oh, Tae—how do I leave you?* She must conquer Seliam's sword, shatter the ice, then they would see. Tae would not be idle, nor Nara. Alaina would be plotting their way on Umar's maps that she held so well in her mind.

"Come."

Kyrin stepped onto the flags after Tae, walking toward the shade of the orange tree beside the gushing horse-head fountain. The men and women of the house who waited about the kitchen and the men's quarters parted for them. Wrapped in the sound of the fountain, Kyrin bowed her head. Tae and Alaina's warm hands sweated in hers. They were companions again, and she would fight.

Jesu! Let me follow the falcon to your heart. At the top of the wall light flushed gold-green through new leaves and waving branches. "Give me your fire of justice . . . your will be done . . ." She licked her dry lips.

Quiet talk crossed the court, back and forth. Kyrin scuffed the pavement, pulling her braid, uneasy under the wondering stares and voices.

She had hoped for a glimpse of Jachin, but he was nowhere. A red canopy raised a festive cover under the colonnade. Shema sat in one of three chairs, her cushion almost swallowing her small form, clad in white robes. Ali's chair from the Blue Flower room sat to her right, with another seat beyond. Sirius's seat.

Shema stared at her across the court. Did she clench her hands in her lap? She had no word that Ali would hear, and she was going to lose her friend whether Kyrin won or lost.

Kyrin straightened and gave Shema a full bow.

Her mistress raised her henna-spiraled hands, miming a restrained slap. A reminder of their first meeting. Kyrin thought Shema's lips quirked in a shaky smile, and her own mouth twitched. Shema trusted her strength to overcome her enemy.

Near the front gate, twenty of Sirius's askars stood about the pool, some sitting on the stone edge. Their thawbs were brilliant red, their deeper scarlet sashes bearing a small gold sigil on the ends. Red fluttered from the hilts of swords and the tips of their spears.

Sirius strode in through the gate, Seliam behind him. The askars' yell crashed over the courtyard. Two of Sirius's men escorted him to the canopy, where he sat before Kyrin on the left side of the dais.

His set face made him a stern leader and judge of men. His rich brown thawb waved in the lazy breeze.

Seliam left his master with a nod and strode across the flags in white trousers and a red sash, his tanned shoulders gleaming with oil. A sash of scarlet, bearing a wink of gold. Askar.

Jesu, and the falcon and I—we bear the right. For Alaina and Tae, Nimah and Zoltan and Nara, I do not bear the sword in vain. Heat welled in Kyrin. *So he is trained, as am I. A test indeed, though my master has made it far more. Indominable spirit. For my mother, for them. One Arab will know it.*

Seliam searched Ali's gathered household, his head turning slowly. His eyes found hers. He gave her a deep, deep bow. She tipped her head in return, not stooping to his mockery.

The crowd heaved and muttered. On either side of Kyrin, Tae and Alaina bowed to Seliam, the precise bow of declaring opponents. One side of Seliam's mouth turned up. The crowd stilled.

"Remember," Tae said in her ear, "*move,* stay out of his reach, draw him in. Until he is where you want him, be afraid."

That would not be hard.

"Do not hold your blade from him, but your hate."

Hate? Seliam would find justice.

The sun was bright on the flags, on the red canopy, on the silver hilt of Seliam's sword. It surprised Kyrin that it did not cling to the long edge in fire.

The flags burned her toes while Arabs watched, waiting for the moment her blood would spill and her mouth mew in defeat. Nasrany, slave, disobedient—to them, her pain was justified. Kyrin touched her jet earring. *Indominable.*

30

Nemesis

Fight the good fight.... ~1 Timothy 6:12

Appeared in the door of his house. Umar and Jachin flanked him, hands on their blades thrust through black sashes. Umar was bare but for a loin wrapping, his golden limbs shining. Clad the same, Jachin looked over the court, his ebony face taut, beaded with sweat.

His eyes rested on her, or was his gaze on Tae behind her? Kyrin smiled at him and hoped he saw.

The sound of the crowd was a growl. Hungry, impatient, a dim swelling cloud of sound. Then Tae's embrace lifted her from the ground, and she felt his quick heartbeat through his blue thawb. He set her down and kissed her forehead. "I am proud. Remember how you stand with the Master of the stars."

Alaina caught her in a painful hug. "A slave won't beat you." She pulled free, tears glistening on her face. "Burn his askar ways to dust!"

Ali sat in the third seat on the dais. In a voice that silenced all else, he cried, "Let the askars come forth!"

With a male's easy strength, Seliam strode to a wide circle marked in white chalk on the flags before the canopy. Sirius's askars and his retinue roared approval.

Kyrin laid her damp hand on her falcon. She would not stumble on the way to her enemy, though her muscles were wood. She walked forward, and did not stumble. The guardsman's askars hooted. Ali's household roared back, surprising her. Zoltan stood among the foremost, shaking his dagger over his head.

Seliam eyed Kyrin through his hair, and tossed it from his face.

She stopped. Close enough to embrace him, Kyrin smelled musky myrrh, olive oil, and sweat. It brought back the scent of sea wrack, storm, and cinnamon. A high tower with a cheerful fire; her mother, dressing for supper; flickering torchlight against dusk. Kyrin cradled the falcon blade.

§

Ali concealed his smile. They made a spectacle, his worthless one all in black, sharp-faced and pale, her bold eyes and jet earring distinct against the opposing bronze circle of his ownership. Sirius's slave stood proud and strong in askar scarlet. Ali snorted. He would find a challenge indeed. Sirius Abdasir waited, idly watchful. Ali leaned back. He would seek out the guardsman's purpose, and if he must, he would thwart it.

Shema twisted her fingers in her lap, and he glared at her. When his desert mouse learned the strength of his house and his will, saw the tempering of his slaves, she could but admire. It was time to prove the substance of his forging, the hardness of his jewels. Ali raised his arm. In this courtyard, he decided fates.

§

At Ali's gesture, Seliam bowed to his master and drew his blade.

Kyrin stepped back and spread her arms wide as Seliam's sword whispered from his sash. "I do not desire to fight you." She gestured at her bronze falcon dagger. "This contest is not in honor. Ask a blade for me." She would use every dragging moment.

Seliam tossed his head, raising his sword. "They told me you could do more than speak, fearful one." His two-handed grip whitened his knuckles.

The thin blade held sun and shadow and burning-cold crystals that crept toward her heart. Kyrin willed her gaze past the edge to his contempt. "I am not afraid, but a trial of skill lies between the strong."

He blinked and laughed, and his mouth fell into habitual lines of petulance. "I will gain a beautiful gazelle, and your blood will flood these stones, loosing her to me. You, Nasrany, will beg of Allah."

She took a breath and slid the falcon free. Her chest cramped. "I would sooner plead with a djinn!" The ice shattered. Seliam swung—short and hard.

Kyrin sprang in behind the blow. Too late. His backswing ripped her sleeve and drew a line of red along her forearm. She slid away, looking to Ali, who waved her on. Her arm stung, but the blood did not run. Heat spread through her.

Seliam laughed, harsh with taunt. "That is your first taste, Nasrany!" He worked toward her and lunged, pulling his sword down in a cross-body blow. Metal grated on metal as she diverted his blade with the dagger. Sirius's men yelled encouragement.

"You know the price, my askar!" Ali called to Kyrin.

Seliam lunged again. Kyrin watched his blade—and smiled.

He cut at her head with driving strokes, she retreated.

Ali screamed at her, beating his hands on his knees. Kyrin slipped aside—and her back foot slid with a scritch of sand on flags. Just so had her mother fallen. Kyrin rolled back into the fall, over her shoulder, and sprang to her feet.

Seliam ran in, swinging. His blade would cut her in half. Kyrin evaded the edge by a hair. And found her opening. With a scream of defiance, she struck.

The falcon slid clean, around his stomach to his back. She followed the blade and slid her other arm about his neck from behind. Her dagger tip pricked his spine. His body arched back.

With bated breath, the crowd waited for his belly to spill. On the gutting blow, she had reversed the blade to the unsharpened edge. Seliam wavered, sword loose in his hand. His breath wrenched hollow through him.

Ali leaned back, and Sirius struck his knee with a curse. Shema put a hand over her eyes.

Kyrin cried, "Yield!"

Seliam fell limp. She staggered, unable to hold him with one arm, but unwilling to slide the falcon into her sash. Kyrin's hand quivered at his back.

If she killed him now, she broke Ali's wager. Her falcon's blunt haft sped toward his temple. The biting prick of the falcon signified blood enough.

Sliding down to drop onto his knees, Seliam unfolded with a snap. His oiled skin defeated her wild swipe. He whipped around and his blade point raked her ankle as she sprang back. Kyrin shook her leg. It burned, but he had not cut the tendon. Seliam crouched, wary, his sword guarding.

Ali yelled, "Bring him down!"

It should have been finished. She could have killed Seliam. All knew it.

The white receded from his face, and his burned-corn hair was lank with sweat. He feinted, studied her sideslip with passionless eyes, every sense focused. His eyes were slits, his mouth tight and bloodless. He meant to kill her.

And their masters meant to let him try.

"Never take your eyes off your enemy." I won't, my father. Kyrin slid into Seliam's reach, and retreated. With a cross-body slash, he followed, a moth to the flame of her body. He missed, and thrust one-handed for her stomach.

She side-stepped then sprang. They thudded together. Kyrin aimed a stroke under his arm, and Seliam's elbow slammed into her dagger hand as he desperately pulled back to shield his ribs.

The falcon dropped from her fingers. Then her hands captured his wrist and twisted. She kicked at his front leg. It gave and she spun him about. His sword fell.

Kyrin took him to the stones with the dull smack of flesh on rock—and landed with her knees in his back. This Arab would learn the cost of treachery.

Confused noise thundered in her ears as she crouched over him, panting. Kyrin wedged her heels further into his sides and shoved his arm up behind his back. Seliam's sword lay loose on the flags. She shifted her weight to hold him and reach it. She held up his blade. "It's done!" Her voice was a gasp.

Seliam bucked. Kyrin dropped to his back. He stiffened and his choked voice cried, "I yield!"

Sirius Abdasir rose from his chair, gaze dark with wrath. "Get up, worm!"

Kyrin did not move. Jachin and Umar touched their sword hilts. Sirius's escort stood from their seats about the court, but under the guardsman's glare they sat again. Ali said nothing, but gave a low laugh. Jachin looked from him to Umar, and loosed his grip.

Carefully, Kyrin laid Seliam's blade down. Using the wrong weapon would absolve a man like Sirius of many things. She leaned across Seliam for her dagger, and he shoved up. Kyrin dropped the falcon clanging to the flags and flattened, sliding her arm around his throat, wedging his arm yet higher with her body. Again he strove to rise. Tae's voice rang in her mind. *Stay with him!*

Her stranglehold on Seliam's throat pulled yet harder when he rolled onto his back—with her under him as he sought to crush her. *No, you will not!* Clinging to him like a leech, Kyrin worked her other hand under her head, and anchored to her opposite shoulder. She arched her back, tightening the choke. He made one frantic effort, and rolled onto his face without a groan.

Kyrin screamed past his unhearing ear at the caliph's guardsman, "Do—you—yield!"

Sirius stared over her head as if she did not lie on his slave's back, betrayed, her arm choking away his life. The sun beat from the flags into her sweaty face. Seliam's neck throbbed relentlessly against her arm.

The ice was melted. *Mother, I did it. I beat the Arab and his blade.* But there was a price to be paid.

The falcon was warm and heavy in her hand as she released her enemy's neck. In a small room her mother smiled at her for the last time. Tae groaned, suspended by Ali's ropes. Her master raised his whip over her cowering form, then Faisal tossed the falcon blade at her feet. Ali dragged Alaina by her hair to Seliam. To a slave who dared gloat in cruelty and pain.

Seliam's musled back rippled feebly under her as he stirred. She braced, and waited for Sirius's protest. It did not come.

Ali glanced from her to Sirius, who gave no sign.

Justice was in her lawful reach. She would protect Alaina and Tae. No one could stop the falcon's strike—as she could not stop the blade that took her mother. Triumph shook through her heart.

Seliam's life would spill. The red would dry to flakes, black flakes to mingle with the snowy powder of her mother in her fiery death. Ashes. Never did her mother want ash.

A tear ran down Kyrin's face. Her arm shook. *She* did not want ashes. *As you have been forgiven . . .*

Ali dropped his hand to his knee in a chopping motion. The guardsman stared, and stroked his chin, saying nothing. The moment widened in a pool of silence. Seliam's sweaty hair spilled over his neck, and his back heaved in small jerks. Had the nerve point she hit thrown him into convulsions?

Then Kyrin knew.

Seliam was crying. She flinched despite herself. Her dagger hand rested beside his shoulder.

It was Ali's command. Kyrin's grip tightened, and she lifted the falcon.

Indrawn breaths swept around the court and caught at her, a ragged blade-edge. *Alaina, oh, Alaina.* Heart aching, teeth bared, she reached to her burning ankle, then flung out her arm. Men and women jerked back from the pattering drops of red.

She knew the right place at the back of the head. Her grip on the haft was numb. With the blow, the world crashed back in.

Loosening her legs from Seliam, Kyrin stood. She leaned over, and her blind, searching hand found his sword. In her mind the tiger and the falcon were a whipping blur of beating pinions and paws, of flame fur and slate feathers. *You remain captive.*

Kyrin whirled, a blade in each hand. Lungs heaving, she blinked hard. And hurled the sword across the court, past the colonnade and Ali's seat. *Tae would call it practice, striking the precise point.*

Umar twitched. Kyrin almost smiled. Sirius' men watched. The blade winked into Ali's largest rosebush then rustled and thumped into the depths. Tears cooled her cheeks. Staring at the rosebush, Kyrin sobbed once. *I am sorry, Alaina.* Seliam broke the law of the match—and she broke her master's command.

Slaves and askars in red goggled. Their mouths opened and shut. Then Shema clapped once, and smiled. Nara broke into a ululating cheer. A wave of stamps reverberated through the flags under a rising roar of approval.

There was a slight smile on Ali's face. She would give much to wipe it off. Kyrin rubbed her cheek. The wind tugged her sticky hair from her temples, flapping a torn black sleeve. Next to Nara stood Alaina, face tracked with tears, fear in her uncertain glance.

Kyrin stared at her hands. She hoped Tae, at least, would understand. But she could not find him among the heaving sea of faces.

It was over, except for her punishment. Kyrin sank down cross-legged, laying the falcon dagger in her lap. Every muscle had its own fire, and she wished she could go to the pool and drink and drink. It hardly mattered.

Behind her on the flags, cloth rustled as Seliam moved; he would have a headache. She fingered the falcon. It had another scratch that revealed the steel.

The stamping cheers died. Whispers rose as footsteps approached. Without looking, Kyrin knew who stood behind her.

Umar ripped the dagger from her unresisting hand. He and Jachin seized her under the arms and hauled her before the dais. Her stumbling feet would not follow her will. They let go, and she fell on her knees. It hurt more than it ought, more than Seliam's blade.

A harsh step beside her, and Kyrin saw Jachin's foot, the tip of his bare sword resting on the flags. Umar snorted on her other side. He would see his revenge.

Ali's chair vibrated with the force of his drumming fingers. Kyrin looked up as Shema whispered something in his ear, but she could do less than nothing.

Sirius Abdasir considered Kyrin, dark eyes sober. Hers burned into his. *Snake. You should have stopped it.* He blinked slowly, his mouth curving neither up nor down.

But it mattered not. Kyrin turned her head to stare at a corner of the canopy, at a lonely, bobbing tassel, battered by the wind.

Ali smiled grudgingly. "Well, O my askar. You have learned the strength of the mercy of the house of Ali Ben Aidon." His gaze lingered on Sirius, who stared over the crowd with a frown.

The strength of the mercy—the murderer! Kyrin's mouth opened in hopeless outrage. She would have lunged up beside his chair and stabbed him if Umar did not have her falcon blade. She gripped her ankle harder, until the pain anchored her to the flags.

Sirius Abdasir sighed. At last he shrugged, and inclined his head to Ali. He conceded the match.

The caliph's guardsman looked past Kyrin. Through the quiet, his voice carried. "My most generous host, your askar has your mercies. I am instructed: a hand may be over generous to a slave, or an askar. Your slave fought well, and her teacher is restrained, worthy of reliance. The golden-haired slave is a skillful scribe. My master will be pleased. But a man should not be bereft of his wives. There will be no divorce and no marriage. My master accepts."

What? Her head was muddled. *What* did the caliph accept? If Tae was not to be broken in Ali's house, and Alaina not to marry Seliam?

"It is well, O my brother." Then Ali nodded to Shema. Smiling, she stood and unfastened a string of polished pearls and blue shell from around her neck, holding them high. Ali intoned, "On behalf of the light of my eyes, here is a token for the one who fought for our house." There was a pause in which every eye admired the drops of swirling, milky cloud inter-spersed with bits of blue sky. Shema bent and laid the necklace in Kyrin's hand.

The crowd erupted. Kyrin stared down at the necklace. Ali's decree of crippling or freedom, of Tae's binding, Alaina's forced marriage: all had been lies? Her smile was bitter. So, Ali found worth to wring from his flawed jewel. An afternoon's entertainment.

As if sensing Kyrin's inner war, Shema said low, "Kyrin—" her voice begging her to accept Ali's gift. With a wave and an expansive grin, her master invited her to put the necklace on.

Kyrin gave Shema a watery smile and closed her hand on the pearls, cool in her hot hand. These she would take, in memory of her master's word broken, of other words kept, and her word to keep.

Her father kept his blades clean, as he did his word. *Oh, Father—Ali never meant ought but evil—but your honor is true. I will try to uphold honor also. I will find you.*

"Ah ha! There, you see, I have also learned from you of a gift fitly given!" Ali turned to Sirius, ignoring his wife and Kyrin. Shema called for Qadira to help her inside the house. The star-ing askars and Ali's overjoyed household gathered before the kitchens, joining in a general celebration of sweetened tea and chattering their amazement at what each had seen of the fight.

Jachin lifted Kyrin to her feet by an arm. He shook her with a wide grin, chortling and bowing his head to her at the same time, then pulled her into a hug. When he released her, she inclined her head with a shaky smile, and on his mighty arm limped to-ward the kitchen and a cool drink. Umar had disappeared.

So. She would see him again. That did not seem so bad, now. Several young Arabs of Sirius's retinue hovered close as two askars carried Seliam toward the men's quarters. Good. Not even Seliam should be deserted as Faisal's companions left him on the sand. Would Faisal approve her fight? *Oh my brother, I hope you smile for me.*

Tae appeared at her shoulder, his herb bag in hand, and leaned down to wrap a cloth about her ankle. It sent fire up her leg. Kyrin yelped. Alaina caught her other arm to steady her. Her sister hugged her, and her face was wet. She had forgiven her, then. Kyrin closed her eyes. They were safe.

§

Sirius kissed Ali on both cheeks and dropped a clinking sack in his hands.

Ali smiled and handed the sizeable fruit of his private wager to Umar, who appeared at his elbow. It had been a most satisfying day. He brought his hands together loudly. His slaves straightened, surely with pride, and their shout echoed from wall to wall. "The house of Ben Aidon is merciful and great!" At his dismissal, they boiled happily about the kitchens.

Ali fingered his chin. There was a banquet to come, and he must speak of his worthless one's prowess. She had pleased Sirius, the delight of the caliph's eyes, so she pleased him. Yet she seemed less a jewel for his setting than before. He frowned. He *would* see her in a place to bring him gold. Yet he must take care that the jewel did not shatter in his hand.

§

Kyrin limped through the breezeway with Tae and Alaina. Nara stepped from the line of other elated women on their way to prepare the feast in the kitchen. Her glowing eyes were full of tears. "Oh, girl, girl," she whispered, wiped her eyes, hugged Kyrin again, and disappeared inside, where Kyrin heard her calling loud, cheerful orders.

Every eye followed them, and many watched Tae. He bowed, mouth curving with his small smile, his eyes missing nothing.

Tae had disappeared during the fight. She had to know why. "You did not watch?"

He tipped up her chin gently, his voice full of pride and joy. "I saw."

"But where did you go?"

All expression fled. "A place I had to be."

31

Vengeance

I desire compassion, and not sacrifice. ~Matthew 9:13

"Kyrin! It's time!" Alaina called. She bounced into the darkening room and shook what she grabbed first. Her sister sat up and retrieved her unbandaged foot. Kyrin looked wan as an inside-out thawb Nara had squeezed dry.

"Why do I have to eat with Ali in front of everyone?" she muttered. "And I have to wear that cursed necklace."

"Oh, come, the pearls truly come from Shema, and you will feel better with some of Nara's honey-almond cake and heavenly curried oryx inside you." Alaina helped her up and lit the lamp. She brushed Kyrin's thick hair, curling a little from her braid after a hasty bath, before she collapsed on her rug.

"Now, beautiful ones," Tae said softly. Alaina turned. Tae slipped through the door quietly, drew a pair of black hairpins from his sash, and laid them in Kyrin's hand. The hard wood was glossy as rock. A falcon's head, it's beak open in an uncompromising scream, adorned each pin. Opposing, carved whorls circled the black shafts down to their sharp points.

How fitting that he carved falcons for Kyrin. Alaina wound the pins into her sister's hair with a few deft twists. *She saved me from Seliam in a backwards kind of way. And I, the scribe who beat old*

387

Qadira's poetic lines, I had no words for her in her needful moment. Tae at least asked Ali to give her a staff, bless him. Tae tested her creation with a tug. Alaina captured a stray brown lock and wound it about one of the pins. *If she would but listen . . . but she has been drawing away into her Subak.* Alaina's brow pinched. *She is not always right. But, creeping lizard, monkey without a mouth, why did I say nothing?* At last the falcon pins held firm, an elegant canted *x*, the falcons nestled at the top edges of Kyrin's glistening coif.

"There," Tae said. "It is fitting that you face Ali and his table tonight with these. This night you are a warrior. You will wear the half-veil but not the hair wrap unless Ali commands otherwise. I do not think he will. The necklace is your spoil of war."

Kyrin grinned at him.

Alaina felt alone, more lost than she ever had before. "They are beautiful, wait until you see them." She shrugged her unease away and turned Kyrin about. "Let us find a mirror!" Shema had one of bronze, and she would clap her hands over Kyrin's hair. Almost a Greek weave, almost the coronet of the women of the Eagles, she'd given Kyrin's hair a twist of her own.

"Wait." Tae smiled, beckoning, two honey-colored pins in his hand.

Alaina felt her blush, and the tears that followed. *Burn it.* She fingered the wooden heads, the tiny ridges and smooth leaves. Delicately carved ferns circled the shafts. "Thank you," she said, and gulped.

Gently Tae coiled her hair and slid in the golden pins. "Great women of my country wear these, and you are worthy."

Alaina turned and hugged him hard, and Tae laughed. He did not often laugh. And her sister, Lady Kyrin. She had beaten Seliam's sword. *They* had beaten Ali, for the moment. But for how long?

Alaina shook the thought away. It was high time to see Shema. She smiled at Kyrin, and they slipped out of the room with the most un-warrior like of giggles.

"Bear them well!" Tae called.

Determination welled in Alaina. "I will!" She fingered the pins again. They could be a weapon, yet they also made her feel a lady.

"Here." Kyrin stopped before the Blue Flower room curtains and fixed Alaina's slipping hair. "Few men have the touch to make it stay. I am sorry I growled when you woke me up. Come on." She grinned. "Just watch Nimah's face when she sees you."

Alaina's smile widened. Nimah would admire her robin's egg blue trousers and short thawb patterned off the black Persian clothing Mey had made Kyrin, with three inch cuffs at leg and arm. It had taken nothing to sew, and with the honey-gold pins in her hair it made her as exotic as Nimah could wish. The garments reminded her of home in Britannia and set off her white silk sash.

Alaina spun in a happy twirl down the passage. Tae would have to make a pair of pins for Shema . . . She stopped short. "Kyrin, you can't wear those old oak beads with our master's pearls—" Her protest died. By the stiffness of her face, Kyrin was going to wear them.

§

Sirius inclined his head when Kyrin approached the table, and Ali directed her to sit beside Shema. Kyrin sat, as uneasy as a falcon on her first man-made perch, clenching her cup so her hands would not move aimlessly. Shema nudged her with her foot and picked up a fruit. Kyrin took a date and some oryx, but her hunger was gone. She forced a bite down. The feast was long and loud.

Throughout the procession of dishes of lamb, pigeon, rice with raisins, dried fruits soaked in milk, and curried oryx, which *was* heavenly, Kyrin's female servers offered her their favorite tidbits with indirect glances. She could not refuse, and soon her plate was piled.

Sirius's gaze kept returning to her across the table, and Kyrin ate so she did not have to meet his eyes more often than she must. It did not save her from his regard.

"My master is intrigued by a woman who knows a blade."

Was that mild rebuke? Or an interest of his own? He had touched her hand once.

Ali broke in with a cheerful smile. "Ah, but who can know the depths of an infidel's heart? They thrive from their first squall on the milk of false teaching. But they amuse us, and Allah knows the hour of his vengeance."

"A jewel of truth." Sirius's mouth curved without mirth.

Her master had diverted the conversation. Kyrin was content. Ali did not speak either to her or to Shema. *His* regard had not changed. Kyrin chewed the rice in her mouth and swallowed.

"I would see the blade that defeated my askar." Sirius watched her.

That must be answered. Kyrin bowed where she sat, pulled her falcon dagger in the rabbit-skin sheath from her sash, and leaned past the lamb to lay it in his hand. She forced her restless hands in her lap.

Sirius turned the weapon in his fingers, eyeing the bronze head; the jet eyes, amber in the light; the defiant beak. The muscles in his cheek flexed, his mouth thinned. Kyrin held her breath.

He paused. Then drew the dagger with a sharp movement, far enough to see the gleam of bronze. With a twist of his mouth he replaced the blade and tossed the falcon to her. Kyrin caught it. What had he expected to see?

"A worthy enough dagger for this one, is it not?" Ali smiled. Sirius nodded, sober, and Kyrin wondered what troubled him. "It is like to the dagger of one I once knew." He shrugged. "But this blade is of little worth."

Ali chewed. "A blade that resembles your traveler's is a favored gift for one such as she." He turned to snatch a sugary plum from Nimah before she removed the platter. Sirius measured him with a cool glance.

Kyrin let her eyes fall to her hands. Sirius did not like Ali. *Join the household.*

At last Ali dismissed her. As Kyrin rose she managed to touch Shema's foot in thanks. Trying to hide her smile of relief, she made her way towards the curtains, past three endless tables of guests, askars, and many of Sirius's retinue, who ate and drank amid endless jokes. Ali had invited them to celebrate, and the young men serving their table scurried among them.

Why, as her teacher, had Tae not sat in honor here, or at Ali's table? Intent on ducking through the curtains, wrapped in thought, Kyrin stumbled over someone's leg. She looked down, mouth open to ask pardon.

Seliam sat bonelessly against the wall, not glancing up in protest. The young Arabs who had carried him away from the court flags rested on the other side of the doorway, carefully not looking at either of them. They dared not soil themselves with Seliam's presence.

Seliam's face was haggard. His head must hurt. He should be resting. Probably Ali demanded he be here, though he huddled as close to the door as possible.

The curtain bulged, and a hand reached around it. A smaller boy with shaggy black hair looked around the blue silk edge. He had dared sit at Seliam's feet. Eyeing her cautiously, he nudged Seliam with an elbow. After a moment Seliam raised his eyes, full of hate.

She struggled with her thick tongue. "I don't hate you," seemed a wrong choice at the moment.

Someone touched her shoulder and she spun, off balance, her ankle twinging. Nimah steadied her and held out a sweet cake with a wide grin. Several of the women crowded behind her, giggling. They held empty platters, cups, and jugs. Among a chorus of warm greetings, one said, "Was the askar hard to trip?" And tittered, high and shrill.

Kyrin's ears heated. She could think of five ways to take Seliam down, but not five words to turn this moment. "Let's go to the pool!" she blurted.

"Oh, yes! And you must tell us everything. . . . Give the dishes to Nara quickly, Nimah." They grabbed leftover honey-cakes from another tray and hurried out.

Kyrin did not look at Seliam as she followed, favoring her leg; her face was forge hot. For him or for herself? She did not know. Arabs did not regard mercy unless it served them.

Outside, the air was warm, light with the fragrance of flowers, and the stars were bright. Much splashing and laughter followed Kyrin's skin-tingling plunge to join the others. She gasped when the water hit her scraped arm. Though it stung, it smelled of moss and life.

She swam to the edge of the pool and began to work the stiffness out of her legs with her hands, resting her ankle on the stone side above the water. She smiled at them all, adding an occasional splat to a water fight that erupted. There was more laughter than she had ever heard in Ali's house, and Umar did not appear to quiet them. It felt so good to laugh with them. Maybe they understood her a little now.

Nimah admired Kyrin's hair-pins more than a little, and the other women looked over her shoulder with "oohs" and "ahhs." Kyrin took them out and shook her hair loose, and Nimah handed the pins around. Tae would have many requests for more.

Kyrin gave brief answers to their deep curiosity about her fight with Seliam. She could not laugh at him. With one misstep she would have been him.

The night wore on and the women quieted, settling to wash each other's backs and hair. Nimah rewound Kyrin's hair. One by one the women left, walking by Kyrin to kiss her goodnight before they strolled toward their quarters. Alaina finished serving at Ali's table and came out to bathe. Then she hugged Kyrin and went to her bed. She did not seem to want to speak.

Kyrin slipped deeper into the pool and lolled in the water, listening to the night, overlaid by the clatter of dishes in the kitchen and muffled voices. Nara was up late.

She fingered one of her pins loose and regarded it. Huen must love Tae. A good man, and worthy of her. Huen had doubtless sworn to wait for him.

Kyrin sighed. As she must wait until Tae returned from his and Alaina's task in Baghdad. She would serve well until she could be made free, as Alaina did. *When we leave this place, I hope Tae takes the doll to Huen, a sign of his faithfulness to stand in honor in their home.*

Home. The whispering oaks and rustling beeches and Samson flying to her fist in a rush of wings. Did Father shoot his great bow with armsmaster Nith—and think of her? His brown face, his strong smile, his loving laughter, how she knew them. Kyrin gripped the pin and hugged her knees.

A blade no longer turned her to a statue of ice. She had beaten a sword with the falcon dagger. Father would want to see the

Damascus steel that had beaten a sword. She laughed softly, and found tears on her cheeks.

She slid the pin back in her hair. She did not want to see the round city, quite content with Shema and Jachin. She knew their faces, and someone needed to keep a finger on the news here, for nothing must be missed. Jachin had hinted that Ali meant him to teach her a little of the sword while Tae and Alaina were gone in Baghdad.

Frogs and insects sang louder as the kitchen quieted. Merriment from the house came faint. She lay back, holding her breath while the water lapped to her nose, and stretched every finger and toe as far as she could. The last knot and the fever-pitch of the day slid from her muscles. Alaina was not to marry Seliam, and Tae remained their protector.

She had faced the Arab and vengeance. When the ice gripped she could assess the hand and the mind behind her attacker's weapon. She could act when she feared.

Heaving herself up onto the flat pool edge, Kyrin felt one with the warm night. Her body was whole, her ankle but a scratch. Her creator had been merciful. She gazed at his sky, spangled with the brightest, best jewels, and the kindness of his night seeped in. *Thank you.*

A mischievous wind wafted her wet shoulders, and the scent of pool-watered earth and the vine's sweet white blooms hung thick. Kyrin got to her feet.

She had best sleep. Nara would cuff the back of her head in the morning if she burned the rice she had promised to show Nimah how to cook. Again. Even if she did beat Seliam, sunrise was another day. Water dripped from her and tinkled into the pool.

Thoughtfully she wrung water from her black thawb. She would hang it in the window where it would dry by morning, and

Alaina would mend the tear in the sleeve from Seliam's blade. Tonight she would sleep in her blue thawb.

Kyrin walked toward the gate, humming. The day had been long, with a good end. No one died.

A shadow detached from the black outline of the gate and struck her a glancing blow. Nimah—no, the small figure was not her. Others closed in. Kyrin sprang away, spinning, too late.

She was borne to the ground with a "whoof!" the air dashed from her lungs. Without breath to scream she thrashed and twisted and hit.

Many hands forced her onto her back. Someone held her head, digging steel fingers around her ears, under her jaw. She bit and bucked, straining against their weight holding her arms and legs. Dirt was thrust into her mouth. Kyrin heaved against the ground, spitting, struggling to breathe.

One of her legs slid free. She heard a grunt when she lashed out. Then her arm was loose. She clawed at the person clamping her head and snagged an ear, dug her fingers in and jerked, trying to pull him over, into the way of the rest. She was working free.

A foot stamped in her stomach. Kyrin curled around the pain, arms around her head. Blows ripped into her sides. White sparks circled her.

Pain, pain, and then foggy awareness. Several people close by panted. A savage voice said, "I will teach you the mark of mercy!"

Kyrin barely tightened her belly before another stamp almost dropped her into the darkness creeping up around her. A hand clawed at her neck and tore the pearls off over her head. She couldn't move. A tentative voice asked, "Is she . . .?"

A blow sank into her side and drove air from her mouth in a sobbing "hunnh."

"No," the savage voice growled. "She will not feed my seasons of work to the wind." He hawked and spat. Warm and sticky, it dribbled across Kyrin's neck. Somehow it was the worst.

There was a shout from the dark at the gate. "You! What errand do you have here?"

Kyrin struggled to open her eyes. It was not so dark as it had seemed. Starlight caught a tall figure with pale hair that sprang up beside her. Seliam.

He cried low, "The vines!" He leapt over her, and looked down, and cursed.

Kyrin blinked. She listened to his feet pound thrice, then turn into climbing rustles. Quick, light steps drew closer. The vines quivered and Kyrin sank into half dream and the sound of wings.

Had the falcon been freed? No, it was Truthseeker who flew toward her, wings beating at the night—or *was* it the tiger's queenly captive? Kyrin could not see if it was the youngling with the wispy feathers or the chained queen. Torchlight slid over her, and she closed her eyes against the stabbing glare. The falcon was gone.

There was a surprised intake of breath, then Jachin bellowed, "Get Tae! Run!" Someone near the gate pattered away, and painless silence closed around Kyrin.

Voices and movement and lights woke her. She tried to squeeze her eyes shut against the yellow confusion.

From a misty distance Tae called her. "Kyrin! Do you hear?" His voice echoed through her head. Gentle fingers touched her throat. They felt rough.

Alaina's voice shivered near. "Kyrin! Oh . . . Kyrin."

Someone squeezed her hands and tapped her feet. For some reason she could not answer. They lifted her and she passed through the gate. She caught snatches of cavernous faces swimming in lamplight and the stones in the passage ceiling. Then she went back to the warm, painless darkness.

§

Old Qadira peered in the room then her inquisitive face disappeared, and Alaina heard her whispering with the other women outside, their voices the rustling of uneasy mice. Alaina turned to Kyrin. The left side of her face was a swelling purple bruise from temple to chin. Her sister needed more than their words or embroidery needles or quill pens.

Alaina held Kyrin's wrist in her hand and counted, measuring the life-beats as Tae had instructed. She touched Kyrin's hair and adjusted the wet cloth on her blood and dirt-masked forehead. Tae swung through the door and hurried to her side, crackling dried herbs, small clay bottles, and clean bandages in his arms. "Nimah, bring the hot water. Nara, open the myrrh bottle and the powder."

Nara, frowning with concentration, had Tae's myrrh tincture ready almost before he asked. Jachin watched from beside the door after delivering a brazier full of coals. He had insisted on carrying Kyrin into the house. Alaina gave him a small smile. He nodded, sober. His shaved head bent, beaded with sweat. His eyes moved from Tae to Kyrin.

32

Wounded

*I am convinced that He is able to guard what I have entrusted to Him. ~2
Timothy 1:12*

In moments, Tae had the herbs inside a pot over the brazier.
He poured in boiling water. Gouts of steam rose, laden with
the aromatic scent of yarrow, feverfew, mint, and myrrh.

Kyrin whimpered when Tae touched her face, and tried to
push him away. Alaina held her sister's hands, kneeling beside
her, aching with tears. *The blows she's taken.*

Kyrin jerked.

"Alaina! Keep her still!" Tae said sharply. He paused in his
careful search of her skull.

Alaina bit her lip. "Why did they do it?" she gasped. "Oh,
Kyrin!"

Nara laid her hand on Alaina's shoulder, and it was too much.
Alaina sobbed. Ali had broken his word of freedom, dangerous
though their freedom would have been. What had that done to
Kyrin? And now she was hurt. What if she never opened her eyes
again?

Nara hugged Alaina and guided her aside to her rug then
knelt in her place. Alaina wound her blanket around her and
watched, wiping tears from her face.

Tae busied himself over the brazier and said a quiet word to Nimah's mother. She stripped Kyrin gently, quickly, and laid a thin sleeping rug over her, leaving her feet and shoulders bare. Then Nara stepped in and helped Tae examine her more closely, lifting her legs and arms, while he felt along her joints and bones. He laid her leg down. Sweat dripped from his face and he rubbed it away.

With boiled shears he shaved Kyrin's hair on the left side of her head, removing a patch from around a long cut. Nara argued with him, her voice low. "Licorice is the queen of herbs for wounds in my land."

"I know myrrh. Using a new herb—"

"I know how to make the right dose in a poultice. It is harmless." She glared at him. "Leave it out of the tea if you wish."

Alaina swallowed her tears. "Why not use the licorice *and* the myrrh?"

A smile flitted across Tae's face. "Will licorice lend itself to another herb?"

Nara nodded, with a quick smile.

They applied the poultice to Kyrin's bruised face, her head, her stomach, and other cuts. After they laid the second moist, hot pack over her stomach they sat back with a sigh and looked at each other, long and wordless.

"She is going to be in pain." Tae dug into his bag of herbs. "She was kicked many times, and stamped on here, by the marks." He indicated an area of the rug from Kyrin's stomach to her ribs, hip to hip. "I pray nothing is hurt inside. At sunrise we will know more. There will be punishment for this." Weary creases about his eyes and jaw thinned his face.

"Yes." Jachin's terse rumble of agreement from the door made the hair rise on Alaina's arms.

Kneeling over his bag, Tae turned his head. "There is something I would know, Jachin. Did you draw your sword over her at our master's word?"

"No." Jachin clenched and unclenched his hands, hands that could break a saluki's neck mid-leap. A shudder shook him, but he held Tae's eyes. "She walks—in kindness. My blade was for Umar, and then—" He slid his hand across his own throat. His lips twitched up on one side. "*You* sat by Mistress Shema, Hakeem, behind our master. You came from the kitchen."

Alaina eyed Jachin, whose mind was sharp. Tae had his bag in his hand afterward, and Jachin said he had gone to Shema. Was he there at her command for her faintness, or to bind Kyrin or Seliam's wounds, or for something else? Behind Shema's chair, Tae was two lengths from Ali's back.

Jachin said, "The caliph's guardsman says you are—controlled. He sees."

"Yes. Two of his men stayed close. I was glad not to test them."

Jachin nodded. "Death to touch our master. Life is better."

Alaina held her breath. His words held more than one meaning.

Tae's eyes narrowed. "What do you know of death touches?"

"Your gift." Jachin was impassive granite again.

Alaina shivered. When Sirius named Seliam a worm and commanded the slave to fight, his men had been ready.

Tae had known. Hah, *restrained*. Burn Sirius! She snorted. Tae was the wisest man she had ever known. *When I am weak then am I strong.* He relied on Another.

Tae looked at her. When she blushed a twinkle came into his eyes, as if he knew her thoughts.

Nara, and Nimah's mother, wound a cream-colored cloth about Kyrin's face and head and slipped her into her faded, worn thawb from the desert. It billowed about her, flooding over her rug.

She lay in it small and pale, a bandage hiding half her purple face. But for the belled cap, she looked a lord's jesting fool. Alaina imagined Kyrin's scornful lift of her head at such a thought and giggled. Tae turned to see what she laughed at, and his mouth twitched. Kyrin's eyelids fluttered, her breathing picked up and deepened. Tae smiled then his own laugh burst out, deep and long. Nara's comfortable chuckle and Jachin's throaty joy twined around them.

§

Kyrin opened eyes as heavy as lead. Nara, Tae, and Alaina stood around her, laughing, their eyes bright. Somehow she was on the floor on her rug, looking up at them. The Nubian grinned in the doorway. No, Jachin, his name was Jachin. How had she forgotten? She frowned. Outside, Nimah and the women giggled.

"What's so funny?" Pain stabbed her head, and her mouth was stiff. Qadira's cackle hurt her ears. Her throat was sore. "Go—away," she said thickly, with infinite dignity.

"Oh, no," gasped Tae. "You ought to see your purple indignance, surrounded by that white sea! It is . . . beyond words!"

Kyrin raised her hand to her aching cheek and jerked her fingers down. Stiffening against that pain brought more. She gasped.

Tae leaned over her in instant concern. "Lie still, lie still. It will pass."

She eyed her muddy fingers. "What happened?"

"Someone beat you. Do you remember?"

"No."

"We found you a little way from the pool. Jachin heard something, and he found you."

The pool. The gate, the blows, and the running shapes flooded back. Ali would kill Seliam and the others. And she did not
know who the others were. Kyrin closed her eyes, frowning in
pain within and without.

Tae said, "We will not speak of it now. Are you dizzy or sick?
What pains you most? You took hard blows."

"I hurt here." She slid her arm across her middle.

"You will hurt there a while. Open your eyes." Tae held a
lamp close, peered in them and grunted. "Good. Tell me if you
get sick or if your sight goes round. Can you see this?" He lifted
a cup from beside her. She nodded the smallest bit. "Poppy and
myrrh will take your pain. Do not be anxious, we will find those
who did this."

§

Alaina stood, awkward and sudden. She had one easy guess
who hurt her sister. Tae laid another blanket over Kyrin, and
Alaina touched her foot. "They will not touch you again."

Kyrin reached out, and Alaina grasped her hand, gulping
remorse.

"Alaina, be easy." Kyrin grinned, one side of her mouth curving. "I am not killed."

"I . . . I thought, they did." She choked.

"Alaina! I am all right. Ow." Kyrin sank back.

Alaina thought of Tae's sword against the wall. Her sister's
arms trembled with pain. She defied their master, risking all to
let Seliam live, and they beat her for it. "Jachin, Tae, and I—
they will not escape, Kyrin."

"No, no! He *is* a jackal," Kyrin said very fast, "I know that—"
She grabbed at Tae's sleeve. Alaina stared at her. "But Umar
will bring out the dogs—his Hand—no one should fall to them."
She turned in appeal to Jachin. "Not the pack. Ali does not have
to know."

"We will learn who, and what, when the sun rises." Jachin's rumble ceased. Tae stared at him. Jachin showed all his teeth, and ducked out.

Kyrin sighed, and Nara echoed her, and patted her shoulder. Outside, Nimah answered a question of Jachin's, her voice high and eager. The news gathering began this hour. Alaina did not attempt to soften her smile that held something of Cicero's eagerness in the hunt.

"I love you," Kyrin said on a breath. She rolled a little on her side and her lashes fluttered down.

Alaina blinked, her own eyes dry and hot. Snatching her pillow, she wedged it behind Kyrin's back. She would take Tae's sword to the pool.

Nara set the cup in Kyrin's hand. "Drink."

Alaina watched her wake with difficulty to swallow. Red finger marks laced her throat.

Tae wrung out a cold wet cloth, and Alaina gently held it to Kyrin's head. Presently she would go. Woe betide the one she caught.

33

Flight

For with Thee is the fountain of life. ~*Psalm 36:9*

Kyrin floated away from stabs of pain. She would not mind if Alaina found Seliam.

Wings beat, and beat. The falcon was loose in the night. Kyrin tipped her head back. She wanted to fly after her, but she had forgotten to ask.

The black expanse pricked with stars blazing to life. Then she was tumbling, her arms helplessly flapping, down through the darkness toward moonlit desert.

Wind rushed around her, tingling and cool. She lifted her wings—and left the fire in her stomach behind. She rose toward the moon, her muscles strong, reveling in the dry night air seeking through her feathers. The high barks of salukis came to her.

Below, a silver shape ran over the sand before the dogs. She folded her wings and dived. Wind tugged at her, but her speed did not cloud her eyes.

The hairs on the tiger's swiveling ears and every mark on his flowing body shone in the moonlight. A drop of mud marred one outstretched paw. She landed with a thump between his ears. He squalled.

His fur gave her good grip against his violent swerve, and his head drove toward the sand. They struck hard—and fell in a dizzying whirl of sand which became damp earth.

Kyrin found herself on her feet a little distance from the pool. The tiger shook himself beside it. The night was silent. The falcon sat proud on the tiger's head, her broken chain dangling around one of his ears. She turned to preen her feathers. The torque clasped the tiger's neck, amber jewels deep, watchful as falcon's eyes.

Ten lengths from Kyrin a sword stuck upright in the ground before the gate. It looked like her father's.

The earth chilled her feet. A vine tendril tickled her arm with lacy blossoms. She walked to the sword. And gripped it.

It slid free. And pain tore at her throat and middle as if all her wounds opened again. She doubled over. Blood trickled down her arm, onto the pale blade. Her necklace snapped and slipped from her quick snatch.

The fish tinked against the sword, and slid along the edge. It dropped to the ground, a huddle of dark and white. The blood on the sword blackened, caked, and fell. The steel was cleansed.

On the ground among beads of oak the fish faced the moon, a pearly nimbus of joy. The joy of a love so strong it touched the deepest hurt. Kyrin stooped and picked the handful up.

She woke with the fish necklace clenched in her hand. The walls were bright with morning. A shaft of sun fell across the room and her rug. She rubbed the fish with her thumb.

Rainbow tints rippled across it. Kyrin lifted the oaken beads in her hands. A rain of dark red flakes drifted into the sunlight—flashed like silvery sparks—and were gone as if they had never been. Kyrin stared.

She lifted her hand. The scar at her throat did not feel bare. It was a mark, of what, she was not sure. One thing she did know. Never again would her heart break under the cry, "Coward."

Tears pricked her eyes. *Mother, it happens so fast in a fight. The step that saves, the move that fells. I wish I could have saved you, but the Master of the stars took you, not my fear. I miss you. And I want to find Father. I need him, and—I hope he needs me.*

The sun warmed her arms, and she sighed. The Master of all was here. It was enough. She bowed her head, and her hurts caught at her breath. But the falcon was free, and she was healing.

Seliam. Where was he? Ali's pearls were lost. What would happen now? She rolled over, and stilled. Alaina slept below. She did not want to wake her.

Alaina stretched with a snort. "What . . . oh, Kyrin!" She uncurled from her cushion and rolled out of her blanket in a rush. "How do you feel?"

"I'm thirsty." *I could drink the pool.*

While she drained a cup of water in small sips, trying not to lose it out of the swollen side of her mouth, Alaina said, "Seliam is hiding, burn him. We searched outside, in the house, and then asked at the doors of the men's quarters. Sirius's askars said they had seen and heard nothing. Seliam had been sick and retching since the feast. They did not know where he was, and would not let us in. They would not disturb their master—but we will get that miserable beast. Jachin is going to speak to Ali."

Kyrin ached all over. "I never said it was Seliam—"

"Who else could it be?"

"It could have been Umar." Kyrin gasped a laugh at Alaina's amazed disdain and stopped. There was a molten bar in her middle.

"Yes, but it was *not* Umar," Alaina growled, trying to smother her smile.

"No." Kyrin sobered. "But Alaina, I do not think—justice is wanted, this time."

"You want to spare him, *again?* Where is your tinkling fool's cap? He tried to kill you!"

"No. There were no daggers." It was strange there had not been. And what work of his had she fed to the wind?

From the door Tae said, "How are you feeling?" He went to Kyrin's side and meditatively laid his fingers on her wrist.

"I hurt, but I could eat." Kyrin tried to peer past the edge of the door. Jachin did not seem to be lurking. She blinked. Her eyes seemed fuzzy.

"Um hum."

"I can get a platter for her," Alaina offered. "She kept the water down."

Tae smiled. "Come, then. You"—he pointed a stern finger at Kyrin—"will not get up alone."

Kyrin nodded. She doubted she could. She hoped Alaina hurried back so she could help her to the privy.

"We will bring fruit and more tea. Nara has some grapes from the village. You will mend."

§

Kyrin was leaning against her pillows, spooning mashed dates and milk past the bandaged side of her face, when Umar came in. She saw the reassuring shadow of Jachin behind him and swallowed, setting her bowl in her lap. Umar stopped at her feet. He was not wearing his sword. He glanced at Tae's rug, his sword and stick beside the wall, and into her face. "Young Zoltan says your saluki found this." He leaned over and dropped a broken hair-pin in her palm.

"I—thank you." They found none of the pearls. But then there would not be any. Seliam's friends would see to that. She was rather glad. Her pouch would hold the oak beads of her fish necklace in honor, without any thought of Ali to sully them.

Umar shifted. Kyrin's face heated. One of the others could have brought her the pin, what did he want?

Umar waved his hand. "There is a small matter." His gaze pinned her. "Who did this foul thing? I must know."

Kyrin's mouth opened. Umar called her ambush *foul?* "I am not sure, I mean, I do not know—" If she told him she would never see Seliam's face again. Or she would have to watch the shadows.

Tae entered behind Umar, silent, and cleared his throat. Umar spun, and Tae said evenly, with a bow, "How may I serve?"

"Ali wishes knowledge of the one who marred her."

"Yes." Tae glanced at her, and Kyrin made her face empty.

"Did you see him?" Umar asked her again. Never had he used her name, but he did not seem to want to call her "worthless one" this morning.

Kyrin stared at him helplessly and her headache roared back. If she did not lie, it would lead to murder. She winced.

"I will speak with her. Her head was hit, and some of her memories may have fled." Tae rubbed his chin, rocking on his heels.

Umar leaned toward him. "Ali is not pleased. She is valuable to Sirius Abdasir and the caliph."

"I am not pleased, either," Tae said very dryly indeed.

Umar stiffened in startlement, then he grinned. "Seek and punish as you will," he murmured, "but leave his death to Ali." He turned, lithe and sure.

"I will, son of my master." Tae's voice held no mockery.

Umar paused, his back to Tae, then went out and down the passage. His steps died away.

"Now," Tae said, "tell me what your heart holds."

Kyrin poured out everything she remembered, ending with a worried frown. "I know Seliam was there, and I can guess at the others. Ali will kill them all, and that is not just."

"Are you sure they would not have killed you if Jachin had not come?"

"I think not." The younger voice *had* asked, and Seliam's savage voice answered in scornful denial.

Tae bent his head, his lips tight. "You are right. There were no blades. But he should be punished. And about your lying to Umar—remember the woman long ago who hid the Master of the stars's spies at her inn?"

"Yes."

"So you have done." He smiled. "I will bring the story for you to read, for you will be sore for some days. Alaina scribed it. She is almost through David's songs."

§

Two days later Ali called Kyrin to the Blue Flower room. Birds twittered outside the high windows. She limped in on Tae's arm and nibbled soaked, dried figs from a dish Ali set before her after Tae left.

Ali's slippers slapped the stone floor as he paced. She had never sat in his presence while he stood, and she could not escape the feeling she should take the platter to the table and kneel. Her jaw and stomach were still sore, and she ate slowly, but the bowl comforted her hands.

He paced before his chair, his wide mouth flat, and Kyrin wished the figs in her mouth would melt so he could tell her what he wanted and she could put on her veil again. She had unveiled at Ali's command. Tae had taken off her bandage for the first time this morning for the air to do its work, and she felt as ugly as Shema's mirror had revealed.

Her shaved spot made her near bald, what hair was left to her was mussed, and her thawb was wrinkled from days in bed.

Ali stopped with a grunt, inspected her head, tilting her chin with an impersonal hand, then grunted again and let her go. Kyrin was cautiously relieved and puzzled. No one else was present, not even Nimah. Ali paused at the far end of the table from her and glanced toward the door. Did she offend his nose? Kyrin sniffed surreptitiously. She did not wear perfume as it made her sneeze. But she liked cinnamon and mint, yet she had not bathed since . . . A whisper rose outside the closed curtains and Ali clapped his hands. "Come!"

Six young Arabs sidled in under Kyrin's stare. Ali directed them into one line. Two of the young men she did not know must be from the village, one was Qadira's runner, and the last three wore Sirius's askar red and black. "Nimah!" Ali barked, and Nimah and Zoltan bolted through the curtains to stand at the end of the line.

Nimah blinked back tears, rubbing her bruised chin, and Zoltan strained to still the quiver of his lip. All of them bore a bruise of some sort, yellow-purple and fading or virulent and new. Ah, bruises. Likely gained on her behalf. Or not.

Nearest Kyrin, the shaggy-haired boy who had sat beside Seliam at the feast had a black eye. His head a little too big for his body, he peered at her under his coarse fringe like a trickster fool, still standing close to Seliam, glaring. No one else looked at her. Seliam threw his head back in defiance, but his shoulders slumped as he stared at the empty air before him.

Kyrin swallowed, remembering his vicious curse and his twisting foot in her belly. A scabbed scrape blazed across Seliam's throat. She did not remember that. One cheek was dark. She might have broken the bone. Was it from the sword fight or after?

He deserved more. He ought to see one of his friends die, to feel that pain. But the Master of the stars carried the sword of justice, and he had not set it in her hand. Jachin said one of Seliam's friends had even asked after her. She rather thought it might be the shaggy one. His glare covered fear.

Ali would give unjust punishment to all involved. So. She was left with hot coals of mercy for one whose fire was going out. They rather burned her. *In Thy light we see light.*

Kyrin nodded to Zoltan. He straightened. Nimah's hand crept into his, and she looked up at her brother with eyes that said, See? She knows it wasn't us.

Ali frowned impatiently. "Is he here?"

"My master?"

"Did any of these worthless ones harm you?"

The relentless discipline of Subak schooled her expression. Kyrin clamped her hands on her bowl. Yes, or no. Seliam's fate turned on such a word. *Father—a clean sword.*

"No. No, my master. He was bigger."

"Did he appear like anyone you have seen in my house?"

"I could not see him well. I think—he was as tall as Jachin, but—thinner than me." She tilted her head. Everyone looked at the floor except Nimah and Zoltan, who stared at her wounded head, fascinated.

Then some of the others dared looked up. Kyrin touched her ragged hair, and Seliam and the shaggy boy fidgeted. Well they should. Let Seliam call insult if he dared.

Ali frowned. "I will find the desecrator of my house before the moon turns," he grated. "The rest of you may go." He flapped his hand toward the door.

Nimah beamed and raced out, while Zoltan followed at a dignified walk. The others shuffled after him.

§

In the door of the merchant's judgment room, under cover of rubbing his mane of hair from his face, Shafiq nudged Seliam. Seliam looked back through the arch, his gaze pulled against his will. The stealer of his life inclined her head, watching him with her amber stare. The stubbled patch of hair and her purple, green, and yellow-marbled cheek made him want to laugh. The black earring in her ear killed the amusement in his throat.

There was judgment in her face, still. She said nothing, doubtless waiting for the moment to destroy him, fingering the necklace at her throat, tracing the only bright piece in it, a fish of opalescent seashell. A saluki in his host's courtyard barked, and Seliam looked to the window. Sweat pricked down his back. Then her gaze was broken, and he was out.

Seliam let out a quick breath. She who bore the evil eye shamed them all: the caliph's guardsman, his askars, and the most excellent caliph. She had to be punished. Sirius had avowed his innocence to their host, though later he glanced sharply at Seliam. He should have been pleased, if he suspected.

Seliam frowned. Did the most excellent Sirius Abdasir shield himself? If so, Baghdad would not shelter a slave if his master discovered his wrong. Why did she wait to denouce him? But he was less than dung if he could not be an askar, a seeker for Sirius Abdasir and the caliph, the light of his eyes. If they only threw him out, the streets would receive him back. He must get out. Seliam almost broke into a run for his host's door.

There was tumult in the kennel. Umar's Hand. The sound of the dogs turned him down the breezeway and outside to the askars' guest quarters instead. If condemnation found him, a blade would take his head—much better than being torn to pieces, the death of the worthless.

He went to his rug and drew his knees up, facing the wall, hugging his flat pillow. Why had the unnatural askar not told his host she knew him? Though an oily merchant, he pressed her hard. Her glance had pierced him in the moonlight. Seliam gritted his teeth. He had beaten her down—the one who shamed him and the caliph's askars—beaten her to the ground. His heart still rose at the memory. Why did she wait? Did she enjoy his torture? Seliam stiffened and sat up. He put his back to the wall. When they came, they would not find him weak with fear.

Evening fell, and Seliam lay down. He stared into the dark. Sirius's guards and his call to the blue judgment room did not come.

§

Kyrin woke to a soft touch. A hand lay light across her mouth. When she stiffened it withdrew. She said softly, "What?" and felt a tug on her sleeve.

Tae and Alaina breathed gently on their rugs. Kyrin sighed. She was not Alaina with her healer's bag, but she would walk out to the privy, the usual meeting place, since she had to use it anyway, and find out who needed her sister's help. Alaina had been up tending her the last three nights, and she needed the rest.

The bisht-shadowed figure slipped to the door, and Kyrin followed, careful and slow, curled slightly around her stiff stomach, wishing a pox on Seliam's head. They went down the passage, through the breezeway, and over moonlit flags past the women's court. She envied the other's easy walk. The silvery figure flitted by the salukis that whined in their kennels. By the turban around the figure's head it was a man, who gained black solidity in the shadow of the privy. He was blessed Jachin had not caught him at her door. He sat on his heels in the shadow, bowed his head, and seemed content with silence.

"What do you seek Alaina for?" Her blanket was not getting warmer, and Nimah had not put enough ashes in the stinking privy.

"I seek an answer." Seliam's voice was calm.

Kyrin leaped back against the saluki kennel. Edging along it, she groped for anything she could swing, searching for other figures in the moonless corners. The gate guard was used to voices here. He would not take easy alarm.

Seliam did not move. After a moment he extended his hands into the moonlight. A sash lay across his palms. "You may bind me—if you wish." The sash trembled a little.

She was seven lengths from him and any hidden blade, and he was seated.

"Stay where you are." She shivered in the chill and resisted crossing her arms. "I hear you."

"Why do you keep silence?"

"My master would not give you justice." There had been a stick somewhere about Cicero's kennel. She groped. Which side of the door?

"Ha!" Seliam leaned forward. "What should be my reward, gold, silver? No." He sat back in the shadow. "It would have been better if my master never saw you that unpropitious day."

"Unpropitious day? I first saw your master on a feast night."

"Ah, but you caught his gaze in Gaza."

Gaza—her fight with Faisal had started Sirius's interest? Kyrin shifted, fingers searching, fumbling. No stick, but Seliam remained motionless, eyeing her. Best keep him thinking. "What does your master desire?"

"Does the great one speak his thoughts to a slave? But all are weapons in Sirius Abdasir's hand. I would have been a keen blade among his askars, swift to obey and gift him with glory. "

Though he approved your death. "That is what I took from you." Kyrin paused. *Poor slave of an askar.* She cleared her throat and felt her way forward. "We could be matched again. When I come to Baghdad and you have time to study my skill. A bout for honor between an askar and—an askar of another land. You might drop such a word in your master's ear. Our way of the warrior is far from any fighting skill you have seen. "

"Did I hit your head so hard?" It was scornful.

"My master should not have you by Umar's Hand—or his own sword." Stubbornly blind, he thought her weak. "You did not kill me, you know." Kyrin wondered at the laughter in her voice. But—her mother laughed, and in the face of death.

"How can you give me gifts when another would take the debt of the Light of Blood?"

"It is not so strange when you know the one who made us. He is like that." Seliam was still dangerous.

"Is your tongue true?" His voice was spun glass.

"Yes."

"I will leave, Nasrany." His voice was so brittle as to break at a touch.

She snorted, and a sliver dug into her finger. She grimaced. "I do not lie. He had mercy on me and tells me to give it, though you do not seem to want the coals."

"You would give me mercy with fire? Your words hide from me. Fire burns."

Kyrin leaned against the wood kennel, reaching to the utmost. "Vengeance is his own. He says to feed my enemy if you are hungry, to give you coals if your hearthfire goes out. He desires me to forgive you." Her fingers found a hard length. "So I do."

The stick nestled solid in her hand. Kyrin breathed out. "He also tells me to defend my life. If you seek to attack me again, I will stop you until the day of eternity."

Seliam stared at her a long while. Kyrin did not look away. She did not bring the stick into the light. Her hand trembled.

Enough, enough pain. A horse in the stable snorted, and Cicero whined behind her, his paws whispering. She yearned for home.

In shadow, Seliam rose slowly and ran his hand over the side of his face. Kyrin's heart thundered. He walked past her toward the men's quarters, and she let him go.

The courtyard was silent. Her back was cold against the kennel door. Kyrin laid the stick against the woven wall and breathed in the relief and the quiet and the moonlight. *My grace is sufficient for you, for power is perfected in weakness. Mother, I remember— and all is not ash.* Her heartbeat slowed.

Cicero stuck his nose between the withe gaps and licked her hands. She whispered to him. After a few moments she rubbed her cold arms and went to her rug, and slept without dreams.

Sirius Abdasir, the caliph's guardsman, left with the dawn for Baghdad. His loaded camels clattered over the flags and through the stable gate. The askars wheeled their horses and formed up on the road outside the wall.

Sirius kissed Ali on both cheeks and invoked Allah's blessings on him and his house, for Ali's household had turned out to bid their departing guest peace. Kyrin hung back, Nimah and Nara on either side. Kyrin was grateful Qadira hovered at her shoulder.

Sirius Abdasir did not seem to see her among the others. He stalked away down the road, a lord of men. Kyrin grinned, and lifted her veil to cover her face. His askars did not escort Alaina among their ranks.

In the tail of the caravan, eating the first dust of his disgrace, Seliam turned his gaze to Kyrin, ignoring Alaina's crossed arms and forbidding frown. Alaina glared and pressed her lips tight, but Kyrin nudged her with an elbow, and motioned Seliam nearer. She laid a roll of paper in his hand.

"You give me a gift?" His eyes were wide.

"The book of John—some of my creator's words in your tongue—and other words."

"You would give me so much?" His amazement made her laugh.

"Yes. My sister is a scribe. And within the book I ask a boon."

Seliam shook his head and looked at her from the corner of his eye. He muttered, "The sun has taken you." But he shoved the roll in his sash and nodded to her. Veilless for once, Alaina inclined her head, unsmiling.

Kyrin lifted her chin. "I will see your face across my blade." She hoped he heard her smile in her voice. Would Seliam speed Tae's letter hidden inside the book to Huen? The caliph did cultivate trade with the Eastern lands.

Seliam gave her a cautious grin and kicked his loaded beast after Sirius's camels.

As the men and women of Ali's house called, "As salaam alaykum!" he caught up with the last camel. Among the baggage beasts there was a distant, growling cough. If she closed her eyes, Kyrin could see a hint of orange and black, and a flash of sun on beating wings.

She was outside the wall. Kyrin stepped onto the road and knelt. The air smelled of rich green, the free wind, and new things. Cicero nudged her hand and she stroked his back—it was not yet time to run. He whined deep in his throat.

A falcon cried, climbing higher. Kyrin smiled.

Tae had woken her with the sun. "You are ready." His words brought the heat of healing. When she saw her father's face she would know how to hold a blade. She was to learn the sword with Jachin, for Tae thought it good for her to have another teacher. And she would study the Book of the Master of the stars, whose word shattered her chains.

Ali had ordered her to learn the scribe's pen. She did not think she would be good at it. Awkward and ugly with fledgling feathers—not good at catching the wind, were young falcons— but the Master of the wind called. Kyrin drew in the earth with a finger, and touched her black earring. She rose.

The falcon spread her wings. With her, she dared the challenge of the drop, the vast world before her eyrie. Though storms beat her down, a bolt of wet feathers, the wind would catch her.

And bear her to the heights.

34

More Books

A reader of epic fantasy and new worlds, Azalea Dabill loves grand adventure and a satisfying, happy ending. Noblebright characters, the fate of the world, and tension between characters fascinates her. She will never stop learning about how words shape and hold meaning. Words wield power like a well-aimed bow.

Her debut novel was released in 2015. When she isn't writing you can find her growing things, raiding bookstores, or hiking the wild.

If you want to know more about her literary adventures you can join her here https://azaleadabill.com/ Her website is the hub for all her books, news, and reader resources.

Kyrin's medieval adventures continue in Falcon Flight, and you can get your signed books from the author's website store and support her directly at https://azaleadabill.com/store/

It's usually cheaper than Amazon with shipping.

She is active on her Facebook page Mythic Fantasy https://www.facebook.com/azaleadabillmythicfantasy, or you can join her on Instagram https://www.instagram.com/azaleadabillauthor/?hl=en and GoodReads https://www.goodreads.com/author/show/13802917.Azalea_Dabill

Share Falcon Heart with a friend, Falcon Heart Wide Universal Book Link: https://books2read.com/u/bP1rpl. It's free!

Or tell me what could be improved or what you liked. Please leave a review on Amazon https://www.amazon.com/review/create-review/?ie=UTF8&channel=glance-detail&asin=B00VOEQXIO or at your favorite retailer. Thank you!

35
_____

Sneak Peek Falcon Flight Chronicle II

A prince's ruin. ~Proverbs 14:28

Kyrin Cieri strode toward the curtains of the Blue Flower room. More than two years of slavery. No word of home, her Britannia of rushing streams and whispering oaks, or of her father, Lord Dain Cieri of Cierheld.

And no way of escape.

Tae said the circle of circumstance was incomplete. Alaina told her the next stitch in the Master of the stars's pattern was not clear. Ali Ben Aidon guarded his slaves too well.

Would she ever walk in Cierheld with her father again? It was five years since her twelfth name-day, when she took the oath of first daughter in Cierheld hall. Esther would say she never had a first daughter's qualities, one who bore the old blood in her veins, and maybe she had not. Yet no one from home could call her "sprite get" now. She was stronger than they dreamed, though she carried the blood of the hills in her slight bones, dark hair and eyes.

She could not return to her people and her land. Her stronghold key rusted away in Ali's possession. She would not see her father again, and Cierheld would die with him.

Stronghold first daughter. She had never entirely felt like one. Kyrin bit her lip. Two things of Britannia remained to her.

Alaina Ilen, dearer than blood, her sister of salt and sacrifice, forged under threat of death. Walking at her side, Alaina's red-gold braid swung with a soft swish against her leather and cane body armor, laced over her white *thawb.* The intricately embroidered tunic displayed swords and flowers in delicate silver, blue and green. The staff Alaina held across her body was a harsh line dividing blade and bloom.

Kyrin's lips quirked. But for its leather handgrips, the staff was smooth as silk from Alaina's use. Her sister gave her a smart blow during their last training bout, before she wrested the weapon away. What new trick would Alaina bring against her this night, besides her proven mastery of the scribe's pen and her embroidery needle?

Ali's first bodyguard, watchful as a leopard, paced before heavy curtains of dark silk. With a glower, Umar thumped the hilt of his sword against the stone arch of the Blue Flower room. The solid thunk of his hilt announced their presence to the feasters within, and to their master, Ali Ben Aidon, merchant and murderer. Mouth wry, Kyrin dipped her head to Umar.

He held out his hand, demanding Alaina's staff. She laid the weapon in his palm, his skin nearer gold than white.

Kyrin wrinkled her nose. Her master's unacknowledged son could never quite wash off the smell of meat, rice, and saluki: the scents of the kennels, and the savage beasts of his Hand. Umar ran with them often, teaching his hunters of men patience and endurance in the desert sands. He glanced at her, expressionless.

Had he forgiven her for her eye of evil intent he once swore tipped the glowing brazier on Ali's ship, that gave him the burn scar across his sword hand?

No matter. Umar never spoke of it since. She had grown strong. She'd stolen every moment she could from serving Ali's table the past two winters to learn the demanding ways of *Subak*.

Tae Chisun, her husband in name, a second father in fact, had taught her well his ancestral fighting art of the hands and feet. Also, under the tutelage of her master's second bodyguard, Jachin, she knew one end of a sword from the other.

Umar glared at Alaina, free of her blue veil and serving robe for this brief moment, as he examined her staff for hidden blades. Umar never sought to interfere with Kyrin's training with Jachin, knowing their master wished her and Alaina's skill to impress the *caliph* in Baghdad—and those the caliph favored. Such as the caliph's *wazir*. Kyrin clenched her hand at her side.

She and Alaina would demonstrate the fighting art of the East to Ali's guests at table—and Sirius Abdasir. Once guards-man to the caliph, now first wazir, Ali's most honored guest pro-fessed a liking for close-in combat. So it would be dagger work this night, among other things. Kyrin touched her blade.

The cool haft of the weapon in her sash did not have the bal-ance of her bronze falcon, the second thing that remained to her of Britannia. She'd left her mother's falcon dagger in their quarters. Tae was right.

Ali Ben Aidon must never discover the Damascus steel under the bronzed surface. It was her last gift from her mother. Never was the weapon for common wear. The falcon drew interest to its piercing amber gaze and beautiful strength.

Umar's smile widened, unpleasant. He kept Alaina's staff. "Wait until the master calls you."

Alaina glanced at Kyrin, who frowned. When would he let them in? He loved to play the sand cat with the mouse, she knew. But they were not his prey.

36

Falcon Chronicle Summaries

Falcon Heart:

In which a slaver kidnaps Kyrin Cieri from Britannia and takes her through many adventures across sea and sand to his house in Araby. Followed by her fear of blades, Kyrin is still determined to wrest justice from the murderer for her mother. A tiger stalks her dreams, and a falcon dagger she found on her mother's breast is a symbol of fearlessness, hope, and freedom.

Befriended by a mentor, Tae Chisun, a slave from early Korea, and Alaina, a peasant girl who is closer to Kyrin than a sister by blood, Kyrin learns martial skill and finds courage in the face of battle in the desert. A last confrontation in the slaver's house in Oman pits Kyrin against a slave wielded by a guardsman to the Caliph. Dagger against sword, Kyrin must face her fear of the blade and gain the heart of a falcon to save Tae and Alaina from horrible fates.

Falcon Flight:

In which Kyrin is sent back to Britannia on a dangerous quest by the wazir to the Caliph, to earn her freedom. The wazir holds Tae hostage to keep Kyrin and Alaina to their task. Defying him, the girls free Tae and flee into the desert. Reaching the port of Jedda, Kyrin takes ship alone, while Tae and Alaina seek refuge in the black tents of a prince of the desert until she can remove the price from their heads.

At home in Britannia, Kyrin travels disguised as a boy. But that does not protect her. After being attacked and rescued by an unexpected friend, she finds her father at last then discovers her people and her hold are under siege. Kyrin finds the wazir's daughter and returns her to the wazir. The siege is broken, and near death overcome. Reunited with Tae and Alaina, and facing her test for the black sash of mastery in her martial art of Subak, Kyrin has little to fear. Yet a greater threat lies in wait in the cryptic last words of an erstwhile friend, 'Ware the asp'. When the wazir comes to demand judgement, the secret of the falcon dagger spells their deliverance and their doom.

Lance and Quill:

In which Alaina flees the wazir's Hand, who pursues her and Tae even to the black tents of a Prince of the sands.

Foiled in her desire to rise as a renowned scribe in the court of the Caliph, Alaina finds herself tending an ailing sheik disguised as Tae's apprentice healer. But the prince pierces her deception, and soon has her scribing for him. Struggling to be worthy of his grandfather's seat as sheik, Prince Faisal has enemies Alaina would gladly shield him from. But she must keep her identity hidden from the tribe and the traitor among them, even as she faces Faisal's rival.

Alaina falls in love with the prince she is not worthy of, and fails him yet again before his rival's cunning schemes. When the wazir's Hand discovers them and enemies known and unknown converge in a last battle, Alaina must rise and break the webs of deceit. If she can discern her uncertain heart before it is too late.

<u>37</u>

Imaginative fiction is a key to our future . . .

Beauty, mystery, and adventure are vital to our spirits. Fantastic journeys invite us to search beyond what we see for truth, to dig deeper for courage.

The soul of fantasy adventure benefits us on three levels:

- The spiritual arena
- The wide world of ideas
- And the sphere we breathe in

Why do the quest and the hero's journey draw us all? What difference does it make? Have you ever wondered how to find the best fantasy adventures for your children, yourself or your friends?

We bring up select jewels from the deep and explore mountain troves of fiction with seventy authors to whet your appetite for the riches heaped on untold shores. The inspiring adventures we explore are beacons of extraordinary story.

Most of them are lights by contrast, guiding us to enchanting lands of danger in the ocean of fantasy and speculative fiction. Heroes and heroines show us how to identify true gems and sell them not. How to discern enemies, friends, and endless possibilities with our inner eye, and to touch and to taste the truths of life in realms near and far.

Take a deep breath before our first plunge into the sea of fantasy. And we will discover that which is the wealth of souls.

CHAPTER 1.0

Discover the Irresistible Beauty of Truth in Fantasy
Who does not wish that at least one moment in a beautiful epic fantasy were true? But some of those moments are true, and some of those places. The mystery of beauty, and sacrifice, the brave call of loyalty, and the torch of true relationships make us yearn for something we often cannot name. But we feel it in epic fantasies of courage, perseverance, and friendship that illuminate selflessness. We behold spiritual heights, physical depths, and in far realms we learn to refuse evil and choose good until it influences our adventures in our own sphere. Fantasy relates to deep reality.

Some people may say there is little truth in the ocean of fantasy. They claim the very words *fantasy fiction* are a double negative of reality. Others say that fantasy involves Wicca, witchcraft, magick—at the very least, it means New Age muddled thought. They claim fantasy is not for serious Christians because it does not encourage spirituality and faith. They say idealism or fantasy doesn't apply to real life, and abstract ideas in fantasy rarely touch real things.

In truth, real things and the ideals we hold are as closely connected as our body and spirit. Abstract ideals are intertwined in the physical and spiritual in every occurrence in the spatial universe. Every idea we believe, experience, and come to understand moves the breath, blood, and bone we call our body—*because* ideals first move our heart and spirit.

Fantasy mirrors reality, showing the abstract in sharper facets. It casts reality back at us in a thousand reflections, penetrating deeper into our souls at times than any physical blade on this earth.

<u>38</u>

Story Chat

§ After reading Alaina's story, are you more aware of martial arts and interested in its past? Was there anything about the martial art that surprised you?

§ Several themes of this desert tale are events in different times and places, with people of various cultures. The book refers to Kyrin and Faisal's parting over different beliefs. Where did they find common ground? What divided them? How did they part in peace, and in what areas?

§ Kyrin admires falcons. What meaning does the bird embody for her, both in her mother's dagger and the living bird?

§ In chapter 3, we meet Tae, who becomes Kyrin's mentor. He urges her to forgive Ali, her kidnapper. Does she forgive him? Have you ever forgiven someone who hurt you badly?

§ The story shows the difference between vengeance and self-defense. What is the difference?

§ Revenge is the opposite of forgiveness. Besides Kyrin, who else in the book seeks revenge? Against who?

§ What does Kyrin love? What does she hate? Who does she love and hate? How do these things you named frame her life? How do they affect her decision to forgive? Why?

§ Kyrin fears blades because of the danger and loss they can bring, because they were used to murder her mother. How did she overcome her fear? Do you have a similar fear? What step can you take to begin overcoming it?

§ At first Kyrin believes the falcon dagger is a bronze blade of low value, though precious to her, before she discovers it is Damascus steel. In the context of the story, what does this mean?

§ For Kyrin, the falcon holds memories of both fear and courage, looking from a place of captivity toward freedom. In what ways do you look toward freedom?

39

Glossary

*
    These terms and names span the world of the Chronicle. Not every entry or book will have every word. Mispronunciations and mistakes are my own. For easier pronunciation I have reduced some words to phonetic spelling. May contain slight spoilers. Enjoy the adventure!

Britannia:

Armsman—"Arms-mun" a lord's sworn man who protects the lord's person and stronghold

Bells—Lauds "Lawds" (just before dawn), Prime (just after daybreak), Terce "Terse" (third hour), Sext (sixth hour), Nones "Nons" (ninth hour), Vespers (eleventh hour), Matins (just after midnight)

Britannia—"Bri-tan-ee-uh" ancient name for Britain

Brooch—"Broach" a pin often worn in pairs, used for cloaks

Death touch—Possible with a strong man trained in Subak—a death thought to be brought by a single blow. Most often the culmination of several deadly nerve points or blows

Eagles—"E-gulls" an ancient name for Romans

Evil eye—Ali believes Kyrin can bring evil with her dark stare and brands her with a jet earring in her ear, besides his bronze ring of ownership in her other ear

Eyas—"Ee-ass" a young falcon in the nest

Eyrie—"Ear-ee" a falcon's nest high on a cliff

Falcon, Peregrine—"Pear-uh-grin" the bird Kyrin loves, which draws her to follow the Master of the stars

Falcon dagger—a mysterious dagger shaped like a falcon that Kyrin finds hidden in a cloak on her murdered mother's breast

Girdle—"Gir-dul" a kind of belt for women, often braided of leather or linen

Hose—like leggings but for men, usually fastened by cross garters attached to leather shoes

Mantle—"Man-tul" a woman's wrap, with a central hole for the head, like a poncho

Stronghold key—a large key that signifies authority over a stronghold. Women often wore them on their girdles

Tunic—"Tune-ick" a medieval shirt-like or robe-like garment worn by men and women, worn over an under-garment or shirt, often of linen, flowing to the knee for men and the feet for women

Names of important characters:

Aart—"A-art" Kyrin's horse, means like an eagle

Alaina Ilen—"A-lay-nuh I-len" Kyrin's peasant sister, closer than blood, means one who harmonizes, noble, stone

Aunt Medaen—"Ma-day-en" her father's tart-tongued sister, who Kyrin hears in her head more than she'd like

Father Annis—"Ann-iss" an important monk who opposes Kyrin

Brother Rolf—"Rawl-f" a sympathetic monk who plays a part in Cierheld's fate

Father Ulf—Kyrin's uncle, pivotal to events in Falcon Flight

Berd—a young armsman in training who becomes Kyrin's armsman

Celine Loring—"Suh-lean Lore-ing" a childhood friend who antagonizes Kyrin. I liked the name for a red-haired girl

Etain—"E-tain" Alaina's mare in Araby, means fairy

Esther—a stronghold daughter, and Kyrin's beautiful rival

Cernalt—"Sir-nalt" an old armsman and hawkmaster to Lord Dain Cieri

Dain Cieri—"Dane Si-eery" Kyrin's father. His name fit the time and place, to my mind

Willa—"Will-a" Kyrin's mother. The connotations of the name fit her gentle strength

Elinore—Kyrin's stepmother in honor of Sam's Elinore in LOTR. It sounded right

Gwenith—"Gwen-ith" the saluki pup that Alaina gives Kyrin, means blessed

Hal Loring—Celine's father and Kyrin's first student in Britannia

Kyrin Cieri—"Kai-rin Si-eery" I liked the sound, the name reminds me of dark hills, Celtic times, and Elizabeth Moon's Paksenarrion

Lord Bergrin Jorn—"Bur-grin Jorn" Myrna's brother, who holds Kyrin captive for a time, and is an ally in war

Lord Ludwin Mornoth—"Lud-win More-noth" who is Cierheld and the strongholds' nemesis

Lord Nidfael Keffer—"Nid-fi-el Keff-er" Mornoth's second in command, and Kyrin's nemesis

Meric—"Mare-ick" Kyrin's stepbrother. His name fits his scholarly bent and nature

Myrna Jorn—"Mur-nuh" Kyrin's friend, means tender

Nell Trinley—a girl with mismatched eyes that Kyrin rescues, who becomes a healer

Nith—an armsmaster, first in command of Cierheld in *Falcon Flight*

Ragad—"Ra-gad" shipmaster of the Howler, Sirius Abdasir's ship that brings Kyrin on her task to find Hamal

Seliam—"See-li-am" the wazir's slave, an askar who threatens everyone Kyrin loves in *Falcon Heart*

Sirius Abdasir—"Sear-ee-us Ab-duh-sir" wazir to the caliph, who holds the secret of the falcon dagger and threatens to destroy Kyrin and all of Cierheld

Talik—"Tal-ick" a messenger between the strongholds who rescues Kyrin, loves and quarrels with her

The Master of the stars—the meaning of this name is for you to discover

Wolf-ship warrior—another name for a Viking

White Christer—a Viking's name for one who follows Christ

§

Araby/Arabia:

Aba—"Ab-uh" an Arabian women's cloak

Aneza—"A-nez-uh" a tribe of Araby people in Kyrin's world

Askar—"Ass-car" means fighter, warrior

Bisht—"Bi-shit" an Arabian men's cloak

Bedu/Bedouin—"Bed-du" or "Bed-o-in" a name for those who live in the desert

Caliph—"Kal-iph" Araby ruler in Baghdad

Dalil—"Dal-lil" a caravan guide, often across the desert

Djinn—"Jin" jinn, genie, jinni

Empty Quarter—Al Ramlah, the ocean of sand south and inland of the coastal mountains

Hattah—"Hat-tah" the desert women's light head covering. Not a veil, though it can be used to cover the face

Kaffiyeh—"Ca-fi-yuh" Araby men's head covering

Mahr—"Marr" a desert maiden's dowry, often precious metal anklets, bracelets, and coins sewn into a bridal headpiece or veil

Nargeela—"Nar-gee-la" a water pipe

Nasrany—"Nas-rany" an infidel unbeliever

Nur-ed-Dam—"Nur-ed-dom" oath of the Light of Blood, or blood-feud oath

Reem—the black-horned gazelle and others of its kind

Shaheen—"Sha-heen" Arabic for a falcon, also the name given to Kyrin

Sheyk—"Shay-ick" a desert leader of a tribe, such as Gershem Ben Salin of the Twilkets

Souk—"Sook" an Araby market

Thawb—"Thaw-ub" an Araby tunic

Twilkets—"Twil-kets" an enemy tribe until events bring unforeseen secrets to light

Umar's Hand—"Oo-mar's Hand" Umar's pack of salukis he trained against their gentle nature to hunt men

Wadi—"Wad-ee" a watercourse, usually dry except during the rainy season

Wazir—"Wah-zeer" the advisor to the caliph

Names of important characters:

Ali Ben Aidon—"Ali-ben A-don" Araby slaver, a common Arabic name

Basimah—"Bass-i-mah" means one who smiles

Cicero—"Siss-er-o" Kyrin and Alaina's saluki, named after a wise man

Faisal—"Fie-sel" desert prince of the Twilkets, loves both Kyrin and Alaina. Means a wise, just judge

Farook—"Fa-ruke" the wazir's slave forced to betray Alaina, means one who discerns right and wrong

Gershem Ben Salin—"Ger-shem Ben Sa-lin" Twilket sheyk and Faisal's grandfather. I liked the name

Hafiz—"Ha-feez" first warrior, and Alaina's opponent in Lance and Quill. Means the guardian

Hala—"Hall-uh" Sirius Abdasir's daughter, means halo around the moon

Hamal—"Ha-mall" the wazir's lost traveler, means gentle as a lamb

Jachin—"Ja-chin" Ali's bodyguard and Tae's friend. I liked the sound for a friendly Nubian

Kentar—"Ken-tar" caravan guide and Tae's eyes and ears. I liked the name from *The Blue Sword*

Mey—"May" Shahin's wife and Rashid's mother. I liked the sound of the name

Nara—"Nar-uh" Umar's Egyptian mother, Ali's cook, and Kyrin's friend in Ali's house, meaning unknown

Nimah—"Nim-uh" first to welcome Kyrin and Alaina to Ali's housem, means blessing

Neddra—"Ned-druh" an Aneza girl who admired Kyrin's falcon dagger, the sound drew me

Qadira—"Ka-deer-uh" head concubine in Ali's house, means powerful one

Rashid—"Ra-shid" the young sheyk's son, means the well guided

Sahar—"Sa-har" Faisal's red saluki, means the dawn

Sarni—"Sar-nee" the name a desert prince gives Alaina, means the elevated one

Shahin—"Sha-hin" sheyk of the Aneza, shelters Kyrin during the desert war for saving his son, Rashid

Truthseeker—the falcon eyas the Aneza tribe gives Kyrin

Umar—"Oo-mar" Ali's treacherous and unacknowledged son, means flourishing, long-lived

Zahir—"Za-heer" Faisal's stallion, means shining, radiant

Zoltan—"Zol-tan" Nimah's brother, means a ruler

§

Land of the Morning Calm/Korea:

Ap bal Chagi—"Op-ball-chagi" front-kick—a snapping kick that best attacks the groin or stomach

Barow—"Ba-row" means return to starting position

Chin-gol—"Chin-goal" means true bone. It was one of the highest military ranks after head-rank five.

Choson—A name for the early Korean culture, specifically applied in my books to the Silla dynasty.

Death touch—death thought to be brought by a single blow. Possible with a strong man trained in Subak, but more often the culmination of several deadly nerve points or blows

Dwi Chagi—"Dwee-chagi" a back-kick. The strongest kick, this one stops an attacker like a stone wall

Hwarang—"Huh-waa-rang" flowering warrior or leader of 500 to 5,000 hwarangdo—one trained in martial arts, literature, the arts, sciences, and one hundred and eight different weapons

Jun be—"June-bee" stance ready for attack. There are several variations

Kum-sool—"Come-sool" means sword skill

Kuksun—"Kook-sun" a commander or general, a lord who led by example

Naryu Chagi—"Nari-yu-chagi" an axe-kick or spinning kick often used to attack enemies on horseback

Open hand—attack with the fingers, palm, or knife-edge of the hand to the eyes, temples, neck, etc.

Pil Sung—certain victory through courage, strength, and indomitable spirit.

Poomse—"Poom-say" a sequence of training techniques done in flowing order, often with multiple techniques hidden within

Hwarangdo—"Huh-waa-rang-doh" or "Rang-do" a martial art student who learned under a hwarang master and followed Sesokokye

Seajok—"Say-jock" a command to begin (the fight, etc.)

Seon—"Say-on" Tae-shin or Tae Chisun, after his name was changed—left Seon to follow the Master of the stars, means the way of Zen

Sesokokye—"See-sok-o-kye" be loyal to your country, honor your parents, be faithful to your friends, never retreat in battle, use good judgment before killing any living thing.

Silla—A dynasty spanning the first century B.C. to 935 A.D. Our story happens around 830 or 840 A.D.

Subak—"Soo-bok" a component of Tae-shin's way of the warrior, means hand technique

Tiger—a beast of terrible power that haunts Kyrin's dreams

Yeop Chagi—"Yee-op chagi" side-kick. This can cripple, used against the knee at an angle

Names of important characters:

Cho Seung—Tae-shin's treacherous hwarang master, means candle, beginning, or second, and rise or achieve

Jeong Jin-ho—"Jee-ong Jin-ho" the rebel kuksun who honors Tae-shin when he is cast outside his clan as a traitor. Means quiet or loyal, and great, brave, heroic, or chivalrous.

Ha-nuel—Tae-shin's brave student who carried an essential message for the life of his people, means sky

Kim Jin-dae—"Jin-day" the name of Tae-shin/Tae Chisun's wife, means truth, or jewel, and greatness. "Hu-en" (pet name) may be associated with judgement. "Kim" means gold. I liked the sounds of these names

Kim Paekche—"Kim Pack-chi" is Tae-shin's father-in-law who exiled him. "Kim" means gold, "Paekche" is thought to mean one hundred crossings

Ryu Tae-shin—"Rue Tie-shin" where "Ryu" means willow tree, "Tae-shin" means great, and belief, faith, or trust. He came to be named Tae Chisun "Tie Chee-sun" by his captor, in his exile. Tae (great) is the first name of a grandmaster, Tae Hong Choi. I also liked the sound for a hero's name. Choi, as in Master Choi in *Path of the Warrior*, means governor of the land and the mountain, or high, superior, lofty.

Young-sool—means dragon or valiant one, and martial art technique

40

Sneak Peek Lance and Quill

Alaina stared into the darkness beyond the glowing coals. Sand whispered, sliding up the dunes with the wind. Doubtless Faisal did not know he treated her as Nara's kitchen help when he gave her his dish to scour with sand. Around the night fire, she broke her silence. "You were kind to take my message to Seliam."

Faisal rested his arms on his knees, his strong hands quiet. "He did not tell the *wazir* of my presence, which was all I asked. Do not judge Seliam too harshly. Captain to Sirius Abdasir, the wazir of the caliph, he is torn between debt of blood and debt of word—between your sister who held his life and his master who holds his oath—and now you, who hold his friendship."

"I? Hold his friendship? I think not." *Traitor.*

"The prince's words are true." Kentar nodded agreement. Veteran camel driver that he was, his *thawb* was drawn close against the desert chill. His old gaze was sharp, the wrinkles of his dark face driven deep by many caravan journeys.

Eyes prickling, Alaina bit her lip. The prince lived up to his name. Faisal Ben Salin, the just judge. Where thanks was due, she would give it. Yet she would *not* quickly absolve Seliam, once a friend. He deserted them when his master held those she loved captive to his dangerous will. It did not matter whether Sirius Abdasir was the caliph's wazir, or the caliph himself. A friend did not leave friends in danger.

The firelight blurred. Alaina pulled her knees up, laid her head down, and stirred the edge of the fire into flame. A Twilket prince must not see her tears. She *could* be as fierce as Kyrin.

Soon Tae banked the fire and they bedded down. The exiled healer and warrior was dear to her as a second father, but he could not comfort her heart this time. She was too weary for more words, but in the bottom of the dune-bowl, sleep left her. She could almost hear Kyrin stir restlessly, see her long shadow beyond the eyes of the coals. But her sister closer than blood did not sleep there, and might never return.

Alaina bit the back of her hand against tears. Kyrin had given her word to Sirius Abdasir that she would fulfill his task, but it was not enough. The wazir had taken Tae as their bond. Alaina's lip curled.

She and Kyrin did not trust Sirius to keep Tae from harm in the roiling currents of the caliph's court in these days of heavy taxes, uneasy slaves, and whispers of rebellion in Baghdad. They snatched Tae from his hands and rode into the desert. After that defiance, Kyrin refused to let her and Tae within Sirius's reach. Her sister had boarded the wazir's ship on the Red Sea at Jedda alone, bound for Britannia on the wazir's errand.

Now Kyrin searched the hills and forests of Britannia for a life in exchange for theirs. When she found Hamal, the one lost to the wazir, would the wazir lose interest in their heads? Doubtless he fixed their price, when he knew she and Tae fled back to the sands.

For every act there was a price. Alaina squeezed her eyes shut, and her mouth twisted in pain. Why had Tae shown Kyrin the touch of death and not her? They had always trained in the way of the warrior together. From the beginning.

She heard his voice again in the night silence of the dunes. A stray breeze had brought his words from behind a mountain of sand where he took Kyrin aside. "The touch of death is for none other than your hands. Do you hear me, my daughter? . . . You go into peril. The death touch is for greatest need . . ." The rest of Tae's words had been swept away.

Alaina shivered and curled into a ball. She might also need the death touch. Umar led his Hand of salukis and the wazir's men after them, seeking that very knowledge. And when he learned it—but the wazir must catch them first.

The night chill carved icy holes for the stars, and her breath plumed. She could feel Tae behind her, a hunched blot sitting against the sand ridge, his back to Kentar, who was his eyes and ears among the desert tribes.

Alaina rolled over. Near the top of the sand-bowl, Faisal kept watch with his stallion. Zahir was a beast clean of limb, with the small Araby head and proud carriage, a veritable dark wind of the desert. Like his master, he belonged to this harsh land.

She sniffed, not altogether disdainfully. Faisal must keep the peace in the Oasis of Oaths, which stood as witness between Aneza and Twilket, with a swift lance, swifter horses, and a heart as wild as the dark wolf that haunted the mountains in the cool shadows before the dawn. Doubtless when he lifted his lance many Twilket warriors answered his call.

He and Kyrin walked after the same Lord now, rode the same wind. Once they had not. But her sister was gone from his reach, bound to seek Hamal. She returned to her father, a lord in Britannia in his own right, for Kyrin was heir to Cierheld stronghold.

Alaina looked at her hands. They smelled of gritty earth. She was only a peasant, though a sister to Kyrin, closer than blood.

She closed her eyes. A tear tickled around her ear, headed for the sand below. Her family was gone, killed the day she was enslaved, fallen alongside the baker's boy she might have hand-fasted. All gone.

Now all was taken again. She had been so near to being a scribe to the caliph, the highest ruler in this land. Her delicate, dedicated hand in his court would have won her freedom. Her hand was skilled at many things. The softest silk and cotton thawbs, rose and jasmine scents for her skin and hair would have been hers, with embroidery thread of all hues for every garment she could imagine and put her needle to, which would have gained her the favor of the women of the court.

She had been so near, so close to a name as a scribe, even a poet of verse. A creator of word and writ who drew all who heard her into a place of vivid thought and sharpened spirit. Alaina choked on a bitter sob. Now she would be surprised to see *Alaina Ilen* gracing the odd scrap of untanned hide she might rescue from some tentmaker and pen a few words on. She drew a breath and wiped her face. Enough.

Desert Bedouin had little use for writing, and less for a female scribe. She was done with rosewater. But Faisal's ailing *sheyk* would need her knowledge of herbs, though many others had that skill. Tae had taught her well in it.

The sand behind her hip was rough and cold and hard. Her exile was just begun. Were only herbs and her needle to be left to her?

If she could but see Kyrin again and hear the bards raise their clear, thunderous voices around the fires under the oaks of Britannia. Better now if she had gone to scribe for her sister.

For if Umar's Hand caught them, or a warrior betrayed them for coin before Kyrin found Hamal . . . Alaina swallowed.

Did Cicero hunt or did his paws carry him far over the sand, his loyal hound's heart yearning for Kyrin? His comforting nose was elsewhere, his moon-shadow form blending with the night. Would Umar's Hand tear him to shreds also?

Chilled, Alaina turned over. Dawn was coming in a few bells. Did Kyrin see the same stars spangled across the sky—did a dark and dangerous expanse lean over her?

40

Acknowledgements

There are so many wonderful people who assisted me on my writing journey. So, if your name is not here and you dropped a word of encouragement or helped me on my writing journey, know that I appreciate you very much.

My thanks to my dad, mom, and family for their support in so many ways, and to Sandy Cathcart, Lynn Leissler, Jeanette Windle, Susan May Warren, and Kathi Macias for their teaching and encouragement at pivotal points in my writing.

My deepest thanks to my crit group, Fantasy for Christ. More recently during the book updates, I thank Charlotte Lesemann and Emily Moore for their encouragement, beta reading, and help with the things that make a book worthwhile. And I also thank you, my readers. You're the best! I deeply appreciate your invaluable advice and honest reviews!

If you have not reviewed this book yet, you can leave a review at Amazon https://www.amazon.com/review/create-review/?ie=UTF8&channel=glance-detail&asin=B00VOEQXIO GoodReads, or at your favorite retailer. I highly value your feedback and insights, as does the rest of the reading world. Thank you!

Azalea Dabill ~ Crossover – Find the Eternal, the Adventure

Made in the USA
Middletown, DE
04 November 2023